Theros couldn't believe what he was seeing. Dragons, small red dragons that seemed to be made of flame, were crawling off the sword that now glowed red in the heat of the blazing fire.

He shut his eyes, rubbed them, looked again. The dragons were still there . . . scuttling across the white-hot coals. One jumped out of the fire, landed on a wooden bench. The dragon vanished, changing to flame. The bench began to smolder and smoke.

The firepit was filled with the tiny dragons now, hundreds and hundreds of them. They dashed up the wooden beams that supported the roof. They crawled to the worktable, dropped among the tools. And everything they touched—even metal—burst into flame.

"Come away, master! Come away!" called Theros's apprentice. "There's nothing you can do! Give up!"

"By Sargas!" Theros roared. "Never!"

Then one of the dragons jumped on his leg. It burned through his long leather apron in just an instant, touching his flesh. The pain was excruciating, far worse than any burn Theros had ever received.

He felt himself starting to black out . . .

DragonLance ®

Saga

**From the Creators of the
DRAGONLANCE® Saga
WARRIORS**

Knights of the Crown
Roland Green

Maquesta Kar-Thon
Tina Daniell

Knights of the Sword
Roland Green

Theros Ironfeld
Don Perrin

DragonLance® Saga

WARRIORS
Volume Four

THEROS IRONFELD

Don Perrin

DRAGONLANCE®
Warriors Series
Volume Four

THEROS IRONFELD

©1996 TSR, Inc.
All Rights Reserved.

Cover art by Jeff Easley. Interior art by Valerie A. Valusek.

First Printing: March 1996
Printed in the United States of America.
Library of Congress Catalog Card Number: 95-62196

9 8 7 6 5 4 3 2 1

8375XXX1501
ISBN: 0-7869-0481-X

TSR, Inc.   TSR Ltd.
201 Sheridan Springs Rd.   120 Church End, Cherry Hinton
Lake Geneva WI 53147   Cambridge CB1 3LB
U.S.A.   United Kingdom

Book One

Chapter 1

The town was a tiny speck on the side of a pristine shoreline of azure and green. A battered war barge glided slowly toward the coastline, the vessel barely under sail. It was obvious that the barge and its crew of minotaurs and human slaves had recently seen action. Only one sail remained aloft, and most of the rigging was down, tangled in masses on the decking below. The mainmast had been shattered, and its remnants lay strewn about, making life difficult for the crew.

"Port Five!"

A minotaur barked course corrections to the wheel. He stood on the forecastle, staring at the tiny dot of civilization through a spyglass. The spyglass symbolized life for the vessel. Originally of human design—possibly from as far back as the Cataclysm—the glass was just under two feet in length, made of brass. It counter-twisted to focus the two lenses on distances as great as a mile or more.

The markings on the side were foreign to the minotaur, but he didn't care what they said or meant. The device did what it needed to do. It magnified items in the distance, warned of the approach of either enemy or victim, and that was what the minotaur captain wanted. The price had been right, too. It had been part of the booty from a raid years ago. Everything on the barge had either been stolen in raids, or was rigged as needed while at sea.

The minotaurs were the masters of the vessel. They were the sailors and the warriors, the heart and the muscle and the brains. They did not swab decks or empty the slop buckets. The drudge work was handled by the slave contingent—humans, also taken as booty. Some slaves escaped, some slaves died while fighting or being disciplined, but that never worried the minotaurs. There would always be more humans. They bred like maggots.

The barge shuddered its way through the course correction. On deck, thirty minotaur warriors prepared for battle. Some strapped on leather armor, while others adjusted straps holding grappling ropes or scabbards containing all manner of weaponry, from Solamnic long swords to Seeker flails to elven dirks. Still others sharpened the blades of their axes or the points of their morning stars. The town ahead was unknown to the minotaur ship of war, but it was on the north coast of Nordmaar, and that made it highly likely to be a human settlement.

Slowly the barge approached land. On the shore, several humans had noticed the curious vessel, were pointing and shouting. It was not uncommon for a ship to be at sea on a day such as this, but landing before noon sun was curious, and the ship was of a strange design. It was a long barge, with a fore and aft castle rising at either end of the long, flat deck. The sails were arranged on two evenly spaced mainmasts rooted in the center of the ship. A third mast jutted out of the front at a jaunty angle. Here, the steering was adjusted, in conjunction with the huge rudder on the aft of the ship.

Ship designs were very different in Nordmaar. The ships were shorter, deeper. They were primarily fishing vessels, designed to drag huge nets and to process the fish once the catch was brought on board. They were not even close to resembling the huge bargelike vessel that approached the shore this day.

A small crowd, mostly women, had gathered on the dock. Their men were out fishing, the minotaur captain knew well, having made certain that the small fishing fleet they had passed earlier had not noticed them. The minotaur ship had closed to within a hundred yards of the harbor entrance before someone had sense enough to call for a town guardsman. The guardsman could see it was a battered warship, and further, that the horned creatures on the bow were not a group of tourists to the quaint fishing locale.

Far too late, the alarm was sounded. A bell in the tower of the town meeting hall began to toll. Moving with ponderous slowness, the barge smashed straight into the first pier. All thirty minotaur warriors rushed forward to the barge's bow and leapt onto the pier.

An ancient human stood inside a provisions shop located near the pier. He held a short bow and beside him rested a quiver of fine arrows—all on display for sale moments before. Taking careful aim, he loosed his first shot and the lead minotaur came crashing down, the staff of an arrow protruding from between his eyes.

"Take that, you damned cow," the old man yelled.

He drew another arrow, and fired. An advancing minotaur fell not twenty feet from the window of the shop.

"I hope your damned cow god is waiting for you," the old man shouted.

Furious, having expected little or no resistance, the minotaurs rushed the shop. The first reached the window just as the archer straightened from retrieving another arrow. The minotaur's battle-axe came crashing down, catching the old man in the back, shattering his spine. Blood spattered the minotaur, who leaned back and howled with a killing lust.

5

"And you take that, you godless wretch," the minotaur grunted in his own language.

Closer to the center of the village, the guardsman who had sounded the alert stood his ground, along with a comrade. A group of minotaurs quickly encircled them. The minotaurs did not press the fight, although they had overwhelming numbers. The first guardsman lunged at the lead minotaur with his short sword. The minotaur jumped back, parrying clumsily. Several minotaurs made gestures to the guardsmen, indicative of dropping their weapons.

"They want us to surrender," said one, half-gagging from the stench of the hair-covered bodies.

"They want slaves," said his companion, still jabbing away with his sword.

"We're smarter than these bastards. We'll escape," said the first. "It beats dying."

"Maybe. Maybe not," said the second.

The guardsmen looked around quickly, in vain, for any support. Seeing none, they lowered their swords. The ranking minotaur warrior stepped forward and took the weapons. The two men were manacled and hauled back to the ship.

By noon sun, the town had capitulated. All inhabitants who had not escaped (and there were very few that did) were rounded up at the pier. The few men—mostly merchants and teenage boys—were separated from the women, who were to be left behind. Minotaurs did not fancy human women. Hornless, snoutless and hairless, human women were hopelessly ugly. The women were given charge of the younger children—with one exception.

A young child, a boy no more than ten years of age, glared in outrage at the minotaur who shoved him to the women's side. The boy marched over to stand with the men. Two of the minotaurs guarding the women began to laugh at the audacity of the young lad.

Speaking broken Common, the minotaur ship commander yelled at the boy, "You! Go back to mama!"

The boy shook his head, did not move.

"You! Yes, you!" The minotaur poked the boy with the butt of his axe. "Go back. I have no need for cubs. Slaves not plenty here, males out fishing. Take only ten males here. You not one of them."

The boy didn't budge. His eyes cast down at the parched wood of the pier decking, the young boy said in a low voice, "I want to go with you."

He raised his eyes, then looked the minotaur captain in the face. "When I was younger, my mother went to the sky, and my father hates me for causing her to die. I will go and be a slave and work your mighty ship for you."

One of the women screamed, and tried to rush over to snatch the boy to her side. The minotaur warriors caught her, threw her back.

"Take the cub, Captain," called one of the minotaurs in their own language. "He has more spirit than most of these wretches!"

"I was like that myself, when I was his age," the captain remarked to his lieutenant. "Very well, cub! I take you to sharpen my blades, clean my thongs and boots. You are now my personal slave."

Eight men and the boy, whose name was Theros, were marched aboard the barge and taken down to join the two guardsmen that were already below. The minotaur warriors, under the direction of the ship's captain and mates, raided the town to collect rope, lumber and sailcloth for repairs, along with drinking water and provisions. They took anything that looked useful, and hauled it all aboard. They weren't paying for anything, anyway.

Within two hours, the barge was loaded and under way. Its damage was unrepaired, but the minotaurs now had fresh, new slaves and provisions. The men of the town would not return from their fishing until sundown. By that time, the minotaur ship would be easily six hours ahead of any chase—if there were any chase. Fishing folk were no match for even a damaged minotaur war barge with a full complement of warriors. Smarter, cooler heads in the town would counsel against pursuit.

A town can lose only so many men in one day.

Chapter 2

The ship headed straight out to sea. As soon as it was out of sight of the coastline, the crew went to work. Minotaur warrior and human slave worked side by side to repair the damaged ship. The second mast's sails were raised, to give the ship some forward motion, but the sails flapped and fluttered in the light breeze. No one paid much attention to them. All focused instead on the damaged masts. The sailors did not even bother to steer. They lashed the rudder and headed north.

The new "recruits" were held prisoner on the forecastle. Each man was given to another, more experienced slave, who taught the first the ropes. In this way, the new slaves were quickly adopted into the fold, as it were.

No one paid any attention to Theros, who was not strong enough to be of much use. Told to keep out of the way or he'd be thrown overboard, he sat on a pile of tangled rope and watched.

Two of the human slaves had attained some measure of status on the vessel. They were, Theros noticed, the only two slaves with beards. These two spoke the minotaur language and directed the repairs to the ship. The minotaurs appeared to treat them with a small amount of respect, more than they gave the other humans.

One was a tall man with dusky black skin and a graying beard and mustache. He was strong, well muscled, and might have been from Theros's own village, for he looked vaguely familiar to the boy. There had been minotaur raids in the past, but Theros was too young to remember much about them. He remembered the stories, though. Now the villagers of Nordmaar would have a new story to tell.

The second human was a white man, with skin tanned as brown as the hide from a mule. His beard was bushy and full, reddish-blond in color. His eyes were blue, so blue that one could see their color from the opposite end of the ship.

Under the direction of the first man, the minotaurs and the slaves had lifted the downed forward mainmast from the central deck of the ship, and using pulleys and ropes, pulled it back into an upright position. Four brawny minotaur warriors wrestled the butt end of the beam onto the remnants of the mast that were still in place and jammed them together. Weaving in and out between the four minotaur warriors, four humans—under the direction of the bearded, black-skinned man—began nailing in supports to connect the two pieces. Next, they lathered the seam with a strong-smelling tar, then wrapped the beam with rope.

The rope was pulled as tight as possible, the minotaurs tugging on it until it had been coiled around and around the beam, as high as a man was tall. Next, the minotaurs added a lower crossbeam to the mast, and secured it to the sides of the ship, immediately giving it better stability.

While all this commotion was going on, the two guardsmen edged over to the side of the deck, near where Theros was seated, and began to whisper to each other.

"Jump for it," one was saying.

The red-bearded human loomed up behind them.

"Get back to work, you lubbers!" he shouted roughly.

"Look, mister, you're a slave like us. Let's jump for it. We're still close enough to swim to shore."

"I said, 'Get back to work!' " the red-bearded man snarled, reinforcing his order with a fist to the jaw that sent the guardsman reeling.

Bruised and bloody, the guardsman picked himself up off the deck, and went back to work.

Repairs progressed throughout the ship. Minotaurs and humans worked alongside each other, except for the captain and his officers. Most of the time the officers remained in the cabins below the forecastle, but occasionally they would come out to check things with either of the two human foremen. The ship continued to sail north, out to sea.

When the sun was nearing the edge of the horizon, the black-skinned foreman climbed up onto the forecastle. Removing the cup from the side of the water barrel, he took a long draw. He replaced the cup back on its hook on the side of the barrel, and sat down, inspecting the work with a satisfied air. Theros, bored, stood up.

"What do I get to do?" he asked, excited.

The man looked up at the boy, shook his head and motioned for him to sit back down. Theros, disappointed, pretended he didn't understand.

"I'm stronger than I look. What can I—"

The man frowned and cut Theros off with a curt hiss and a sharp hand motion. He pointed emphatically to the ropes where Theros had been sitting. Theros had not been much in the habit of obeying his father, who cared little one way or the other. Theros started to make another protest, but— at a look from the man—the boy swallowed his words and returned meekly to his seat.

As the sun sank into the water, the minotaur warriors went below. Through the open hatch, Theros could smell cooked fish and meat. He hadn't eaten since morning.

"I'm hungry," Theros announced. "When do we eat?"

The foreman did not answer. He sat staring at his hands. He might have been dozing, but his eyes were open. The

sound of booted feet, clomping right behind him, caused
Theros to turn. A minotaur warrior marched up to Theros,
grabbed him by the shoulder and yanked him to his feet.
The warrior, not used to the lack of weight in a human
child, nearly threw the boy across the deck. Recovering,
the minotaur kept fast hold of Theros, lifted him off his
feet, let him dangle about four feet in the air.

"No talking! Next time I whip you. No talking!"

The minotaur released him. Theros fell in a heap on the
deck. Tears welled up inside him, but he choked them
down. He had learned from his father's scoldings not to
show any tears. He had vowed when he left the village that
he would never allow anyone to batter him down, either
physically or mentally.

The words of his mother echoed over and over in his
memory. The only thing he could remember about his
mother was the time, right before she died, when she had
called to him from her bed. She had rested her hand on his
head.

"The old gods have left us. I don't like these new gods,
who seem to have nothing to do with us. Until you find a
god to watch over you, Theros, I give you my blessing. Be
courageous and do not waste the gifts you have been
given."

Theros didn't know what gifts those were, but he knew
he possessed them and that made him as good as any
man—or any minotaur.

He held back the tears, and did not move until long after
the minotaur had gone below.

When it was nighttime, the minotaur warriors began to
come up from below deck. They laughed and talked
amongst themselves. Once the last of the minotaurs had
come up onto the deck, the guards started to herd the
slaves below. At last, the black-skinned foreman rose to his
feet. Walking over to Theros, the man tapped him on the
shoulder and motioned for him to follow.

They climbed down the ladder from the forecastle, then
down the ladder beneath the hatch to the galley below.
Theros went down first, managing the ladders and stairs
clumsily. The foreman came after him, pausing to see if any

humans were left on deck before closing the hatch.

They entered a hot cabin crowded with humans, including the red-bearded man, who came to a sort of ragged attention when the black-skinned foreman appeared. A long wooden table was covered with platters of fish and meat and bread.

Theros had never smelled food so wonderful in all of his life. He had never been this hungry, either. Theros's father, a fisherman, may have yelled at and neglected the boy, but at least there had been food on the table. There had been no time in the boy's short life when he had ever been denied a meal. His stomach growled, his mouth watered.

The foreman nodded to the red-bearded man. Everyone began talking at once, albeit in hushed tones.

The foreman put his hand on Theros's shoulder, and turned the boy around to face him.

"So what's your name, lad?" the man asked.

"I'm Theros." He added, with pride, "I'm a new member of this crew."

The foreman grinned. His hand on the boy's shoulder tightened painfully.

"Get this straight from the beginning, Theros. You are *not* a member of the crew. You are a slave aboard this ship. My name is Heretos Guntoos. I am the repair foreman of this ship, but unlike you, I am not a slave. I am an equal member of the captain's crew. I am paid and paid handsomely for my work. You, however, *are* a slave, as are all the other humans aboard this ship, except for Timpan the Red over there. Now you must learn, and learn quickly. Listen to what I say."

Theros let his glance stray to the food. Heretos cuffed him on the ear to regain his attention. "I said listen!"

Wincing, Theros returned his attention to the foreman.

"Good. Now do not speak at all in the presence of a minotaur, unless he has spoken to you first. We may talk down here only because there are no minotaurs here now. If one were to enter, then all talking must stop. The sail foreman, Timpan, over there"—he gestured toward the red-bearded man—"and I are allowed to speak in order to direct the work on deck as is necessary. You do not have this privilege. You may notice, lad, that I did not speak to

you on the fo'c'sle. You would have been whipped for such
a transgression. Understand?"

"Yes . . . sir," Theros said.

Heretos nodded. "You seem a fast learner. What I'm
telling you is for your own good. I've never seen a slave as
young as you. Normally they take only able-bodied men.
So why is it that they've brought you on board? What is it
they're going to have you do here?"

Theros saw true interest in the man's eyes, more interest
than his own father had ever showed in the boy.

"I don't know what my job is yet, sir, so I can't tell you
what I do."

Heretos smiled.

"You'll be kept busy, I'm sure. First, let's get some food
and water into you."

The foreman marched the boy up to the food server, a
short, flabby human who smelled of fish. In a low tone,
Heretos said, "This is Theros. He's one of the new ones. My
guess is he'll be helping you out down here from time to
time. Take care of him when you can, eh?"

He then turned to Theros. "This is Aldvin. He's the cook.
He makes one meal for the minotaurs, and then one for us.
Timpan and I usually eat with the minotaurs, but for the
next week we eat with you slaves, to teach you what is
proper. Slaves usually get only what's left over, but it's
always good when Aldvin's on the job. We eat at sunrise,
and just after sundown. You can get water on the fo'c'sle
any time during the day, if your duties permit."

Theros nodded, but he was far more interested in the
bowl of steaming fish stew now in his hands, and the small
hunk of black bread the cook had dumped on top.

"Go on, boy. Go and eat."

Theros found a bench and immediately devoured his
food. Finished, he brought his bowl back to the cook.

"That was really good. I'll have some more."

He was startled and chagrined to hear everyone in the
galley start to laugh, including the cook.

"Sorry, lad. You get what you are served and no more.
The rest goes for morning meal, and the mainstay of that is
for those doing the heavy work. When you need more, I'll

give it to you, but you don't need it now."

Theros started to argue, but the laughter ceased suddenly. Silence fell. Two minotaurs had descended into the galley.

"I am Kavas, the captain of this ship of war," the minotaur said, speaking passable Common. "The ship is called *Blatvos Kemas*, and it has brought great honor to me and my crew. This is my second, Rez."

Kavas was bigger than the other minotaurs, and Theros wondered if that may have had something to do with why he was captain.

Kavas continued. "Repair foreman, take six of the new slaves for your shifts. Sail foreman, take the rest. After main repairs are finished, four go from repair to sail. I want this ship in fighting form in two days. Each day, from noon sun until two hours later, the bow of the ship is to be cleared for warriors to practice. That is all."

The minotaurs turned to climb the ladder. Theros began wildly waving his right arm in the air.

The captain turned to Heretos. "What is this arm-thrashing about?"

Heretos lowered his head slightly. "It is a custom taught to young human children. He is trying to get your attention to ask you a question, sir. He knows he is not supposed to speak without permission."

The captain turned to Theros. "You have permission to talk, boy."

"What do *I* do, Captain?" Theros demanded. "What do *I* get to do?"

Captain Kavas hesitated for a moment, as if wondering that same thing himself. Then he said, "I have decided I not need a personal slave. Instead, you will be slave to my warriors. When they need anything, you will provide. Repair foreman, bring this cub to my fighting contingent commander at sunrise."

The captain did not await a reply. He climbed up and out of the galley. The second minotaur followed him.

As soon as the two minotaurs had left, the slaves began to talk and eat.

Theros, still hungry, watched them.

Chapter 3

It was still dark when Theros was roughly and rudely awakened by someone whacking him across the stomach with a stick. Theros sat bolt upright, startled and indignant.

"Get up! Time to start working," Heretos told the boy. "You will help Aldvin down in the galley this morning, and later you will begin your job of assisting the warriors. You got that?"

Theros nodded. Groggily, he hopped down from the bunk and wandered over to the water barrel. He started to plunge in his hands to wash his face. Heretos grabbed hold of him and turned him to another barrel that was brackish and smelled of fish.

"You wash in seawater, my lad. Never waste drinking

water on anything but drinking. First rule of the sea, and she doesn't forgive mistakes."

He handed Theros a small metal bowl and a rag. Theros poured seawater into the bowl. He scrubbed his body with the wet rag, even going over his teeth to get the scum off of them. Finally, he rinsed his mouth with a bit of the water and spat it back into the bowl. He had learned early in his life that drinking seawater was a good way to lose your breakfast. It would make you sicker than a half-drowned dog. He took the bowl, and as he had observed others doing, lifted the cover of a porthole and dumped the water out.

The taste of the seawater was awful. Theros took a long draught of fresh water from the drinking barrel. Ready for the day, he looked over to see Heretos slapping around one of the guardsmen, who was apparently not used to waking up this early.

Theros climbed the ladder and made his way onto the deck. The sky was beginning to show color as the sun teased the world with hazy light. The sea was calm again this morning. Theros hurried across the deck, trying to remember the way to the galley. He was nearly knocked down by the other guardsman, who had just climbed up onto the deck.

"Get out of my way, boy," the guardsman snarled.

A minotaur whipped around. "You spoke, human dog."

He poked the man in the stomach with the butt end of his axe. The slave cursed loudly, and spat on the deck.

The minotaur backhanded the man with the handle of his axe, sent the guardsman flying. He landed like a heap of kelp and lay very still. The minotaur walked away.

A tap on his back reminded Theros that he had work to do. Heretos, standing behind him, shoved Theros along the deck. Theros stared at the slave's body as he climbed down the access ladder to the galley. He could not rid himself of the image of the warrior brutally swinging his axe handle, connecting with the man's jaw, sending him sprawling.

Aldvin was already at work in the galley. He had started the fires and begun to heat water. He motioned to Theros.

"Here, take this bowl and fill it with fish from last night.

Over there in that barrel. Yes, that's the one." The boy looked over at a barrel tied to a main support beam. "What is it, lad?"

Theros opened his mouth, then shut it again.

Aldvin laughed. "It's all right, lad. We can talk down here as long as none of the minotaurs come down, and they won't be down until the sun's fully risen. Off you go, there, lad. Oh, and if you find any bones in the fish, throw them in this bucket here. Got it?"

The boy nodded and went off to do as he was told. Aldvin prepared the fish, adding new seasonings and heating the mixture over the galley fire. Theros cleaned all of the serving bowls and put out large jugs of drinking water. Just as he was setting down the last jug, a minotaur, ignoring the ladder, jumped the distance to the deck below. The noise of impact jarred the boy. He sloshed water all over the table.

"You! Small one! Bring me my morning meal!"

Theros ran over to Aldvin, who handed him a steaming bowl of food. Theros took the bowl to the minotaur.

He placed the food in front of the warrior. The minotaur grabbed Theros by the shirt collar. "You saw me handle that unruly slave, didn't you? I warn you. Never cross a minotaur warrior on this ship. What you saw is what I will do to you if you disobey me. Go! Get me water!"

The boy stumbled backward. At Aldvin's gesture, Theros raced over to the sea cupboard where the flagons were kept. He grabbed one, filled it from the fresh barrel and brought it back to the warrior. By this time, several other minotaur warriors had climbed down the ladder into the galley. They laughed as they saw Theros running, fetching, serving, and made comments in their own language. None sounded at all complimentary. Theros's ears burned.

He was becoming addled with the heat, the shouting, the confusion. The warriors yelled at him to hurry with their food, to get them water, to clean up spills, to go faster, always faster! Aldvin watched, enjoying the show. The minotaurs were having fun now, sending the panic-stricken boy to fetch this and that, hurling it back into his face when he brought it with a command to go fetch something else.

"Stop!"

The voice was huge, deep, imposing. All heads turned. The captain stood at the bottom of the ladder. He glared at the warriors before him. He spoke in the minotaur language, which Theros didn't understand then. Aldvin would translate it for him later.

"You call this honor? You call this the code of the warrior? You have your fun screaming at a cub, forgetting that this cub actually chose to come with us. He, in that one act, has shown more courage than all of you mighty warriors this morning. Eat and get back to work. I will hear no more of this."

The captain, now flanked by the first and second officers, walked over to Aldvin and demanded food. The cook gave each a heaping bowl of fish and a full flagon of water. They moved forward to a table, and ate with their backs to the rest of the warriors. They never once glanced at Theros.

The warriors fell silent, ate quickly. When they finished, they climbed up to the deck. Soon, all of the warriors had left, leaving only the three officers at their table, eating.

Aldvin motioned to Theros to begin collecting the bowls and flagons, and to wash them in the basin. Theros did so, but kept his eyes on the three minotaurs sitting with their backs to him. They talked in hushed tones to each other.

Theros took all of the bowls to the basin, dumped the remains of the meals into a bucket and began to scrub the bowls. He tried desperately to ignore his own hunger. He turned only when he heard voices. Human voices.

The three officers had finished and left. The slaves were now climbing down into the galley. Theros started to go fetch the three sets of flagons and bowls that he thought would still be on the table from the officers' meals. He headed for the table, felt a hand on his shoulder. Theros stopped, looked up. Aldvin smiled and motioned to the three bowls beside the basin.

"I took care of it for you, lad. They were a bit rough on you, weren't they? I'll tell you a secret, though. "

Theros looked up expectantly.

"Don't let them see you're afraid. Do what they say, but keep your chin up, your head high. They'll respect you for it."

Aldvin looked across at the men starting to seat themselves. "All right, lad, go and fetch some food for everyone. I'll serve it, you deliver it."

The rest of the morning's duties in the galley were uneventful. After all had left, Theros and Aldvin ate what was left over and then cleaned up. When that was finished, Aldvin sent Theros back up the ladder.

"Go up and find the warriors. You'll be working for them for the rest of the day. I'll be down here cleaning the fresh fish for tonight's meal. You'll help me wash up again after we're all done eating. Now, stay out of harm's way."

Already so tired that he could barely walk, Theros climbed the ladder back to the deck. He shielded his eyes from the near-noon sun, now blazing in the clear azure sky. It took several seconds, but his eyes adjusted to the bright light. Looking around, he saw that the rear raised deck had become a practice yard. The warriors were swinging, lunging and dodging as they practiced with battle weapons. In other parts of the ship, slaves were working to restore the ship back to seaworthy condition. Already the foremast was re-rigged and the men had turned their attention to the new mainmast.

One minotaur sat apart from the other warriors. He had a pile of weapons beside him, and was working on the leather sheaths and belts. Theros walked up to the warrior and stood in front of him. The minotaur was busy with a scabbard and at first did not notice the boy.

Theros remained standing, not knowing what to do. Finally, he sat down, and picked up a sword and a sharpening stone. His father had shown him how to sharpen a fish knife and this looked much the same. He began to work.

The minotaur glanced up with a start. He seemed about to protest, then noticed that the boy was doing something useful, so the minotaur went back to his work.

Theros sharpened a sword, an axe, then another sword. The work was easy in his hands. He scraped the stone across the blade of the weapon, grinding it ever so slightly. Over and over the process was repeated, all along the blade, until finally the weapon felt sharp from tip to basket. After sharpening, he knew enough to dip the tip of the weapon into a small vial of oil, then spread the oil over the blade and basket to ensure that it didn't rust. He slid the leather scabbard back over the weapon and started on the next.

The minotaur worked beside him, never saying a word, keeping a watchful eye on his work, handing him another weapon when he was finished with the previous.

Sitting in the sun, Theros soon grew thirsty, but he was afraid to leave his work. He licked his dry, parched lips. At that, the minotaur working beside him grunted. Theros looked up. The minotaur pointed to the bow of the ship, grunted, and returned his attention to a leather belt.

Theros made his way forward across the deck. He was fascinated to observe the different tasks being performed. The ship was looking more like a sailing vessel again. Debris had been cleared away. The repair crews had all the rigging up. The ship had picked up speed as the sails were unfurled.

A ladle hung on the side of the water barrel on the forecastle. A man stood beside the barrel, dipped the ladle, drank gingerly from it. Theros recognized the man as the former guardsman. The man's lower jaw was purple and black from bruising. His lip was split. It was obvious that even the act of drinking was a painful one. He glared at Theros.

"All your fault, you little bastard," he muttered. "But I'll show them."

He hung the ladle back on the side of the barrel. Theros took down the ladle, drank thirstily. He had been in the sun all afternoon, and had not noticed that he was beginning to become dehydrated. He took another long drink, put the ladle back.

From beneath the forecastle, the captain emerged onto the main deck. He took a few steps forward and began to survey the rigging and masts. His eyes seemed to move in slow motion as he scanned every knot and block of rigging, every bolt of sail.

The guardsman beside Theros shivered slightly. Nervous hands plucked at his clothing. He climbed down to the main deck. Turning from the ladder, he took two steps forward, putting him only a pace behind the captain. The minotaur did not see or hear the human. Reaching inside his shirt, the man pulled out a knife.

Later, Theros would often wonder why he did what he did. Perhaps it was because the captain had praised his courage. Perhaps it was that he felt no man—or minotaur—should die from a stab in the back.

Theros yelled at the top of his lungs. "Captain! Behind you!"

The captain turned just as the guardsman's knife plunged down. The natural reflexes of the warrior let Kavas sidestep the attack, and at the same time pull his knife from its scabbard. The human and the minotaur stood facing each other, both in a fighting stance, knives brandished. All work on the ship stopped.

The warriors on the rear deck of the ship rushed forward to get a better look. The two other officers stood near the forecastle, each armed with a battle-axe. No one interfered with the fight, however. It was the captain's right to kill this would-be assassin.

The human and the minotaur circled each other. Passing by the foremast, the man grabbed a three-foot-long shoring peg out of a hole. He now had two weapons. Half a revolution more and the human made his move. He lunged forward with the knife, holding the peg—now a makeshift club—to ward off any blow. The captain dodged the thrust and swung his own weapon. The man batted the knife away, but the swing had been a feint. The captain brought his knee up and smashed it into the man's chest.

The man dropped his weapons and crumpled to the deck. He rolled to the side, clutching his chest and gasping for air, and then he stopped moving. The captain stood above him, ready and waiting. Moments passed. The man lay still. Finally, the captain put his knife away. The other two officers walked forward. One turned the human onto his back. He was dead.

The captain, suddenly remembering the cry that had

saved his life, turned to look at Theros. He nodded once to the boy, then marched back into the cabin below the fore-castle. The other two officers followed their captain back into the cabin. The dead man was left on the deck.

Timpan and Heretos scrambled forward from the rig-ging to where the man lay. They both looked up at Theros, then back to the dead man. Both shook their heads. Theros couldn't tell what they were thinking, but he saw the other slaves on board glaring at him with hatred. The two fore-men lifted the body and shuffled to the port side of the ship. Heretos shut the man's eyes, then they lifted the body over the side rail and let it fall to the sea below. No one said a word.

Theros watched as the body bobbed in the sea behind the moving ship, finally losing sight of it as it slipped beneath the waves.

"What—" Theros said to himself miserably, "what have I done?"

Chapter 4

Theros woke with a start. He shook his head and tried to peer into the gloom. He did not recognize his surroundings and could not for the life of him remember how he had gotten to be where he was. The floor refused to stay still. First, he slid to his left, then moments later to his right. Everywhere around him were hushed voices, mumbling in the dark. Suddenly, he remembered the events of the previous two days.

His eyes began to adjust. It was not as dark as he had first thought. He could make out hammocks slung around, and berths along either side of the cabin. He had been assigned to a berth along the port side. There were more men than sleeping places, but that worked out, because some of the men were always on night watch. When the watches shifted, they would trade places in the berths. No one had to worry about who had what berth or hammock, as they were all functionally identical. As slaves, they owned nothing, and therefore could not claim one over another.

The voices he had heard weren't voices at all, he realized. It was the sound of the waves slapping against the side of the ship.

Theros sat up, trying to recall the noise that had awakened him. He heard the hatch above open, and saw someone slowly climb down the ladder. The figure made no sound at all, which was strange, considering that he wore armor and more weapons than the boy could believe possible. The figure moved directly toward Theros. If anyone else was awake, no one stirred.

As the figure came closer, Theros could see that this was a minotaur, but no ordinary minotaur. He was massive, with huge horns. He wore leather armor with gold accoutrements hammered into it. Theros had learned his lesson, and did not move or say anything. The minotaur went straight up to Theros's bunk, and finding that the boy was awake, motioned for Theros to follow him.

Theros clamored down to the floor, and followed the giant minotaur up the ladder and onto the forecastle. No one was in sight. What had happened to the night crew? The minotaur pointed to a crate for Theros to sit. He sat, looked up expectantly at the huge being. Theros remembered Aldvin's advice: *Don't let them see you are afraid*. He clasped his hands together tightly.

You do not know who I am, do you? The minotaur spoke, but the words made no sound. They made their impact only in Theros's mind, and nowhere else.

Theros shook his head.

You may speak here with me. I am not a member of the crew of this ship. I am Sargas. I watch over the minotaurs, among others.

Theros opened his mouth. "I am—"

Stop, little human. I know who you are, and what you are. You are one of my children. Do you know of the gods, young Theros?

"There are no gods, sir," Theros answered. "The man in

our village says that the old gods left us after the Cataclysm and that—"

Enough! The minotaur growled and looked very fierce. *I know of men who say such things. They call themselves Seekers in human tongue. They say that they are the only clerics left on Krynn.*

Let me tell you what you need to know of the gods, little Theros. There is only one god you need to concern yourself with. That is the god who rules your life, and that is me. I am Sargas, god of minotaurs, and god of honor, warfare and revenge. Worship me, Theros, as I am your master of masters.

Theros looked quizzically at the minotaur. "You are not a god, you are a minotaur. I don't understand." A thought came to him, something the Seeker had said. "If you're a god, prove it to me."

Rage contorted the giant warrior's face. His voice thundered, though he never made a sound. *You truly do not know anything about gods, do you, little Theros? It is up to mortals to prove themselves to me, to prove that they have the honor to be recognized by me, to prove that they have the warrior skills and the devious mind of tacticians.*

Theros was frightened, but he forced himself to remain calm.

Sargas, watching him, actually smiled. *You are brave. I like that. This time, I will swallow my pride and prove to you that I am a god of unparalleled power.*

As he spoke, the minotaur grew larger and larger, until his form straddled the entire ship. There was still no actual sound, but the words pounded inside Theros's head. Suddenly, the minotaur's arms grew longer, and sprouted feathers. Theros could not believe his eyes. Within seconds, the colossal minotaur had changed into a giant black crow. It took to the air, a red glow outlining its form. It flew above the ship, and then, claws extended, it dove down toward Theros at a terrifying speed.

The gigantic bird would tear Theros apart. He couldn't move, not because he was courageous, but because he was frozen with terror. The crow hurtled toward the very spot where the minotaur had stood, then, at the last instant, changed back to the minotaur. Sargas stood before Theros, and smiled.

Theros could not believe, could not comprehend what he had just seen. He rubbed his eyes, pinched himself (to ensure that he was awake). Still the minotaur stood there before him.

Sargas bent at the waist, stared straight into the boy's eyes. *Two days ago, Theros, you stood on the beach, a boy in a village whose destiny it was to be a fisherman. You had sense enough to detest such a life. You threw your lot in with the minotaur warriors. That pleased me a great deal and I began to keep my eye on you.*

Yesterday, you revealed yourself to be a champion of honor. You could have let the human warrior plunge his knife into the back of the minotaur, who was—after all—your enemy. Instead, you saw the cowardly act for what it was, and warned the captain in time. Again, you pleased me.

You are a human whose life is promising. I am here now, revealing myself to you, in order to guide you on the correct path.

Theros looked up into the pools of darkness that were Sargas's eyes. His mind fell into the pools, diving into the center, seeing everything and nothing.

Theros believed. "What am I to do, Lord Sargas?"

Sargas straightened. *You must at all times remember honor. Bring honor to me by bringing honor to yourself, and recognize honor for the true virtue that it is. Learn the art and skills of warfare, and be aware that you are a human of destiny. Do not cast away your life, but take it and use it, and bend it to your will, as you did on the beach two days ago, and as you did yesterday on this ship.*

I will come to you three times in your life, Theros, this being the first. You will have no warning of these visits, but they will come at moments of crisis, so that I can help you learn the path I wish you to take.

Without warning, the minotaur once again turned into the black crow, whose wings seemed to be made of fire. It flew into the air. Theros followed the glowing bird as it rose higher and higher into the night sky, until it became just a speck, replacing one of the stars.

Theros made his way back to his berth below the deck. He intended to stay awake and go over the events of the past day in his head, to make some sense and order of it all. Instead, he slid into a deep, deep sleep.

When he awoke, he found the minotaur crew marveling over a black crow's feather they'd discovered on the deck. They were too far from land, they said, for crows to be flying over the ship.

Book Two

Chapter 5

"A good morning to you, Master Smith."

"Bah! Why is it that you humans must always try to grow flowers out of crap? It is a horrible day. The rain does not cease, and the mud does not cease, so why do you say the morning is good, Theros?"

The minotaur glared at the young man, who was tall and sturdy for his eighteen years. His arms were well developed, his hands large and capable. He kept his curly hair short, his face clean-shaven, as was the custom for humans in minotaur servitude.

"It is a good morning because it is a day of battle, Master Smith," Theros said.

The smith shook his horned head and snorted. "I doubt

that the elves will attack today. It does not seem to be weather to their liking. I'd wager on battle tomorrow. That means we have an immense amount of work to do. I will work on the arrowheads. You work on the spearheads. We can never have too many. Warriors use them as if they were rocks lying at their feet. They never seem to notice how long it takes to make them!"

Theros grimaced. "You spoil me, Hran. You know I hate to do arrowheads. They require such detailed work! But you have a harder time with them than I do. Your hands are far too big. Let me do the arrowheads. You do the spears."

"You see, you are learning. Knowing who is good for what job is how you get the work done. Now stop talking and start working. You humans are always talking. . . ."

Theros turned to stoke the fire. The battlefield forge had been set up the day before, but this was the first day they could use it. The fire took almost a day to build up enough heat to be useful.

The minotaur Hran was the master weapons-smith and armorer to the Third Minotaur Army. The army had campaigned most of the summer months, waging war against the elves in the forests of Silvanesti. A year ago, a group of minotaurs had decided that the coastal area would be ideal for minotaur settlements. Led by a sea pirate named Klaf, these minotaurs had built a walled village on the coast.

It was the first minotaur settlement on the continent since the Cataclysm had removed the land links between the minotaur homeland and the rest of Ansalon. The plan was to have the village grow into a town and later into a coastal fortress. Once entrenched, the minotaurs would be impossible to uproot, and home territory advantage would be granted to the minotaurs in any defense. The elves would have to strike while the minotaurs were still establishing their new colony on Ansalon.

The elves had done just that. Acknowledging that the minotaurs were masters of the sea, the elves were building up their strength, preparing for an all-out attempt to retake the coastal area using inland armies. The minotaurs would have to fight for this ground.

Klaf, the minotaur in command, petitioned the Supreme Circle for an army to conquer the elves. If the elves could be defeated, then the coast and sea were the minotaurs' for the taking. From there, the minotaurs could conveniently raid most of Ansalon.

The Emperor, through the Supreme Circle, awarded Klaf the command of the minotaur army and ordered him to remove the threat of elves from the site of the colony. It was stressed that the honor of Klaf's entire clan rested on the success of this campaign. There was only one small problem. No combat-ready minotaur army could be spared. The Third Army was a ceremonial and parade ground army, normally housed at the capital in Lacynes. The Third Army had never seen battle. It would take a monumental effort for Klaf to turn the Third Army into battle-ready warriors.

During the last year, Klaf had done just that. For seven months now, the force had campaigned against the elf units in the area, slowly and inexorably pushing them back inland. Klaf had seen victory in the offing and then, two weeks ago, his spies brought him word that a new force had arrived—an elven army of eight thousand that threatened to challenge the minotaurs in open battle. Although weaker in infantry than the minotaurs, the elves possessed excellent archers and their light cavalry could wreak havoc among the slow-moving minotaurs.

Klaf was firm in the belief that only amateur soldiers plotted strategy and tactics. Professionals studied logistics. He knew that archers were his army's weakness. The booty taken from the first few battles enabled Klaf to hire mercenaries—human archers—to round out his force.

By keeping his supply lines from the sea open, he had ensured that his army was well fed and well equipped. Hundreds of artisans, cooks, skilled woodworkers and taskmasters had been taken from the ships in the minotaur fleets, and put to work in the coastal village. One of these had been Theros, who had served on board a minotaur ship for the past eight years, since the age of ten.

The job of sharpening weapons, which Theros had picked up almost by accident, had proven to be one in which he was highly skilled. Theros had been so successful at his work of repairing leather and maintaining the ship's complement of weapons that his reputation spread far beyond the war barge on which he served.

The warriors of the *Blatvos Kemas* had done well in battle. They credited themselves, to be sure, but the captain had also done Theros the rare honor of including him in the reports. The captain claimed that the quality of armor and weapons was such that a warrior could rely on them to enable him to rise to his true potential. Unfortunately for the captain, this praise of Theros caught the eye of a wealthy Supreme Circle member. The captain lost Theros in a wager on a sea battle with the council member, much to the regret of the crew and warriors.

Theros was not the only valuable object won by the Supreme Circle member. Several ships, with their complement of slaves, crew, warriors and supplies, went to the high-ranking minotaur. He sent most of his winnings to the revitalized army of Klaf, as a show of support.

Theros was assigned to the chief armorer of Klaf's forces. Hran was wise, powerful, with legendary skills when it came to bladed weapons. His axes were much prized and widely sought after. At first, Hran had been skeptical of working with a human. He assigned the young man the job of making arrows and spears. These were not the weapons of any fabled warrior, yet they were the daily tools of an army. They could be made in abundance, and an army would run short of them in two days of fighting. When Theros proved skilled in this task, Hran began to think that the human might make a fairly decent smith.

Hran took care never to tell Theros that, however.

The new elven army posed a great threat to the minotaur army. The elves had to be defeated or there could be no consolidation of the coastline. The place of battle was not a hospitable one, and the clouds had not stopped raining for the past week. The ground was soaked through, and wherever the large wagons of the baggage train moved, mud churned in their wake. The ground around the smithy was the only dry ground for a league in any direction. A huge tent had been set up, with the center post being the chimney for the forge. The heat of the fire under the tent baked the ground to a hard clay.

The fire was finally hot enough to melt metal after a day of feeding the flames. Theros took blocks of steel and bronze and melted them in a large cauldron. Under the watchful eye of Hran, he tossed in small amounts of different powders to add special properties to the metal soup. White powder ensured that the metal would not crack when cooled. Gray powder helped the two different metals mix together to form a stronger alloy.

The cauldron bubbled and boiled. Using a small knife, Theros cleaned the mold for the arrowheads. Very carefully, he peeled away any remnants of previous castings. When he was satisfied, he arranged the wooden plates around the fire. With a huge pair of tongs, he lifted the cauldron and poured molten metal into the first mold. The metal flowed into the arrow-shaped crevices carved into the wooden block and began to congeal. The wood burst into flame from the intense heat. Theros moved on to the second mold, and repeated the pouring. He did the same again and again until all of the ten molds were filled, all were on fire.

Theros placed the cauldron back into the forge flame, and dropped the tongs. He ran to the water barrel, filled a bucket, and ran back to his burning molds. One by one, he doused the molds in water, putting out the fire and curing the metal. The steam rose, mixing with the smoke from the forge, curling from the top of the tent.

"I'd say three more uses for these molds. After that, they'll be far too burned. What do you think, Hran?"

The large minotaur grunted. "I would say that you could have at least four more uses if you put out the fires faster. For a young cub in the prime of his physical condition, you are exceedingly slow and as clumsy as a dwarf. You are hopeless! You will never make a smith!"

The young man was not disheartened. He knew that he had put out the fires in the molds in near-record time. Hran was always trying to push Theros to better, higher standards. Theros refilled his bucket of water. This time he cooled the metal to the point where the raw arrowheads could be removed from the molds. He dropped them into a metal grate that hung just below the water's surface in the water barrel. Bubbles and steam sputtered from the water. Soon, two hundred raw arrowheads from the ten molds lay cooling in the water.

"Hey, Hran! When do you think Klaf will march the warriors out to battle?"

Hran stopped sharpening an axe blade for a moment, and looked up. "If Klaf has his way, it will be two more days before the battle will begin. I think that Klaf will not get his way, though. I do not see those soft and dainty elves becoming more and more drenched while waiting for us to build up to fighting on our terms. No, I think that they will push soon. Too soon. We must be ready."

Theros pulled the arrowheads from the water one by one. He fastened each one into a vise. Next, he took a large metal file and began to sharpen the raw shape into a honed tip. Four or five scrapes with the coarse-toothed file would shape one side of the arrow, and four or five scrapes with a fine-toothed file would put a sharp edge on it.

"Don't you think that our infantry is better than theirs, though?" Theros asked.

Hran continued sharpening the sword. "Infantry is only one part of a battle. We have no cavalry, and the elves make good use of theirs. Normally that means nothing to us. We stand and fight until there are no other enemies to be fought. In this case, I can see trouble. If our supply lines are cut and the infantry are separated into small groups, the elves can concentrate their forces and crush the survivors."

"Klaf knows that," Theros said. "We will prevail if given the chance."

He removed the arrowhead from the vise, turned it over, put it back and repeated the process on the other side.

"You've got to admit, my friend, that our weapons are vastly superior to those of the elves." Theros regarded his work with pride. Every few moments, he would finish an arrowhead and throw it in a pile. As they talked, the pile grew steadily larger.

"Bah!" Hran snorted again. "You know nothing of weapons. I have taught you as much as I know in the months you have worked for me. We deal with weapons and armor designed for an army's everyday use. Axe, sword, arrow, spear, knife—these are the weapons of the warrior. Shield, breastplate, shin plates—these are the armor of a warrior. We mend and beat out the dents and make arrows, but we don't have the time to do truly excellent work. Take this sword, for example. It's a weapon for a true warrior. Only an expert can craft such a blade. I wish I had the time to teach you the art of making a good sword."

Hran gazed at the weapon fondly, then, with a sigh, he slid the sword back into its sheath. Setting the sword aside on a table, he picked up a huge breastplate. The piece was ornate with inlaid silver pictograms and symbols, each depicting a heroic act or a battle scene. The armor had separated from the leather backing.

Hran threaded a leather-working needle with sinew and inspected the piece. The leather had ripped in the backing, causing the shoulder straps to come loose. The piece had probably came loose in a battle, and the warrior had ripped the plate away, causing most of the damage.

Hran grunted and threw the work onto the ground. "Bah! Theros, you do this. The work requires smaller hands than mine. Why they want me to waste my talents on repairing armor is beyond me."

Theros finished the last of the arrowheads and left them in the pile, ready for shafts. Later he would carry them down to the fletcher to have the shafts and fletching added. That was not a weapons-smith's job.

Hran picked up a huge axe head with a broken shaft hanging from its center mount. "Ah! Now this is a fine piece of work! I can see the craftsmanship in this axe head. A new handle and it will be a worthy weapon for a warrior!"

Theros laughed. He picked up the armor to inspect it. "Of course, you think that. It is obviously one of yours!"

He turned his attention back to the armor breastplate. Using leather shears, he began cutting away the upper right corner of the inner pad, as well as the right shoulder strapping. The leather was badly corroded from being wet and not properly cared for. It had probably never seen saddle soap in its history. The piece looked as if it had been handed down for several generations, a marvelous piece when it was new—a breastplate fit for a brave, honorable warrior.

Theros turned to Hran to continue the conversation, but at that moment, Hran began beating the axe handle remnants with a huge hammer and a wood awl. The pounding made further conversation impossible.

It was nearing the middle of the morning, and the haze was beginning to lift. Even the light drizzle began to subside. Theros could now make out the fletcher's tent, the commissary tent, and the quartermaster's wagons. The weather was indeed improving. Minotaur warriors moved in and out of the tents. Human slaves moved about. It was business as usual in the rear guard of an army.

A large warrior with overly large horns entered the weapons-smith's tent. Hran did not notice, and kept on hammering at the axe handle remnants. Theros rose. He recognized the minotaur—he was the officer in charge of the rear guard. Huluk was his name and he had a reputation for being a quarrelsome warrior whose only joy was fighting, either in battle or with his fellow soldiers.

The big warrior shouted over the din. "Is that my armor you are working on, slave? Let me see that."

Theros gestured that the right strap wasn't finished, but the minotaur ignored him. Theros was a slave, after all. Theros held out the half-repaired piece to the officer for his inspection. The minotaur took the breastplate, slapped it on and fumbled for the straps. When he couldn't find the right strap, he was furious. The minotaur flung the plate back at Theros.

"This is not good enough! I want this ready in one hour."

Hran heard the words over the din and stopped hammering. He turned to watch the officer stomp away through the mud.

"In Sargas's name, what was that all about?"

Theros shrugged. "The commander doesn't like the work I have done on his breastplate. I tried to tell him it wasn't finished. He wants it in an hour."

"Tell him he will have it when he gets it."

Theros smiled, but it was a bitter smile. "I don't dare tell him that. I'm a slave, or have you forgotten?"

Hran gazed at him. "Sometimes I think you're the one who has forgotten, Theros. You speak of 'we' minotaurs and 'our' army. It almost seems that you consider yourself a minotaur. Why is that?"

Theros muttered something to the effect that it was probably because he'd lived with the minotaurs for eight years. He'd never told anyone about his meeting with Sargas. He didn't think he ever would.

Hran eyed him, evidently guessing there was more to this than Theros's words. Theros bent over the leather.

The smith mumbled something about less talk and more work, and went back to pounding out the wood in the axe head.

Theros began by taking a fresh piece of leather and cutting it to shape. The leather needle was still threaded, and lay on the table beside the other tools. With it, Theros stitched the new leather to the old piece that was still attached to the plate. He sewed the new leather in place, then added cotton tacking to pad between the leather and the metal. Next, he connected the sides of the leather to the edging, using the fasteners that were still there, and hammering in new ones where there were none.

He laid the plate to one side. Picking up the old leather, he placed it in the vise. He broke the strap harness away from the old piece by severing the rivet with pliers.

He threw the rest of the leather away. Lifting the buckle, he dunked it in grease. His fingers began to work the jammed buckle, loosening the rust to the point that the buckle could be used again. The last thing to do was to reattach the buckle to the breastplate.

Theros turned to pick up the rivet pliers. The clouds broke. Yellow sunlight streamed through to the ground.

From the front, a lone horn sounded.

It was the call to battle.

Chapter 6

Theros looked at Hran. Both of them stopped work.

The call to battle was too early.

The moment of inactivity passed, just as quickly replaced with commotion. Everything and everyone moved as fast as a jackrabbit spotted by a hound. The warriors poured out of their tents, hastily donning armor or breastplates.

Hran dropped what he was doing. "Quick, lad, finish that piece! We've got to get ready! Great Sargas alive! This is not the time!"

Theros sewed as fast as he could. He concentrated on his sewing, while the whole world swarmed around him. Sub-commanders were streaming into the tent, demanding arrows or spears, leather-covered shields, or metal bullets especially shaped for the slingers. They grabbed what they needed, then rushed out.

Hran dashed over to a large storage box sitting to the side of the tent. He threw it open and lifted out a piece of his own armor—a leather jerkin with metal strips, designed to turn an arrow or blade before it did damage. He strapped it on, and fumbled for the next piece.

Theros could not get his fingers to work fast enough. He knew he would never finish in time. He was right.

Huluk, the rear guard commander, burst into the tent.

"You, slave! Give me that breastplate. I need it now!"

Theros started to protest, to tell the officer that the piece wasn't ready yet, that it was only barely sewn together. The officer backhanded Theros across the face, sending the young man sprawling.

"Damned slave! This armor is not done yet! How am I to fight with garbage like this? Get this on me!"

Theros, flat on his back from the blow, rolled over and jumped to his feet. He tried to strap the armor to the torso of the huge minotaur. It would not hold. The seam was already giving way as Theros tried to pull the strap tight.

This time Theros reacted as the warrior's shoulder muscles tightened and the minotaur began to turn. Theros ducked just in time to miss another blow.

"I am sorry, Commander. I did not have time. . . ."

The officer shouted at the smith. "You will pay for the insolence and incompetence of this slave under your control. Mark my words, Hran. This will not go unpunished."

Hran waved his hand. "Do as you will, Huluk. But now, there is a battle, and you must lead your warriors. Stop wasting my time and my slave's time and get to your fight!"

Huluk shook with rage, turned, and stormed out of the weapons-smith's tent. As he walked, his leather breastplate banged against his chest, only partly attached.

Theros stood glumly, his hands at his sides, his head down. He had failed. He deserved his punishment.

Hran walked over, gripped Theros by the shoulder. "Listen here, Theros. One warrior's panic is not another's emergency. We will defeat this elven army, and then we will return to the new village on the shore, where we will forge wondrous swords only warriors from antiquity have seen!

"First, the task at hand. You begin on the left side, I will start on the right. We roll the tent canvas off the support poles toward the center chimney. Now move!"

Theros dashed off to his side of the tent and began rolling up the wet sides of the canvas.

They had to take the tent down, and stow the equipment in the wagon before they could properly prepare for battle. The hearth remained stoked and hot, but the tent was to be removed. If they won the battle, they would set the tent up again. If they lost, they would form part of the army's baggage train, then retreat with the rear guard. Hran would leave nothing behind for the elves, not even scraps.

The canvas was heavy, soaked after days of rain. Hran finished his side, rolling it to the edge of the hearth. He began to disconnect the two sides of canvas from one another. Theros struggled. The heavy canvas rolled slowly, getting heavier with each inch.

"Come on there, lad! Put your back into it!" Hran yelled.

Between the two of them, the roll moved faster. It thumped up against the side of the hastily built stone hearth before stopping. Together, they went to the right end of the roll, and lifted it over and onto the other half. Both bending, they hoisted the canvas onto the wagon.

Hran grunted as they shoved the canvas securely into place in the wagon. "Quickly now, collect all of the tools!"

Theros ran to where the tent had stood moments ago. He stooped to grab the two sets of tongs lying in the grass. As he reached for them, the mournful sounds of the regimental trumpets began to wail.

"The call to form ranks." Hran looked worried. "Hurry, lad! Hurry!"

Now Theros could hear the sound of shrill elven trumpets. The enemy was close at hand.

They had taken too much time with the canvas. He and Hran were going to be caught in the midst of the battle.

Chapter 7

The clouds were beginning to break and dots of sunshine began to play across the field separating the minotaurs from their foe, the elves.

Theros was but one small cog in the minotaurs' huge war machine. As he labored in the rear, the machine geared up to creak forward.

The minotaur leader, Commander Klaf, hastened out of his tent, near the back of the assembling troops. He shouted to the standard-bearer and bugler. "What is going on? Why did you sound the battle call?"

His officers pointed. Klaf looked across the field. Elves were pouring from the woods and beginning to form around their own standards.

"Great Sargas! Bugler, sound the 'officers to me' call."
The bugler brought the great horn up and blasted out the
notes. The entire camp had come alive when the call to
arms had been sounded. Now it was time to get moving,
not stand around like children waiting to be fed.

Klaf stood with his arms crossed, studying his enemy
from across the nearly mile-wide field. As always, the elves
were taking their time, forming into pristine companies, all
in precise lines and columns. The elf commander had three
infantry corps in his command. He placed one corps forward and the other two side-by-side behind the first. Klaf
motioned to the standard-bearer.

"So what do you think, Olik? Where would you say all
of their archers are going to be? That's what we worry
about most."

The younger officer hesitated for a moment, still studying the enemy formations. "The rear two corps must con-
tain their archers, sir. I cannot believe that the elves are
stupid enough to challenge us with their infantry alone.
Surely they will use their might in archery to try and bring
our numbers down. I don't see any cavalry, either, Commander. Do we know if they have any?"

The older minotaur nodded. "They must have cavalry,
but I do not see it. Damn them! The elves always play these
silly games. Why don't they just come out and fight?"

Three minotaurs ran up to the officers, two more racing
behind. All were in various stages of dress, none fully
ready for battle.

The tallest, Bak, spoke first. "Are they forming to attack
now? Great Lords of the Abyss! We aren't ready!"

Klaf turned to the huge warrior. "Set the example, damn
you! I expect your troops to be formed before the enemy is
ready. Now go! *Go!*"

The officers turned and ran back to their tent lines, all
bellowing orders to their subordinates.

Olik planted the army standard in the ground. It was a
twelve-foot pole with a crosspiece attached near the top.
An orange and red banner hung down from the crosspiece,
showing a black raven with glowing wing tips. The very
top of the pole was adorned with a gold spearhead, and

two gold tassels hung down. The banner was normally cased in a leather sock, but when the horns of battle rang out, clear as the morning sun, Olik decided it was time for the banner to be unfurled. The banner would show the enemy that they were fighting against a mighty army.

Olik had been chosen specially as the standard-bearer for the Third Army because he was a foot taller than any other minotaur in the army. His job was to keep the standard flying at all costs. To let it fall would be a disgrace for the army. To let it be captured would be the worst of all possible fates, worse even than defeat. Olik would fight to the death to defend the standard.

The elves had begun to straighten their lines and close together for the march across the field. The minotaur officers were shouting at their warriors to form into regiments and straighten their own lines. Across the field, a fanfare of trumpets sounded, and with a great shudder, the three corps of elves began to push forward.

Minotaurs were still coming out of tents, still pulling on pieces of armor, still fumbling for weapons, still tightening straps. Officers and junior leaders were doing everything in their power to get their troops in place.

One minotaur was completely drunk. An officer raced up behind him and bashed him on the back of the head in an attempt to sober him up. The soused minotaur fell facedown into the grass. His officer left him for dead and went back to his unit.

Olik, still watching the advance of the elven army, shook his head and looked over to Klaf. "We have to slow their advance, sir, to allow our troops enough time to get into formation. We don't even have our skirmish line out yet!"

Klaf shook his head. "We can't engage them with archery. My archers aren't in place. Such an attack might even cause them to quicken the pace. What if we . . ." He hesitated, looked over at his standard-bearer and friend.

"What, sir?"

"What if we offered to parley?" Klaf said.

Olik was shocked. "You can't be serious, sir? Parley . . . with elves?" He almost spat the word.

"It will slow them down," the commander noted.

"True. . . ." Olik was not yet convinced.

Klaf had made up his mind. "Quick, go back to the tent line and grab some tent canvas and a spear. You and I, along with several warriors, will go forward under a flag of truce. They will honor that. They have to honor that!"

Shaking his head, Olik ran off at a trot. A few moments later, he emerged from a tent with a spear and a ripped section of white cloth. He ran back to the command group.

Olik looked miserable. "Do you really mean to go through with this, sir?"

Klaf turned his attention away from the enemy. He glanced back to see his troops rushing about in confusion.

"If the elves reach us now, they'll cut us to pieces. Do you know of a better way to stop them?"

Olik said nothing.

"Right, come with me." Klaf marched forward, through his assembling troops. As he walked past his warriors, he yelled out to some of them, calling them by name, attempting to boost morale.

"Ready to kill some elves today, Rajan?

"Good day for a fight, eh, Bratag?

"Muddy enough for you, you giant lug, Mosex?"

The soldiers waved and shouted. Klaf and his small group moved forward through his own troops' lines and out toward the enemy. Halfway, Klaf ordered the white banner raised.

"No need to get shot for this," Klaf said. He looked back at his own army. Units were jostling to get into line. The mercenary human longbowmen hired to provide the army some mode of long range missile fire were too far to the left side. The skirmish line had not yet deployed.

The whistling of an arrow brought the minotaur warriors in Klaf's party back to the situation at hand. They froze as the arrow slammed into the soft ground not a foot in front of Olik. Three elves on horseback rode forward from their center positions. As they did so, elf commanders all over the field ordered their units to halt. Seconds later, the elven army had come to a standstill. The three elf officers moved forward, one holding a spear with a white scarf attached.

The four minotaurs stood and waited. The diminutive horses of the elves seemed to dance across the field as they approached. At a distance of a hundred feet, the group stopped.

The lead elf stood up in the saddle and yelled in Common. "Minotaur warriors! What is this? Some sort of a trick? Or are you truly wanting to parley?"

Klaf began to laugh, then checked himself. He yelled back. "This is a parley. We want to talk."

The elves moved forward cautiously. All kept their hands away from weapons, as did the minotaurs. The minotaurs knew that they were in range of some skilled archer somewhere, or more likely a unit of them. The elves knew that if the flag of truce was violated, then they would have to face in hand-to-hand battle these four well-armed and experienced minotaur warriors, one of whom stood nearly nine feet tall!

Two of the elves remained mounted when they came within hearing distance. The third dismounted.

"I am Harinburthallas, son of Harinbutthal. I command the Northern Wing of the Imperial Army."

"I am Klaf, son of Klak, son of Krak. I am the commander of the Third Minotaur Army. I come to discuss the terms for your surrender."

The elf looked astonished. "My surrender? Are you blind? I outnumber you at least two to one. My archers are far superior to that rabble of humans that you have on your left flank, and you do not even have your skirmishers deployed. Most assuredly *you* are going to offer your surrender to *me!*"

Klaf stared at the elf in feigned amazement. He looked over at Olik, who shook his horned head no, indicating they needed more time. Klaf took a step toward the elf.

"Do not *dare* to insult the honor of my army, or of any minotaur warrior. We are servants of Sargas! I will not surrender to you! You do not have enough honor among you all to lace up the strap of my boot, much less accept my surrender, even if I had the intention to do so."

He glanced over again at Olik. The huge standard-bearer was looking over his shoulder. A second later, his gaze returned to his commander, and he nodded yes.

Klaf concluded. "I see that a parley with you elves is to no avail. I wish you honor on this day of battle." He turned, and so did the other minotaurs in the party. They marched back to the army lines.

As they headed back, Olik rode over to Klaf. "So, do you think they took you seriously about surrender?"

Klaf shook his head. "I have heard of this General Harinburthallas. He is one of their best. He knew that we were delaying. He could have refused to talk, however even elves have some smattering of honor. But that is why they rode horses, to speed things up. Notice that already the elf general is back with his army."

Klaf broke into a trot, followed by the three other minotaurs. A minute later they cleared their own skirmish line and continued to the space between the skirmishers and the main infantry line. The skirmish infantry were armed and armored lightly. Their job was to slow the main advance of the elves, and to force them to form into battle lines early. As they formed, the main infantry would charge through and hit the elves as they were still changing formations.

Klaf stopped to look over his troops. The minotaur warriors all fell silent as they saw their commander eyeing them. Klaf reached over and took the spear with the white cloth from Olik. He turned it over, and thrust it into the mud as deeply as he could. The white cloth was almost completely obscured.

A huge cheer went up across the army, spreading from the center, where every warrior could see their commander, out to the wings. Even the human longbowmen cheered. Klaf took his battle-axe from the harness strapped to his back, and held it aloft. As he did so, Olik raised the standard high above his head. Again, the cheer went up.

The small group passed through the front lines and positioned themselves on a knoll between the front corps and the rear reserve corps. The rest of the army staff, four officers and a phalanx of twenty of the best bodyguards, joined the commander.

Klaf looked up to find his skirmishers racing forward to

engage the enemy's front line of infantry. The middle of the first elven wing split down the center in an obviously rehearsed move. From their rear, elven light cavalry charged forward to engage the minotaur skirmish infantry.

The fight was on.

* * * * *

Theros could hear the battle raging. From his vantage point in the rear, though, he could see nothing. Barracks and supply tents stood between him and the field of battle.

He knew only that somehow, someone had gained them some time. He and Hran worked at a feverish rate collecting all of the tools, benches, anvils and spare parts that went into the smithy. The stone forge remained where it was, its coals still red-hot.

All around them other parts of the rear were also packing up, getting ready to move—either forward or back. The commissary unit across the road had eight human slaves loading meat and other edibles into covered wagons.

Hran stopped Theros as he picked up the last of the arrowheads that he had been working on earlier. Hran handed Theros a shovel.

"You've seen a minotaur army only in victory. You've never seen what happens in a defeat. I do not like the omens of Sargas for this battle today, so here is what I will have you do.

"Dig a small pit here near the forge. If the going gets rough, I want you to hide in it. You have no armor or weapons, and you'll die if there's fighting around and you're in the way. I'll ensure that the forge is stocked up and ready to get back to work in case we win. Now start digging."

Theros hated the thought of hiding in a pit, but he had to face facts. He had no way to defend himself. He began to dig.

Hran kept leaving his work stoking the fire, raising himself up to stare in the direction of the battle.

"What is it, Hran? What's troubling you?" Theros asked.

"Get back to work! Now dig!" Hran searched around the

ground for tools or other pieces of armor or weapons that should be stowed.

Behind them, the sound of thunder began to build.

Behind them?

Chapter 8

Klaf pounded his armored fists together. "Yes! Yes! That's it! Keep up the pressure."

From the command group's vantage, they could see clearly only the front lines. The left and right were obscured by the troops of the center regiments. The skirmish infantry, out in front of the main lines, had driven the elven archers from the front of the elven battle line. Most of the skirmishers had fallen when the front line of the enemy army stopped advancing and fired a devastating volley of arrows. Then, the minotaurs had hit them. The elven archers were no match for minotaur warriors in hand-to-hand combat.

Klaf could see the two armies moving closer and closer.

Both sides were taking casualties now from archery. Klaf's mercenaries on his left flank were pouring their own long-range archery into the elven lines. The two battle lines closed to within two hundred yards.

Klaf turned to the bugler. "This is it, lad! Sound the charge!"

The bugle call rang out clearly across the battlefield. Within moments, it was drowned out by the minotaurs' war cry. The sound was like banshees howling. Forward they went, battle-axes and swords swinging, hungering for elven flesh to tear and rend.

The elves stopped cold at the sight. Their officers ordered the ranks to close up. The front rank knelt. They fired a volley into the charging, near-berserk minotaurs. Hundreds dropped, but many hundreds kept coming on. Elves fumbled to reload. Many dropped their bows and drew swords, preparing to receive the charge.

The two lines met with a huge crash of steel and bone. The sheer size of the minotaur warriors, combined with their crazed battle frenzy, were enough to smash holes in several places in the front regiments of elves.

Klaf was well pleased. His heavy infantry was making short work of the first corps of elves. The charge had cleared over a third of the elven infantry from the first elven corps, or so he could see from where he stood. If he could get that front corps to rout, then they would run back through the following corps, panicking them or at least disrupting their ranks. The morale of his troops would shoot up like an elven arrow to the sun. The key was shock of impact and follow-through force. He had to commit his reserve force of warriors.

He slapped the bugler on the right shoulder. The din of battle was incredible. It would be difficult to hear the call. Klaf yelled, "Sound the advance!" and motioned to Olik to carry the army standard forward. The clear notes of the bugle sung out over the crash of armies.

The reserve corps began to march forward into the melee.

A bright flash in the center of the minotaur line drew Klaf's attention. An explosion ripped apart a ten-foot circle in the front lines of the lead minotaurs. Twenty warriors fell in the blast. Klaf could not see the source of the explosion, but he knew what it was. Every seasoned battlefield commander knew the sight of battle magic. Somewhere there was an elf war-mage. He had to be close to the front lines, too. The range of spells was limited in field conditions.

Klaf turned and motioned for two of his bodyguards. "Did you see that explosion down there?" The two nodded. Klaf continued. "Get down there, find that elf wizard, and rip him to pieces!"

The two warriors saluted and ran off as fast as they could. This was their moment of glory. They skirted past the warriors in the first corps, and through one of the developing holes in the elven line. Breaking out behind the lines of the first elven corps, they ran straight down the rear of the elven ranks. Several elves turned to fight them, but the minotaurs moved so quickly that the elves lost sight of them.

Klaf kept his eyes fixed on the two warriors. If the war-mage was to continue, Klaf's whole battle plan could become unhinged. The minotaurs were not magic-using soldiers. Honor and glory lay in battle, not in spellbooks and trickery.

He spotted an elf surrounded by a small group of four bodyguards. Klaf did not notice the elf before, but now he was obvious. The elf in the center must be either the commander of the first corps or the wizard casting the spells. Either way, his death would aid the minotaurs. The two warriors crashed into the group, axes swinging.

Another explosion rocked the front of the minotaur line. This time Klaf saw the elf in the group conjure the fireball. It was to be his last spell. Seconds later, the wizard fell. The attacking minotaurs had cut down the bodyguards and were hacking the wizard limb from limb. Elf soldiers from the rear of their brigade turned and engaged the two elite warriors. Four more elves fell before the two minotaurs were cut down. Klaf nodded in satisfaction. The warriors had completed their mission, and died with extreme honor.

Up and down the line, elves and minotaurs were exchanging blows. The minotaurs had the upper hand, though.

Their size and battle skills outweighed the elves' finesse with swords. The main elven advantage of archery was useless in close-quarter fighting. Still, the minotaurs were paying the price of battle. Many warriors fell in the fight. Their deaths only drove their comrades to fight harder.

* * * * *

Theros dug faster. The thunder rumbled over the ground. The source of the sound was from the rear. He glanced up to see Hran buckling his great battle-axe onto his back. Theros recognized the sound now—it was the thunder of horses' hooves.

Hran unhooked the weapon from its holster and tested its weight. It was a finely balanced weapon, carved from end to end with markings and symbols and scenes of battle. While Theros watched in amazement, Hran stepped out into the roadway and readied his axe in a battle stance.

A white stallion with armored barding burst out of the forest, flew past Hran. An elf rider in armor plate sat atop the beast, sword held high.

A second and a third galloped past Hran, without coming close enough to bother him. The fourth rider yelled an elven war cry and headed straight for the smith. The horse threatened to plow the minotaur under, but at the last moment, Hran neatly sidestepped the horse and brought his battle-axe up into the horse's path, slicing into its chest. The animal pitched forward, throwing its rider onto the ground. Before he could recover, Hran embedded his axe into the elf's back. Hran recovered his axe, almost too late.

Elven armored cavalry streamed through the camp, killing anything that moved. Very few minotaurs offered resistance. Hran was one.

One rider came around the side of the wagon. He swung a gleaming sword at Theros, who very nearly lost his head to the elf. The rider's horse was forced to jump over the forge, causing the rider to falter in his swing.

Wishing desperately that he had a weapon, Theros could do nothing but dive headfirst into the shallow pit. He was up almost immediately, trying to see how Hran was doing, but the forge was in the way.

The elves kept coming. One rode past with a burning torch, and tossed it onto the smithy wagon. The pitch from the torch spattered onto the wood sides and immediately caught fire. Within seconds, the whole side of the wagon was in flames. Even the wet canvas that they had rolled up was beginning to burn.

Theros rose to his knees just in time to see another armored horse bearing down on his position. Again, he threw himself into the dirt. The horse and rider flew over the forge and onward, probably never even noticing the human slave that hid there.

Theros rose once more. The thunder of hooves was now behind him and going the other way, toward the armies battling on the field. There was a sudden hush. Theros stood and looked around. The wagon with all of the smith equipment and supplies was blazing.

Hran stood in the road, an arrow protruding from his shoulder. He paid it no heed. A group of the mounted elves turned and charged back through the camp, herding those who ran before them, cutting them down when they caught them. Hran did not run.

The first of the elven heavy cavalry charged straight for Hran. Weaponless, Theros could do nothing but watch the unequal battle. The elf yelled a war cry and brought down a thin lance. Hran tried to sidestep the blow as he had done before. This time he was too slow. The lance split open his side, cutting straight through the leather armor. Blood spurted out. Hran grabbed his side with one hand, but brought the axe up with the other. His swing was wide, the rider sped past him.

The elf behind the first came on with the same maneuver. This one, however, held the lance point too low. Hran swatted the point of the lance into the ground just in front of him. The elf vaulted straight out of his saddle before he knew what had happened. The horse ran past, the elf fell a few feet to Hran's right. Quickly, he hobbled over and brought his axe down on the elf's head. Blood and bone and brains spattered.

Hran charged forward to meet another elf mounted on

horseback. Blood ran from the minotaur's side. Hran was weakening. The elf dropped his lance, and drew his sword. As Hran approached, the elf slowed his mount and caused it to rear up. Hran went for the horse's underbelly. He was too slow, though. The lack of blood and the sheer exertion were just too much for him. The horse kicked Hran in the chest, sending him sprawling backward.

The elf jumped off the horse, and ran forward to finish the smith where he lay. The elf brought his sword down in a mighty swing, but Hran rolled away. He staggered to his feet, but the elf was ready. The elf thrust forward with his long sword, striking Hran through the heart.

Hran looked down at the wound. He tried to bring up his axe, but it slipped from his grasp. The elf withdrew his sword, and Hran pitched forward into the dirt, face first. The elf ran off after his mount. The rest of the elven cavalry were already far off across the camp.

Sudden fury shook Theros. He sprinted to Hran's side. Theros rolled the big minotaur over, and pulled him to a sitting position. Hran stared out unblinking into the destroyed and burning camp. He was dead.

Tears that pain could never wring from him welled up in Theros's eyes. Hran, his slave master, had been mentor and friend.

The bodies of eight elf warriors lay strewn across the road. Theros dragged Hran away from the forge and pulled him up beside the shallow trench that had saved the young man's life. Hran had died a true warrior. He had slain eight of the best elves that the Silvanesti Nation could muster.

Theros began to dig again. As he dug, anger welled up inside him. This was no act of honor that had cost Hran his life. The elves had intentionally circled around the back and attacked the rear guard while the minotaur main forces were arrayed on the field. Looking over to the commissary wagon, he could see that the elves had slain the human slaves, as well as the minotaurs, all mostly unarmed.

It had been the plan of a coward. A coward without honor.

Theros continued to dig.

Chapter 9

Klaf turned and raised his huge battle-axe. He started running forward. The rest of the command group followed him. A cheer went up from the reserve corps, and they, too, broke into a run, closing the distance between their position and the front lines.

"Make sure they can see the army standard up there," Klaf commanded. "Don't let some hot-headed elf take you down."

Olik roared a battle cry and raised the standard high. In his other hand he held an exquisite long sword. It was of Solamnic origin, but now it was decorated with the designs of Olik's clan.

The noise was horrendous. Klaf's bodyguards cleared a

path around the commander and Olik. Two elves spotted the banner and charged toward the standard. If it fell, the morale of the minotaurs might be broken and the day go with the elves.

One of the elves was immediately taken down by a minotaur's sword. The other elf broke the circle. With a great cry, he raised an ornate blade high above his helmeted head. Olik stood his ground. He planted his back foot and kicked out with his front foot just as the elf came within reach. The foot smashed in the front of the elf's helmet, and shattered the face inside. The elf crumpled like a sack of leaves. Klaf brought his axe down on the battered body.

Suddenly, the elves routed.

Many threw down weapons and ran. Some just ran. Within seconds, the only elves left were the dead ones or those trapped by fallen bodies of minotaur warriors. They soon joined the ranks of their dead comrades. The minotaur force let out a huge cheer.

But the cheer was short-lived and died suspended in the air. Klaf looked around in confusion. He turned a full circle, and another. Then, he realized what had just happened.

In front of him, five hundred yards away, were two fresh corps of elven infantry, probably heavy infantry with archers in support. To his rear, he could see smoke staining the sky. Arrayed between him and his camp stood the elven heavy cavalry.

The quiet that had engulfed the minotaur army suddenly shattered as officers ordered troops into line again. The minotaurs moved slowly. Moments ago, it was to have been the elves who were running from the field, their morale crushed and their vanquishers chasing them down. Now, it was the minotaurs.

Klaf's heart sank. He realized that he had marched his army into a trap. The elves had intentionally placed an inferior force before the minotaurs to keep their attention on the battle in front. To their rear, the elven cavalry had slaughtered the rear guard and now threatened to sandwich the minotaurs.

The sound he dreaded and knew was coming echoed across the field from the elven lines. Thousands of arrows arched their way through the clearing sky toward the army. Before they hit, a second volley was loosed.

The impact of the first volley was devastating. Because the minotaurs did not wear substantial armor, their leather padding and shielding did nothing to stop well-fired arrows. Klaf stared in horror as warriors all around him fell.

He swung his battle-axe over his head and began a deep growl that slowly became a howling war cry. Leaping forward, alone, he raced toward the elven infantry.

His warriors stood and watched in stunned silence. Olik, suddenly realizing that this was the only way to an honorable death, couched the army standard like a lance and sprinted after his commander.

The minotaur army rallied and charged.

After one hundred yards, a quarter of them had fallen to arrows. They kept going.

After two hundred yards, another quarter were dying in the mud, but the rest kept going. The arrows were less effective at this range.

After four hundred yards, the minotaurs that were left were sorely winded. Still they kept charging. There was death in anything that they did now, but the only way to honor was one hundred yards ahead.

Klaf's own fear of defeat with dishonor fired him forward. He screamed and swung his axe in huge arcs. At twenty yards, Olik, running beside him, stumbled a few steps. An arrow protruded from his chest. The giant minotaur shook his head, tore the arrow from his chest, tossed it on the ground, and caught up to Klaf.

Klaf hit the elven line first. The elves were jammed together in a tight defensive formation, swords and spears bristling outward. Klaf died almost instantly, but his body, as it fell, carried with it four elves, opening a hole in the lines.

Olik plunged into the hole after his dead commander, swinging his sword with one hand, using the army standard as a club in the other. Four, six, eight elves fell before the giant. More elves rushed forward, only to be bashed to pieces. Finally, two archers fired four arrows each into the big warrior's torso. Even then, Olik kept swinging standard and sword. Finally, he fell to his knees, then pitched forward into the dirt.

The standard fell. The minotaur army fell with it.

* * * * *

The minotaur army had died an ignoble death. Maybe one tenth of the minotaurs who began the battle were still alive. They stood in one group, prisoners of the elves. The death toll had not been only on the losing side, however. Hundreds of elves lay where they had been battered and hacked to death.

It was unclear whether the elves had lost more, but they weren't counting. They had won the day. The threat of minotaur intrusion into their coastal areas had been effectively negated. All that remained was the mop-up of remaining enemy forces.

The captured minotaurs were herded into one large group and surrounded by elf warriors and archers. All of the prisoners looked dejected. Their dishonor weighed heavily upon them.

The surviving elves went through the battlefield looking for dead and wounded warriors of their kind. The dead were taken back to the tree line and laid out with their weapons and the weapons of dead minotaurs near them as trophies. The wounded were taken back to a makeshift aid station in the rear. Here the healers worked their craft, some with arcane herbs and lore, others with brute force of bone-setting and flesh-cutting and the searing brand of cauterization. The healers had much to do this day.

Those minotaurs they found who were still alive but badly wounded were quickly dispatched. The elves had no regard for minotaur life. The prisoners might be useful for an exchange with the minotaur Supreme Circle for some political concession or other.

When all the elven wounded had been found and taken to the healers, the soldiers began the monumental task of burying their own dead, and burning the minotaur corpses.

Harinburthallas, the elven army commander, ordered one regiment, now numbering less than two hundred elf soldiers, to clear out the minotaur camp. The regimental commander, Llantoes, formed his soldiers into a column, and marched them across the field. They passed the site of the first engagement. The dead had been removed, but the mud was stained red, and a forest of arrows, embedded at the angle of impact, looked like stocks of straw that were bent by the wind. The mud was thick. The soldiers slogged forward.

Fewer than twenty minotaurs had survived in the rear area, all that was left of a mighty army. Most deserted their posts and disappeared into the woods, looking to get away. Several dozen human slaves lived too, Theros among them.

Fires burned everywhere. The camp was a complete ruin. From where Theros stood he could see the burning commissary wagons and the quartermaster's site. He could not see any minotaurs, other than those that had fallen in the brief battle with the elven cavalry.

Theros leaned on his shovel for a moment to catch his breath. The ground was soft for the first few feet, then turned to a thick, hard-packed clay. Digging was slow.

The smell of burning wood and canvas permeated the air. The smoke rose up and stained the cloudy sky. To the west was blue sky, but it could be seen only every once in a while through the pall of black, acrid smoke. The smoke caught in Theros's nose and throat. He tied a piece of cloth around his face to try to block the fumes.

He bent back to his digging. His young arms rippled with the effort. The blade dug only a few inches into the clay. Theros pried back the shovel, and a brick-sized chunk of clay broke loose. He bent down, picked up the piece, tossed it aside. He repeated the process, again and again.

He reached a depth of five feet in the trench. Deep enough. And who knew how much more time he would have before the elves found him? He tossed the shovel to the side, and climbed out. Hran lay several feet to the side of the trench.

Hran weighed close to three hundred and fifty pounds, with his armor and weapons. Theros dragged the body to the newly dug grave and rolled it in. Climbing down into the grave, Theros rearranged the body in the restful pose of death. He closed the eyelids, straightened the body, crossed the arms over the chest. It was not exactly how a minotaur would have honored the dead, but it was as close as the young man knew. He climbed back out, and stood silent.

The minotaur had been a strict master, but Theros had learned much from him in the past few months.

"Sargas, hear me," he began, and said a prayer for Hran.

* * * * *

Huluk, the rear guard commander, crouched behind several water barrels. Beside him crouched Nevek, another minotaur warrior.

Nevek shook his head. "We've got to leave. If we don't leave now, we'll be killed or captured like the rest."

Huluk grunted. "That was our army that was just slaughtered out there. Sargas strike us down! We should have died out there like the rest. We should have fought like the true warriors that they were."

"Yes, sir. Look, sir, our army is gone. We have a duty to warn the coastal village and the Supreme Circle. Our honor is in reporting the valiant sacrifice that our warriors made this day."

Huluk's face contorted in rage. This insolent young cub was telling him, a senior officer and a valiant, decorated warrior, about honor. "You! You know nothing of honor! Have you ever been victorious in battle? You . . ."

The officer paused. The young minotaur actually had a point about reporting the events of the day. Huluk's mind was racing. He had witnessed the deaths of many warriors that he knew and respected. He had lost his command to a surprise attack from heavy cavalry. He would be blamed for the failure, that was certain. But perhaps there *was* a chance to regain his shattered honor . . .

Nevek brought Huluk back to the here and now. "Sir, the

elves are moving this way!"

Huluk jumped up and peered over the barrels. While he had been sitting and brooding, a column of elf warriors had been slogging its way toward them. They were no more than two hundred yards away.

Huluk made his decision.

"You have a point, young warrior. We must get back to warn the village garrison. Now, we're going to need a few things. It is a four-day trip back. Gather up weapons and anything else that will be useful."

Nevek nodded. "I'll grab as many skins of water as I can find. The water barrels here are full. I'll try to find some food, too. Hurry, sir, they're almost here!"

Huluk nodded. "Right, meet me at the far end of the camp, near the weapons-smith's tent, or what's left of it. Go!"

Nevek ran. Huluk raced back through the burning camp. The broken breastplate banged and chafed against his fur. He stopped just short of the commissary wagons, the flames now beginning to burn low, and gave the armor a good yank. The leather straps disintegrated and the piece fell to the ground.

"Useless. Damned slave."

He bent and picked up his axe from the back harness built into the failed armor. He'd have to find a replacement.

The commissary area was strewn with bodies, minotaur and human. Several elves with their horses lay on the roadway. At least some enemies had fallen in the short-lived battle. Huluk rooted through the wreckage. Near the wagons were a stack of produce crates. He searched through them. The crates contained mostly raw meat and vegetables, some fish and a case of spices for the preservation of food. The bottom crate held baked hardtack. He rummaged around the tent site and found a cloth sack. He filled the sack halfway with food.

Weapons were next. He had to carry his axe, but he had nothing to carry it in. A bow would be good. A sword and scabbard would be useful, too. He crossed the commissary area and entered the smithy area. Several metal pegs and an anvil marked the edge where the tent had been. The stone hearth still stood in the middle of the tent area, its coals beginning to cool.

A movement from the left side caught Huluk's attention.

A young human stepped from behind the forge. He was dirty, and blood covered his clothes. Huluk recognized the human as Hran's slave—the same slave who had done a useless job on his armor.

Huluk nearly burst a vein. Here, in the middle of the carnage and destruction of an entire army, with everyone dead or gone, the only sentient being he could find was the moron who had ruined his armor.

The urgency of the situation left him no time for the luxury of expending his anger and fear upon this human slave. "You! Help me here! I need two bows, quarrels of arrows, a sword and anything else you've got that I can use. Hurry! I need them now!"

Theros turned to the nearly burned-out wagon. He picked up a stick, and began to sift through the remnants of the wagon's load.

Huluk did the same with his axe. Most of what they sifted through were tools or bits of tools that had been burned, their wooden parts no longer of any use. There was no sight of anything like a bow or an arrow or anything close to being useful.

"I'm sorry sir, this is all there is left," said Theros. "We had very few bows to begin with. They must have—wait!"

Theros ran out into the roadway to where some elves had fallen. Two horses lay dead in the street beside their riders. Pulling at the underside of one of the horse's saddles, Theros pried loose an elven short bow. The second yank yielded a full quiver of arrows. He held them up for the minotaur officer to see.

From a distance down the street, a high-pitched voice shouted in Common. "You! Yes, you! You will die for defiling an elf warrior in death!"

Theros turned to see four elf infantrymen running toward him, swords drawn. He looked back at the officer, who had also heard the shout. Huluk ducked down behind the remnants of the still-burning wagon.

Huluk waited, axe at the ready. Theros ran back and knelt beside the officer. He heard the light tread of soft leather boots. Huluk waited. Just as the first elf rounded the corner of the wagon, sword drawn, Huluk swung his axe with a backhanded motion. The exquisitely crafted blade sliced squarely into the elf's chest, caving it in, and pirouetting the elf onto his back.

Huluk jumped out into the open where he could fight without hindrance. He tossed the axe back and forth between his hands. The second elf rushed the big minotaur. Huluk easily leaned out of the way, tripping the elf as he lunged by, and embedding his axe into the soldier's helmet. The elf died like a leaf in a fire.

The other two elves circled the minotaur, who was trying to yank his axe from the body of the dead elf. One elf lunged. Huluk twisted as only a trained minotaur could, turning what should have been a deathblow into a painful slice across the side. Blood welled up out of the wound. Huluk went into a rage.

He jerked up violently with his axe, freeing it, and turned to the elf who had just wounded him. The elf blanched. Huluk brought his axe up as if he were going to charge. The elf immediately braced for the impact, hoping to sidestep the huge minotaur's lunge. Instead, Huluk thrust forward with his arm and let the axe sail forward. The elf never knew what hit him. The axe embedded in the elf's chest, crushing it.

The fourth elf lost no time. He charged the minotaur while he was off-balance. The hit was good, and the minotaur went sprawling. The elf brought his sword down, but Huluk rolled to one side, avoiding the blow. The elf was too close.

Huluk kicked at the elf's boots, knocking them out from under him. The minotaur was immediately on top of the elf, pinning him. The minotaur easily outweighed the elf by two to three times. Huluk placed his hands around the elf's neck, strangled him.

After the death rattle, Huluk rose. His side bled profusely.

Theros ripped off his shirt, pressing it against the side of the minotaur. Holding the cloth in place, Huluk pushed Theros away and retrieved his axe.

"You won't need that where you're going, minotaur."

Both Huluk and Theros turned around to see who spoke. An elf officer in gilt armor with gold fittings stood on the road. With him stood eight elf warriors, each with a bow. Eight arrows pointed at the two.

Huluk moved toward the elf. As he did so, the elf warriors began to circle around the minotaur, surrounding him.

The elf officer laughed. "So it has come to this, eh, warrior? We elves, so small in comparison to you huge beasts, have crushed your army. Our victory is the product of a finely honed military. We are no accidents of the gods like your horrible excuse for a race, or so the old text teaches. We were the firstborn, the pure. You are a race of abominations!"

Huluk breathed slowly, the wound in his side throbbing, but beginning to seal. The wound was not deep, but the blood loss was making him weak.

"What of it, elf?" Huluk sneered.

The elf mocked the warrior. "What of it? I want you to attack me. You are an officer in this once oh-so-mighty army, aren't you? I want to take the horns of an officer back to my fellow officers as a prize, so I want you to attack me."

Huluk did not move.

The elf immediately to his rear loosed an arrow right into the minotaur's buttocks. Huluk jumped straight up at the unexpected pain, howling like a wolf on a full-moon night.

The elves laughed. They were taunting their prey before killing it. They had forgotten about the human slave.

Silently, moving slowly and cautiously, Theros edged over to Hran's grave. His shovel stood where he'd left it, plunged into the mud. Grabbing the shovel by the handle, he returned to Huluk's side.

Huluk could barely stand; the pain of the arrow was maddening. He dropped his axe, grabbed the arrow sticking out of his rear and tried to pull it out.

The elf officer was highly amused. "What have we here? A little human slave come to aid his master with a weapon of the ages, the mighty shovel of Palanthas!" The elves laughed, enjoying the show being put on for their benefit.

Theros turned around in a circle, eyeing his foes, assessing his chances. They were zero and none. He turned back to the elf officer. He had not really regarded himself as a slave, even after all these years of captivity. After all, he had asked to come with the minotaurs. If they hadn't been kind to him, at least they had never tortured him as he was sure these elves would. He wanted to be free, to be sure, but he wanted freedom on his own terms.

Theros stared into the elf officer's eyes. "You have no honor, elf. If you did, you would fight me like a warrior."

The elf officer laughed so hard he could barely stand. "Oh, I like this! A human slave is challenging me to personal combat. Very well, I will bring in the horns of a minotaur and the head of a human, too. All right, let him come forward. I will accept your challenge, human slave!"

The other elves backed off, but still kept their arrows trained on the wounded minotaur. Theros held the shovel with two hands and began to circle the elf officer. The elf drew his sword from a jewel-encrusted scabbard, its blade flashing in the day's sunlight. The elf danced around Theros in a circle. As he circled the second time, he thrust.

The blow was so quick that Theros could not counter, could not parry. A gash opened on his upper arm. The blade gleamed and sang and gave Theros two more such cuts. Theros tried to lash out with the blade of his shovel, but the elf easily eluded him.

The show was most amusing, or so the elves thought. They laughed and jeered as the fight continued.

Theros knew the elf was only playing with him. At any moment, when the elf grew bored with the contest, he would sink his blade into Theros, who could do nothing to stop him.

Outmatched, Theros circled with the elf. He had a plan. The elf faked a chest thrust and sliced across the young man's hip. Theros ignored the pain.

He lowered the shovel. The elf thought Theros was giving up. Instead, Theros scraped the shovel across the earth and upward, tossing dust and dirt into the elf's face. The elf gasped, blinded. He dug his fists into his eyes, trying to clear them. Theros brought the butt end of the shovel up and smacked the elf squarely in the face. The elf fell over onto his back. His sword went flying through the air.

Theros stepped back. The sword landed on the roadway just off to his side. The elf sat up and shook his head, holding his broken nose between his fingers. The other elves brought their bows up, preparing to shoot the arrogant human.

"Stop! Lower your weapons!" the elf officer called in a tone more nasal than normal, due to his injury.

Theros planted the shovel into the ground. He picked up the elf's sword, tested it in the air.

"It is truly a fine weapon, sir elf. The blade is perfectly balanced. I admire the craftsmanship."

Theros handed the blade back to the officer, hilt first.

The elf paused, seemed on the verge of ordering his men to fire. Then, with a rueful smile and a shrug, the elf accepted the blade, clasping it in a bloody hand.

"You have bested an elf warrior of the Silver Birch Circle, young human, and you did it with a digging implement. You are a brave warrior and deserve to live. There has been enough killing this day.

"I release you. You may go where you will. We will not harm you."

Theros looked at the officer, then back to the bloody, half-fainting minotaur. "I will accept your offer, but I will go only with my master." He went to the minotaur's side.

Huluk regarded Theros with amazement. Theros grabbed the shaft of the arrow with both hands, and yanked it out. Huluk gritted his teeth against the pain. The human helped the minotaur to his feet. The elves said nothing and did not hinder them. Theros picked up the warrior's axe, and, with Huluk leaning on his shoulder, walked down the road, away from the field, away from the battle.

Neither looked back.

Chapter 10

Two miles was all that Huluk could manage. The road deteriorated into a cart track and the forest encroached on both sides, making the going difficult. The big minotaur finally collapsed. He had been walking, supporting himself on Theros's shoulder, but the pain was too much. He lost consciousness and slumped to the ground.

Theros checked the minotaur's wound. It was bleeding still, as were several of the cuts on his arms and torso.

"Damn. He can't go any farther, but we've got to get off this road. And we need food and water," Theros muttered to himself.

He left the minotaur where he lay, and went to explore the forest. Fifty feet from the track, Theros heard the sound of running water. Another twenty-five feet along he found a small stream. He bent to taste the water. He had forgotten about his own wounds. He was weak and light-headed and very nearly blacked out.

Dipping his hand into the small stream, he tasted the water. It was pure. Theros drank deeply.

Slowly, he rose, trying not to repeat the near-blackout. He looked around and found a small knoll where a great oak tree had fallen. Its roots formed a shield from the road, and gave easy access to the water.

Theros went back to the minotaur officer. Huluk hadn't moved. His breathing was still strong, but he was unconscious. Nothing Theros did would rouse him. Finally, Theros clasped the minotaur by his two arms and began to drag the unconscious Huluk into the woods.

Theros stepped on a loose rock. It turned beneath his foot, pitching him backward. As he lay, smarting from the fall and disheartened by the day's awful events, a shadow fell across him, blocking out the setting sun. Theros found himself staring straight up at the towering form of a minotaur warrior.

The minotaur put his axe head under Theros's chin, and using the weapon, forced him to stumble to his feet. "So, little slave. I see you have done well for yourself. I suppose you think the elves will reward you for killing this officer."

"I didn't kill him! I was trying to help him!" Theros protested.

"Shut up, you useless excuse for a human. There was no justice on the field of battle today, but there will be justice here. Pray for Sargas to take you, as death is your next destination. Justice is served, human!"

The minotaur drew back with his axe, and swung. To Theros's astonishment, the axe halted in midair. Instead, the warrior stumbled.

"Ah, Nevek," growled Huluk, holding onto the haft of the axe. "I was wondering what had happened to you."

Huluk slumped back against a tree, barely able to keep upright.

"But—but, sir," Nevek cried. "I thought you were dead!"

"For an up-and-coming officer, you are not terribly

observant. Next time check to see if I am breathing."

Nevek shook his head. "Officer?"

Huluk laughed softly. "You are the second-in-command of this fine army of ours." The strain was too much. He slid down the tree to the forest floor.

Still suspicious, Nevek glanced at Theros. "Yes, sir. I see your point. But if I am an officer now, who is the army? This slave?"

Huluk looked up at Theros. "This slave taught me honor today, and he saved my life. It is wrong for a slave to teach a minotaur honor and so you should no longer be a slave. What is your name, human?"

"I am Theros, slave to—"

Huluk interrupted. "You are Theros, a free human currently in the employ of the mighty Third Army of the Minotaur Supreme Circle. Or should I say, you *are* the mighty Third Army of the Minotaur Supreme Circle."

Theros was hesitant. "Do you mean it, sir? I am free?"

"You are free, Theros, and you are to be commended for your bravery and honor. Now, do I hear the sound of running water?"

Theros and Nevek hoisted the minotaur officer between the two of them, and Theros led them to his hiding spot. The sun was beginning to fall into the hills beyond the forest, casting long shadows.

They set Huluk down on the moss-covered side of the river. He started to peel off his armor and coverings, but the pain was too great. Nevek came over to help. The blood had encrusted around Huluk's wound, and continued to seep out.

Together, the two minotaurs waded into the water. Nevek helped Huluk wash the minor wounds, then they did their best with the more serious wound. The slow-moving water grew red with the washing away of blood.

Theros remained on the river shore. He was searching for a way to start a fire. Without one this night, Huluk might die. Theros needed Huluk to go back to the coastal village to let authorities know that he, a senior officer in the military, had released Theros from servitude.

Theros couldn't believe it. He was free. He thought he

should be happy over this, was surprised to find out he wasn't. What did freedom mean to the young man? It meant no one would take care of him anymore. No one would see to it that he was fed, clothed, had a bed at night. He was on his own. He shook his head.

There was work to be done. Nevek had brought two empty wineskins, a smoked hindquarter of pork meat, a hunting knife and a small tinderbox. The forest floor was littered with twigs and dried branches. Hran had taught Theros how to make a hearth that did not smoke much, and he used the lore to build his fire.

Dried leaves served as the kindling. Using the tinderbox, he started a small fire. Twigs, then small branches followed, until he had a little fire going. They had nothing to boil water in. There were wild onions and a few mushrooms around. They could have used the pork with the fungus and vegetables to make a small stew, but there was no pot.

Huluk and Nevek clambered out of the cool water and onto the shore. "How is the commander doing?" Theros asked.

Huluk collapsed beside the fire. He closed his eyes and he was shivering.

Nevek said in a low voice. "He is not well. There must be some infection. He may not live through the night."

"Can't we do something? Cauterize the wound or something?" Theros asked.

Nevek looked dubious. "I know that's what we should do, but I have no idea how to do it. I do not have the experience."

"When I was on board the ship, the second mate sometimes had to do it if there was a wounded warrior or injured slave," Theros said. "All you do is heat a piece of metal until it is white-hot. Then you stick it in the wound. It burns the area around the wound, but kills the infection and closes the hole. I can get the fire hot enough and we can use your knife. I can't do the surgery, though. I wouldn't be able to hold him down when he starts to thrash. You could, though."

Nevek's eyes widened. "You want me to stick a searing

hot knife into Huluk's buttocks? He would kill me with his bare hands alone!"

"He'll be dead if you don't."

Nevek nodded. It had to be done. The sky was turning a deep shade of red. The lower depths of the forest were becoming obscured in darkness. Night and its chill would soon be on them.

Theros dug a shallow pit with the hunting knife. He patted down the sides to make it smooth, then crawled to the stream's edge to pick up small pebbles. He brought these back to line the bottom and sides of his pit. Then, he took two sticks and picked up the hottest burning embers, transferring them to the new firepit. Next, he built up the fire. Every so often, he would stop and blow on the fire, building its embers.

Theros showed Nevek how to keep the fire hot by blowing on it. He went back to the stream and cleaned the knife that he'd used to dig. It had to be used as the instrument of cauterization.

Nevek wrapped a wineskin strap over the knife's handle. Theros inserted the knife into the fire. He kept the inner embers white-hot by blowing on them and shifting the coals, just as Hran had taught him.

It took nearly an hour for the knife to heat so that it glowed red on the outside and yellow in the center.

"It's time," Theros said. He glanced over at Huluk. "Fortunately, he's unconscious."

Nevek swallowed hard. He rolled Huluk onto his back. "I'll do the burning, but you sit on Huluk's head, between his horns. Don't let him get up, or we're both dead. Hold that burning brand above so that I can see what I'm doing."

Theros sat on the minotaur's head. Nevek picked up the white-hot knife and moved to the officer. He sat across the small of Huluk's back. "Hold the brand higher. I can't see."

Theros did as he was told. Nevek struck.

Huluk woke with a howl, began to buck and thrash about. Theros held on for the wildest ride of his life. The brand went flying backward, falling on the forest floor. Theros held on to the two horns with all of his strength.

The sound of sizzling flesh, followed by a sickening smell, turned Theros's stomach.

The smell dissipated. The thrashing stopped, ending in a groan. Theros stood up.

"How did it go?" he asked.

Nevek retrieved the brand, stomped out the tiny brush fire that it had started. He walked down to the creek edge and dropped the knife in. The sizzle indicated that the blade was still hot. He washed off his hands and face.

"I think it went all right. I sealed the wound, and it stopped bleeding. We should wash it out again, though."

Theros agreed. He found his shirt that he had used to stem the bleeding earlier in the day. He washed it out thoroughly in the running stream, rubbing out the hardened bits of dirt and blood in the cloth.

Scooping water in the shirt, Theros went back to Huluk. The minotaur still lay as he had when they had finished. He had not moved. Theros cleaned around the wound and poured water into it, letting it drain. He then gently cleaned out the wound.

Nevek sat down, took out his axe and set it across his lap. "I'll take the first watch. I'll wake you in a couple of hours. You wake me when you can't keep your eyes open anymore. I'll take it from there to sunrise. I'm not good with humans—I can't read your emotions or what you are trying to say under the surface of your words. But I do think that you need more sleep than I do right now."

Theros nodded. He didn't bother to respond. He pitched back onto the moss and fell asleep.

* * * * *

Nevek nudged him in the morning. The sun was rising over the trees and there was no sign of a cloud in the sky. Theros started. "You were supposed to wake me!"

"I know. I rested and was comfortable. I had no problem just sitting here. Huluk suggested I leave you to rest. He said you had earned it."

"Huluk?" Theros looked back to where the minotaur had been lying. He was not there. Theros looked over to see the big minotaur washing in the stream.

"How is he?" Theros inquired.

Nevek nodded. "He is much better. He is not well, by any measure, but he is better than he was. I think his fever has broken. He awoke halfway through the night, sweating like a pig. I gave him some water. He felt better and went back to sleep."

Theros breathed easier. It looked as if Huluk would survive. He was kneeling gingerly in the stream, cleaning his wound as best he could. Theros stripped off his trousers and went down to the stream to join the officer in a bath.

Huluk looked up. "Ah, it is the army! I see you are looking better than yesterday. I am glad to report that I am, too. My back end feels like it has been shot with an arrow, which it has, but it does not feel like it is on fire, which it did yesterday.

"Today we must make many miles. If I cannot keep up, Nevek will go ahead without us, to warn the village and send word to the Supreme Circle. You must help me. You will be my support."

Theros nodded. "I understand, sir. We should eat and drink, then be on our way."

Huluk agreed. Theros helped the wounded minotaur out of the water. They dried in the sun as they ate and prepared to move out. The road was four days' march for an army. Nevek could probably make it in two. Theros and Huluk would take at least three.

By noon sun, it was clear that Huluk had overestimated his strength. They rested by the path in a glade and sparingly ate of the meat and drank from the water-filled wineskins.

Nevek was clearly nervous. Huluk regarded him with interest. "Are you looking around because you hear something I do not, or are you trying to figure out a way to tell me that I am too slow?"

Nevek avoided his superior officer's eyes. "I am sorry, sir. I must abandon you here, by your own orders! I will send help back as soon as I arrive."

Huluk nodded and grunted. "Yes, you must go. Now that you do not have us as a burden, you must hurry.

Here." Huluk handed the young warrior the rest of the meat, the full waterskin and the commander's own axe. "Take these. We will find other food along the way. The axe is to prove that I still live, and that you have not deserted. Send help for me. I will not be stranded here on this damned elf-infested mainland!"

Nevek took the supplies, and left without another word. He broke into a run on the other side of the glade.

"Well, my army, are you ready to aid your commander for another few miles?" Huluk struggled to stand up.

Theros sprang to his feet to support the minotaur officer. They continued down the road.

They were still moving as night began to fall. Theros left Huluk by a tree and looked around for a place to conceal a fire.

The trees changed to pine and spruce in this area. The flat land gave way to gentle, rolling hills. As they drew closer to the coast, the hills would be greater. There was no stream.

Theros found wood. The tinderbox in his pocket was all they needed to start the fire. They both drank from the waterskin. Huluk took the skin back for a second drink.

"I will take the watch tonight. You are still wounded and need the sleep." Theros said.

Huluk handed the skin back. "No, we will both sleep tonight. Let the fire burn out. We are far enough away by now that no elf will find us." Then Huluk added, with a wry smile, "If the elves find us, lad, they will miss Nevek."

Theros understood. If they were indeed being hunted, they were to be the decoys.

He stacked up the fire. Huluk lay down on his side, and almost immediately went to sleep. Theros lay down, but he stared at the small sparks rising above the fire, wondering what it really meant to be free.

Chapter 11

Theros awoke with a start. The fire had gone out. Only embers remained.

A very distant scream, one of terror and pain, had stopped as suddenly as it had started. It was so distant. Theros had no idea from which direction it had come.

He sat up, hurriedly tossed dirt and sand over the glowing embers. Could it be elves? Who was doing the screaming?

Theros continued to listen. His nerves were stretched. He could feel his heart beat, hard and strong, the adrenaline keeping him awake and alert.

The scream came again and now sounded quite close. Theros was on his feet, Nevek's axe swaying gently back and forth, waiting. Huluk was awake, too, propped up on his side. A red glow erupted from behind them. Theros turned around. The glow intensified. A tree was burning. He saw, in silhouette, a body flailing, black against the flames, but he heard no sound.

As suddenly as it had appeared, the red glow vanished, as if the tree's flame had been snuffed out.

Sorcery. It had to be.

Theros crouched, afraid to move, not knowing what might leap out at him from the darkness. And then, the flapping of the wings of a huge bird, black in the night, nearly bowled Theros over. The bird came and was gone. A red glow shimmered where the bird had vanished. Theros was reminded of something, vague childhood terrors came back to him.

He maintained his crouched stance and waited. The attack was sure to come.

After a good hour of silence, the sounds of the woods began to return. Crickets began to chirp, leaves rustled in the wind. Huluk had fallen back to sleep. Puzzled and tired, Theros sat back down, rubbing the knots in his aching legs. He leaned against a tree, the axe across his lap, but he stayed awake until daylight.

The sun was nearly halfway up the trees before Theros dared to move. With the light, his courage began to revive. He stood up, looked around and woke Huluk.

"What is it?" Huluk asked in an urgent tone. Then he sighed. "Oh, it is morning." He rolled gingerly onto his stomach, then stood.

"We had visitors last night," Huluk said, recalling the incident. "Very strange. Did you find out who it was?"

Theros shook his head no. "I did not leave your side. I saw a tree on fire and a body and a . . . well, that's not important. Now that you are awake, I'm going to search for tracks just up the hill."

"Wait, help me. I will come with you."

They did not search long before they found the site. Blood had been spattered everywhere. An elf's body was propped up against a tree. Its arms and legs were missing. The eyes had been pecked out.

The two stood staring for several moments.

"An elf scout. He must have seen us, but he certainly didn't report back. What exactly did you see?" Huluk demanded.

"I saw a red glow, then a bird," Theros answered reluctantly, afraid he would not be believed. "It flew past me. But surely a bird could not have done this!"

Huluk lowered his voice. "Not a bird. It was Sargas. He came to answer my prayers of vengeance against the elves, to aid our cause. I have been blessed by a sign from my god. We are to continue our fight."

"Sargas?" Theros asked. "Surely you cannot believe that Sargas came here to save us from elf scouts . . ."

Theros's words died away. Memory returned clearly. The first night after he had been taken into slavery. The giant black bird glowing red in the night, flying above the ship and swooping down.

Theros murmured to himself. "It was real. He *does* exist. Honor, I remember."

Huluk placed his hand on Theros's shoulder. "Feel blessed. Sargas, the god of the minotaurs, must find us worthy. To be saved by him is a great honor."

Theros helped Huluk back to their camp. They drank the remaining water, picked up their possessions and headed back down the road.

Several minutes later, they came across two more elves, both killed in the same manner as the first. Sheer terror was mirrored in their faces, their features locked in the scream they had never finished.

The two travelers did not tarry long. They continued on. Three hours later, they took a break. Theros thought he heard running water, and went in search of it. Sure enough, he returned in ten minutes with a filled waterskin and several large mushrooms.

"Here, eat!" he said to Huluk.

The minotaur gave the mushrooms a scathing glance, shook his head. "Without meat, I cannot eat such things. My stomach would reject them. I will be fine as long as I get meat in the next day or two. Here, give me some of that fresh water."

Theros handed over the skin, then wolfed down the mushrooms. They settled the growls in his stomach.

"Do you really think that was Sargas back there?"

Huluk handed the skin back. "Yes, I am sure. We all have been taught the signs. He appears to our enemies first, blazing a path of terror before him. It is said that he always exacts some form of revenge for the defeat of a minotaur on the field of battle. When he appears to his own kind, he is seen as a bird—"

"—glowing red but appearing black," Theros finished. "That is what I saw last night."

Huluk looked incredulously at the human. "So you said, but I couldn't believe it. You saw Sargas, too? Are you a believer of Sargas? You would have to be, or he would not have shown himself to you. There have been very few actual sightings of Sargas. All have been chronicled in the great books by the followers. I know of no incident, though, in which a human witnessed such an event. And lived to tell of it, of course," Huluk added offhandedly.

They continued down the road. Huluk was having more and more difficulty keeping up. The wound stayed sealed, but the pain was intensifying. His muscles and joints were stiffening. Without proper cleaning and salves, the wound could putrify again.

An hour later, they had to stop for Huluk to rest. Huluk took another drink from the skin, but lowered it quickly. He pointed into the forest.

"I saw movement. It could be another elven patrol. Leave me here and circle around, and see what you can find out."

Theros tried in vain to see anything. Taking the axe, he circled into the brush. He moved forward, half crawling, half running, bending over to conceal himself.

He stopped when he saw movement ahead. A large figure was peering out from behind a tree. The horns sticking out of the side of his head showed him to be a minotaur. Breathing a sigh of relief, Theros stood up. The minotaur's eyes widened. He reached out with his axe held high, ready to strike.

Theros dropped his axe. "Stop! Stop! I am on your side!

Stop!" he cried in the minotaur's own language.

His pleas were echoed from behind the first minotaur. Another minotaur voice shouted, "Stop!"

The first minotaur halted, looked up the road. Nevek stood on the roadway, out of breath with his exertion. His wrists were manacled. "This is the human that aided Commander Huluk. He carries my axe!" Nevek motioned.

Ten more minotaurs emerged from the trees and walked forward, each with his weapon at the ready.

One of the minotaurs glared suspiciously at Theros. "If that is true, where is the commander?"

Huluk appeared, limping through the trees. "Here. Good to see you again, Nevek." He turned to face the suspicious minotaur. "You see, Nevek didn't murder me and make off in the night. You could learn much about trust and honor from this human."

The other minotaurs bowed at the approach of the officer. Huluk's horns were wider than the rest. His medallions showed him to be a skilled warrior.

"Commander, it is good to find you alive!" said one of the minotaurs.

Huluk chuckled. "I take it that you found Nevek here, running down the road. He carried my axe with him and you naturally assumed that he had murdered me and made off with my fine weapon. He had deserted from the Third Army, and you were keen enough to catch him. Is that it?"

The junior officer nodded his head slightly. He was the one now carrying Huluk's axe. "Yes, sir. Well, not exactly, sir. Surely no one could expect me to send part of my patrol back to the village to report on the warrior's wild story of the Third Army being completely wiped out, and to ask us to believe that a human slave who is not a slave was helping you to escape the elves?"

If Huluk had been well, he would have bashed the young officer across the jaw and sent him sprawling. Instead, he growled in high displeasure. "All of what Nevek has told you is true. And take those manacles off of my officer!"

The other minotaurs grunted and shook their horned

heads. One removed Nevek's manacles. All looked incredulous.

"No, listen," Huluk continued, "I believe that Nevek and I, along with this human, are the only survivors of the army. The elves tricked us, routed us completely. Send your best runner back to the village to update the garrison commander. Tell Blevros that I am alive and not as well as I could be, but better than the elves had planned. Tell him that the army has been defeated, and to make whatever preparations he has been ordered to make by the Supreme Circle in this contingency. Further, tell . . ."

Huluk wavered, sagged, collapsed. The young officer yelled for two of the large warriors to aid the senior officer. Theros, standing to the side, was forgotten. He quietly cleared his throat to get the officer's attention.

"Sir, I think that we should make a carrying seat from two strong branches and take Commander Huluk back to the village. He is not well, and I think his fever is returning."

The officer clearly did not want to take advice from a human—slave or no slave. "Fetch branches," he ordered his men. "We will make a carrying seat for the commander." He glared at Theros, daring him to say something.

Theros kept a straight face, did what he could to make Huluk more comfortable.

The minotaurs returned with two straight branches, each about six feet long and about six inches wide. They had cleared off the attached branches and twigs with their axes. They held the poles like a stretcher, then lowered the poles to permit Huluk to straddle them. The minotaurs lifted the poles, allowing the commander to sit on them with only mild discomfort. Theros found a small branch to use as a crossbeam and asked for some rope. One of the warriors produced a length. He cut it in two, and the two of them secured it across the two beams, forming a backrest.

They were once again mobile. Huluk barked at the junior officer. "Don't you damned well drop my axe! It's been in my family for more than ten generations. Lose it or damage it and you will face me in battle! I've already lost a valuable breastplate." He glanced at Theros and winked. It was the nearest the minotaur would ever come to an apology or to thanks.

Theros, understanding, smiled and nodded.

The officer grunted, obviously not understanding. He fastened his own axe to the holster on his back. He carried Huluk's axe with the sort of reverence usually reserved for religious objects.

They headed for the village on the run.

Chapter 12

It was good to be back on board a ship. For seven years, Theros had lived on or around ships like this, a long galley—one of many evacuating the minotaurs from their failed colony on the coast.

Once Huluk had been safely transported to the village, the governor had met with him. It was confirmed that the Third Army was indeed destroyed, and that the elves were planning to eradicate the minotaur encampment from "their" land. The governor immediately sent a swift corsair to the Supreme Circle with a request for aid.

It had been an extremely orderly evacuation. The governor had ordered the defenses strengthened, and used his small force effectively to stall the elves on their march to the village and harbor. They had laid traps and ambushes, forcing the elves to abandon their heavy cavalry in the dense woods. The elves were forced to fight in ways in which the minotaurs were superior.

Those minotaurs not capable of fighting had been ordered to dismantle parts of the encampment. Tools, stores, war machines and personal belongings were all crated up and stacked by the pier, waiting for transport.

Ships stationed at the harbor were loaded and sent back to the minotaur homelands. All of the necessary equipment and belongings were put aboard, as were the females, children, slaves and wounded. Both Theros and Huluk were among the passengers. Nevek, now a junior officer in the garrison, stayed behind to aid in the defense. Huluk had personally recommended him for the field promotion. The governor agreed. Nevek's horns seemed to grow almost a full inch overnight.

The ship rocked gently from side to side. Its sails were completely unfurled, catching the breath of the sea. Theros watched the minotaurs crawl among the rigging, wondered if he himself still had the knack. He longed to try, but his skill was needed in weapon-making. Standing on deck, he recalled old Heretos, his first master.

"I am not a slave. I am an honored member of the crew," Heretos had stated proudly.

Now Theros could say the same. He was sought after to sharpen and re-hone the edges of weapons, to refit axes with broken handles. He was skilled in carving the intricate designs that the minotaur warriors placed on their weapons. Through the years, he had become skilled in leatherwork and knew the secrets of fastening metal to leather to form well-made armor.

And he had Hran to thank for it.

Memories of the smith returned to Theros, including the first time they had ever met.

Theros had been one of fifty slaves ceded to the commander of the Third Army. The commander had been informed of Theros's skill as a smith, but the minotaur had not believed that a human could do such exacting work. Theros had been put to work in the commissary section of the rear guard. But instead of peeling and slicing for preparation of food, Theros was usually found out back of the tents, sharpening the kitchen knives or sewing and repairing the tents.

One day, right before the army shipped off to Silvanesti, a large minotaur, dressed in the leather apron that marked him as a blacksmith, watched Theros as he sharpened knives.

"Don't you work in the commissary section, slave?" Hran asked.

Theros stood up respectfully. "Yes, sir. But the cook says I am more useful sharpening and sewing than I am preparing a meal. This is what I used to do on board ship."

Hran grunted. Grabbing the young man by the arm, the smith dragged Theros inside the commissary tent. He found the minotaur in charge. "Perjaf, this slave tells me he sharpens knives and sews cloth for you. Is he lying?"

Perjaf wiped his hands on his apron. He had just finished slaughtering a pig. "No, the slave tells the truth. Why, was he not doing as he was told? Was he snooping around your shop? If he was, I'll beat some manners—"

"You have the brains of a goat, Perjaf. This slave is much too valuable to waste sharpening knives to cut onions. I want him to work for me."

Perjaf scowled. "He is quite valuable. He does leatherwork, too."

"What do you want in return?" Hran was older, senior to Perjaf, but they held comparable positions, so they had to barter.

Perjaf hesitated a moment. Hran had been good to him, had provided him with excellent knives and other implements over the years. He could not, however, just hand over the slave to him. It would demean him in Hran's eyes.

"Have your new slave make me a leather harness for my battle-axe. My old one is worn through, and will split before too long. Do we have an exchange, Hran?"

Hran nodded, grinned broadly. "Done. Come along, slave."

Theros could not believe his luck. At last, he was going to learn from a master.

"Where did you acquire the skills you have?" Hran eyed the boy as if he were a gift sent from Sargas. Theros looked eagerly around the forge, his gaze fixing on several fine swords.

"I was a slave to the warriors on the *Blatvos Kemas*, a war barge under the Velek hierarchy, until it was signed over to Supreme Circle member Kronic. He sold the ship, and most of the slaves, including me, were sent here."

Hran nodded approvingly. Seeing Theros studying the swords, the minotaur asked, "Do you know how to make a forge hot, to hammer metal into a fine blade?"

Theros shook his head. "No, sir, I don't." He looked down at his feet. He felt two inches tall.

Hran slapped the human on the back, nearly sending Theros headfirst into the forge. "We have much work to do! You will be my apprentice, and will learn what I can teach. Remember that you are still a slave, especially outside of this building. In here, though, you are my apprentice first and foremost. What is your name?"

Theros stared, amazed. Always before, he'd been known as "slave."

"Theros."

"Now, Theros, get to work." Hran had grinned.

The movement of the ship jolted Theros back to the present. He sighed. Hran would be pleased if he could see him today. Theros was free, and no longer had to do the work of a slave on the ship.

But even the lowest-ranking minotaur would rate higher than Theros. He would always have to wait to speak until he was spoken to. He could have no say in politics or administration, nor could he hold any official position. He could not own property.

So what was Theros to do now? Where would he go? He had no desire to return to his own homeland, somewhere in Nordmaar, which he barely remembered. He imagined himself catching fish, day after day. He was a warrior, not a fisherman!

Three days out to sea, Huluk finally appeared on the deck. Theros walked over to greet the minotaur officer and extended an arm in support. Huluk refused the help.

"The surgeon says that I will always walk with a limp, but I will be fit for fighting in a month or two. I need the exercise. Walk with me and keep me company."

"Commander, could I ask you for some advice?" Theros fell into step beside the minotaur.

Huluk grimaced. "Oh, now that you are free, you have decided to adopt me as your father, is that it?"

Theros smiled. "No, sir! I wouldn't dream of . . . well, that is, I would be honored to . . . I mean . . ."

"Relax, Theros. I was joking. Now what is it that you want advice about?"

Theros hesitated, trying to frame his thoughts into words. The two walked over to the rail. Huluk leaned against the bulkhead.

"They've done wonders for me down below, but it will take weeks before I can sit in a chair. Sargas be my witness, I hate elves! Now, what is it you want to ask me?"

Theros turned to the minotaur officer. "Where should I go from here, sir? I am a weapons-smith. At least, I *was* an apprentice weapons-smith. I can't work as a smith in a minotaur army. Minotaur law forbids it because I am a human."

Huluk was thoughtful. "We can be so shortsighted sometimes. If you want to continue as a smith, Theros, there is only one option open to you. You will have to go back to your own race. Freedom in minotaur society is not equality. You need the respect of the people for whom you are working. It seems that you must find yourself a human army."

"I don't even know where to look. How do I get to human lands? How do I present myself?" Theros was perplexed.

"Ah, yes." Huluk said, nodding. "You have been a slave most of your life. You have not been among very many humans. When I was younger, I was a junior officer, much like Nevek. We were in central Ansalon, fighting alongside Dargon Moorgoth, a mercenary human commander from somewhere called Sanction. We were fighting with Moorgoth to conquer the island of Schallsea, in the Newsea. The raid that we jointly planned went poorly, but not because of any mistakes on Moorgoth's part. He might be someone to try to find."

"Sanction? Where is that?" Theros asked.

"It's a city somewhere in the middle of continental Ansalon. I do not know where, exactly. Yes, Sanction is where I would look for humans who might have need of a skilled smith."

"Thank you, Commander. I will take your advice."

"I will introduce you to a ship's captain named Olifac. He is supposed to be running weapons in that area. He will take you where you wish to go, provided you work for your passage."

Theros nodded. "Thank you again, Commander."

"Before you go, you should at least spend some time as a smith in Lacynes. You are a free human in minotaur society, and we minotaurs are among the most skilled smiths in all of Krynn. Why not sign on for a year or two, and then go looking for your human army?"

Theros thought for a moment. "I don't know, Commander. It will not be the same, working for someone other than Hran. Will Olifac still be there when we get to Lacynes?"

Huluk waved a hand. "Stop calling me 'commander!' I have been promoted by order of the Supreme Circle to *group* commander. Now address me as I am to be addressed."

"Yes, sir, Group Commander." Theros smiled.

Huluk nearly permitted himself a smile. "Looks like this brutal war with the elves has been good for promotions all around. About Olifac, I have no idea if he will have his ship around or not. We will find out when we land."

They landed four days later.

Chapter 13

Crowds of minotaurs gathered on the docks to glimpse the returning colonists. All wanted to know the same thing. Had the Third Army truly been wiped out? Had it really been destroyed by an elven army? They shouted questions and jammed forward.

The port authorities tried to keep the calm, but to no avail. Disaster had struck the colony on the Silvanesti coast. The people wanted to know the details.

The city guard was called out. Once the crowd was shoved back, the passengers began to disembark from the first ship and other ships that sailed into the harbor.

Theros and Huluk were on board the first ship. The settlers who had bravely gone off to the new land walked down the gangplank with their heads and horns held high. They had nothing to be ashamed of, nothing had cost them any honor. It was the soldiers who had failed.

When the settlers left, Theros helped Huluk off the ship. Those in the crowd jeered at the officer.

"Where is your army now, warrior?"

"You saved your skin. What happened to the others of the brave Third Army? Where are they to tell their tale?"

"Why did you not die like the brave soldiers of the Third Army?"

Huluk held his head up high, hobbling as he walked down the pier. Soon enough they would know his story. He had been ordered to go directly to the Assembly of the Supreme Circle and make his report.

Theros helped the officer to the steps of the massive building in the center of the city. It was a monument to minotaur freedom and a holy shrine to the Cataclysm, when Sargas had thrown off the shackles of the foul King-priest of Istar, releasing the minotaurs to be free once again.

Theros wished Huluk well and turned to leave.

"Wait, Theros! In this city you will be treated as a slave unless you can prove otherwise. Take this coin." Huluk handed him a coin with the emperor's face on one side and the family symbol of Huluk's clan on the other. "It is a clan coin. You are now a member of my clan." He growled in mock ferocity. "Do us honor or you will not live to regret it." Then, the minotaur smiled. "In truth, I have no fears for you, Theros. Keep that coin as a symbol of your freedom, and good luck."

Huluk walked up the steps. Theros remained behind. Only a command or invitation by the Emperor himself would allow Theros to enter the great building, or the adjoining Imperial Fortress, where the Emperor resided.

Theros went back to the docks. At one end stood the harbor offices. Theros entered and waited at the counter for someone to help him. He waited a long time. Every minotaur who entered was given assistance before Theros. Finally, when the offices were empty, a minotaur cast a bored glance at Theros.

"What do you want, slave? Do you have an errand for your master? Speak up. Can't you see that we're busy?"

Theros remained polite. "I would like to know if Captain Olifac and his ship are in harbor."

The minotaur grunted. "Who wants to know?"

Theros pulled the coin from his pocket and placed it on the counter with the clan emblem facing up. "I do," he replied.

The minotaur came up to the counter and examined the coin. "So, you're a member of the Hrolk clan. My clan and theirs are very close." He eyed Theros suspiciously. "I never heard of their taking in a human. Perhaps you stole this."

Theros stood his ground. "I am Theros, and I have been granted my freedom by Huluk, Group Commander of the Third Army."

The minotaur looked at him with new respect. "So, you are the slave who helped old Huluk escape the elves. The tale of your valor has spread. You proved your honor. I can respect that. Olifac has just left for a raiding tour. He will be gone for several months, maybe longer. We will not hear from him until he returns."

Disappointed, Theros thanked the minotaur and went back outside. What was he going to do now? The thought occurred to him that even if Olifac had been in the harbor, he might not be able to work for his passage from Mithas to the continent. Theros had no money, no treasure of any kind. He had to earn a living.

He headed off to the lower markets.

The street vendors and shops had all manner of goods for sale. One shop sold freshly cooked strips of meat. Another sold stoneware for serving food. Finally Theros found what he was looking for. One shop had an assortment of weapons. He checked the quality and inquired within.

"Excuse me, sir. I was wondering if you could tell me the name of the smith who made the weapons that you have on display."

The shopkeeper was gruff. "You would be looking for Hrall, slave. He charges too much for the damned things.

Still, with this new elven war and all, I may make some money on them yet."

Theros thanked the minotaur and headed for the area of the city where smiths, leatherworkers, cobblers and coopers lived and worked. He stopped at the first smith.

"What is it you want, slave?" the minotaur smith asked.

Theros looked around the shop. It was clean but small. The metalwork being done was for all manner of implements and tools except weapons.

"I was looking for a smith named Hrall. He is a weaponssmith."

"You are right, human. He is at the end of this street. His forge is a good one."

Theros bowed slightly to show his respect and left the shop. He found the smithy and entered.

A huge minotaur had his back to the door. He was pounding the blade of a long sword into shape. As he pounded, sparks of steel and fire leaped from the weapon. The smell of the fire, mixed with that of oiled leather and wood smoke, was a whiff of nostalgia for Theros. He missed working in a smithy and, especially, he missed his friend Hran.

The minotaur put his tongs and hammer down and turned around. Theros nearly jumped out of his skin.

In front of him stood Hran! It was as if Theros had conjured him up. He had just been thinking about Hran, and there his old friend stood, right in front of him.

The big minotaur cleaned his hands on his apron. "What is the matter, slave? You look as if you had seen a death knight!"

Theros bowed. "I am sorry, sir. I thought that you looked like another minotaur that I once knew. He was also a smith and a very fine one."

"You must have met my brother, Hran. I am told that he is dead now. It is left to me to carry on the family name. Where did you know Hran?"

"I was an apprentice to Hran in the Third Army. I was there when he died. I buried him." Theros said quietly.

"You were there? You buried him? Tell me, did he die like a warrior? Did he die with his axe in his hand?"

"Yes, sir! He died fighting the elven cavalry that raided our camp. They finally overran us, but he killed eight elite warriors, the ones with the plate armor and barded horses. They fell surrounding him. He died with his axe in his hand, a true warrior. You should be proud of him! He fought well!"

Hrall grunted. "Do not think I am surprised. I am not. He was truly a great warrior, and a great smith, too. We did not get along well, my brother and I. He decided to take the path of military service. I decided to make weapons as a commercial venture. My fighting is done in the Circus. He decided to do battle as a soldier. But he still wanted to be a smith. He achieved his goals, I achieved mine. We didn't see each other much. I am sorry now that we did not. Truly sorry."

Theros had no idea what to say to the minotaur, who was obviously deeply affected by his brother's death.

"You were a slave in my brother's shop, were you?"

Theros nodded.

"Fine. You will work here. I will buy out whoever owns you now."

Theros produced the coin that Huluk had given him. "Sir, I am a free man. I am owned by no one. I am now a member of the Hrolk Clan. And I was not Hran's slave. He made me his apprentice."

Hrall was surprised. "I had no idea that they were still freeing slaves these days. This makes things different. I would have to pay you, and I cannot do that. I do good work, but I do not make enough money to hire someone else."

"Sir, if you could hire me, I would work for just food and board, at first. Hran taught me well. I will bring in enough work to make you more money. When your business grows, then you can pay me."

Hrall peered shrewdly at the young man. "You say you were my brother's apprentice. Are you any good? Can you do leatherwork?"

"I am not new to smithing, sir, but I am not a master smith, either. I can do the small jobs that require doing, so that you can concentrate on the bigger and more demanding pieces. And I can sew leather."

Hrall had heard enough. "You are hired. You can live in the back shed behind the shop. You'll have to clean it out yourself. I have never been able to work leather like my brother could. If you can work leather, I will teach you the trade where my brother left off."

The minotaur and the human shook hands.

* * * * *

Theros returned to the Supreme Circle chambers to find Huluk, tell him that he had a job. Theros waited for Huluk for hours. Nobody bothered or even noticed him. He was human, and might have been a bug as far as the minotaurs were concerned.

Suddenly, near nightfall, the bells in the tower crowning the Supreme Circle building pealed out.

From all directions, minotaurs came rushing up the street. They crowded in front of Theros, shoving him out of the way. Their attention was fixed on the large wooden doors at the top of the stone stairs. More and more minotaurs poured into the streets.

"What are they all here for?" Theros wondered uneasily if this had anything to do with Huluk.

Nearly a hundred minotaurs were waiting when the doors finally opened. Two guards in ceremonial garb came out first, followed by the eight minotaurs of the Supreme Circle. Lastly, several other military officers, including Huluk, walked out. Huluk was easy to spot because of his limp.

The crowd grew silent out of respect for the Supreme Circle. One of the eight took two paces forward.

"Minotaurs of the Empire! We of the Supreme Circle have found Klaf, now-dead commander of the now-dead Third Army of Minotaurs, to be guilty of grievous errors in judgment. He put the entire colony in Silvanesti, as well as the lives and honor of warriors of the highest order, in jeopardy. His clan will be stripped of its honor, and must regain their honor in the Circus. The clan shall be known as Nar-Klaf, until it has proven itself worthy."

The crowd roared its approval. One minotaur, standing near Theros, shook his head from side to side. Someone, spotting him, pointed and shouted. "Bastard Nar-Klaf!" This minotaur turned and ran, perhaps to warn his family. A few minotaurs tossed rocks at him, but most turned again to listen to the speaker.

"To take Klaf's place, we appoint Huluk, surviving officer of the Third Army, to be its new commander. He will raise and train a new Third Army from veterans and recruits. We will not be going back to the land of the elves, at least not in the short term. We will, Sargas be praised, have our vengeance on them, but now is not the time.

"This concludes the announcement of the Supreme Circle. Let all know that its words are law, by the grace of the Emperor."

The minotaurs stepped back, and it was Huluk's turn. "Warriors of the Minotaur Empire, I call upon you to join the new Third Army! For those of you whose clan members participated in Nar-Klaf's slaughter, hear this! All clans, save the Nar-Klaf clan, are hereby absolved of the defeat in Silvanesti. I personally witnessed the honor and courage of the combatants, and how they sacrificed themselves."

Nods and praises to Sargas were whispered through the crowd. Every clan in the capital had a member in the Third Army.

"The warriors held prisoner by the elves will be released and transported back to Mithas in one month's time. That is all."

Huluk stepped back. The members of the Supreme Circle turned and re-entered the great hall. The officers followed, then the bodyguards, who closed the doors.

The bells pealed out one last time, then fell silent, not to be heard on Mithas until ten years later, the year the armies began to marshal for the War of the Lance.

* * * * *

Theros waited two more hours. Huluk still had not emerged. It had been night for some time now.

Theros decided to return to the smithy. The streets were dark in the administrative part of the city. A glow came from the outer part of the city, where there were inns and drinking and eating establishments. Many minotaurs went straight to these places after a day of work. Theros wished he could join them.

He had no trouble finding his way around the city. The roads in Lacynes were well laid out. It had been a planned city dating back several centuries, and had suffered little from the Cataclysm, even though it was not far from Istar. This was Sargas's way of repaying the minotaurs for their suffering at the hands of the clerics and holy men of Istar.

Theros opened the door of the smithy, entered and sat down by the hearth. There was no one around. He was hungry. His stomach's rumbling probably could be heard for a block. He thought about begging Hrall for a meal, but pride and good sense counseled against such a degrading act. Hrall would lose all respect for him.

Theros slept in the smithy that night. Despite his hunger, he smiled as he breathed in the smell of the leather, the wood smoke, the sweat. The heat from the hearth kept him warm.

Theros was up at the first crack of sunlight. Hrall came to the shop about an hour after sunrise. Theros was already busy investigating all of the tools and the half-made weapons.

The booming voice from the door caught him off guard. "What in the Abyss are you doing with that?" the minotaur yelled.

Theros was holding a half-finished axe in a battle stance, as if he were ready to fight the elven cavalry by himself. He jumped at the voice and dropped the axe. Guiltily, Theros turned around to see his new employer, scowling and clearly not happy about the unaccustomed disarray in his shop.

Hrall picked up the axe. "Play with the toys in this shop and I will spit you and cook you over my hearth."

The threat did not worry Theros. The hint of food only made his mouth water and his stomach growl.

"So, you haven't eaten, eh? I can see the wolf in your

eyes, lad." Hrall sounded exactly like Hran—gruff on the outside, a friend beneath.

"Come on, then. I guess we should get some food in you."

They went behind the shop, past the storage shed that was to be Theros's new home. A path led to the next street. They turned right and entered the first building. It was Hrall's house. Hrall's mate brought out meat and fruit cider, along with some hard black bread. Theros thanked her and ate quickly, keeping his eyes on the food, for it would never do for a human to gaze directly at a female minotaur. After the meal, he belched loudly to indicate to his hostess that the food had been good.

After eating, he and Hrall returned to the smithy.

Hrall started with the rules of the shop. He emphasized that what he said was what Theros did. No questions asked.

Theros listened and smiled. It was the exact speech that Hran had given him.

Theros felt right at home.

* * * * *

Theros stayed two years with Hrall, learning the techniques and tricks of a master smith. When he had learned all that Hrall could teach him, he decided it was time to move on. In fact, in many areas, such as leatherwork, he was far more skilled than his master. He could have been the master of his own smithy, but he would never accomplish that goal in Mithas or Kothas. The minotaurs themselves would never allow a human to be the master over other minotaurs.

After that day at the Supreme Circle chambers, Theros never saw Huluk, except at a distance. Huluk was a hero now, leading a new Third Army in parades and military exercises. He was constantly challenged in the ring of the Circus, but never defeated.

One day, Theros bid Hrall farewell. The master smith was sorry to part with him. He gave him good advice and, as a gift, the axe Theros had been using for practice when

Hrall first walked in on him.

Leaving the smithy, Theros headed down to the port. He had a ship to catch—the *Jelez Klarr*. Its captain was a minotaur by the name of Olifac.

Now, Theros would pay for his passage.

Book Three

Chapter 14

"I will not leave you in the Abyss. Your blood would be on my head. Your clan would seek revenge. If you want to get off here, you must pay double the fare."

"This isn't the Abyss!" Theros snorted. "It's a city, like any other, except that it is reputed to need a good smith more than most. I've paid my passage. Take me into port."

The minotaur captain shook his horned head. "You must pay for the privilege. That way no friend of yours will accuse me of selling you."

Grumbling, Theros paid. The minotaur ship sailed into port. Olifac hustled Theros off without ceremony. The minotaur crew lined the rails, armed to the teeth, ready for any hostile action. This done, they weighed anchor and sailed with the tide, off to find glory in battle.

Theros walked along the docks and entered the town of Sanction. He had to admit he was not much impressed with what he saw, was beginning to think he'd made a mistake.

Sanction had the reputation of being an evil place. Nestled in the cradle of three large volcanoes—the Lords of Doom—the town of Sanction even smelled evil. Smoke choked its alleys. Canals of molten lava flowed through the town as waterways would through other cities. The heat and gases pouring off the flows made breathing difficult. People went about with their faces muffled, mouths and noses covered. Yet Sanction was a bustling, thriving town. Perhaps because it was a town that never asked questions of anyone.

The business section was crowded with warehouses, shops and markets. People shoved and pushed their way through the crowded streets. No one smiled or muttered a hello or good-day to Theros. Each person appeared to be engrossed in his or her own private business.

Theros spent his first day in Sanction roaming the streets, watching the people. He'd never seen so many different races. Humans were the predominant race, but mingled among them were the small chattering kender (of whom Theros had been warned), grim stocky dwarves, the occasional skulking goblin or hobgoblin, and half-breed mixes of every sort.

Theros was astounded to note that wizards—of both red and black robes—actually had the effrontery to set up mageware shops in Sanction. No other town would have permitted it. Theros gave the shops and shop owners a wide berth. He had no use for wizards.

He was, in fact, attempting to avoid falling into a refuse-filled gutter on one side of the street, while avoiding a wizardess on the other, when he brushed against someone.

"Sorry," Theros said, starting to continue past.

"What do you mean, sorry?" A hoarse voice roared in his ear.

Theros looked down. A man clad in a bright maroon coat glared up at him, blocking Theros's way. The man was of average height, but he reached only Theros's broad shoulder. "You got dirt on my boots!"

The man pointed to a bit of mud on the toe of one boot.

"I said I was sorry, sir," Theros repeated and started to walk around the man.

To his astonishment and ire, the man doubled up his fist and punched Theros hard in the chest.

"Clean it!" snarled the man.

"Clean it yourself," said Theros and again started past.

Steel flashed. Voices growled. Theros was surrounded by six men in maroon coats, all carrying swords. Each sword was now pointed at his throat.

"Clean my boot," the man repeated.

No minotaur alive would have suffered such an insult. Theros was just contemplating the fact that his stay in Sanction had been incredibly short—as had his life—when he felt the touch of a hand on his shoulder.

"Do as he says," advised a voice, speaking the minotaur language. "There is small honor in dying in a gutter in Sanction. And you were in the wrong."

Theros looked up to see a large minotaur, towering head and shoulders over everyone else in the street. What the minotaur said made sense. By now a crowd had gathered. Theros, feeling his skin burn, knelt down on the sidewalk, and using the cuff of his shirt, cleaned the man's boot.

The man lifted his foot, planted it in Theros's chest and shoved. Theros toppled over backward. Laughing, the man and his comrades strolled off.

Theros jumped to his feet, with half a mind to go after them. The minotaur stood eyeing Theros.

"I saw you leave Olifac's ship. What are you? A freed slave?"

"Yes, sir," said Theros, dusting himself off. He did not ask about the minotaur. For one, it wouldn't be polite and for another, he noticed the notched mark on one of the minotaur's horns—a badge of dishonor, made by the minotaur's own relations. This was an outcast.

"Take my advice," said the minotaur. "Forget it. No one gets the best of Baron Moorgoth's men. They run Sanction, at least for now, until someone stronger comes along. You can either fight them and lose, or use your cunning and let them make your fortune for you."

The minotaur walked off. Theros never saw the minotaur again, but he thought long and hard on the advice.

Baron Moorgoth. Could that be Huluk's friend? Huluk never mentioned the fact that Dargon Moorgoth was a baron.

Now probably wouldn't be a good time to go to the baron and remind him of old friendships. Theros had too much pride. He'd make it on his own. When he was successful, he'd go visit Moorgoth.

* * * * *

It took Theros almost a year of working odd jobs before he had saved enough money to purchase an old smithy in the merchant quarter. No smith of quality operated in the town, and this one had gone out of business years before. The shop had been turned into a warehouse, but the forge, central chimney and most of the workbenches still stood. A huge anvil languished in the corner. When Theros found it, it was stacked with crates of produce. To Theros, it was worth its weight in steel.

He purchased the building for a mere pittance, which was, in fact, all he had. He was forced to begin his business by sewing leather, in order to save up for the tools necessary to start metal smithing.

Six years later, he had an established shop. He owned one of the largest smithies in Sanction, with a reputation for making fine quality swords and daggers. He had Baron Moorgoth and his men in their maroon uniform coats to thank for his success.

Baron Moorgoth had arrived in Sanction with a large amount of wealth that he claimed was his inheritance. Rumors followed of a murdered uncle and stolen jewels, but no one could ever prove anything and Sanction wasn't the town to believe all the gossip it heard. Through a number of wise investments in various businesses, Moorgoth doubled and tripled his wealth. He used his earnings to buy men and steel, and backed by these loyal supporters, he bought up even more of Sanction.

He claimed himself as nominal ruler of the town, although he refused to be bothered by such mundane matters as keeping law and order or making civic improvements. He had, by now, amassed a small army and was, rumor had it, looking to expand his holdings.

What Moorgoth did or didn't do was now of no interest to Theros. He had worked hard over the years to develop his skills as a weapons-smith and was just now beginning to enjoy the fruits of his labors. He had even been able to take on an apprentice to do the tooled leatherwork and other chores, leaving Theros more time to concentrate on the craft of swordsmaking.

The smithy stood several blocks from the port area. The sign out front read, in Common, "Weapons and Armor. Theros Ironfeld, Proprietor." Ironfeld was a name Theros chose for himself. It served both as a name and an advertisement. The name also showed he was proud of his skills. The sign's lettering was crude, but the populace of Sanction didn't mind. Most of them couldn't read it anyway.

One of Moorgoth's maroon-coated guardsmen was his first customer into the shop this day. Theros glanced at the man, nodded, but continued work. He hammered on hot metal, fashioning a new sword from molten steel. The guardsman, knowing he would not be heard above the din, waited impatiently for the smith to take a break.

Theros had not grown much in height during the past seven years, but he had increased his girth immensely since his days with the minotaurs. His arms were massive, muscles rippled. His chest was as big around as an enormous water barrel. His black skin glistened in the light of the forge. Compared to the minotaurs, he had been viewed as short and puny. Among humans, he was head and shoulders taller than most men. Now, when Theros walked the streets of Sanction, people skirted out of his way.

Theros straightened, groaning from the strain. The guardsman coughed to attract Theros's attention. He turned to see who it was.

"Ah, Morik. You are here for a new scabbard! I told you you'd be back. That horrible, tattered scabbard is no house to keep the jewel I made for you."

Theros was proud of the work—the first long sword of the season. A good sign, coming so early. It looked as if it was going to be a good year for business.

The guardsman pulled the blade from its scabbard. "Actually, no, Master Smith. The scabbard will do. Could you make a dirk to match the sword, though?"

Theros smiled. "I see you like the finer things in life, Morik. Yes, I can make you a matching dirk. Do you want your family crest on it, as before?"

The guardsman nodded.

"Very well," Theros concluded. "It will cost you forty steel. Pay me half now and half on completion. It will take me two weeks."

"Forty steel!" The guardsman gaped. "I could get it for fifteen down the street at Malachai the Dwarf's!"

"Then do so," Theros said. "You know the way."

"Twenty pieces," the guardsman bargained.

Theros didn't even bother to answer. He turned back to his work. He was not interested in haggling. He was the only smith in the town capable of making a weapon of such fine quality. Malachai the Dwarf could not do much more than forge horseshoes and building nails.

The guardsman fretted and fumed and walked out, glancing over his shoulder, obviously hoping Theros would run after him. Theros continued to work. A few minutes later, the guardsman came back in. He had his purse in his hand.

"Yuri!" Theros bellowed.

A boy of sixteen dropped the leather gauntlet he was stitching and came forward from the back of the shop.

"Sir, that will be twenty steel in advance, please."

It was the boy's job to take the money.

Theros thrust the sword on which he was working back into the fire to reheat it. He overheard the conversation between the two.

"Doesn't that bastard ever bargain?" the guardsman grumbled.

Yuri shook his head. He was proud of his master. "He doesn't have to. He knows that if you want the weapon, you will pay. If you don't, you won't." The boy held out his hand.

"He should watch who he offends in this town," the guardsman muttered as he emptied the steel coins into the lad's palm. "Some people might think he's getting too big for his boots."

The boy counted, nodded and went to the back of the shop to deposit the money in the strongbox. The guardsman stormed out.

Yuri returned. He paused a moment, gazing out the door to watch the guardsman leave.

"You have offended him, master. He is one of the baron's top lieutenants. He thinks his position should have garnered him more respect, and thus a lower price."

Theros snorted, a habit he had picked up from his days among the minotaurs. He paid no attention to the politics of the town of Sanction or any other town.

"Get back to work," Theros said. "And I believe I've mentioned before that you're to speak only when you're spoken to."

"Yes, master." Yuri sighed.

Theros pretended he didn't hear. He was training Yuri as an apprentice the same way Theros himself had been trained by the minotaurs. If that way was a bit harsh, it was the only way Theros knew and, he assumed, as good as any. Yuri lacked discipline in his life. And if Theros had to treat Yuri like a slave in order to instill discipline, Yuri would be the one to gain in the long run. At least, that was Theros's view.

Yuri finished the gauntlet, began working on a small leather jerkin, putting metal strips inside the jacket to conceal the armor. The jerkin was bright green and decorated with painted designs across the front and back.

Theros, spotting it, glared at the boy. "Isn't that jerkin done yet?"

Yuri looked up, flushed. "No, sir. I'll be done within the hour. The kender will not be back until late this afternoon, so I have time to finish it."

"You be sure that you do. I don't want that damned kender wandering around my shop, 'borrowing' my tools and weapons. When you're done, wait for him outside and give it to him there. Don't let him in the door! And make certain you get good money for that, too."

It had been a week since the kender had shown up in the shop. Usually Theros was quick to throw them out, but this time he'd been busy engraving a blade and hadn't been able to leave his work. Yuri had foolishly allowed the kender inside and, once there, they couldn't seem to get rid of him. He had wandered around, picking up this, looking at that, chattering all the time about his father—Trapspringer or something was the name.

Finally Theros was able to stop his work long enough to collar the kender, catching the little fellow just as he slipped a pair of steel tongs into one of his pouches. Theros grabbed the kender by the lapels and began to shake, trying to loosen his tongs and whatever else that may have dropped into the pouches and pockets. He turned the kender upside down, shook him by his ankles. All the while, the kender screeched and tried to whack Theros across the legs with his hoopak. A mountain of objects cascaded down onto the floor. Theros's anger at the small being was replaced by wonder.

Theros was sure there was even more in the kender's possession, but the pile was nearly a foot and a half high—nearly a hundred items lay there—when he set the kender down.

The kender was offended. "Never before in the history of the Trapspringers has such an injustice been performed!" The little fellow jumped about, trying to retrieve his precious possessions. All attempts were blocked by the huge smith.

"Yuri," Theros ordered, "sort through that stuff and take out everything that is mine."

Yuri sifted through the items, discovering the pair of tongs, a leather needle, a small dagger and leather thongs. He set these aside. The remaining items were a marvel. There were, among other things, maps of all shapes and descriptions, jewels, a purse of gold, an apple pastry that looked as if it had been through the Cataclysm, tiny mechanical items that neither Yuri nor Theros could fathom, a book of dwarven recipes, several buttons from a fancy tunic, a pair of wrist restraints, a silver goblet with Solamnic heraldry on it, and a small bag of glass beads.

Yuri looked over a knife, handed it to Theros. "I don't think it's one of yours, sir."

Theros studied the weapon. Sure enough, the design was good, but not one of Theros's. He tossed it back into the pile.

"That's for slaying rabbits!" Trapspringer proudly announced. "It was given to me by my Aunt Slipjail! That's what I came to talk to you about."

From still another pocket, one Theros had missed, the kender pulled out a purse. "Look, I have money. I want you to make me something."

Theros eyed the purse. "That's a woman's purse. How much gold is in there?"

Yuri picked it up and counted the coins. His eye caught something else in the pile, and he pulled out another purse. This, too, had gold in it. "He must have stolen it."

The kender was outraged. "Steal? Steal! How dare you! That's a present from some ladies I met in Palanthas. Or was it Solace?"

Yuri counted the money in the second purse. "All told, he's got ninety-one gold pieces!"

Theros shook his head. He turned back to the kender. "What do you want us to make for you? A knife? A small sword?"

The kender's eyes brightened. "I already have a knife. And I don't think I'd be much good at using a sword. What do you have to offer?"

Theros thought for a moment. During the scuffle, he had ripped the kender's jerkin. "How about a brand-new jerkin?"

The kender hopped up and down. "Will it have lots of pockets? Could you make it in bright colors? Will it have a fancy fastener in the front? Could I hide things up the sleeve?"

"Yuri will make you a colorful leather jerkin with lots of pockets. He will put steel strips inside to armor it against small blades, and line it so that it is warm in the winter. It will cost the same amount of gold that you have in those purses. Is it a deal?"

Trapspringer's topknot had swung back and forth as he nodded vigorously. Theros had ordered the kender to return in a week and Yuri had begun work immediately.

The week was up. The jerkin was nearly finished. Yuri was inserting the last of the metal strips, fastening them to the material, then covering them. From the outside, there was no indication that the coat was anything special. There were, however, thirty-one different pockets and pouches built into the lining and sleeves of the piece. Yuri was pleased with his work. He had designed it himself.

Theros thought it was fine work, but he never said so. Discipline must be maintained.

Yuri was, as usual, prattling. "I think I'd make a good kender, you know, sir! Wouldn't it be a fun life? Always traveling about, meeting interesting people."

Theros grunted. He was in no mood for banter. He was never in the mood. Life was harsh and hard and the sooner young people like Yuri learned that lesson, the better.

"Hurry up and finish. I don't want that kender back in this shop."

Yuri finished within the hour and took the jerkin outside. He waited for only a few moments before Trapspringer came dashing up the street.

Theros, interested in spite of himself, kept watch through the window. The kender flung his arms around Yuri in a friendly hug. Yuri was probably thankful he'd been careful to empty his pockets before coming out.

"Is it done? Is it done? What's it look like?" Trapspringer hopped up and down with excitement.

Yuri held up the finished jerkin. The kender was ecstatic. He actually kept quiet with joy for about three seconds.

He tried the jacket on. It fit well. The three brass fasteners were actually crate fasteners, but the kender didn't know that and they held the coat together. He explored every pocket and seam. Finally, the kender took off the jacket and inspected the exterior. The back and front had been painted with clothing dyes of different colors, which effectively concealed several of the hidden pockets. The seams were all but invisible. Theros thought the color combination was truly hideous, but it appeared to be perfect for Trapspringer.

"So, it is to your liking?" Yuri asked.

"And you say this has armor built right in, do you?" Trapspringer was too excited to answer. "Well, fascinating! Now, I am fully prepared to give you this rather nifty purse—"

"Two purses," Yuri reminded him. "There were two of them."

"Um, well, I don't have both purses anymore. I have just the one." The kender rummaged through one of his pouches and came up with one of the purses. The gold was still in it, but where was the second purse?

"What do you intend to give in place of the second purse? After all, we did have a deal. It is a matter of honor." Yuri lowered his voice to try to sound like Theros, much to Theros's secret amusement.

The kender looked puzzled for a moment, then began rooting through the pouches again. He came up with a dog's skull. "These are the bones of an ancient dragon from way back in antiquity. You could have it, I suppose, but—"

"That might be an ancient poodle," Yuri said in disgust. "It's certainly not a dragon."

The kender dropped the skull back into the pouch and kept looking. "Not interested in any maps, are you?"

Yuri shook his head.

A shiny rock fell from the pouch as Trapspringer dug deeper inside. The rock was a silver nugget easily the size of a man's fist. Yuri bent down and picked it up. "What about this?"

"That? My paperweight? Oh, sure, if you really want it. I have better rocks than that."

Yuri held the nugget up, examining it. Theros, just by looking, figured that the nugget was easily worth thirty gold pieces. Yuri counted out another thirty from the purse. The kender was still short by about thirty pieces of gold. Theros kept quiet, waited to see what Yuri would do.

The kender had doffed his old jacket and was transferring all of the items from the old to the new. Half an hour later, after "oh, that's where that went," and "I didn't know I had one of these!" he put the new jerkin on.

"Is it a deal?" the kender asked eagerly.

Yuri obviously liked the kender and was pleased with the fact that the kender liked the jacket so much.

"A deal," Yuri said at last.

Theros frowned.

Trapspringer shook Yuri's hand, pumping it up and down, and thanked him for the jerkin. Yuri extracted himself, quickly, checking that he still had the purse and the silver nugget.

Trapspringer ran off and Yuri went back inside the forge. Theros put down his work. "So, did he pay what he promised?"

"No, sir, not exactly. He had thirty pieces of gold and a silver nugget worth at least thirty. I think—"

Theros smacked the young man across the face.

"An honorable deal is an honorable deal. He should have paid what was agreed, or you should have kept the jacket and called the guard on him!"

Yuri shrank back. "I'm sorry, sir, it's just that I—"

"That's all I want to hear from you. 'Sorry' doesn't cut it when honor is breached! He will spread the word that I can be made a fool of!" Theros went back to his work and began pounding with vigor again.

Yuri crept back to his work.

The young man certainly had a lot to learn.

* * * * *

Near closing time, when the sun was casting long shadows across the town, a man entered the smithy. He was dressed in a brown cloak. His hood was pulled low over his head and face. He shut the door behind him and stood for a moment, letting his eyes become accustomed to the contrast of dark intermingled with the bright fire from the forge. Saying nothing, he pulled the hood from his head.

The man was probably in his late forties or early fifties, judging by his short-cropped gray hair. His teeth were jagged, with a few missing, and he sported at least two scars across the left cheek. At this, Theros had the feeling that the man looked familiar, but he couldn't place him.

A soldier, Theros determined. A veteran, at that. Theros knew he'd seen him before. But where? Probably in the street or the tavern.

Theros kept hammering. He had finished with the raw shape of the new sword, and was now honing the blade to a fine edge. A minute later, he put down the hammer and thrust the sword back into the fire. He turned to the new-comer.

"What can I do for you, stranger? New sword, or a dagger perhaps?"

The man stood motionless for a moment, studying the smith. "You are Theros Ironfeld, once a slave to the mino-taurs, now a member of the Hrolk Clan. Am I right?"

The old names and faces returned to memory after a long absence. "Yes, I am Theros Ironfeld. Not that it should matter to you who I am. Do you want a weapon or armor?"

The man raised a leather-clad hand. "All in good time, Ironfeld. I understand that you charge high prices for your services and that you won't bargain. Are you truly as good as you claim to be?"

Theros shrugged. "Ask anyone in Sanction. They'll tell you whether or not I am worth the price. You judge the quality of my work yourself."

The man glanced at several swords lying on a table, but did not touch them.

"I also understand that you came to Sanction looking for Dargon Moorgoth. But you lost interest, apparently. You never came to see him. Would you be interested in seeing him now?"

"I am making money, and I don't have to go looking for anyone now," Theros replied. "No, I am not interested in meeting Baron Dargon Moorgoth. Why?"

The brown-robed man studied him intently "It turns out that Dargon Moorgoth is looking for *you*, Ironfeld. He wants to meet with you tonight. Will you come?"

The idea of finally meeting the great Baron Dargon Moorgoth was an appealing one. Theros was going to close down his shop for the night anyway. He had no one to go home to, so why not? Perhaps Moorgoth needed a fine sword. Behind the man, Yuri was listening and nodding wildly. This could make both their fortunes.

"Tell Baron Moorgoth that I will meet him at the Belching Fury Inn and Pub on Center Street. Tell him to bring his purse, because he's picking up the tab. I will be there an hour after my shop closes."

Theros turned his back on the stranger. Taking the sword out of the fire and going back to the anvil, he picked up the hammer and began pounding again. The stranger left.

At least, Theros thought, I'll get a free meal out of it, if nothing else.

Chapter 15

The room in the Belching Fury was dark and smoky. The fire on the far side wall wasn't vented very well. Some days, it was difficult to see through the haze of wood smoke and smoke from pipeweed. The food was tinged with the same taste as the smell; smoke permeated everything.

Theros didn't care. It wasn't half as bad as standing near a hot forge all day, pounding metal into shape. The real secret of the pub's success was its method of keeping ale cold. No one—at least no one who was talking—would reveal the secret of how the kegs were kept chilled. The barmaids would descend to the basement and retrieve large mugs of the brew and bring them back up. No one else was allowed down there.

The contrast from hot food and hot fire to the icy cold drink was truly something to cherish. Theros finished his first mug at a draught and hungrily tore into half a loaf of bread and a bowl of chicken stew. He couldn't taste the smoky flavor that everyone complained about. It was lost on him. Minotaurs were far less delicate in their eating habits.

Theros remembered back to his lean days working as a slave on board the minotaur ship and he was thankful for the change. Then he'd had to wait until his betters were served before him. He'd had to make do with the scraps and leftovers.

Now he ate and drank enough for three men, but he *did* the work of three men. He was just finishing his third bowl of stew when the man with the brown cloak entered the inn and stood to one side of the door, looking around carefully, much as he had done when he'd entered Theros's smithy. After a few moments, the man threw back the hood and walked up to the table.

People in the inn, catching sight of the man, rose to their feet. The innkeeper dashed out from behind the bar, bowing and bobbing until it was a wonder his head didn't tumble off. The barmaids dropped curtsies and anything else they were carrying.

Theros kept on eating. The man in brown walked straight up to him.

"Theros Ironfeld. I am glad that you decided to keep your appointment. Very glad indeed."

Theros looked up, still chewing. "Why should you care? Does Baron Moorgoth pay you extra if I show up?"

The man sat down without invitation. Theros motioned for the barmaid.

"I'll have the usual," the man said, "and I'll have the same stew as my friend here."

"Don't call me friend. I'm here to meet your commander. You I can live without." Theros went back to his eating.

"Oh, sir!" The barmaid looked scandalized. "Don't you know—"

"Hush, Marissa. Go about your business," the man ordered. He seemed to find something highly amusing. He leaned back in his seat. "You really don't know who I am, do you? I am Dargon Moorgoth. Baron Dargon Moorgoth."

Theros eyed the man with indifference. So that's where he'd seen this man. Riding about town in his fine carriage or reviewing his troops in the market square. Lately, the baron and his army had been gone for months at a time, coming back with wagonloads of loot.

"So what if you are Baron Moorgoth? What am I supposed to do? Bow and kiss your feet like everyone else in Sanction? And why the disguise? Why not just come out and tell me who you are and what you want?"

Moorgoth smiled. "I heard you were a man who did things your own way. I also heard that you refused to give my guardsmen special treatment. I decided to see for myself. They were right. You treat me no differently now than you did when you thought I was an ordinary soldier. I like that."

"Good. I'm glad." Theros had little use for game-playing. "Now what's your business with me?"

"Business? My business today is conquest. I am preparing to expand my holdings beyond Sanction. My men need good weapons and good armor. My job is to train my men and lead them into battle. Your job will be to equip them. To make it short, I need a new smith in my army."

Theros thought back to his days with the minotaur army. He remembered the excitement of preparing for the battle, the hours of fast and furious labor, making ready for the fight, the pride in knowing that his weapons and armor had done their duty. He found the prospect interesting, for a moment. Then came back to Theros the hardship, the backbreaking labor, sleeping on the ground, eating cold food, driving wagons over rough terrain in all sorts of weather.

He thought of his snug little dwelling—not big, but comfortable. He thought of chilled ale and hot stew.

Theros shook his head. "What could you possibly offer me that I couldn't get here? I made over fifty gold pieces for a single armored jerkin today. Could you offer me that sort of money?"

Moorgoth laughed. "You mean that jerkin that your lad

made for the kender? Good work, I agree, but the little rat never knew the worth of what he was trading."

Theros frowned. "Do not suggest that I am a thief, Moorgoth. It is no way to begin a business discussion. The kender got a bargain. Whatever I do, I am fair."

"You are a soldier, Theros Ironfeld, and honorable as a minotaur, Huluk says. Huluk sent me word about you. Unfortunately, we already had a smith at the time, and he was good. I still have the letter from Huluk, of the Clan Hrolk, introducing you. I remember Huluk. He was quite a warrior. Someday we will see him again here on Ansalon. I hear that his new Third Army is second to none."

He paused to take a drink of ale. Theros finished his meal, shoved his plate aside.

"My smith is dead," Moorgoth continued. "My rear area was attacked last month when I raided a dwarven camp. I defeated the force on the ground, but not without loss. We took what we had come for, and left. The hole in my unit still remains, however. I have found a new quartermaster and a new fletcher. I need a new smith for weapons and armor."

Theros grunted. "I'm not interested. I am doing fine where I am."

Moorgoth shoved aside his plate, leaned back. "I am willing to pay you one thousand pieces of steel to join, and one of these gems a month for as long as you stay."

The mercenary held up a clear jewel, exquisitely cut. It caught the light and splashed it around the room. The baron quickly concealed the bauble.

"It is worth at least a hundred gold pieces, and probably a lot more. I captured a huge load of these from the dwarves. I will pay you one per month. Further, I guarantee that I will buy them back at a rate of one hundred gold pieces if you cannot find a better deal elsewhere."

Theros motioned for Moorgoth to hand over the jewel for inspection. The baron dropped the jewel into Theros's huge calloused hand. Theros eyed it and then handed it back. "You should have come to me seven years ago. Then I would have been interested. Now, I can buy one of these myself if I have the mind."

Moorgoth continued to try to make the sale. "You can keep your shop, Ironfeld. Just close it down while you are away. I will hire you for a three-year contract. I will even hire a guard to keep watch on the shop while you are gone, at no additional expense to yourself."

Theros was impressed. He couldn't help but be a little interested, in spite of himself.

"So what will I do to earn this wealth? It seems to me that if you paid everyone in your force with the same generosity that you are showing me, you would have to be raiding the Halls of Thorbardin, not a single dwarf camp."

Moorgoth took a long swig of ale. "You know as well as I do that finding good infantry is never difficult. Young men and women are always out to prove themselves, to risk their lives for booty. And I have good, solid veterans who keep the backbone of my small force strong. It is the skilled labor I need and I don't have three years to wait while some smith learns the fine art of sword-making. I need a skilled smith, one who can do fast work and good work in a field situation. You can bring your assistant along to help. I will pay him double what he is making now."

The barmaid, Marissa, hustled over, asked if the baron would like a refill on his ale.

"Thank you, yes." He gave her a pinch.

The barmaid flashed him a smile, left with a twirl of her skirt that revealed her shapely legs.

Theros gazed after her. In all the years he'd been coming to this bar, she had never looked at him like that. Granted, he was not the most handsome man in the world and he supposed his manner was crude and abrupt from living so long among the minotaurs. Still, the baron was no prize and the woman had smiled prettily for him. Money and power, Theros thought. That's what makes the difference. She'd smile for me if I put that jewel in her hand.

From deep inside, a voice asked, "And would you want a woman who will smile only if she's paid to smile? And do you truly want to work for this man when you don't like him?"

Theros grunted. He leaned forward. "No, thanks, Baron. Like I said, seven years ago—maybe. If you're looking for a smith, I suggest Malachai the Dwarf. He might be interested. I'm not."

The baron tried this angle and that, but Theros continued to refuse. At length, it seemed that Moorgoth gave up. He didn't appear to have any hard feelings about it. He had turned his attention to other things.

The barmaid came back to the table with two full mugs of ale. Moorgoth grabbed the woman around the waist, pulled her close. "My men and I will be going out to battle soon. Shall I bring you back a little something?"

The woman giggled and tried—but not very hard—to pull away. "Oh, yes! That would be wonderful, my lord!" She snuggled up. She knew how to win friends.

"I would really like this man, Theros Ironfeld, to join my army. Do you suppose you could persuade him to do that for me?"

The girl's eyes widened. She had seen Theros in the pub many times over the past years and had paid little attention to him. She now eyed him with more respect.

"I'm not sure what I could say to him to make him reconsider," she said.

Moorgoth gave the girl a nudge toward Theros. She wobbled and landed in Theros's lap. "I'm sure you'll think of something, my dear."

Marissa's eyes darted over the massive muscles of the smith in admiration. She ran her hand over his shoulder. Three gold pieces had been shoved into her hand while she sat with Dargon Moorgoth.

Theros didn't know this at the time. He put his arm around the woman's waist. "Say anything you like to me. You are a very lovely woman!"

The barmaid snuggled close and looked into his eyes. "Oh, sir. Do you really think so?" she asked coyly.

Moorgoth smiled and stood up. "I am off to bed, Theros Ironfeld. I hope you change your mind and decide to join Moorgoth's raiders. Perhaps I'll stop by tomorrow and we can have another little chat." With that, he turned and left.

The barmaid stood and began clearing the dishes and mugs from the table. She took them to the kitchen, then went over to the bartender. The two whispered back and forth for a few moments, and a few coins were passed to the man.

She returned to Theros's table and picked up his now-empty mug. Leaning forward, she let her hair fall softly across Theros's face and whispered in his ear. "Meet me upstairs in Room Two in half an hour."

She turned and took the mug away.

Theros's heart pounded. He had admired the barmaid for a long time. Now, he was being admired in turn. He was no longer just the town smith.

He went upstairs.

He found the room without any problem, even in the poorly lit corridor. The candles in their sconces illuminated the number on the brass door. He hesitated in front of the door, then opened it without knocking. He quickly looked around. No one was in the room.

The bed was large enough for two, and there was a desk and chair standing in the corner. Next to the door stood a small table with a washbasin and a full jug of water. Beside the basin sat a razor. A small hand towel hung from a peg in the wall. It was definitely a comfortable room.

Theros gingerly tried the bed. It was soft. A down quilt covered the straw bedding, neatly hiding the scratchy stalks below the cloth. Sheets and a blanket covered the quilt.

He lay back on the bed and shut his eyes. He felt like a man of destiny today. He had been invited to join up with an army. He had refused, but the memory of old times made him wonder what its objectives were, how many men and what sort of equipment it had. He was thinking about this when the door opened.

The barmaid slid in and shut the door behind her. She came over and sat next to Theros on the bed.

She put her hands on Theros's chest and looked down into his eyes. "My name is Marissa."

Theros started to tell her what his name was, but she stopped his words with a kiss. He put his arms around her and brought her close.

Marissa pulled back from him, ran her hands through his curly, short black hair. "I know your name. And I'm sorry I never noticed you before, Theros Ironfeld," she said softly, breathlessly.

Reaching into the bodice of her dress, she drew out three gold pieces and handed them to Theros.

"What's this for?" he asked in astonishment.

"You overpaid me for the meal," she answered, smiling.

"But—"

Marissa kissed him again. There was no more talk about money. Nor did she once mention the notion that he should join Moorgoth's raiders.

The night was one Theros would never forget.

Chapter 16

Theros awoke when the sun hit him in the eyes and he looked around, not recognizing his surroundings. Then the last evening and his liaison with Marissa came back to him swiftly.

He lay back down in the bed, noticing that she was gone. He could still smell her perfume on the sheets. The sun was yet level with his window, meaning that it was early. He didn't have to leave at once. Perhaps Marissa would come back.

Today would be a good one for Theros. He would go to his work, start that new shield he'd promised to one of Moorgoth's men. Now that the army was planning to march, Theros would undoubtedly have as much work as he could manage in the next few days. He'd work long hours, but he'd charge more for the extra time. Then he'd visit the Jeweler's Guild, buy one of those jewels Marissa thought were so lovely.

Marissa. Last night had been the first night Theros had not slept alone since he had arrived in Sanction seven years ago. Women had glanced his way on more than one occasion, but he'd never done much to encourage them to do more than look. He didn't know how to talk to women, who seemed to expect a man to talk about things like moonlight and roses. The only thing Theros knew about moonlight was that it permitted night marching. Women never seemed the least bit interested in talking about the things he liked to talk about—the best stone to use for sharpening swords, how to make fine quality steel.

Not until he'd met Marissa. Last night, they'd talked and talked, and not about moonlight, either.

He rose, rinsed his face in the basin, and shaved. Dressing, he went down the stairs to the pub. Breakfast was being served.

He looked around to see if he could find Marissa. She was nowhere in sight. Theros ordered a plate of eggs and bread, with tarbean tea and a piece of apple for his meal. He ordered an apple cider to wash it down.

After his meal, he went back out onto the street, walked to his shop. Yuri was there already, opening the shutters. Yuri was a good worker, skilled in tooling and sewing leather. He was not strong enough to make a smith, but he could do all of the odd jobs that Theros didn't have time to do—leatherwork, arrow and spearhead making, armor work. Yuri was young, but he caught on quickly.

Sometime, perhaps, Theros would tell Yuri that. Then Theros thought of Hran and his training. Praise gives a person a swelled head. Better to keep Yuri in line. He'd learn faster.

Arriving at the smithy, Theros was not surprised to find one of Moorgoth's men loitering about the street in front of the smithy, obviously waiting for the smith to open for business.

Theros gave the man a nod, unlocked the latch, opened

the big doors. He went inside and started to heat up the forge. The guardsman stepped inside. He was holding a sword in his hand. Theros, eyeing the weapon, was quick to spot the notched blade.

"Yuri!" Theros bellowed. "Get in here!"

The young man was in the back room, where he slept. He ran into the smithy, looking fearful, as if there were a fire, or—worse—he had forgotten to do something. "What is it, sir? The accounts are in order. I counted them down myself this morning! I—Oh! Hello, sir." Yuri flushed. He was supposed to watch for customers. "What can we do for you today?"

"Look at this blade!" the guardsman said in disgust. "Can you believe it? Just for hitting a blasted dwarf over the head. Sure, he had on a steel helm, but still! I paid good money for this sword in Flotsam. I expected better. Moorgoth sent me to you. Can you mend it, Master Ironfeld?"

Theros smiled. So Moorgoth was sending his men over here. That was excellent! "Certainly. Put the blade on that table. I'll have it ready for you tonight."

"Fine. Moorgoth said to send the bill to him."

Theros nodded. He'd make it double what he would have charged anyone else.

The guardsman left the forge. Yuri took the sword, placing it on the table. Theros went back to his work, heating up the fire, when he noticed that Yuri was wasting time, staring at the sword.

"In Sargas's name, what are you doing, boy? Haven't you ever seen a sword before?"

"Not one like this, sir," said Yuri. "It's got funny little marks all over the blade."

"Bah!" Theros snorted. "That's the problem, then. Let this be a lesson to you. Engraving a blade is well and good, but if you don't know what you're doing, you ruin the blade's effectiveness. Now get back to those gloves you're stitching."

Yuri ran off, giving the sword a last parting glance.

Theros, now curious, left the fire to itself and went over to examine the weapon.

The marks on the blade were, as Yuri had said, curious.

Theros had expected them to be Solamnic in nature, for the knights were forever putting family crests, roses, kingfishers and every other heraldic symbol they could find upon their weapons.

But this. . . . Theros turned the blade this way and that and finally made out what the "marks" were supposed to represent.

Dragons. Dragons twining up and down the blade. Strange-looking dragons with long, snakelike bodies and no wings. And interspersed among the dragons appeared to be letters, although they belonged to no alphabet that Theros knew. Not elven, certainly. Not dwarven either.

Obviously, though, he'd been correct in his assessment. The engraving had marred the integrity of the blade. He thrust the blade into the fire to heat, and began sorting out and preparing the proper tools.

A strange hissing caught his attention.

"Yuri, stop making that fool noise!" Theros shouted.

"Stop what, sir?" Yuri walked in from the back, a half-finished glove in his hand. "I wasn't doing anything—sir! Blessed Gilean! S-s-sir! L-l-l-look!"

Theros turned. Yuri was stammering and pointing at the forge fire.

Theros couldn't believe what he was seeing. Dragons, small red dragons that seemed to be made of flame, were crawling off the blade of the sword that now glowed red in the heat of the blazing fire.

Openmouthed, Theros stared. He shut his eyes, rubbed them, looked again. The dragons were still there, more and more of them. Now they were scuttling across the white-hot coals. One of the dragons—a bright, fiery red creature—jumped out of the bed of coals, landed on a wooden bench. The dragon vanished, changing to flame. The bench began to smolder and smoke.

The firepit was filled with tiny dragons now, hundreds and hundreds. They were leaping and dancing and jumping, and everything they touched burst into flame. Yuri was now shrieking at the top of his lungs. At least he had the presence of mind to grab a bucket of water and throw its contents on the flaming bench.

Theros couldn't move. Sorcery! This was wizard's work. Theros would have faced the prospect of cold steel in the belly without blanching. The sight of that ensorceled sword left him as weak and shaking as a terrified child.

The fiery little dragons were dashing up the wooden beams that supported the roof. They crawled to the work-table, dropped among the tools. And everything they touched burst into flame—even metal. The only effect the water seemed to have on the flames was to spread them. Yuri might have been pouring oil on them.

Yuri was clutching at Theros, trying to drag him out of the forge. The building filled up rapidly with a particularly toxic, choking smoke.

"Come away, master! Come away! There's nothing you can do! Give up!"

"By Sargas!" Theros roared, coming to himself. "Never!"

Grabbing hold of a piece of uncut leather, he began beating at the flaming dragons that were running along the hard-packed earthen floor of the smithy. The dragons jumped onto the leather, and it caught fire so fast that the heat of the flames singed all the hair off of Theros's arm. He dropped the leather, started to try to stamp out the flames with his foot.

"No, master, no!" Yuri was howling.

"More water, you fool!" Theros shoved the boy out of the forge. "Bring more water."

He stomped on the dragons, and every time his foot hit one, it gave a little squeak and turned cold and black. But there must have been thousands now and he could never hope to put them all out. The smoke was making him cough, burning his eyes. The wooden beams on the ceiling had caught fire now. The heat was forcing Theros back toward the open door.

Still he fought, until one of the dragons jumped on his leg. It burned through his long leather apron in an instant, touched his flesh. The pain was excruciating, far worse than any burn Theros had ever received in his long years of working the forge. It seemed that his flesh was going to burst into flame. The pain was so intense, he felt himself starting to black out.

He staggered out of the burning forge and collapsed upon the ground, clutching his leg and moaning. Looking up, he saw that a crowd had formed around his forge. Most of his neighbors were there, plus many more of the citizens of Sanction, attracted by the billowing black smoke. Among these were several of the maroon-coated men of Moorgoth's raiders. And standing among those was a black-robed wizard. He stood with his arms folded across his chest, a slight smile on his face.

Not one person sought to help put out the blaze. Not one person grabbed a bucket or shouted for the town guard, or did anything else typical of such emergencies. They all stood in silence, watching the fire, staring at Theros.

Yuri came running up, panting, carrying the bucket of water. He stared, aghast, at the shop—it was engulfed in flames.

"Never mind that now!" Theros shouted. "Pour the water on my leg!" It might help or it might make the flames worse, but Theros was frantic with the pain. He didn't much care.

Yuri dumped the water on Theros's burning clothes. The fire went out instantly. Theros lay back on the ground, panting and sweating. The pain of his burned leg made him almost sick, as did the smell of his own charred flesh.

The black-robed wizard walked up to Theros, knelt down to examine the smithy's injured leg. Theros growled, but he was in too much pain to say anything.

"Nasty burn," said the mage calmly. "It will leave a bad scar, I'm afraid. But I have something that might ease the pain." He placed a jar of ointment at Theros's side. "Oh, don't worry about paying me," the wizard added, with a sly grin. "I'll send the bill to Baron Moorgoth."

The wizard strode off, black robes trailing in the ashes, which were just about all that was left of the forge. Even the stone chimney had burned in the magical blaze.

One by one, Theros's neighbors drifted away, went back to their work. The townspeople, now that the excitement was over, wandered back to the bars and taverns. Moorgoth's men stood around, talking amongst themselves.

"Isn't that a coincidence? For the smith's forge to catch

fire like that. After he turned down the baron's generous offer. My, my. I wonder what Master Ironfeld will do now?"

"Lost his tools and everything. You know, it's a strange twist of fate, but Baron Moorgoth's well stocked with tools. Kept them from the last smith we had."

Yuri helped Theros to his feet. "Master!" The boy's face was white, streaked with black. His eyes were wide and frightened. "Master, even the strongbox melted!"

"The money?" Theros knew the answer.

Yuri shook his head. "Gone. All gone."

"Well, Ironfeld," said a voice behind him. "This is a terrible accident you've had. Just terrible."

Theros turned. Baron Dargon Moorgoth stood behind him.

"What will you do now, Ironfeld? Oh, I guess you could start up your business again, but you know, I have the feeling that you wouldn't get very many customers."

A minotaur bested in contest who has fought well is permitted to surrender without shame or dishonor. Theros knew when he was beaten. The best thing to do was to accept his defeat, surrender, and carry on. But do it with dignity. Always with dignity.

Theros, limping on his injured leg, pulled himself up, faced Moorgoth.

"Do you still need a smith?"

"As a matter of fact, I do," said Moorgoth.

"I will take you up on the job, then," Theros said coolly. "You will pay me what you offered me last night—one thousand steel to join. You can hand it over now. I'll need to replace what I've lost in the blaze."

"Agreed," said Moorgoth, smiling. "Though I might say that you are in no position to bargain—"

"You might," said Theros. "And I might say that you could go looking for your weapons-smith in the Newsea." He took the purse that Moorgoth held out to him.

The baron started to walk away. His men, laughing and talking, fell in behind him.

Theros raised his voice to be heard. "Plus, I want a percentage of any take that your army makes, over and above my pay. Is this clear, Baron?"

The baron turned to stare at Theros in amazement. "What did you say, Ironfeld? I thought you made more demands."

"I did." Theros was calm. Yuri, standing next to him, was shaking in fear and making signs to Theros to be quiet. Theros ignored him.

"I want a percentage of the take. I'm worth it. You must think so, too. You must have paid that foul wizard a small fortune for his work today."

"I don't know what you mean," Moorgoth said. "This was a terrible accident. Still, I imagine that I can agree to the deal. My former smith had a two percent cut. You will receive the same. If you stay past the first three years, I will increase that. Anything else you want, Ironfeld?"

"Nothing for now, Baron," Theros said. "Where do I join up?"

"Meet us at the center of town." Moorgoth eyed Theros with new respect. "I think we're going to get along fine, Ironfeld. Just fine."

He sauntered off, his men accompanying him. Yuri was looking at Theros with round-eyed wonder.

"What?" Theros demanded, irritated. Bending down, he spread some of the ointment on his leg. Sure enough, the burn immediately ceased to hurt. "Stop gaping at me like that. You look half-witted. Now take some of this money and buy yourself some warm clothes and a blanket. You'll need them, sleeping out in the open—"

"I . . . I don't want to go!" Yuri protested.

"Of course you're going. Don't be a fool. You'll make good money and learn the art of battlefield smithing."

"But . . . it's dangerous, sir. And . . . and . . ."

Theros turned his back, looked at what remained of his forge. There might be something left he could salvage. He was ignoring Yuri's blathering—until Theros heard the words, "I hate you, Theros Ironfeld!"

Theros turned, shocked.

The young man was seething. Fear had given him courage. "I'm not a slave like you used to be! I'm a free man and I have a right to decide if I'll go with you or not!

Don't make decisions for me. You treat me like a dog—a dog you don't like. I work hard with never a word from you except if I get things wrong!"

Theros regarded the young man in silence. A minotaur would have slammed the boy into the ground, taught him how to speak to his elders.

Yuri was spewing out words. They must have been stored up inside him for months. "I can't believe that you're going to go with that horrible man! His army's nothing but thieves and rascals! He burned down your forge, for Gilean's sake! And you just stand there and take it! Now you expect me to go along? After this? After what he did to you? To us?"

Theros swallowed an anger-filled response. Yuri was young. He couldn't be expected to understand that sometimes you had to knuckle under to fate.

"The pay is good," Theros said stiffly. "More than I can afford to pay you. And you are worth it. I want you to go. I need your help."

Yuri stared, stunned.

"Well?" Theros demanded impatiently. "Are you going with me or not?"

Yuri tried a tentative smile. "Do you mean that, Theros? Do you think I'm worth it?"

"You wouldn't be hanging around here taking up space if you weren't," Theros said curtly. "Now go do as you're told."

Yuri, clutching the money, dashed off down the street.

Theros picked up a stick and began to sift through the still-glowing ashes of what once had been his life.

Chapter 17

"Get a crate for these tools," Theros ordered Yuri. "We'll need to take them with us. And gather up those leather tools and supplies. Secure what we aren't taking into crates and nail them shut."

Theros was standing in the shop of the army's former weapons-smith, gathering up tools and other supplies.

Yuri did as he was instructed. "Sir, I'll have to go down to the carpenter for more crates. We have just two left. He'll want to be paid for them."

Theros handed over the money. He was busy going through the back stock of weapons, deciding which ones to take. He gazed at most of them in disgust. No wonder Moorgoth had gone to all the trouble to burn down

Theros's forge. The baron needed a good weapons-smith badly. Theros almost felt flattered.

Almost.

Yuri came back an hour later with two men from the carpenter's shop, each carrying a large crate. They set the crates down in the middle of the smithy. Yuri had just started to load tools into the first crate when Baron Moorgoth entered the shop.

"Good! I see that you are nearly packed. I will send a horse and wagon around in two hours."

Theros was preoccupied. "Yuri! Hurry up with those weapons!" He glanced at the baron. "Where is the army camped? Outside of town? How many men do you have?"

To Theros's amazement, Moorgoth flushed in anger.

"You're asking a lot of damned questions, Ironfeld. From now on, you're just another officer under my command. You'll go where I tell you to go and do what I tell you to do. You'll be told where to go when you report with your wagons."

Moorgoth left, saying something about meeting the new logistics officer.

Theros stared after the man. It had been a simple question, nothing more. It seemed logical that the weapons-smith should know how many men were in the army he was to be responsible for outfitting. And why shouldn't he know where the army was camped? Eventually, he returned to his work.

Yuri completed packing the box of tools and extra weapons. The crates were heavy, but they were going to be loaded onto a cart, not carried by hand, so the weight didn't matter.

"What should I do now, Theros?" Yuri asked.

Theros wouldn't admit it, but it pleased him to hear a new note of respect in the boy's voice.

* * * * *

The wagons arrived at precisely the hour Moorgoth had named. Theros was ready. He and Yuri and the wagon's driver hoisted two of the crates onto the wagon. Theros and Yuri carried two more to the back storage area of the smith for safekeeping. Then came the hard part—time to move the anvil.

Yuri and the driver both stared at the anvil blankly. Neither could even budge the heavy object.

Theros waved them both away. He dragged the anvil from its place in the abandoned forge to the back of the wagon. Once there, Theros paused to rest. Then, flexing his muscles, he bent down in a crouch. With a forceful grunt, he lifted the anvil and, sweating with the exertion, maneuvered it carefully into the back end of the wagon, placing it directly over the axle.

The wagon driver told them that they would meet the rest of the force near the center of town. Yuri hoisted his small bag of personal belongings onto the wagon. Theros carried his somewhat larger sack over his shoulder. Now that he had recovered from the shock of losing his forge, Theros found himself almost looking forward to this new adventure. In his mind, he could already hear the call of the trumpet. He climbed up onto the wagon.

"Roll out," he ordered.

* * * * *

Four more wagons were assembled in a side street off the plaza. Theros's wagon joined in at the end of the line. The baron was on hand to make introductions.

"Cheldon Sarger, our quartermaster," said the baron.

Cheldon Sarger was a middle-aged human with a face that looked as if it had been dipped in his own cooking oil. He was broad, much like Theros, but Cheldon's girth was made of fat, not muscle. Cheldon's job was to keep the army supplied. He maintained the food, clothing, uniforms, weapons and armor in stock. The weapons and armor would be provided by Theros. The rest Cheldon would have to acquire from the locals, either by bartering or buying or, as Cheldon said with a wink, stealing.

Theros thought the man was kidding.

Belhesser Vankjad was the new logistics officer, the person in charge of both Cheldon and Theros. Belhesser was a tall, thin man, with a pointed face like a ferret. Belhesser looked like a half-elf, but always declared vehemently that he wasn't. He had previously worked in the port authority. His job was twofold. He handled supplies, maintenance of weapons and armor, and acquisition of new materials. He was also like Huluk, in that he was responsible for a section of line soldiers who would defend the rear area in case it was overrun. In addition, he was responsible for transport— the wagons and horses that would keep the army rolling.

The final man that Moorgoth introduced was named Uwel Lors. And if Belhesser resembled a half-elf, Uwel resembled a half-goblin. Theros had never imagined one person could be so ugly. An older man, in his late forties, Uwel looked every bit as tough as the steel armor chain mail that he wore. Uwel appeared to be friendly enough, however. He saluted smartly, then shook hands with Theros.

"Good day, sir. It's a pleasure to have a new smith with us, sir." Uwel had a strange, clipped way of talking. "I am responsible for the dress, drill, deportment and most of all, the discipline of the rank and file in this army. I am not an officer like yourselves, sir, but I am the senior ranking nonofficer in the army. If you have a discipline problem, come to me.

"Now sir, I understand that you've fought with minotaur armies before, but never with a human army. Is this true?"

Theros frowned and nodded yes. He was angered, thinking that Uwel might mean this for some sort of insult.

"Not to worry, sir!" Uwel said brightly. "We're run a little different, and with a lot more discipline than those huge beasts. Still, we get the job done."

Uwel saluted and went back to the front of the wagon train to confer with the drivers.

Baron Moorgoth slapped Theros on the back. Whatever ill humor the baron had been in back at the forge, he seemed to have regained his good temper among his men. "Introductions are over. Let's get on the road!"

The army commander barked an order to Uwel in the

front. The drivers mounted their wagons. Uwel called "Forward!" in a voice that seemed to echo through the city, and the first wagon lurched into motion.

Everyone walked except the drivers with their loads. There were four officers, including the army commander and Theros, and twenty other men, not counting the drivers.

The wagon train rounded a corner, rolling past the Belching Fury. At the sight, the barmaids poured out of the tavern and into the street. They exchanged banter with the passing men.

Theros looked around to see if there was any sign of Marissa. From inside the inn, she saw him and waved, then suddenly ran outside to the line of men. They all tried to catch hold of her, including Baron Moorgoth, who clearly thought she was running out to greet him. She avoided them all and came straight to Theros. Putting her arms around him, she gave him a warm, deep kiss.

"I heard about what happened to your forge. Don't worry. You'll make your fortune with the baron. When you get back, you come and look me up!" Marissa said and, laughing, she ran back to the inn.

The men cheered. Theros felt his face burn, but it was burning with pleasure. The baron, looking back, was clearly displeased. He motioned to Uwel Lors, said something to the half-goblin. Uwel nodded and fell out of the line of moving wagons. Theros, who could still feel Marissa's kiss on his lips, didn't pay any attention.

The wagon train continued on through the city, moving north.

Theros could think only of Marissa. "Why is it," he muttered to himself, "that good things only come to me when I've got to leave them behind?"

* * * * *

The men and wagons joined the road that would take them across the north pass through the Guardian Mountains and then through the Khalkist Mountains, leading to a city known as Neraka. Theros had never heard of it.

It took four days for the wagons to cross the mountains. When they reached Neraka, Theros thought it seemed ordinary enough, much like any other city, with stone buildings and market stalls and more people than it knew what to do with. But he hadn't been in the city long before he decided he was mistaken. There was an eerie feeling about Neraka. It was the feeling that he was being watched, a chill in the blood that he could not explain.

He and Yuri walked its streets shortly after their arrival. Theros kept turning around, thinking that someone was following him. Whenever he looked back, there was no one there. Yet he felt the hair prickle on the back of his neck.

Yuri was obviously feeling something of the same. He jumped at every sound and refused to let Theros out of his sight.

"I've heard that there is a temple of evil here. Do you think it's true?" Yuri asked in a whisper.

Theros laughed, but his laugh was hollow. "How can that be true? Have you not heard the story of the Seekers? They say that there are no gods. I know them to be wrong, of course, but there is no temple to Sargas in Neraka."

Yuri was not convinced. "If there were evil gods, they'd be here," he said softly.

Theros wouldn't admit it, but he knew how the boy felt. Something dreadful was going on here, though no one spoke of it aloud. He could see it in the blank, cold stares of those they passed, in the voices that hushed the moment anyone came within hearing, in the faces that retreated back into shadows.

The other men seemed to feel the same, all except Uwel and Baron Moorgoth. The baron, in particular, was not in the least disquieted, seemed quite at home in the region. He ordered a halt for the evening at the north end of town.

That night, the baron called an assembly.

"I know you've all been wondering where we're headed. For security purposes, I haven't told any of you. It's not that I don't trust you, but ale has a way of talking, so the saying goes. The army has barracks in Gargath, northwest of here by fifty miles. We will join with them and prepare to move north. The campaigning season is nearly upon us."

"North? How far north?" someone asked.

"We will move another hundred miles or so north of Gargath. There are some villages in the area that have proved to be rather stubborn about paying us for protecting them from bandits." Moorgoth laughed, as if at some private joke. "I have reason to believe that we'll find riches there and that we will have a very good year."

With the plan laid out for them, the men all drank to the success of the army.

The next morning, they left Neraka and followed the path to Gargath. The next two days they spent in the mountains. By the start of the third day, they had crossed the Busuk Range and moved into the extended valley that lay ahead of them. By the middle of the fourth day, they entered Gargath.

At the first sight of Gargath, the hearts of the soldiers all cheered. It had been a long trip. A troop of cavalry, twenty strong, equipped with long spears and chain mail armor, rode up to meet them.

The troop commander saluted the baron. "Hail, sir. We're glad to have you back. I see that your mission in Sanction was a success!"

"Yes, indeed. Tell Commander Roshenka to prepare to receive our new officers and men. Have him cook a special meal for tonight. I want to introduce our new warriors to the rest of the army."

The young officer saluted and galloped off toward the town. The rest of the troop remained with the procession. Half an hour later, they entered the gates of Gargath.

Theros was amazed. The entire town looked as if it were here to do nothing but support and house the army. The streets were crowded with soldiers, along with their women and children, all gathered to cheer their commander and welcome him back home. The main street was lined with stables and barracks. An open plaza stood in the center of the town. Across the plaza was the army's headquarters.

Moorgoth called his new officers together. "Here, gentlemen, is where you will be staying."

He pointed to the headquarters building. Uwel Lors

took Yuri and the other men aside and showed them their barracks. They marched off at a brisk pace, Uwel shouting commands as they moved. Theros watched Yuri a bit anxiously. The young man was not much of a marcher.

Sure enough, Yuri stumbled, almost knocking down the man in front of him.

Quicker than the eye could follow, Uwel lashed out with a whip he carried on his belt. The tip caught Yuri on the rear end. Yuri screeched, tumbled out of line. Uwel caught him, shoved him back in.

"Watch what you're doing, fumble-foot!" Uwel commanded.

Yuri choked back tears. Theros could see blood on the young man's backside. He almost said something, then stopped, remembering the blows he'd received from the minotaurs. He'd survived. A little discipline never hurt anyone.

The drivers moved their wagons through the plaza and exited on the other side. They were heading for the army assembly area, where the wagons would be kept until morning.

Theros and the other officers picked up their belongings and walked across the plaza to the headquarters building. They entered through the front door. Two guardsmen saluted.

A third soldier behind a desk rose to greet them. "Good day, sirs! I am Corporal Vincens, the headquarters troop orderly. If I can be of service, I will be here at this desk. But now I will take you to your rooms."

The corporal led Theros up two flights of stairs and entered a long hallway. Three doors down, he stopped. Corporal Vincens opened the door. "Captain Ironfeld, this is your room. You are to meet down below at sundown for the officers' meal. I will take you there."

Theros entered his new room. The others continued on down the hall.

The room was spacious. A single bed stood by the window. The air was clean and breathable here in Gargath, a pleasant change from Sanction. Theros opened the window to let in some light and air.

The presence of the army definitely had its effects. Groups of soldiers were everywhere. Across from the headquarters, on the other side of the plaza, shops and markets were filled with people. This must be market day.

A knock on the door interrupted him. The sun was setting, and the air was turning cool.

"Time for dinner, sir."

All of the officers in the army had gathered in the foyer of the building before the sun went down. The new officers were easy to identify in that they were not wearing the maroon uniform that was the hallmark of Moorgoth's army. All of the other officers wore black trousers tucked into black boots. White shirts with black leather jerkins were covered by maroon surcoats, bearing the crest of the army. They all carried swords at their sides.

Theros shook hands with many of them, exchanging names and looking them over. Just as the sun slid below the level of the far building on the west side of the plaza, Baron Moorgoth strode into the room.

"Gentlemen! I see you have all met our new officers. Excellent! Let us go and eat."

The crowd of twenty officers followed their commander down the hallway to the dining area. The tables were assembled in a long row, so that men could sit at each side of the tables to eat.

As they entered, Theros noticed that a woman in a fine dress was already sitting at the head table. Once all of the officers had found seats around the table, Moorgoth took his place beside the woman.

"Gentlemen, for those of you who are new here, please meet my wife, Charina Moorgoth." The lady rose and bowed, and then sat down again.

"Her word is the same as mine. Her wishes can be taken as my orders."

Moorgoth sat down and clapped twice, loudly. A row of soldiers entered the room, carrying flagons of wine, huge plates of meat, platters of fruit and vegetables, and baskets of bread.

The officer to Theros's right introduced himself as Wirjen Jamaar, commander of the cavalry squadron. "So,

Theros, what do you think of our little army here in Gargath?"

Theros was impressed. "I look forward to setting up shop and getting to work. I'm never happier than when I am banging metal into armor or a weapon."

The cavalry officer, a tall man with wide shoulders, laughed out loud. He raised his goblet of wine and clanked it against Theros's. "Good for you, Ironfeld! I am glad to have an officer who likes what he does. Tell me, have you ever worked horse armor?"

Theros was bewildered. "You mean armor for horses, or for horse soldiers?"

"Ah, you make me laugh, Ironfeld. I like that. I am, of course, talking about barding for the horses themselves. Have you ever done work like that?"

Theros shook his head no.

Wirjen scowled, slammed down his glass. "Damnation! I thought that Baron Moorgoth said he had acquired a qualified smith. What the hell good are you going to be to me if you can't make armor for my horses? It is vital—"

An officer across the table interrupted him. "Ironfeld, pay no attention to Jamaar there. He cares only for his horses. He didn't happen to mention that we've never had barding on our cavalry here, did he?"

Theros wasn't certain what to say, and so he kept silent. The other officer continued. "I command the first battalion of infantry. We met before in the foyer. I'm Gentry Hawkin. We're looking forward to a smith who knows how to keep weapons in shape. I don't need another smith like the last. One of his swords in your hand was as good as having a stick. You knew it was going to break. It was just a matter of when. Come over to my quarters tomorrow and I'll show you what I mean. We want better for the campaign."

Conversation came to a sudden stop when the baron stood. "Gentlemen, it is good to have new officers among us. It will take a while for them to get accustomed to the way we do business around here. Still, let us be patient until they have learned our ways. Now, I know you've all been wondering where we're headed."

The veteran officers murmured their assent. They obviously had not been told where or when the campaign was going to take them this year.

"We will be going north, into the Nordmaar area to remove resistance up there. I understand that there are still pockets of Solamnic Knights, and we all know the treasures that they hold in their castles. We go to challenge them!"

The officers were on their feet, cheering.

Late that night, after much wine and many, many war stories, Theros stumbled up the stairs to his room.

He was, once more, a member of an army, an officer and a smith. He could hardly believe it. And they were going to fight knights. Knights of Solamnia.

Hran would be proud.

Theros couldn't figure out how to work the fastener on his jerkin. It didn't matter. He was sound asleep before his wine-muddled brain had time to work on it.

Chapter 18

The army had been deployed for nearly a month, moving forward in fits and starts. They would set up camp for several days, send the hunters and scroungers out to replenish supplies, then tear it down, move forward for a week, and then repeat the process. They kept on the move as much as possible, for fear the hated Solamnic Knights—reportedly nearby—would hit them before they were ready.

"I will choose the ground," Moorgoth was fond of saying. "They will fight me on my own ground."

It was a ragtag army made up of men and women from all over this part of Ansalon. The backbone was the mercenary force. These men and women were well treated, ate the best, got the best wine, had the best places to pitch their tents. The rest were conscripts or debtors. People who owed the baron money—and there were many in Sanction—could pay off their debts by serving in his army. They were the ones who came in line for the brunt of Uwel's discipline. The mercenaries—who knew their own worth—wouldn't stand for it.

The soldiers were mostly human, with a half-breed or two thrown in for good measure. Moorgoth refused to fight with hobgoblins or ogres, who, he claimed, could not be disciplined.

"We have our standards, sir!" Uwel sniffed.

Theros was relieved, albeit surprised, to notice that the black-robed wizard who had burned down the forge—thereby proving he was handy with fire spells, at least—was not marching among their ranks. He questioned Uwel about the mage.

"If there is one person you cannot discipline, sir, it is a magic-user. Too used to getting their own way, sir, and that's a fact. Plus, they're all dyed-in-the-wool cowards. We tried one once, and the baron said never again. The first time an arrow whistled past his head, the man passed out cold. And when I poked him a bit with my knife, sir, to bring him around, he bleated like a stuck hog. Gave away our position to the enemy. I was forced to clunk him over the head with the hilt of my sword to get him to shut up."

"Did he?" Theros asked.

"Yes, sir. Permanently, sir." Uwel looked thoughtful. "I hit him a bit too hard, I think, sir."

The troops did not know that they were heading out to fight Solamnic Knights, the only organized force that stood between Moorgoth's army and the towns and villages they planned to plunder. The officers knew, but they weren't passing on anything to the men and women under their command. It was the soldiers' job to move and fight when ordered, not to be involved in the discussion of where or why they were moving. They were paid, and that was enough for Dargon Moorgoth. If it wasn't, Uwel Lors, the senior nonofficer, exacted a swift and punishing discipline.

Yuri wasn't the only person to feel Uwel's lash. The man was quite skilled with his whip and livened up an otherwise boring march by snapping it over the heads of the conscripts or licking it at their heels. Any who complained were pulled out of line and dealt with more harshly. Uwel added his fists to his whip for variety. It was sometimes Theros's job to pick up these unfortunates, who were generally left unconscious by the side of the road until the wagons came along in the rear.

Fear and money—or the hope of it—was what was holding this army together. Theros contrasted that with the minotaurs, who fought for the glory of their country, their clan and their own personal honor. The elation Theros had felt at once more being involved with a fighting unit was rapidly evaporating. He said nothing, however. It wasn't his place. It wasn't his army. He would do his job, for which he was being paid—well paid.

After three days of marching, Moorgoth brought the army to a halt. Tents were pitched, but Theros was ordered not to set up the forge and equipment yet. They would be moving again. Theros and Yuri were attending to minor repairs to equipment they could handle with the small forge-fire, when a runner dashed up.

"Sir. Baron Moorgoth requests the pleasure of your attendance at an orders group in thirty minutes. Shall I tell him that you will attend?"

Theros nodded and waved the soldier away. He never quite trusted Moorgoth's grand way of speaking—Theros always had to sort through the polite nothings to get to the meat—but he was pleased to have a chance to talk to him. The last few days, the rest of the army's officers had begun to shun him and the two other new men. They stopped talking when Theros or Cheldon or Belhesser joined them. Theros had no idea what he had said or done to offend anyone. He hoped Moorgoth might be able to provide an explanation.

The command tent stood in the center of the small camp. The army standard—a black serpent's head on a red background—flew from the front tent pole. Four guards stood at the ready in front of the tent. That was double the number of guards in a minotaur army. The guards waved Theros past. Obviously, he was expected. He entered the tent, found the other officers already present.

"I will come right to the point," Moorgoth stated. His voice was tight, his face flushed. "There is a spy in this camp. And one of you three"—he singled out Theros, Cheldon, and Belhesser—"is responsible."

The three officers stared at each other. Cheldon shook his head in disbelief. Theros leaned over to whisper to him. "So that's what's going on! They think it's someone from our organizations! We're the new ones."

Cheldon nodded. He said nothing, but he looked troubled.

Moorgoth went on. "We have a problem, gentlemen. Every time we move, the Solamnic force moves ahead of us, keeping within striking range, cutting us off from our objective. Our army is a small one. We cannot attack a village and still keep back enough to hold off those damned knights.

"According to our scouts, we easily outnumber the knights, but they are nearly half heavy cavalry. They are highly mobile, and that's where the problem lies.

"We're running out of time, gentlemen. We have to take the three villages in this area soon. I need new recruits, money and supplies for my army. Before we attack those villages, we're going to have to take out that damned Solamnic force!"

Moorgoth looked hard at the three officers, staring at each in turn. Each man met his commander's gaze and held it, including Theros. Moorgoth appeared satisfied.

"I trust you men. All of you. But one of you is harboring a spy. Find that person, bring him or her to me, and you will be well rewarded. Understood?"

The officers indicated their assent.

After the meeting, Theros, Cheldon and Belhesser held their own meeting in Belhesser's tent.

"For damned sure, keep your eyes open around your people. You especially, Theros," Belhesser emphasized. "I know all the people who are working with me. They've been with me for years. But you have raw recruits working for you now. Who knows where they came from or who they are?"

Theros had taken on three men to work with him at his smithy. He picked them out of the conscripts because they had the brawn needed to haul about the smith's heavy equipment. Yuri was still the apprentice to Theros, and the three others did odd jobs. They were hardworking men. Theros really didn't know them well yet, and he was forced to admit that any one of them could be a spy. His only complaint about the men so far was that, being older, they teased Yuri and mistreated him when they thought Theros wasn't looking.

Theros had been looking one day. He had started to intervene, but had decided, on second thought, that Yuri should learn to take care of himself. This wasn't an elven dancing school, after all. This was an army. The life, and the men and women who lived it, were rough.

Theros nodded. "I'll keep an eye on them. Still, I think the spy is most likely among the camp followers. The women in what I've heard called the "Pleasure Platoon" come and go as they please."

Cheldon Sarger laughed nervously. Everyone was tense, keyed up, kept glancing over his shoulder. "It could be anyone, for Morgion's sake! We've got to watch our backs. No matter what Moorgoth says, the officer found harboring a spy is ruined."

"Probably dead!" Belhesser corrected grimly.

On this gloomy note, the meeting broke up. Theros walked through the infantry tent lines back to his own tent.

As he passed through the camp, he noticed an unusual bustle. Soldiers who would have been lounging around, dicing or chatting or cooking, were instead polishing their weapons and checking over their armor. Officers ran back and forth from the command tent. Moorgoth had said there would be a fight, but he hadn't said when. Obviously, everyone else in camp knew something Theros didn't. The knowledge made him angry. He had as much as been accused of being a traitor. His honor was being called into question. But he couldn't defend himself. Not until he knew for certain that none of his people were spies.

* * * * *

Theros left orders for Yuri to wake him before sunrise. The sky was gray, and there was enough light to see, but soon the valley would be sun-drenched and hot.

"Bring me some food from the commissary tents, and see if you can't get some extra bread," Theros grunted.

"Yes, sir." Yuri ran off.

Theros watched him leave. "He could be the spy. Any one of them could be the spy! If one is, he will know my wrath!"

He pulled on his breeches and black leather boots. Theros wore the maroon surcoat, and over that a belt with leather shoulder straps attached to form a "Y" in the center of his back. Here he carried a metal holster that held his two-headed battle-axe.

Hran had always maintained that the axe was the perfect weapon for a smith. He could be armed and ready for battle, yet still keep both hands free to do work as needed. The battle-axe was of Theros's own design and his personal favorite.

On the way to the smithy, Theros saw Yuri over in the meal line, collecting his food. The young woman serving him was flirting with the young man. The two spent a long time together, talking. Now and again, the young woman would blush or giggle. Yuri gazed at her in admiration, a feeling that was obviously returned.

All this lovemaking going on while Theros starved! He was just about to stomp over and retrieve his apprentice, when Yuri returned with the food, including the extra bread that Theros had ordered. Theros took the food from Yuri without a word, and hungrily dove into the meal.

The men had eaten earlier, while it was still dark. In this army, the officers ate last. It was the soldiers who had to eat first, to ensure that they were well fed. No army survived when its troops starved.

Speaking of troops . . .

Sudden realization hit Theros like a blow to the head. Where were the horses? Theros set his plate to one side and stood. He looked around the camp. The area where the cavalry had been set up was empty. No horses grazing. No tents, no men.

Theros was a sound sleeper. Still, he should have heard the noise of the troops riding out—unless they had deliberately sneaked out in the darkness, muffling all sound. As if hiding from the enemy. Only this time, the enemy was within!

He shouted to Yuri. "Where in the Abyss did the cavalry go?"

Yuri blinked, astonished. "I'm sorry, sir, I didn't notice that they *had* gone."

"You'd damned well better find out!" Theros growled.

The sharp notes of the "officers to me" bugle call rang through the camp. Cursing, Theros took a long swig of water from the water bucket, and headed off at a run to the command tent.

This time, as he passed through the infantry lines, he saw that the soldiers were ready to march. Their corporals and sergeants had them sitting in ranks, waiting for the order to move out.

"Nice of Moorgoth to let me know what's happening," Theros muttered.

He entered the tent with the rest of the officers. Cheldon and Belhesser stood together in one corner. Theros joined them.

"Do either of you know why the calvary left this morning?" Theros said in a low voice.

They both shook their heads. Neither looked pleased.

"I didn't even hear them leave," Belhesser replied. "Obviously, the infantry officers know what's happening. They're ready to go."

"Everyone knows but us," Theros said angrily.

Baron Moorgoth entered the tent, closely followed by Uwel Lors. Uwel barked an order for the officers to stand at attention.

Moorgoth strode to the front of the tent. "Gentlemen, please be seated. As you know, the cavalry has deployed during the night."

"Begging your pardon, sir," said Theros, "but some of us *didn't* know!"

Moorgoth turned his attention to the three officers. "Quartermaster, Smith and Logistics Officer—I owe each of you an apology. I don't mean to single you gentlemen out, but as I said, I have reason to believe that the spy is somewhere in your organization and none of you has done anything to reassure me."

The three officers exchanged glances.

"You don't trust us," Theros said, anger burning.

"I trust you three," Moorgoth corrected quietly. "That's why you're here."

Theros's anger dwindled. At least his honor wasn't in question. That was what mattered.

Moorgoth continued. "I received word around midnight that the Solamnic force was no more than ten miles north of here and headed this way. We are only ten miles east of the town of Milikas, our intended target. I've sent the cavalry to raid the town. They will hit at noon sun. This attack will cause the Solamnic force to draw off, come out of hiding and force them to meet us in battle—on our terms! On our ground!"

Moorgoth grinned. So did everyone else in the tent. The plan was becoming clear. "While the cavalry is keeping the knights occupied along their front lines, the infantry will strike the Solamnics from the rear. We'll set up an ambush, and take out those bastards before they know what hit them.

"But to make this work, we are going to force-march the army this morning until we're within a mile of that town. We've got nine hours to cover nine miles. Think we can do it?"

A resounding cheer went up. Moorgoth smiled and left. After that, everyone looked at each other. An army of a thousand, each carrying a heavy pack marching—no, running—that distance? Covering it in nine hours? Well, they had said they could do it. Now they were committed.

The orders conference broke up moments later. Officers ran back to their commands to begin the preparations.

Theros barked orders, hurried his soldiers into quick action. He sent Yuri over to bring their wagons forward. When the wagons arrived, the smith was broken down, ready to load. They were shoving the heavy crates onto the wagons when Baron Moorgoth walked up.

"Carry on, men. Good job to you all. Oh, Captain Ironfeld, a word, if you will."

Moorgoth drew Theros off to one side, looked around to see that no one was listening. Certain that they were alone, Moorgoth crouched low to the ground. He drew out a map, rolled it out in front of them.

"Ironfeld, you and the other logistical units will be slower than the rest of the army. I'm going to assign a company of infantry to march with you. When you get to this position here"—Moorgoth pointed out the area on the map—"I want you to set up your smithy. If the plan works, I want you working on arrows and spears when we move back to this area. We'll need new weapons fast. Can you do that?"

Theros nodded. "Yes, sir. But why tell me? Belhesser Vankjad is the commander of logistics."

"I'm telling you because you need telling. I've already told Vankjad. He's telling the quartermaster. Something is on your mind, Ironfeld. What is it?"

Theros scratched his chin. "Sir, I don't like all these secrets. You're setting us apart from the rest of the army. The other officers don't trust us. We are loyal, just as they are."

"Yes, I know," replied Moorgoth. "And I know where the spy is now. I just don't know who. And don't worry, he's not in the smithy. You can relax."

Theros let out a sigh of relief.

Moorgoth smiled, clapped Theros on the shoulder. "I must be going. I'll see you tonight. Be at your post on time. Good marching!"

Theros saluted as the baron went back to the now-forming column. If this plan worked, Moorgoth would be a hero to his army. If it didn't, Theros could find himself running from a victorious enemy again.

He wasn't big on praying for help, but he did ask Sargas to take an interest in them. Theros didn't know that much about Sargas, but he was fairly certain the horned god had little use for Solamnic Knights.

Chapter 19

Baron Dargon Moorgoth walked to the front of the column. His command staff stood ready to move out. The army's standard-bearer, a tall young officer named Berenek, held the flag unfurled in the morning breeze. It was only an hour since the sun had cracked the horizon.

Theros looked around at the baron's staff. There were four officers, Berenek included, and four soldiers, all sergeants. Normally, the heavy cavalry would serve as Moorgoth's personal bodyguards, but today they were off on a different mission. The sergeants—normally his organizers and scribes—would be his bodyguards. Looking at their grizzled faces and calloused hands, Theros guessed that Baron Moorgoth was in safe hands.

"All right, men. Ready to go?"

Every one of them responded yes. The baron waved his hand and then began to run, at an easy pace, down the road. The command staff was only a few steps behind. The infantry battalion commanders yelled their march orders and the entire army lurched to a walk, then to a jog-trot. Like a huge slug, the army started to crawl along the road.

After the first mile at a run, the long forced march was already starting to take its toll. The line of men and women looked tired. But no one would think of falling behind. For one, they'd taste Uwel's lash. And they would be ridiculed as weaklings by their comrades.

Another mile and still they kept going. The troops traveled light, but each man carried his weapon and supplies. Still, they covered a lot of ground. The men and women pounded on, well aware that the faster they ran the distance, the more time they would have to rest when they reached their destination.

They left the slow-moving supply wagons far behind. The wagons would catch up later, possibly even after the battle was over.

* * * * *

After the third mile, Moorgoth called a halt. The soldiers behind him sagged down onto the ground and sat there, sweating and panting.

Moorgoth removed his boots. A good-sized blister was forming on the back of his heel on his left foot. He pulled out his dagger and lanced it. The liquid drained immediately. He put his sock back on and pulled on his boots, tightening the straps as tight as they would go. Standing, he tried the foot. The pain was a minor irritation.

He walked back through the first battalion of infantry, stopped to talk to small groups of soldiers.

"So, Corporal? You and your section going to make it to the other end?"

"We'll make it, sir. There's no question of that."

Satisfied with the answer, Moorgoth moved forward once more to take his place at the front of the column. He felt good now. His foot would hold up.

"Ready?" he asked his command group.

He waved his hand forward, over his head, and began to march, not run. He kept up a brisk pace, but the soldiers appreciated the fact that they were not running. They needed the break.

They did not stop again until they came to a small forest straddling both sides of the road. As they entered the shade of the trees, they met a group of three women driving a donkey cart, coming the other way. Alarmed at the sight of the soldiers, the women abandoned the cart, jumped over the sides, and ran.

"Catch them!" Moorgoth ordered.

His men caught two of the women easily. The other woman ran like a frightened deer down the road, outdistancing the armor-clad man who chased after her.

"Stop her!" the baron ordered, glancing back.

An archer ran forward. He unslung a longbow, took careful aim and loosed the arrow. It flew through the trees with a whistling sound. The woman suddenly stumbled, then fell flat on her face, an arrow sticking out of her back.

"Good shooting, Corporal. Well done." Moorgoth complimented the archer. The soldier saluted and went back to his place in the ranks. The baron made a mental note to remember that man. He would get an extra share of the loot.

The sergeants dragged the other two women back to the main body of the army. The women were sobbing, horrified by the slaughter of their companion.

One of the sergeants came forward to ask for orders. "If we let them go, sir, they'll tell someone they've seen us for sure."

"Kill them," the baron responded.

The women began to scream and wail. One, an older woman with graying hair, fell to her knees, her hands uplifted in a plea for mercy. At this, the men detailed for the job looked uneasy, fingered their weapons, but didn't draw them.

"I don't like this, sir," said one. "This isn't what I was hired to do—kill a kid and an old granny."

"We could bind them, leave them in the forest," said another.

Moorgoth was furious. They were wasting time. He said nothing, however. He merely looked about for Uwel Lors.

Uwel strode forward. Grabbing hold of the older woman, Uwel flung her down on the ground in front of him, drew his dagger, and grasping hold of her hair, jerked her head back and slit her throat. The younger woman screamed and fainted. This made Uwel's job easier. He leaned down and cut her throat wide open. Now that the task was done, the two men who had been supposed to carry it out helped Uwel drag the bodies to the side of the road.

Baron Moorgoth made a mental note of these two men. He would have something to say to them later. Rather, Uwel would have something to say to them. Moorgoth waved the troops forward again, leaving the dead where they lay. The bewildered donkey stood with his cart near the road, braying mournfully as the army marched past.

* * * * *

Theros led the column of wagons that followed after the main army. He and Belhesser marched on foot, accompanied by Yuri and the soldiers from the smithy. The wagons rolled along next, followed by the quartermaster's troops and wagons. The rear guard was made up of sixty soldiers and one officer. The column moved forward at a leisurely pace.

"I can see why they left us to ourselves," Theros said to Belhesser.

"Yes, we're much too slow for the main army. They'll be at the assembly area for the ambush before we're even halfway there."

They marched for four miles without taking a break, entered the same forest that the main force had entered an hour or so earlier. Then they saw a donkey cart standing on the side of the road.

"Curious. What do you make of that?" Belhesser said.

He called a halt. The supply wagons were the lifeblood of the army. And though this looked apparently innocent, no one wanted to take a chance. Wizards had been known to use their cunning craft to make objects as innocent-looking as this donkey and cart into deadly traps for the unwary.

"I'll go forward and check it out."

Theros hefted his axe, motioned for Yuri and the soldiers to accompany him.

Theros was the first to find the women lying in the ditch. He went over to investigate. Flies buzzed over the bodies that lay in pools of their own blood. One of the women was young, no more than eighteen, perhaps. The other, older woman was either the mother or maybe even the grandmother.

Theros, fearing an ambush, glanced around. He saw nothing, however, heard nothing. The woods were quiet, but that was not unusual, considering the large number of soldiers that had just marched this way. He sent Yuri on down the road, then waved the column forward. The infantry in the rear dashed up to join him, weapons drawn.

The commander stopped when he saw the bodies.

Belhesser, coming up behind him, spoke first. "What do you suppose happened? Surely the baron wasn't afraid of two women?"

The infantry commander laughed callously. "Baron Moorgoth couldn't afford to have them running around screeching that they'd seen an army. They could have warned the cursed Solamnic Knights."

Theros shrugged in agreement. Whatever stirrings of pity he felt, he quickly tamped down. "Bad luck for them. They were simply in the wrong place at the wrong time."

Yuri came running back down the road. His face was white and it went whiter when he saw the bodies in the ditch. He made a strangled sound, gagged, and turned hastily away.

"What is it, Yuri?" Theros demanded harshly. He could see the others exchanging glances and grinning. He cuffed Yuri on the ear. "Get a hold of yourself," he said in an undertone. "People are watching!"

Gasping and wiping his lips, Yuri made his report. "There's another dead woman down the road, there." He pointed.

"You're sure she's dead?"

Yuri nodded, unable to speak.

"Well, then, she's no threat to us now. We had best move on," Belhesser ordered.

The infantry and the wagons moved past the bodies in the ditch. At Theros's order, Yuri cut the donkey loose from its harness. No reason to let it suffer from thirst and starve to death. The donkey trotted off into the woods, glad to run away from the smell of blood and death. They left the cart on the side of the road.

Theros passed the body of the third murdered woman. She had been shot in the back with a longbow—the broken arrow shaft still protruded from her back. She lay in the road where she had fallen. The soldiers had walked right over her. The woman was barely recognizable. Her body was a pulp of bones and blood.

Yuri was looking backward, stumbling as he went. "We should have buried them, at least," he said in a choked voice.

"No time," Theros growled.

"I hate this army!" said Yuri suddenly, softly. "I hate the baron. I hope they're all slaughtered!"

"Stupid hope, boy," Theros said, glaring at him. "You've just wished your own death."

"I wouldn't mind much now," said Yuri. "I don't feel fit to live."

Theros said nothing more. He could almost feel the hot, angry breath of Sargas down his back. No minotaur alive would have ever committed such a dishonorable, cowardly act. At that moment, Theros was ashamed of being human.

They marched on.

* * * * *

The baron signaled another halt. They were less than two miles from their destination. It was just past noon sun. If all was going according to plan, the cavalry attack on the village was moving forward at this very moment.

"How do you think they're doing, sir?" asked Berenek,

the standard-bearer. "The cavalry. I hope they're doing well. My brother is with them."

Moorgoth slapped the tall man across the back. "I had forgotten that Wirjen Jamaar was your older brother. He's my best cavalry officer. He will do just fine. Is your family name Jamaar as well?"

"No, sir. My family name is Ibind. Wirjen and I are only half brothers. His father died in a goblin ambush before I was born. My mother remarried."

They were interrupted by a messenger running back from the front lines. It took several moments for the man to catch his breath. "Sir, I am to show you where to meet Sergeant Jogoth. We've got the area all scouted out. You can see the town from where we are."

The baron was very interested. "And how's the cavalry attack going? Could you see it?"

"It looks as if the cavalry has broken into the town. We could hear fighting in the town—probably the town guard—but we couldn't see anything."

"No sign of the knights?"

"No, sir."

"Good."

Moorgoth ordered the men to return to a run. They moved more slowly than when they had first started out. They were all tired. Still, the faster they deployed, the more time they would have to rest, and the more fit they would be when they hit the enemy.

The baron picked up the pace. "Come on, you bastards, hurry up!" he yelled back over his shoulder.

He didn't bother to look back to know that everyone was keeping pace with him. They would follow him at a sprint, if they had to. All knew that to disobey would bring down the wrath of Uwel Lors.

The scout ran beside the baron. After the first mile, the ground began to slope. A large hill stood to the left. They headed down to the wooded bottom of the river basin.

The soldier pointed. "That forest there, sir. That's where we enter. On the other side, about five hundred yards across, you can see the town. There's nobody out here. They're all in the town fighting, I suppose. We scoured the area pretty thoroughly but we found no traces of anyone. They're either not here or they're really good at hiding."

They slowed to a jog, and finally to a march when they entered the forest. Leaving the road, they moved through the trees. As the baron entered the woods, another scout came out from behind a tree.

"Sir! Over here, sir." The sergeant motioned for the baron to join him. The first scout continued to lead the rest of the force through the forest.

The sergeant held out a map, drawn with charcoal on a piece of smooth tree bark. "Here's the layout, sir. Tell me if you want anything changed."

The crudely and hastily sketched map showed the town and the edge of the tree line. The road entered the town about a thousand yards past its exit from the trees. The first and second brigades of infantry were to move into line in the woods, with the archers deployed forward, at the edge of the trees. The command group was shown in the middle.

"Yes, this is fine, Sergeant. When you've finished moving the troops into position, assemble your men, and set up near the road. When our cavalry comes through, stop them and have them form on the other side of the forest, near the road. I want them ready to dash back up that road in a hurry. Send Captain Jamaar to me. Carry on, Sergeant."

The troops were still moving through the woods and into position. Everyone was quiet, too tired to talk. The last run had taken its toll. Now, at least, they had time to catch their breath. Moorgoth returned their salutes as the soldiers moved past him.

Finally, the rear guard advanced. They were the last company of the second brigade. The company commander saluted as he came up to the baron.

"Sir, we're the last of them. We left sixty-one soldiers behind on the road today. Most dropped from exhaustion. They should be picked up by the wagons. We didn't see nobody followin' us, sir."

Sixty-one people hadn't been able to take the killing pace, had fallen out of ranks. Still, that wasn't bad for an infantry force this size. Not bad at all. Any comparably sized army would have lost three times that number, or more. Nevertheless, Moorgoth would ensure that those sixty-one people were flogged and lost pay. He wasn't paying for soldiers who couldn't keep up.

The baron followed the last company through the woods, and turned off to find his command group. They would be facing the town.

The fluttering red flag indicated his tent.

The baron, spotting it, was highly displeased.

"Berenek, get that flag under wraps. I don't want someone from that town seeing a red flag in these woods. Don't bring it out again until I order a move. Now, pass the word down the lines, right and left. I want to see senior officers here in ten minutes."

The waiting game was on. The trap was set. Would the Solamnics take the bait?

Chapter 20

The wagon train moved forward slowly. With the wagons as heavily loaded as they were, speed was impossible. Theros and Belhesser walked along in front of the lead wagon.

The road wound through a series of hills and forests. The going was difficult. The road was sometimes hard-packed and smooth, other times rutted and bumpy. Sometimes it was wide, sometimes so narrow that tree branches scraped the sides of the wagons.

The baggage train rolled to the site Moorgoth had chosen. The place was nearly a mile from the battle site, behind a series of hills that separated the army's position from their own.

"Belhesser, any word of our spy?" Theros asked quietly.

"No, nothing. I think our problem will go away if Moorgoth wins this next fight. If there is a spy, whoever it is will have failed in his task and will want nothing more than to get the Abyss out of here. And nothing cheers the baron like a victory. He'll forgive and forget. Watch your back if we lose, though."

Theros agreed. He could well imagine that the baron would be in a foul mood if his army had to skulk back to Sanction with its tail between its legs. He looked behind to see the progress of the column. Two of his soldiers walked together, talking, followed by the third, driving the wagon with the smithy's equipment and supplies. Yuri was nowhere in sight.

"Where in Sargas's name has he gone?" Theros muttered.

He hung back and let the wagons containing his equipment roll past him. No sign of Yuri. Theros joined the commissary group, which was far larger than Theros's little band of metal workers.

Searching among the workers, Theros found the woman who was in charge of making the bread.

"Have you seen Yuri, my apprentice?"

The woman wore a white cotton man's shirt, the same as issued to the soldiers, tucked into a long buff skirt. Below that, high-laced black boots. Her head was covered with a handkerchief, to keep the dust out of her hair and face. She was in her forties and was, by her weather-beaten face, an old campaigner. She looked at Theros and laughed.

"Of course, he's here! You know that."

Theros scowled. "No, I don't know that. Why should I? Does he come back here often?"

"Morgion bless us, yes! You can't tell me you don't notice that! He's back here every time we're on the march. He even comes over when he's done working in the smithy for you for the day. But then, it's only natural, ain't it, Master Smith?" The woman winked and leered. "Young blood is hot blood, they say."

Reaching out her hand, she playfully tickled Theros on his massive chest. "But there's a lot to be said for experience, my man. Come by my tent tonight. . . ."

Theros was growing embarrassed and angry. He could see some of the men, standing around, laughing and nudging each other.

"Where is he?" Theros demanded, ignoring the woman's offer.

"He's back behind the second wagon. He'll be with Telera, my assistant."

Theros turned and hurried back past the wagons to investigate.

Just as the woman had described, Yuri was walking with a young woman. She wore the same clothes as the first woman. Her long blond hair was braided and put up to keep out the dust and sweat. She probably was not more than eighteen. But now that Theros took a good look at her, he could see that she was different from most of the women who either fought in this army or served it.

Her fair skin was reddened from the sun, as if she were not accustomed to being outdoors much. There was an air of delicacy and daintiness about her that made the shabby clothes she wore seem much more attractive than they really were. No wonder Yuri was drawn to her.

Theros stood directly in front of the two, blocking their path. At the sight of him, the young woman blanched and shied like a skittish colt. Yuri went bright red and opened his mouth to speak.

Before either could say anything, Theros pounced on Yuri and grabbed him by the arm.

"Damn you! What in Sargas's name do you think you're doing? Your place is up with our wagon, not back here flirting with the women."

Yuri protested. "But, sir! I haven't done anything wrong! I only—"

Theros couldn't believe it. The boy honestly had no idea how much danger he was in. He smacked Yuri hard on the back of his head, making him stumble.

"Shut up and get back there, or I'll whip you for insubordination!"

Yuri looked over quickly at Telera. She was pale and frightened.

"Go!" she mouthed.

Yuri looked back to Theros, and then ran forward at a sprint.

Theros glanced over at the woman. She cringed away from him. He saw in her eyes the same fear that he had seen in soldiers' eyes when they were about to be whipped or beaten.

"Don't beat Yuri, sir!" she begged, raising her hands in a pleading gesture. "It was my fault. You"—she swallowed, then said bravely—"you can take your anger out on me, if you want, sir."

Theros stared. He couldn't believe it. This young woman actually thought he was capable of beating her!

"Great Sargas! Where is my honor?" Theros asked himself. "I'm turning into one of those bastards who uses threats and whips to maintain a show of respect that is, in reality, no respect at all. It's just fear. This is no way to lead men."

Theros found he was still staring at the woman. She was pretty, but now that he regarded her closely, she looked worn and much too thin. Moorgoth worked everyone hard, men and women both. And only the soldiers were guaranteed a good meal. When the supplies ran low, those who did the cooking, not the fighting, were the first to go hungry. Her life could not be an easy one. And now she looked almost sick with terror.

A wagon rolling past halted, its driver stopping to watch the interesting action on the roadside.

Theros regained his composure and yelled back to the driver. "What are you stopping for? Nobody ordered a halt!"

He turned on his heel and walked up past the commissary wagons to the front of the line. He couldn't get the woman's fearful eyes out of his mind. He saw them, and he saw the bodies of the women in the ditch. He remembered Yuri's words.

I don't feel fit to live.

Theros walked along alone, immersed in thought. He didn't realize he'd reached his own wagons, until Belhesser yelled back at him, breaking his reverie.

"What is it, Belhesser?"

Belhesser held out his map. "Would you say that hill over there was this hill here?" He indicated a spot on the map just beyond where they were to set up camp.

Theros took the map and studied it for a moment. He found the road on the map, and looked up to compare it to the terrain before him.

"Yes, that's the spot all right."

The wagons continued moving down the road. Theros walked back to his wagons. Yuri walked alongside, his head down. Theros tried to forget that he had struck Yuri, decided to pretend that the incident never happened. Again, he said to himself that it was for the young man's good.

If the spy was among the commissary people, then anyone from Theros's section caught talking to anyone in Cheldon's section would be immediately suspect.

He even tried explaining this to Yuri, who only stared at Theros incredulously, managing to look as dumb as a tent post.

"Spy?" Yuri repeated stupidly. "What do you mean?"

At length, Theros gave up.

"Forget it. Just obey me on this one. I don't ever want to see you with that young woman again. For her sake, as well as yours. Now, run ahead and find me a good site for the smithy. We're to set up once we get the word." Theros turned to one of the soldiers. "Erela, go back and tell the sergeant of the commissary that the place there, in front of that hill"—he pointed—"is where we set up camp."

The two set off at a run.

The sun was at the hilltop ahead of them by the time they had the wagons into position. Yuri had removed the digging implements from the smith's wagon, and he and the soldiers dug a pit for the forge. Two of the soldiers were sent to find enough wood to last them for the next few days. Theros went off to talk with Belhesser.

"Listen, do you know anything about a woman in the commissary by the name of Telera?"

Belhesser leered. "So, you've got your eye—?"

"No, not at all." Theros snorted. "I just need to know something about her."

Belhesser gave him a puzzled look. "I know that she works as an assistant for Hercjal in bread-making. She joined us in Sanction. Said she was orphaned. Fever took her folks. That's all I know. Why do you ask?"

Theros passed it off with an easy shrug. "I thought I knew her from the Belching Fury. I guess I was mistaken. It's not important."

Belhesser winked. "You have got your eye on her. You sly dog. Well, good luck to you. Not that there'll be much time for slap and tickle in the next day or two. Are your wagons in position? Don't set up your forge until I order it. If we're losing, I want to be able to get out of here before those accursed knights catch us."

Theros returned to his smithy and found the forge pit had been built to his liking. The earth in the area was hard and rocky. The men had dug down with shovels and picks, forming a bowl in the center of the spot where Theros had indicated he wanted the smithy. The pit was lined with larger stones that they had found or dug up, forming a good fire reflector.

The soldiers were cutting up the dead wood that they had hauled in and were stacking it beside the pit, ready to start the fire when needed. Yuri was over in the wagon, checking to make sure that none of the tools had shifted or been damaged. Theros left him alone to do his job. He had harassed him enough for one day.

Theros walked up the hill a short distance and sat down, looking over the site. The commissary section was set up at the edge of the hill, forming the close side of the square. The quartermaster's stores were a couple of hundred feet past the commissary, forming the far side of the square. The smithy was going to be on the left side as Theros looked down from the hill. The right side was open, and beyond it was where the infantrymen would set up tent lines.

As the sun sank lower behind the hill and it grew too dark to see, Theros's thoughts turned inward.

What is going on inside of me? I am an honorable man. I should never have agreed to take this job, no matter how much money it paid. Moorgoth has men whipped almost to death if they commit the smallest infraction. He murdered those poor women, when it would have been just as easy to take them prisoner. He destroyed my forge, and instead of killing him, as any minotaur would have done, I came along with him! I took his blood money!

Admit it, Theros, he thought ruefully, you wanted to be back with a fighting unit. You wanted the thrill of battle, the glory of the kill. Glory! He blew air through his nose. We're nothing more than uniformed, organized bandits.

Theros shook his head, stared down at the ground. And how do I explain today? How do I explain the way I treated Yuri? I can't. And this isn't the first time. He was right, that day he yelled at me. I treat him like a slave. And I know how it feels, to be treated like a slave.

Sargas take me! What do I do? I have accepted Moorgoth's money. We have a contract. It would be dishonorable to leave his army. Dangerous, too, Theros thought. Undoubtedly, he would think *I* was the spy. Yet I see no honor in staying. What do I do?

Theros raised his eyes to the heavens. "Sargas, give me a sign. Give me direction. That's all I ask. I'll take care of the rest."

Theros watched and waited, thinking that he might see the gigantic black bird with the fiery wings that had come to him before, No sign came, but perhaps now was not the time.

Feeling more at ease now that he had shared his burden with Sargas, Theros stood up and walked back down the hill. Undoubtedly, someone would be looking for him by now, wanting the answer to some fool question.

He wondered how Moorgoth's army was doing.

Chapter 21

The army hiding in the forest waited for over an hour with no news. The wait was unnerving. Nothing could be seen in the town. Nothing could be seen in the fields surrounding the town. Nothing.

A soldier crept through the underbrush to the baron's side. "Sir, no sign of anything," he whispered. "The scouts have seen no sign of the enemy."

Moorgoth nodded and the soldier crept back into the underbrush, back to his place farther up the line. They continued to wait.

Suddenly, from their front, came a rumbling sound, rolling from the town and growing louder. Moorgoth rose to his feet and looked into the town. He pulled a spyglass from a pouch on his belt, and put it to his eye.

Smoke was rising. Flames flickered on the far side of the town. The smoke was obscuring his vision, but the baron could make out individual buildings and the roads between them. He kept his eye on the main road that led into the town.

The next sound he heard was that of horses, galloping through the streets. He couldn't see them yet, but he knew the sound of hooves thudding against hard ground.

A flash of steel. Another flash. Moorgoth moved the spyglass, followed the road down, and focused on two riders.

They were his men.

The baron put the glass down. He could now see the two clearly, galloping up the road. Behind them, he could see more horses thundering out of the town. He brought the glass up again. Yes, he recognized the maroon uniforms. They were his cavalry.

In a sharp voice, he yelled orders back to a runner.

"Those are our cavalry. Tell Captain Jamaar to hold his squadrons behind the forest until I call for them by bugle. Tell him to send me word of how he did. Understand?"

The young man nodded and was off into the woods at a run.

The first two riders galloped into the woods. Once out of sight of the town, the two riders dismounted. The runner raced forward to confer with the two. One of the riders remounted, just in time to lead the rest of the cavalry through the woods to the rear. The other rider returned with the runner to Baron Moorgoth's position.

"Good day, sir. It was a fine fight, but a tough one," the officer called.

"Lieutenant Boromus, isn't it? You are second in command of the light cavalry. Am I right?" Moorgoth asked the young officer.

"Yes, sir, I am."

"Did you achieve your objectives?"

The officer shook his head. "Not all objectives, sir. We rode into the center of the town. The town guard gave us a fight at first, but they weren't organized. We threw them off. You were right, sir. There is a spy in our midst." The soldier was grim. "They were waiting for us."

"Damn!" Moorgoth swore softly.

"When we beat back the town guard, we began rounding up the civilians, marched them into the central marketplace." The officer paused.

"Go on," urged the baron.

"There were more civilians than we thought and they were ready for a fight. They fought like devils from the Abyss, sir. At one point, they dragged one of Captain Jamaar's heavy cavalrymen from his saddle and beat him to death. We pushed the people back, but there was a lot of bloodshed.

"The town guard regrouped and charged us on the west side of the town square, attacking us from the rear. They killed at least four and wounded four more before we could manage to turn around and make the battle more even."

Moorgoth could see that the man was nearly exhausted. "Go ahead, drink some water." He offered the cavalry officer his waterskin.

"Thank you, sir." Boromus took a drink. "Once we'd whipped the town guard, we dismounted and held the horses on the east side of the town, ready for us to pull out, according to plan. We thought we had the civilians all penned up, but a bunch must have been hiding. They must have sneaked through the buildings, instead of going out in the streets where we could have seen them. They killed the guards we had set over the horses, and then cut the animals loose. We stopped them, but we lost a lot of men and mounts and supplies."

"What happened next?" the baron asked, frowning.

"We fought on, both against the civilians in the square and the guard. We held on until midafternoon, as you had ordered. Then, we ran as fast as we could from that hornet's nest. Sir, I can tell you, I'm looking forward to razing that cesspool of a town. I'll . . ."

Moorgoth let the man rant. He could see that Boromus was cracking from the strain. He needed to let off steam. The baron waited patiently until the man had calmed down.

"You said that you had not achieved all of the objectives," Moorgoth continued. "Your only objective was to have the calvary cause trouble in the town until midafternoon. It sounds as if you did that well enough."

"Sir, I didn't think it was in your orders to lose half of the cavalry! Half, sir. Half are dead. What you saw riding out of the town is it—around fifty of us. There were some wounded, but they're surely dead now."

Moorgoth looked down at the ground. Again he swore silently. He swore vengeance for his men. The town would pay.

"You did well. You held on, and that's what counts. Go back to your captain."

The officer looked at him in tight-lipped anger and despair. "Sir—" he began, but he couldn't continue.

Moorgoth understood.

"Your captain is dead, right? You're in command now. Is that right?"

The young officer nodded.

"Very well, you shall have the rank to go with it. You are now Captain Boromus. I wish it were under better circumstances. The fighting for the day is not yet over. Get your men fed and rested. I may call upon you again. Coordinate with Captain Jamaar. Go back to your unit."

The man nodded, but did not salute. He crawled back through the underbrush to his horse. Mounting, he slowly made his way back to his troops.

Moorgoth shook his head. Half? Over half! Over half of his cavalry was gone. The cost alone was crippling, but the loss of good soldiers was worse. Those had been some of the finest mercenaries ever to come his way.

His attention focused on the top of the rise to the left front. A lone rider stood on the ridgeline. Moorgoth raised his spyglass again, to see the rider better.

Through the glass, he could see an armored warrior on a white charger. He could see the emblem on the breastplate—a bird. The rider was half a mile away and Moorgoth could make out nothing more. Yet he knew what that emblem was—a kingfisher, the symbol of one of the orders of the Knights of Solamnia.

The knight rode down the hill toward the town. The smoke of the fires on the far side of town stained the pleasant summer sky.

Moorgoth lost sight of the knight when he drew close to the town. The baron turned to order his men to get ready, but he needed to say nothing. Everyone was watching the knight. They crouched in their hiding places, ready to move. Excitement rustled among them like wind through tree leaves.

Two minutes later, the knight came charging out of the town, galloping over the hill in the same direction from which he had come.

"Settle down," said Moorgoth to his men, though he knew they couldn't hear him. "Settle down, boys. Now we get into the hard part. We have to wait for the main force of the knights to arrive. We even have to sit here and watch them assemble, right in front of us. And we don't dare make a sound. It's going to be hard."

He motioned behind him for the runner.

"Pass this word to all of my officers. If any man makes a sound or moves so that the enemy finds us before we're ready, I'll cut his throat myself. Go ahead and pass the word."

Another runner came up, crawling forward to the baron's position.

"Sir, Commander Omini sends his regards."

Moorgoth glared at the man. "I don't need Omini's regards! What's his damned news?"

"He wishes to inform you, sir, that his scout reports a force of mounted heavy cavalry and another of foot soldiers moving at a quick pace toward the town."

Moorgoth was immensely cheered. They were racing right into his trap!

"Good," he said to the runner. "You tell Omini that I want his brigade flat on their bellies until they hear my bugle call. Tell him to recall his scouts and hide."

The runner, crawling on all fours, saluted. Moorgoth fought to hide his laughter. Crawling on all fours and saluting looked extremely idiotic.

* * * * *

Sunlight flashed off armor. The knight had returned to the ridgeline about twenty minutes later. Moorgoth studied him with the spyglass. Through the glass, he saw the knight look directly at him.

The baron dropped down to his belly. Quickly, he looked up. He was all right—he'd been standing in the shade. He had feared that the knight had seen the reflection of light off the glass's front lens. The knight must have been just scanning the forest.

The knight was joined by another, then another, and then by twenty more. One held a standard—a white flag hanging from a long pole with a crosspiece. The emblem on the flag was the same black-and-red kingfisher that the knight wore on his armor.

The party of knights stood at the top of the ridgeline for several minutes, looking around. Moorgoth found he was sweating. All it would take was one fool to sneeze and the knights would know they were walking into an ambush.

Silence.

Ten of the knights broke away from the main group and galloped down the hill toward the town. A bugle call rang out across the valley.

The baron looked nervously behind him. One of his men might have mistaken that bugle call for their own. He waited tensely for his soldiers to leap forward—too early.

Nobody moved. Everybody watched the ridgeline.

Moorgoth breathed again.

The main force of knights came down the hill, walking their horses. Over the ridgeline, a column of knights, four across, appeared. Behind the knights came their foot soldiers. They marched eight across and kept up with the cavalry.

Moorgoth brought his glass up again to study the infantry. They all wore leather cuirasses and steel helmets. Most were armed with swords or axes. They carried large shields on their backs. As he watched, he saw a break in the column, and behind came a group of two hundred archers. They did not wear any sort of armor. They carried longbows strapped over their shoulders.

The baron looked around. He could see the anxious expressions on the faces of his soldiers. He gave them a stern look meant to reinforce discipline—that's what mattered most in an ambush. He motioned for his bugler.

The baron turned his attention back to the army crossing the distance between the ridge and the town. When the last of the infantry had cleared the ridge, but the first of them had not yet entered the town, he knew it was time.

He stood up. The bugler, alert, stood up beside him.

"Bugler, sound 'archers advance,' " the baron ordered.

The twelve notes rang out in perfect pitch across the field and through the forest. At first, nothing happened, as if no one had heard the call.

Then, suddenly, a thousand archers, from all across the front of the forest, moved forward, lining up in front of the trees.

They stopped, planted their arrows in front of them, and drew back their first nocked arrows. A lone officer held up his sword. With a single yell and a swift downward motion of his sword, he commenced the battle.

"Loose!"

The arrows leaped from the longbows almost in unison. Quickly, each archer retrieved his next arrow from the ground in front of him, nocked it, and raised his aim to achieve the maximum range.

"Loose!"

The second volley flew skyward, before the first had even hit the ground. Many of them found their targets. A shower of arrows rained down on the unsuspecting infantry, caught out in the open.

Gaps formed immediately in the Solamnic infantry column. Dead and wounded fell everywhere. Their officers responded quickly. They shouted for a charge. Shaken, but certainly not broken, the infantry charged forward.

The Solamnic officers' instinct was correct. If the men had stayed where they were, they would have been cut down. As it was, many more fell from the second volley of arrows. But the third volley missed completely, overreaching their targets. Now came the hardest task for Moorgoth's archers. They had to hit a moving target.

The charging infantry could see only the archers to their front. They were heartened—archers were no match for good heavy infantry. Behind them, the Solamnic cavalry heard the fighting and turned their horses to race back to the battle. Bugles blared, sounding the alarm and ordering the charge.

This was the toughest part of the battle for Baron Moorgoth. He had to keep his infantry hidden. The Solamnics were getting closer, but every flight of arrows took down a few more. Closer they came.

When they got to within two hundred yards, the archers poured on the fire. Their officer ordered them to fire at will, allowing the archers to choose their own targets. The baron yelled over the din of battle to his bugler.

"Sound 'infantry advance!' "

The bugler nodded and brought the brass instrument to his lips. The clear, cold sounds of the order issued out. Men surged forward to join the fight. It seemed that the very trees had come alive. The infantry rushed to meet the charge.

The archers ran back to the safety of the woods. They were no match for well-armed and armored attackers. The baron's infantrymen swarming out of the trees would handle that task.

The soldiers had no time to form into ranks. They ran forward into the tired and depleted ranks of the oncoming Solamnics. The two sides met with a thunderous crash, sounding like fifty trees falling to the ground at once.

Due to their overwhelming numbers, not all of Moorgoth's men could get into the fight. There just weren't that many Solamnics to go around.

The archers caught their breath and watched the fight intensely. If the Solamnics broke through, it would be up to the archers to stop them. Luckily for them, it did not look as if the main infantry was going to break or fail.

Moorgoth motioned for the runner again.

"Tell the command group to fall back from the fight and join me here. Then go tell the cavalry commanders that I want them to ride hard to the back of that hill." He pointed to the ridge that the Solamnics had only recently crossed. "Tell them to listen for my call. When it comes, I want them to charge into the Solamnics' rear. Now go!"

The baron's heart was pounding. He lived for the excitement of battle. He looked out to the fighting not fifty yards away. His infantry was pushing back the Solamnics. They were faltering, their lines starting to give way.

"Push them, damn you!" Moorgoth yelled to no one in particular. As if they had all heard him, the baron's infantry line surged forward. The Solamnic infantry broke.

They were no longer a unit, or a group of units. Now, they were individuals, fleeing to save their lives. The Solamnics ran toward the town.

The baron's infantry started to pursue.

Moorgoth turned to his bugler. "Quick, sound 'form line!' "

The notes carried out over the noise.

Officers yelled and senior nonofficers shoved and prodded men back into position.

The command group of four armored bodyguards and two officers moved toward the baron. Moorgoth motioned for the bugler to follow him and he left the trees to join them. The red-and-black banner flew proudly in the wind.

Moorgoth moved into a run. He ran through his command group and forward to the infantry line just ahead.

"Come on!" he ordered. "Follow me."

The bodyguards and officers did as they were told.

Moorgoth broke through the ranks to see what was going on. His infantry were beginning to straighten into lines. Several infantrymen were forward of the front line, pulling wounded survivors of the fight toward the rear, into the woods. They took only men in maroon uniforms. The Solamnics were either left to die where they had fallen or helped along the way with a stab through the heart.

Then, in his moment of triumph, the baron saw the danger. Instead of attacking piecemeal, as he had expected, the Solamnic cavalry were forming in the field. They numbered around eight hundred, the baron estimated, confirming his scout's report.

Moorgoth ordered the bugler to call "officers to me."

He was infuriated by the arrogance of the knights. Their commander stood out in front of his cavalry, and instead of ordering a charge, it appeared that he was giving a speech!

The baron's own officers came in at a dead run.

"Gentlemen, I'll make this quick. When you hear the retreat bugle call, have your men run back into the woods. Be ready to come out again fighting. Have your archers prepared to pepper them once we're in the trees. Understand?" He looked around. "Good. Once we've broken the charge, the fight's on. Do your best. Now, hurry!"

The officers sprinted back to their various commands and began shouting orders. On the top of the ridge, the knights' commander had concluded with something inspirational. The knights raised a rousing cheer.

Lances up, they began their advance at a trot.

The cavalry was a sight to see. Eight hundred armored knights and horses, moving forward in brilliant lines, all the heraldry of many families proudly displayed. They broke into a canter.

Quickly, the distance between the two armies was shrinking. As they advanced, the command group could see more and more details of their foe. They kept their lines straight as they moved forward to meet their enemy.

At five hundred yards, bugles called out from several places in the advancing cavalry line. Their lances came down into horizontal positions, couched to kill upon impact.

The knights broke into a full gallop.

Chapter 22

Theros came down from the hill and walked back to his smithy. Nothing had been heard from Moorgoth about the direction of the battle. It was late afternoon. If they were going to set up, they would need word soon. Otherwise, there wouldn't be enough light left to do anything.

He hadn't taken two steps when a rider came galloping into their wagon area. The rider went straight to Belhesser Vankjad, the logistics officer.

Theros hurried to hear the news. When he arrived, the rider saluted Theros and then continued to speak with Belhesser.

". . . and we should, if the fight goes well, be here just after sundown. Baron Moorgoth wants you to set up. He feels confident in the day's decision, and wants a hot meal and a ready camp waiting for him and his troops when he arrives."

Belhesser looked up at the sinking sun. He thought for a moment, then turned to Theros.

"What do you think, Ironfeld? Could you set up before sundown?"

"Yes, sir. I can be ready, sir."

Belhesser turned back to the rider. "There you go, Corporal, you have your answer. We will be ready. You can report to Baron Moorgoth that we wish him the best of luck on the field."

The rider saluted, remounted his horse, and sped away, back to the army in action.

"Any news of the fight?" Theros asked. He was confused, wondering if he wanted the baron to win or be soundly defeated.

Belhesser shook his head. "All he knew was that there had been heavy fighting, and that the Solamnics were fighting near the town. Moorgoth sounds confident, though. We're to set up and all."

Theros agreed. "I have to get back and get to work if I'm to be ready to mend weapons and armor tonight."

He turned and ran back to his wagon. Erela was the first soldier he could find.

"Where is Yuri?" Theros asked, then realized that he already knew the answer.

The soldier blinked. "I thought he was around here somewhere, sir. He was a moment ago. I don't know, sir. I haven't seen him for the last half hour. Shall I go look for him?"

Inwardly, Theros cursed his young apprentice.

"Never mind. I'll find him. Set up the tent over there."

In a foul mood, Theros stomped over to the commissary area. People were beginning to move around the wagons, unpacking, setting up. He could see Quartermaster Sarger shouting orders.

And there was Yuri, rushing out from behind a wagon, heading for the smithy. And there was Telera running back to the rear of the wagons, hoping to arrive before someone noticed them. It could all be perfectly innocent—a stolen kiss behind a wagon.

Theros stopped in his tracks and pointed to Yuri. "You! Get over here!"

The men and women working to put up the commissary tent stopped and looked, wondering if the smithy was yelling at them. Yuri ran over. Defiance on his face, he stood in front of Theros.

Theros raised his hand to teach some discipline to the young man. Yuri tightened his jaw, braced himself for the blow.

Theros, scowling, let his hand fall.

"Get to work!" he ordered. "And stop hanging about that wench. People might get the wrong idea."

Yuri blinked, astonished that he'd not been hit, astonished at the order. "What wrong idea? How—"

"Shut up, you fool. People are listening. Get back to the wagon and see that the smithy is set up correctly. Go!"

Yuri ran over to the smithy area where the soldiers were raising the first tent poles.

Theros stood gazing after his apprentice. Yuri did not want to be a soldier. He had never wanted to be a soldier. He wanted to be a blacksmith. He had come to Theros, offering to work for food and board if only Theros would teach him the trade. Yuri had a talent for detail work, but he didn't have the strength or girth to pound out huge axes or swords. It wasn't his fault. He was born thin and wiry and he'd be that way until the day he died. Still, he had the brains to know that he could do good work within his limits.

But Yuri needed discipline. He couldn't discipline himself, apparently, so Theros would have to do it for him. And the first thing Theros had to do was see that this romance came to a halt. For Yuri's own good.

Theros found Cheldon giving his final commands to his section leaders.

". . . and I want the cooking fires lit before it gets dark. I'll want a hot meal for every soldier. Oh, and keep two extra cooking cauldrons on with water boiling. The wounded are going to need attention when they come in, too, and boiling water will be essential. Right, get to it."

The two section leaders saluted and went about their duties. The quartermaster's workers parked their wagons behind their tent lines, setting up long wooden tables to dispense food and supplies.

"Cheldon, I need to talk to you," Theros said.

"What is it, Ironfeld?"

"I've got a problem with my apprentice, Yuri. I keep catching him over here with one of your women workers."

Cheldon laughed. "Oh, is that all? You had me worried there." He winked. "Boys will be boys, eh, Theros? And girls will be girls, praise the Seeker gods. Let them have some fun."

Theros scowled. "Look, I've heard rumors that the spy may be one of your women. She may be getting more out of Yuri than a few giggles in the night. If he gets into trouble, I'll be blamed. All I'm asking is that you keep my man away from here."

"One of my women, a spy?" Cheldon was angry. "Listen, Ironfeld. It's your man who keeps coming over here, not the other way around. If you've got a problem with him, then you take care of it. As for my people, I brought most of them with me from Sanction. I know them a lot better than you do. Now leave me alone. I've got a lot to do!"

Cheldon Sarger stormed away.

Fuming, Theros turned and walked back to his own section.

* * * * *

The bugler stood beside Moorgoth, waiting for orders.

"Not yet . . . not yet . . . not yet—*now!*"

The charging Solamnic cavalry were a hundred and fifty yards to their front. The bugle again rang clear and true, sounding the retreat.

The baron watched the bugler. "I'm going to have to reward this young lad," he thought. "He's never faltered once under such extreme pressure."

As the boy finished the notes, the entire command group

turned and began to run at a dead sprint toward the tree line. The thunder of the knights' horses behind them grew louder and louder.

Many of the soldiers were running so fast that by the time they reached the tree line, they tripped and dashed headlong into tree trunks. Most made it safely. Some were not so fortunate.

The left end of the line was extended out past the trees, stuck out in the open. The knights hit these men hard, catching them from behind, running them down. Nearly half were overrun before the rest made it to the trees.

At the forest's edge, the knights faltered. Their horses balked at entering the tree line at full speed. Several riders were thrown from their saddles. Those who were able to stay seated urged their steeds forward.

Moorgoth gave another command.

Archers sprang up and loosed arrows at the knights.

The baron and the bugler both dodged a sword swung by a knight who had managed to urge his horse in among the trees. One of Moorgoth's bodyguards struck the knight down. The bugler remained standing beside the baron.

"Sound the attack!" Moorgoth yelled.

The boy once again blasted out the call. The Solamnics had just realized that they'd been caught in an ambush. They were trying to organize themselves. Their own buglers were sounding the retreat, the calls sounding raucously together. The buglers were waging their own battle, it seemed.

Moorgoth's soldiers rushed forward. They struck at the knights when they could, struck the horses when they couldn't reach the riders. They outnumbered their mounted foes by over two to one.

The knights were attempting to fall back, but they were surrounded and had to fight on. In front of the baron, five knights stood back to back in a circle. Twenty soldiers surrounded them, yet no one had struck a blow. Moorgoth's men appeared daunted by the knights' proud demeanor, their bright armor and flashing blades.

Seeing the standoff, the baron ran over, shoved his men aside, made his way to the front.

"Surrender or die here on this field. The choice is yours," Moorgoth shouted to the knights.

The knights glanced at each other. It was a hard decision, but finally one slowly nodded his head. Walking stiffly forward, he raised the visor of his helm and held out his sword—hilt first—to Moorgoth.

The baron politely accepted the sword.

"You will be well and honorably treated. Put your weapons down," he ordered the other knights.

They did as commanded, placing their swords on the ground.

Once the knights were unarmed, Moorgoth waved his hand. His soldiers leapt on them, slashing and stabbing.

"Damn you!" cried the knight who had given Moorgoth his sword. "Damn you back to the Abyss where you were spawn—"

Those were the knight's last words.

Chuckling at the look of surprise on the knights' faces, the baron extracted himself from the fight. What fools these knights were! So damned trusting. Glancing back, he saw all five of the knights dead on the field, brutally hacked apart.

The remainder of the knights drew back several hundred yards from the tree line. Their general tried desperately to rally his troops into a charge line. The fight was still on among the trees. The archers could have no effect there, fearful of hitting their own comrades.

The baron went to look to the army's left flank. The battle was not going as well there. The knights had caught many of his men out in the open. It looked as if the left flank would cave in, giving the knights a chance to sweep at him from that direction.

Then he heard the sound of shouting.

Moorgoth looked up the hill to see his own cavalry cresting the top. The Solamnic Knights were already engaged in battle. They could not turn and face this new threat. Moorgoth's cavalry struck the knights from behind.

The reaction was immediate. The Solamnics on the left crumbled. The baron's own infantry took advantage of the disorganization of the Solamnic Knights and fought with renewed vigor.

The Solamnic commander had rallied two hundred of his knights back from the fighting. He had originally hoped to charge back into the line. He now could see that he was outnumbered. To ride in again would be suicide.

He ordered a retreat. Even at that, many of the knights refused to obey. They would rather die than leave the battle to these butchers.

The commander shouted something, ending in the words, ". . . by the Oath and Measure!" He wheeled his charger and galloped back across the field, heading into the town.

The majority of the knights followed. A small number, twenty or so, had apparently decided to die fighting. They headed back into the melee and crashed into the infantry right in front of the baron, killing as they went.

"They're going for the standard!" he yelled to Berenek Ibind, the army's bearer. The large man stood his ground.

"Protect the standard!" Moorgoth yelled, and repeated it several times. He drew his sword and charged into the fight.

His bodyguards gathered around the standard. The knights were crazed, trying to get close enough to take the standard and smash it, thereby winning a moral victory, if not a real one. Infantryman after infantryman fell to the Solamnics. But the baron's men were getting in their own cuts, dragging the knights from their horses, stabbing them when they were on the ground.

Only eight knights were left when Moorgoth reached the fight. A huge man on a white charger turned to meet him. Moorgoth ducked in time to miss the knight's swinging sword. As he came up, he brought his own sword up across the belly of the knight's horse. The horse reared backward, blood spurting everywhere. The knight was thrown to the ground. Immediately, he regained his feet. He faced Moorgoth.

An infantryman rushed the knight from the right, trying to take him from a blind side. The knight saw him coming and sidestepped the assault, slicing the man nearly in two as he hurtled past, killing him instantly. The baron swung while the knight was recovering from the attack, but his opponent narrowly avoided the blow.

The two circled around, the dead horse forming one edge of a small arena for the fight. The rest of the knights were now either dead or dismounted.

Moorgoth did not have the luxury to look around. The knight in front of him was prepared to die, and he wanted to take the baron with him.

Moorgoth parried blow after blow, not able to get into a position to attack. Suddenly, the knight stiffened. To his rear, a soldier had run him through with a spear, jamming it into the man's back, through his armor.

He did not fall. Raising his sword, he brought it crashing down upon Moorgoth in a blow designed to split the baron in two.

The baron's sword came up to parry the attack. The knight's blade hit Moorgoth's sword, breaking it cleanly from the hilt. The knight's blade snapped at the point of impact, its end spinning away and sticking in the ground.

The knight fell face first into the dirt. The baron's arm burned with pain from the shock of the blow. He was thrown backward and landed on the ground. He lay still for a moment, the ringing in his ears drowning out all other sounds.

He sat up a moment later, still hearing nothing but the ringing of steel on steel. He looked around. No knight was left standing. The fight was over. The standard was still flying.

Berenek Ibind stood with his sword drawn, blood dripping from its tip. His left hand grasped the standard and held it aloft.

Victory was Baron Dargon Moorgoth's.

Chapter 23

Baron Moorgoth was elated with the turn of events. The town was his for the plundering. He would see to it that the towns-people rued the day they had dared to cross him. He would avenge his lost men.

The sun was setting slowly in the western sky. There were still wounded on the field, but none were from Moor-goth's army. They had been located and carried into the woods, to be later transported back to the encampment.

The Solamnic wounded were damned to the Abyss, as far as Dargon Moorgoth was concerned. Those who escaped the wrath of his men could suffer all through the night and the following day. Let them fend for themselves. He called his officers to meet with him on the edge of the forest.

"All right, gentlemen, very good work. I congratulate you. Well done! I want the first brigade to set up a picket line around the town tonight. Nobody in, nobody out, under pain of death. If there are any men in this army who want to get a head start on pillaging, they hang in the morning.

"I can't afford any more casualties. I need this army ready to fight. This is just the first town, the first battle. We've got a whole season of campaigning to do, and only six or seven weeks before winter sets in. Tell the men to be patient. We'll get our loot, all right, but we'll do it on my orders. Now, how many prisoners do we have?"

Berenek Ibind was in charge of the army standard and the command group. The baron's bodyguards were holding the prisoners.

"Sir, we hold only twenty knights. The rest were wounded and were dispatched."

The baron rubbed his hands together. "Good. At least we shall have some sport tonight. Move the second and third brigades back to the camp set up beyond that second hill. Make sure that the commissary crew takes hot food out to the first brigade tonight. They'll have a long night of it."

The officers saluted and went back to their commands. Soon, orders were being shouted all over the field. The first brigade began to deploy around the town, keeping a distance of at least two hundred yards between the nearest building and their picket line. The plan was to set up roadblocks at either end of the town, on the roads leading in and out. No one was to leave that night. Any citizen foolish enough to try to do so would be searched for weapons, roughed up a bit, then sent back home.

The second and third brigades headed for the site of the camp. Among these were the command group, bringing with them the twenty prisoners. The knights were tied by the wrists and ankles and had been disarmed.

Moorgoth let them keep their armor. It was heavy and would increase the difficulty of their march.

* * * * *

Theros looked up to see a column appear over the hill. The army was back! His smithy was set up, but the fire was not yet started in the forge.

"Yuri, hurry up with the wood!" he yelled at his assistant, who was struggling with a load of slumak bark and wood.

Theros had set up the grates above the fireplace to heat the metal. Two large barrels of water stood to one side to temper the metal.

Yuri stumbled into the tent and threw the wood down. He began to stack the wood up near the edge of the tent, away from the fire. The last thing they needed was the cordwood catching fire and taking the whole smithy with it.

"We'll be mending weapons all night, it seems," Theros commented, hoping to draw Yuri into conversation.

Yuri didn't even look at Theros. He just turned and went back out into the twilight to collect more wood. The other soldiers came in and stacked their bark and wood, too. Erela—the soldier that Theros had come to know best— entered last.

Theros had already laid a bed of coal rocks. Over them, he had placed twigs and leaves. Now came the slumak—a very hard wood. It took a long time to catch fire, but once caught, it burned long and hot.

Theros and Erela were still building the fire when the second brigade marched past the tent, on their way through to the opposite side of camp, where they would set up their tents. The soldiers looked worn, but pleased with themselves. They had won, and nothing cured minor wounds like winning. They would be well paid. They would start celebrating as soon as their tents were pitched.

The unloaded commissary wagons, pulled by draft horses, headed to the battlefield to carry the wounded back to the camp.

Under Theros's care, the fire started. The flaps of the tent's chimney were tied back to allow the smoke and heat to escape. Yuri had attached a metal skirt around the hole to protect the canvas from getting too hot and bursting into flame. Theros stoked the fire, and for a time, forgot his troubles.

The flames danced, weaving in and out, merging, parting, them coming together again, reminding him of two lovers. He thought of Yuri and Telera. Theros thought back to Marissa.

His heart soared as he remembered his night with her. She was almost a dream to him, a shining moment in a bleak existence. He remembered her kiss at parting. She had made it clear to everyone that she liked him. Maybe she even loved him.

"So what makes me any different from anyone else?" he asked himself. "Why should she choose me? Certainly not for my looks!" He chuckled some at this.

He'd never thought much about his appearance, until he started living among humans. Among minotaurs, ugliness was equated with prowess in battle. Scars and lumps were badges of honor. A slit nostril, a torn and tattered ear, missing teeth—these were outward signs of a proud warrior and were much admired by minotaur females.

Among humans, Theros had been astonished to learn that women liked men with smooth skin, unbroken noses and hands that weren't rough and calloused. He had led a hard life, one that had left its marks on his body. He carried scars from battle—not only battles with men, but also those with his work. When he looked at his dusky face in the shaving mirror, he was always displeased with himself.

His nose had been broken more than once. He'd lost a front tooth during a "discipline" session on board the minotaur ship. Part of his hair had been singed off during a fire and would never grow back. Thinking himself ugly, Theros had managed to convince people he *was* ugly.

But he'd seen a new side of himself reflected in Marissa's eyes. It had never occurred to him that women might be able to see beneath the scars and the roughness, to see the dreams and longings of his soul. He had found himself sharing such things with Marissa during that night. She had listened, been interested in him. He had even told her his dream of seeing the god Sargas. She had not laughed, as he had expected.

Yuri's voice, talking to someone outside the tent, disturbed Theros's reverie, then became a part of it.

Yuri was nearly the same age as Theros had been when he had won his freedom from the minotaurs and had been granted the capability to forge his own life. Yuri didn't have that choice. He was not a slave, yet he didn't seem much better off than Theros had been. Theros realized suddenly, ruefully, that it was easier to yell at Yuri, to hit Yuri, to force Yuri into obedience, than it was to talk to Yuri, reason with him, discuss things.

Theros thought of the girl, Telera, the girl Yuri loved.

Yuri had the right to feel the same way about a woman that Theros felt, but the young man had to learn that there was a time and place for everything—even romance. What if this girl were a spy? The inexperienced and naive Yuri would be an easy target for seduction. And even if this relationship were all perfectly innocent, it looked very bad.

"It cannot continue," Theros told himself. "It's a matter of discipline." But perhaps he should try to talk again to Yuri, explain why it was bad, rather than just order him to quit seeing the girl.

And that brought Theros in a circle back to Marissa. He smiled. When he had served his time in this army, when he felt he had repaid Moorgoth's investment in him, Theros would go straight back to Sanction, straight back to Marissa.

The sound of shouts and jeers woke Theros from his musings. He looked out of the tent to see the bodyguards from the command group marching into the center of the camp. They brought with them the twenty prisoner knights, tied together to form a human chain. Weary, the men stumbled over the rough terrain.

So this is our enemy, Theros thought.

He had heard nothing good about the Knights of Solamnia. The minotaurs had no use for them, claiming that the knights had lost all honor because they'd been given the chance to stop the Cataclysm and had failed, or some such tale. But these knights had, from what Theros had heard, acquitted themselves well.

He came out of his tent to get a better look at them. The bodyguards dragged the prisoners to the center of the enclosure made by the wagons and tents. There, they hammered a large stake and tied the chained knights to it.

"Stand at attention, you dogs," one of the sergeants yelled.

Most of the knights remained standing proudly, but one—wounded, perhaps—slumped to his knees. The sergeant walked over, kicked the man in the face.

The soldiers laughed, jeering and throwing food scraps at the prisoners. Theros was appalled. By all accounts, the knights had fought valiantly. Among the minotaurs, if a foe has fought well in combat, that foe is honored, not tormented and abused.

The knights were trying to assist their fallen comrade. The sergeant started to kick the man again. He found Theros's huge hand engulfing his arm.

Theros glared at the sergeant. "These men are thirsty. Bring them water."

The sergeant glowered back. "Those weren't Moorgoth's orders, sir."

"Those are *my* orders," Theros returned.

The sergeant didn't like it, but Theros was a senior officer. Saluting, the sergeant stalked off.

Theros helped the wounded knight to a seated position, assisting him to rest comfortably against the stake. By taking note of which knight the others looked to, Theros determined which one was the senior officer.

Curious to talk with these knights, Theros questioned the man.

"Who are you? What's your name?"

The knight cast Theros a bitter, hate-filled glance. At first, it seemed the man would not answer, but then—perhaps reflecting that Theros deserved something for having halted the torment of the wounded man—the knight replied.

"Richard Strongmail, Knight of the Order of the Kingfisher of the Knights of Solamnia." The knight spoke his name and rank proudly, despite the fact that he was a prisoner, in chains.

Memories of another battle, another defeat, were strong in Theros's mind.

"I am Captain Theros Ironfeld. I am the master smith of

this army. Tell me, Knight of Solamnia, why are you here?"

The knight was scornful. "If you are referring to why we fought today, it was because the Solamnic Order had pledged its own in the defense of the town of Neugardj from the attack of Moorgoth and you thieves."

Theros didn't relish being called a thief, but he let it pass. He didn't feel he had much to say in his own defense.

"That wasn't what I meant," Theros said. "I mean why did you allow yourselves to be made prisoners?" Minotaurs would have died fighting, if they'd had the chance.

"I was bested on the battlefield," the knight replied, "and I surrendered when it became clear that I would fight only to my death. There is no honor in fighting a lost battle. Vengeance is not a trait of my order."

Theros rubbed his chin. "So you surrendered yourself. You didn't get knocked out and wake up a prisoner?"

"On my oath, no! I surrendered, and surrendered what was left of my command." Sir Richard's eyes flashed. "I was assured that we would be treated honorably. My men have not eaten nor drunk water since the battle. Are we to be starved to death or made to die of thirst? Is that the way you treat your captives?"

Theros was displeased. Prisoners they were, but they were not animals. Even animals should be given water.

"It is not right," Theros said. "I will see what I can do."

Sir Richard eyed Theros with more respect than he'd done at first. "Thank you," he muttered, and turned back to his men.

Theros left, walked across the field to the commissary tent.

Most of the men and women of the second brigade were through the food line, and the third brigade and the cavalry were beginning to line up.

Theros entered the tent where the food was being served. The smell was wonderful. They had cooked up a hearty stew with lots of meat and vegetables. Loaves of fresh bread were stacked on a table. The soldiers came through, had their bowls filled, then grabbed hunks of bread. They headed out the far side of the tent to eat and drink. The wine had already been distributed. It was a night of celebration.

Theros found Cheldon Sarger standing just outside the tent, keeping an eye on his command.

"Ah, Theros. Good to see you. I've set aside a pot of stew and some loaves for the logistics company. We'll eat in here, away from the flies and bugs. Bring your men over when you're ready. Oh, I've been saving a few bottles of good wine from the barracks in Gargath." Cheldon winked. "I think we deserve a few to celebrate!"

"Sure, thanks, Cheldon. Say, I'm sorry about losing my temper over that affair with my assistant. I was worried about the boy, that's all. I'll bring my men back, but first I was wondering if I could get some food, at least some bread, for the prisoners?"

Cheldon Sarger looked at Theros as if he had suddenly grown three heads. "Food! Prisoners! What for? They sure aren't going to need food where they're going!"

Theros didn't understand. "What do you mean? Aren't we going to ransom them back to their kin?"

Cheldon laughed. "And get what for them? Those knights are poor as rats, most of them. No, we'll have some fun tonight. I heard from Captain Ibind that these knights aren't going to last the night. They're to be this evening's after-dinner entertainment! Great fun, eh?"

Theros couldn't believe he'd heard correctly. Moorgoth was going to torture these prisoners!

"They need water, at least," Theros growled. "I can't believe that Baron Moorgoth would allow such a thing. I just can't."

But Theros could believe it. That was the problem. Unfortunately, this news about Baron Moorgoth didn't surprise him all that much.

"Just remember that to the victor go the spoils, and tonight, we're victorious!" Cheldon spoke loudly. "Bring your lads around in about an hour." This said, he drew Theros off to one side, continued in a low voice, "Look, I don't like this 'entertainment' business any more than you do. But what can we do to stop it? I say we stay in here and eat and drink ourselves into a pleasant stupor."

Theros mumbled an agreement, turned and left. Cheldon was right. If Theros protested or tried to protect the prisoners, Moorgoth would suspect the smith of being a traitor. He might even figure that Theros was the spy.

Head bowed, lost in thought, Theros wasn't watching where he was going. When he fell over a tent peg, he looked around, found himself among the tents of the women. He turned on his heel to make a quick departure, when he heard voices coming from one of the tents.

Theros recognized one of the voices.

"We'll escape tonight," a voice said, "when everyone's drunk . . ."

Theros walked up to the tent, ripped open the flap.

Frightened eyes stared back at him. Yuri and Telera, seated together inside the tent, shrank back at the sight of Theros's anger.

"What is the meaning of this?" Theros demanded.

Yuri jumped to his feet, came surging forward, put himself between Theros and Telera.

"I'm the spy, sir. I confess it. Take me away. I'll—"

"No, don't, Yuri!" Telera was on her feet, too, clinging to Yuri.

He attempted to say something, to argue. She shook her head, stepped in front of him and faced Theros.

"I am the spy, sir. I'm the one you want. Let Yuri go. He didn't know anything about it. I'll swear to that—"

Yuri started protesting. Telera was shaking her head.

"Shut up!" Theros said in a low, impassioned voice.

Both of them, startled, fell silent.

Theros raised the tent flap, peered cautiously back outside. No one was around. He lowered it again, turned—seething—to the two in front of him.

"Tell me the truth, damn you," he said.

Telera licked her lips, swallowed. But her voice was strong and steady. "I am the daughter of a knight. My father was murdered by Baron Moorgoth and his men when they raided our castle. I escaped by hiding in the woods. When I came back home, I found the bodies . . ."

She blinked her eyes. Yuri took hold of her hand.

After a moment, Telera continued. "I swore revenge on Moorgoth. But I'm a female and am not trained as a warrior. What could I do? I decided I would join his band, and whenever I could, get word to my father's friends about what the army was doing, how many men it numbered. I used Yuri to get information. He didn't know—"

"I found out, sir," Yuri added. "I was glad to be able to help, even though Telera didn't want to put me in danger. And I'll keep on being glad, no matter what they do to me. Only please, sir, see to it that no harm comes to Telera."

"I'll die at their hands before I'd leave without Yuri!" Telera said firmly. "I could not die in better company than with Yuri and the gallant knights. My only regret," she added bitterly, "is that I failed. Moorgoth and his army live still."

"Not all of them. Not by a long shot. At least you've accomplished that much," Theros muttered the words and he hadn't realized he'd spoken them aloud until he saw the two looking at him with dawning hope.

"Do you mean that, sir?" Yuri could scarcely talk.

Theros didn't answer. He was thinking. "Listen, Telera, do you know your way around this countryside?"

"Yes, sir. I was born and raised not far from here."

"You could find your way, even in the darkness?"

"Yes, sir. And it won't be that dark tonight. The moonlight will be bright enough to walk by."

"Good. On the other side of the hill is a line of trees. No one's around. You won't have a better chance. Head for those trees. Wait there. You'll be joined by others."

"By you, sir?" Yuri was gazing at Theros with the respect and admiration Theros had long sought from his apprentice. "Will you meet us, sir? You'll be in danger yourself if they discover that I've gone."

"Never mind me. Do what you're told for once in your life." Theros growled, but he smiled at the same time.

"Yes, sir," Yuri said softly. "Sir, I want to thank—"

"No time." Theros cut him off. "Belhesser will be looking for us. I'll cover for you. Don't worry about me. I can take care of myself."

Telera rested her hand briefly, hesitantly, on Theros's big arm.

"Thank you, sir," she said, simply.

Theros grunted and nodded. Then, lifting the flap, he went back outside, looked around. No one was nearby. He motioned for the two to come.

Yuri took Telera's hand, and together they slipped out of the tent and dashed into the forest. Theros waited for a moment to be sure that they had made good their escape, then he turned back to his smithy. He had the feeling that, no matter what happened, he would never see Yuri again. Theros wished him and Telera well.

At the smithy, the soldiers were sitting around, waiting for the chance to eat. Theros waved his hand.

"Go on, men. Get in line. We're to eat inside the commissary tent tonight with the quartermaster's staff. He's saved some wine for us, too."

The soldiers jumped up, grabbed their bowls, and rushed off to get in the food line.

Theros took his own cup and dropped it into one of the buckets sitting beside the water barrels. He filled the bucket and walked out of the tent. He looked around to see if anyone was watching. On the far side, he could see campfires, with men sitting around them, eating and drinking and celebrating.

No one was paying attention to the prisoners in the center. There was no need. The knights had given their word of honor that they would not try to escape. Moorgoth respected the knights' word, even though he obviously thought them fools for making such an absurd promise. The baron would teach them their folly tonight.

Perhaps the knights are fools, Theros thought, but only because they believe that other men are as honorable as themselves.

Carrying the bucket of water, Theros walked up to the knights. Most had cast off their metal breastplates and other armor. Theros went to Sir Richard, who looked up warily.

"Here, take a drink," Theros said.

The knight grabbed the cup from Theros's hand and drank it dry. He passed the cup to the next knight, who refilled it from the bucket. One of the knights held the cup to the lips of the injured man.

Sir Richard was on his feet. "Thank you," he said grudgingly. "Perhaps you can tell us what's going on. No one has spoken to us about ransom or prisoner exchange—"

Theros interrupted. "That's why I am here. There will be no ransom. No exchange. Tonight, you and your men are to be made a form of 'entertainment' for the troops. I think you can guess what that means."

By the grim look on his face, it was clear Sir Richard knew what was in store for him and his men. "Baron Moorgoth promised—"

"He is a man without honor," Theros said, ashamed. "As an officer in this army, I cannot stop what he means to do to you, but as a man of honor, I cannot condone it. I advise you to do whatever is in your power to preserve your command. I know you've given your word to an officer that you will not escape. Well, *I'm* an officer, and I release you from your word."

"Are you suggesting that we—" Sir Richard began.

Theros halted him. "I wish you well and hope that Sargas sees you through the night. If you happen to be walking around over by that line of trees, you'll find people there who can aid you. You can trust them."

Theros turned and walked away quickly.

He entered his tent. He'd done what he could for the knights. They were on their own now. All Theros had to do was make certain that no one noticed Yuri was missing for at least a day or so. As Belhesser had said, Moorgoth would be in a good mood following his victory. He wouldn't be worrying about spies now.

Picking up his bowl, Theros left for the commissary tent.

Chapter 24

Theros entered the food tent with his bowl in hand. Cheldon Sarger and Belhesser Vankjad sat at a table to one side. The rest of the tent was filled with workers and soldiers employed by the commissary, quartermaster and smithy. His four assistants were sitting with women from the commissary, laughing and drinking, happy to be away from their duties for a while.

Theros went to join them. The soldiers, seeing him approach, jumped to their feet.

Theros waved them down. "No, that's all right. Stay seated. Have a good time tonight. Don't worry about the forge. I've posted Yuri on sentry duty at the forge tonight. He'll wake one of you at sunrise to take over."

Erela answered for the group. "Yes sir. Thank you, sir."

Theros turned back to the officers' table.

Belhesser looked up. "Ah, Theros, I was wondering where you had gotten to. We saved you some food and wine."

The officer handed Theros a goblet full of rich red wine. Theros accepted it and sat down with the others.

Cheldon leaned back in his chair. He looked up at Theros. "I saw you over with the prisoners. I trust you were just there to make certain that their chains were still good and tight."

"I took them some water," Theros answered, refusing to lie. "They fought well, from what I've heard. They were suffering from thirst."

Belhesser frowned, displeased. He stared hard at Theros. "It'll all be the same when Baron Moorgoth puts them through their paces. They'll wish they were never born on the face of Ansalon after tonight!" He laughed.

Theros nodded. "I suspect you're right."

Hoping this would end the conversation, he dug into his food. Two helpings later, he felt better. The wine was starting to take the edge off the day. He pushed the whole issue of the knights out of his mind, while he tried to work out a way to deal with Yuri's disappearance.

It was getting late. Outside, he could hear the sounds of drunken revelry. Inside, the men were just as loud.

Cheldon nudged Theros. "Cheer up, man! Have s'more wine." He was working hard at getting drunk. "Don't sit there and sulk. What's the matter with you?"

Theros realized he'd been sitting, brooding in silence for an hour, on a night when he should be celebrating. He attempted to make conversation. "I heard that today was a stunning victory for the baron!"

Belhesser nodded, waved his wineglass in the air, sloshing the liquid all over himself. "Damned right. I heard that we inflicted over fifteen hundred casualties today. We had only one hundred dead and another hundred wounded. That's incredible, considering that most of the Solamnic force was mounted knights!"

Cheldon agreed. "They must have really been surprised

when ol' Dargon showed up with an army nearly three times the size of their army!"

They all laughed, Theros included.

"Yes, it must have really been a fine sight to see. Captain Ibind told me that they used the forest to break the cavalry charge. Moorgoth feinted with a battle line in front of the woods, but then had them dive into the cover of the brush when the cavalry came too close. The knights stopped cold, their horses refused to budge. Our boys ran right back out of the woods, and the fight was on! I even heard—"

The sound of a man screaming in agony shattered the night and the merriment. Inside the tent, everyone stopped talking. The scream came again. They all stared at one another. Theros tried to look as if he were as baffled as the rest.

"Maybe the fun started early," Belhesser suggested.

At that moment, Uwel Lors came bursting through the far tent flap.

He strode up to the officers' table and saluted. "Sirs, I have to report that several of the prisoners have escaped."

"Then what the devil was that yell?" Belhesser demanded.

"Ah, sir. Some of the prisoners didn't quite make it. They had a wounded man with them, you see, and—instead of abandoning him—a few of the fools stayed with him. Now, sir, I have received information that one of you was seen speaking with the prisoners earlier this evening. Is that true?"

Belhesser and Cheldon both looked over at Theros.

Theros stood up. He cleared his throat. "Yes, it is true. I took them water earlier this evening."

"And did you notice any of them missing then?" Uwel asked, flicking the handle of his whip casually against his leg.

"No, all twenty were there." Theros shrugged. "They must have escaped after that. How many got away?"

Uwel eyed Theros in suspicion. "I'm going to have to report this to Baron Moorgoth. Fifteen of the knights have escaped. Five were recaptured. We will make an example out of them."

As if to emphasize his point, another scream echoed across the camp.

Uwel saluted again, then left the tent.

Belhesser turned to Theros. "Thanks a lot!" He was bitter. "You're under my command. What were you thinking?"

"Look, I'm sorry if I've caused you any trouble. I'll take full responsibility. I'll tell Moorgoth it was my fault and I'll resign," Theros offered.

Belhesser continued to look grim. "If you had anything to do with those knights escaping, you won't be given a chance to resign. It'll be the Abyss for you. Those knights will get off lucky, compared to what Moorgoth will do to you and probably to me, too. Maybe I can go head off Lors, come up with some sort of excuse."

The shocking sound of the scream and the knowledge of his own danger had sobered up Belhesser. Glaring at Theros, the officer rose from the table and dashed out of the tent.

Theros rose. He didn't want to go out there, but he was afraid that it would look suspicious if he didn't. He glanced over at Cheldon.

"You coming?"

The scream had badly unnerved the officer. He was gulping down more wine. Shivering, looking sick, he shook his head. He managed a strained smile.

"N-no. I wasn't cut out for this sort of thing. Baking bread. That's what I do." He gazed up at Theros. "Don't tell anyone though. Will you?" He gulped more wine.

Theros walked out of the tent and into a scene straight from a nightmare.

The five knights were strapped to large wooden tripods. Each man's wrists had been tied together, then hung over the center joint of the tripod. Their legs had been spread apart and tied to two of the tripod's legs. Their armor and outer clothing had been removed. They were clad in just breechcloths and undershirts.

One of the knights had already been tortured. He sagged limp on his tripod. His face was battered almost to a pulp. His shirt was soaked with blood.

Baron Dargon Moorgoth was addressing the troops. "We've won a great victory today, but at a high cost. Many of our comrades suffer from wounds inflicted by these knights. Many of our good friends are dead. It's too bad that their comrades were so unknightly as to play the coward and run away. But these will be made to pay the price."

A soldier took a burning brand from a nearby fire and brought it forward. Uwel Lors took the brand.

"Time for a little fun!" Uwel announced.

He walked to the unconscious knight and held the flame under the man's left foot. Suddenly, the knight's head jerked back. He screamed and tried to move his foot out of the flame. The ropes held fast.

Even though he was some distance away, Theros could smell the stench of burning flesh. It sickened him, but it pleased the drunken crowd. They yelled for more.

Uwel took the brand and turned to the next knight. By the light of the flame, Theros could recognize Sir Richard. Of course, he had stayed with his command, remained behind with the wounded knight, though he knew full well what his fate would be.

"Sargas honor him," Theros said quietly. "And grant him a swift death."

Uwel lit the knight's loincloth on fire. Sir Richard tried to twist right and left to get away from the searing flame, but to no avail. The skin was bubbling and melting, finally turning black all around his midriff. He tried bravely to stifle his agony, but the pain was more than he could bear. His screams caused the drunken men to laugh more loudly. Mercifully, as far as Theros was concerned, the knight soon lost consciousness.

The crowd loved the show. Uwel moved from knight to knight, burning their feet, hands and undergarments. The first knight didn't move. Theros guessed he was dead. Uwel took his fighting knife and slit the man's stomach. The body lurched and strained, but the knight never regained awareness. Within moments, the body stopped twitching. The knight's soul had moved on to whatever god awaited him.

The torture lasted for another hour. Three knights were

still alive, all of them writhing and twisting in their bonds. The sight was ghastly.

Theros could take no more of it. His stomach clenched. He'd seen man and minotaur die in battle and never felt as sick as this. His only solace was that he had warned Sir Richard in time, and the knight commander had taken his warning and acted upon it. Fifteen knights had escaped and had, hopefully, found their way into the forest, where Yuri and Telera could guide them.

Theros pushed his way through the crowd of soldiers. He needed water, needed to wash out the taste and smell of blood. He stumbled over to a water barrel, took a drink and was immediately sorry. He bent over double, vomiting, every heave accentuated by a scream from one of the knights who still hung on their tripods.

At length, when he had nothing more in his stomach, Theros straightened, drew in a deep breath. He washed his mouth out with water, splashed water on his burning face. He took one last look back in time to see Uwel swing a long sword, chopping deep into Sir Richard's neck. Blood sprayed out over Uwel. Covered in gore, he laughed. Sir Richard hung limp. The knight was dead. All the knights were now dead.

Theros knew his soul would never forgive him for the sights he had witnessed, that they would torment him in dreams for the rest of his life.

He went back to the commissary tent, stumbling like a man in need of more wine.

Chapter 25

Theros strode through the commissary tent, then made his way back to the tents where he had encountered Yuri and Telera and out into the forest beyond. He did not look back. He shook all over with anger and horror.

"I cannot stay here," he said to himself. "Moorgoth is not a general. He is a coward and a butcher. These men are not soldiers; they are animals. These humans talk of minotaurs being beasts, but minotaurs would never treat an honorable enemy like this. They certainly would never do this to their own kind."

Theros unbuckled his field harness, then took off the surcoat with the army's colors. He threw it to the ground, placed his heel on it and twisted his boot into it, ripping and tearing the cloth. He put the harness back on over his white shirt, and walked off into the woods.

He had just resigned.

Theros wasn't certain where he was. Clouds partially obscured the moon and stars. He had no way of telling direction. But he had the vague idea he was heading south, away from the battle, away from the direction of the town. He walked through the trees without really seeing them. He could still see the dying men in his mind, still hear their screams in his head.

How could I have been so blind? he thought. The only thing keeping this so-called army together is the whip and the lash. And I am as bad as the rest. The only way I could keep Yuri was by making him afraid of me. Hran never treated me that badly, and I was his slave.

He continued walking through the forest. The going was slow. It was difficult to see his way in the darkness. He tripped over tree roots. Branches slapped him in the face. He was not overly concerned about pursuit. Moorgoth hadn't tried very hard to recapture the missing knights, and as drunk as everyone was, no one would miss Theros until morning. At the same time, they'd find Yuri and Telera missing, too. Theros smiled for the first time in a week.

"I bet Moorgoth never had so many desertions after a victory and promise of pay before!"

At length, Theros reached a clearing in the forest. He looked up into the sky, hoping that the clouds had broken for good. He was rewarded by the sight of two moons and the stars. Solinari and Lunitari cast enough light to see. He was out of the tree line. Before him were plowed fields, their crops harvested, ready for winter.

Ready for Moorgoth to steal.

Theros walked on, seeing no one. At least he was part of that no longer.

* * * * *

Two hours later, he was climbing over a low stone wall that separated two fields, when the faint thud of hooves caught his attention. He dropped down beside the wall, flat on his stomach, and drew his axe.

Looking at himself, he realized his white shirt showed up brightly in the night. He quickly threw off his leather harness and ripped off the shirt. Pulling the harness back on over his bare torso, he dug a hole and buried the shirt. Then he lay flat on his face in the muck.

Theros kept perfectly still, not daring to take a look. The rider galloped by on the other side of the fence without seeing him.

Theros waited. The sound of the hooves grew fainter and fainter. When they were almost out of earshot, he sat up, looking down the fence line to see if he could see the rider. In the distance, he could make out a shape.

It was a cavalry scout from Moorgoth's army. Either he was a long-range patrol or part of the picket line.

"Or maybe I was wrong," Theros said to himself. "Maybe they're not all drunk. Maybe they're looking for me!"

Instead of continuing on down the fence line, he decided to cut across the field. He reached another fence line and walked down it, until it ended. He started up a hill, realizing that he must have come quite a long way. The sun was beginning to lighten the sky to a deep gray in the east.

The hill was the first in a long series of connected hills, probably the foothills of the Busuk Range. He could wander for days in the mountains, never finding his way back to civilization. Ogres, hobgoblins and others with no love for man were reputed to live in those mountains. Not even Moorgoth would challenge them. Theros was heading in the wrong direction. He began to search for a path, hoping it would lead him farther south.

The sun broke over the horizon and flooded the land with warmth and light. Theros crested the top of a hill, paused to look around. He could see no riders, no sign of any living being. There were no fields, no fences. No villages or farmhouses. He could not see any roads, either.

And if he did find a road, where would it take him?

It occurred to Theros that he had nowhere to go. His smithy was gone. That was how Moorgoth kept his people loyal. He made them dependent on him. Theros wondered how he could have been sucked in by Moorgoth. It was easy, he realized.

I had no self-respect, he thought. I was lured by the prospect of glory and riches. Moorgoth took me for an idiot or for the same type of cowardly cur that he is himself. And he was almost right. He was almost right.

Theros decided to change direction and reckoning by the sun, head west. The army had been east of the main road, and if he moved west, he would eventually cross it.

He forced himself to keep traveling until noon sun. The rumblings in his stomach reminded him that he had left without stopping to pack food. He found a clear stream at the bottom of the hill, walked down to its bank and knelt beside the water. He drank thirstily. The cold water cleared his head and soothed his empty stomach.

Late in the afternoon, after crossing several hills, he came to the crest of another ridge. Down below was the road. It was empty.

Theros climbed down the hill and walked to the road. He had to give Moorgoth credit for one thing—his insistence on good boots for his officers and men. Those boots were becoming invaluable right now.

He continued walking south.

The hills were no less steep, but the road made it easier to travel and Theros made better time. The sun dropped below the tree level, casting great shadows across the road. He was just beginning to congratulate himself on the ease of his escape, and to think that he might be able to take time to rest, when he heard hoofbeats.

He turned to see a mounted rider far back down the road, heading south, toward him.

"Maybe he hasn't seen me yet," Theros muttered.

He dashed to the side of the road and dove into the huge fir trees. He crouched down amid the shadows and waited.

The rider took his time coming up the road. When he was near enough for Theros to get a good look, he reigned in his mount for a moment and gazed around.

Theros recognized the rider's uniform—maroon surcoat with a black design on the front. Another of Moorgoth's scouts. The only reason for this scout to be this far away from the army was that he must be looking for deserters.

The scout leaned over the horse, searching the ground for footprints in the dirt. Theros thanked Sargas that the dirt was hard-packed—there'd been no rain for a week. The scout shook his head and rode on. He had not seen Theros.

Still, Theros thought, I can't go back to the road. This is proof that they're searching for me. Where there was one, there will be others.

He started to stand up, almost fell, and realized that he could walk no farther without sleep. Yet it was too danger-ous to sleep out in the open, with Moorgoth's men on his trail. Theros turned his back on the road, made his way into the stand of fir trees. He crossed the forest, came up on a makeshift wooden fence surrounding a small field. On the opposite side of the field was a barn.

Theros hunkered down in the shadow of the trees and watched.

The barn appeared to be deserted. Perhaps its owner had fled the approaching army. He saw no one coming or going. Theros took out his axe. He crossed the field, hug-ging the tree line, and crept up on the barn. He walked around the entire exterior of the barn. He opened the door and peered inside. It was dark and empty. He took a chance.

Theros entered into the building and shut the door behind him. There was just enough light to still see the general shape of the walls inside.

Hay was piled up in a corner. It looked extremely invit-ing, more inviting—right now—than the finest bed in Sanction.

Theros was desperately tired. He had been on the move since early the night before, and hadn't stopped. He needed sleep. He would stay here.

He burrowed into the hay, covering himself, just in case. He was slipping off to sleep, when he heard the barn door creak. It opened and a bright light shone inside. Theros jumped up out of the hay, scrambled for his axe.

A huge minotaur walked through the door, ducking so that his giant horns wouldn't hit the frame. Theros had been a child the last time he saw this minotaur, but he recognized the minotaur instantly.

"Sargas!"

The minotaur seemed to grow in size even as he stood there. *I am Sargas. You are wise to recognize your god. You do me honor.*

Theros dropped the axe to his side on the floor, and fell to his knees. "Oh, great Sargas! You do me honor in appearing before me."

Great honor indeed, human.

As before, Sargas's words did not come from his mouth. They materialized inside Theros's mind, as bright and as booming as lightning. *More than you deserve!*

Theros stared, astounded.

"What have I done to displease you, great Sargas?" Theros asked.

You have proven yourself a weakling! Admittedly, you have shown that you have honor, but you do not seek vengeance and retribution against those who besmirch your honor. That half-goblin Lors as much as denounced you for a traitor! You did not even refute him, let alone strike him down in his own blood, as you should have!

Theros did not know what to say in his own defense. He remained silent.

Sargas continued. *Your assistant, Yuri. He is a spy, a creature of dishonor. You should have killed him! Instead, you let him escape. And now this! You run from your place of duty!*

"How can you tell me to serve a dishonorable man like Moorgoth, Oh, great Sargas?" Theros demanded.

If you thought Moorgoth's leadership was so bad, then you should have challenged him to mortal combat! Take over his command. Lead the men yourself. That is what a follower of mine would do!

Theros ventured to argue. "He would have refused and simply ordered his men to kill me—"

Then you die with honor for the glory of my name, Sargas intoned. *The stain of dishonor is upon him, not you.*

Yes, but I can't very well appreciate it if I'm dead, Theros thought, but didn't say.

It didn't matter. Sargas heard his thoughts.

Bah! That is the human blood in you talking! I had hoped for better things from you, Theros Ironfeld. You are not the man of destiny I foresaw in your youth. From now on, you must work hard to regain my good will.

You will atone for your sins! You will improve your ways! You will obey me or you will see me no more!

The words boomed like thunder inside Theros's head. He looked up, fearful of retribution.

The minotaur changed into a giant black bird with flaming wings. It took flight, shooting straight up through the roof of the barn and disappearing into the night.

Theros remained on his knees for a long time, long enough for his body to stiffen. Finally, he lifted his head, expecting to see a hole in the roof, the wood ablaze.

The roof was intact. Nothing.

He thought back to Sargas's accusations. They were true and he felt ashamed. He should have challenged Moorgoth. He should have spoken out, made some attempt to stop the torture. There had been others who had been sickened by it. Perhaps they would have joined him and forced Moorgoth to put an end to it.

Theros snorted. "Be realistic. No one would have backed me. I'd be dead, like those wretched knights. I am not a man of destiny, Sargas. You were mistaken in me. I want only to be a good weapons-smith."

He pitched forward, exhausted, into the hay.

* * * * *

Theros awoke the next morning, the sun streaming in from the east. He thought back to the previous day, wondered if it had all been a dream. No, he knew it wasn't. Sargas had come to him again. He remembered the first visit. He had been only eight. Sargas had said that he would appear three times. This had been the second. There would be another time—perhaps. The thought made him shiver.

His empty stomach brought him back to reality. He was dizzy and light-headed from lack of food. He needed clothing, too. He couldn't run around the countryside half-naked. Theros peered cautiously outside. The barn was near an old garden on the edge of a cornfield. In the center of the field stood a scarecrow, its shirt sleeves flapping in the wind.

Seeing no one around, Theros left his hiding place, went to investigate the scarecrow. The pants were ripped, but the shirt was in reasonable condition. He took the shirt from the scarecrow and shook out the straw. Taking off his harness, he put the shirt on. One seam immediately gave way on his arm, but at least the shirt provided some warmth. The brown color would make it easier to hide in the woods, too. Still, he would need warmer clothing for the mountain pass.

He went back to the garden. It had not been tended for years. All manner of wild vegetation grew in the patch, including a good many weeds. But he found carrots and a line of potatoes, too. He dug up several and wolfed them down raw. When he could eat no more, he pulled a few more out of the ground, and stuffed them in his pockets. He would need them later.

He set out, skirting the road, heading south.

Book Four

Chapter 26

"Friend or foe?"

The elf was insistent. The arrow from the elf's bow—pointed at Theros's heart—made it doubly so.

"What do you mean?" Theros hedged, catching his breath. The elf had taken him completely off guard, nearly scared him half to death. "I don't understand."

"Answer me now or die where you stand."

It was obvious to Theros that the elf was looking for only one of two possible answers.

Theros let his pack slide from his back to the ground. He showed both palms forward, to indicate that he was unarmed. "I guess I'm a friend."

The elf nodded, but did not drop his aim. "Good, now

prove it."

"What? How am I going to—" Theros halted. It had been the wrong thing to say. He could see the elf's eyes squint as if he were just about ready to loose his arrow. Theros waved his hands. "Wait! Wait! What do you want me to do?"

Theros had been traveling the road leading to Solace. Night was falling and he hadn't yet found a place to camp. He had intended to move a few yards into the woods, find a stream and a good place to build a fire, and bed down for the night.

He hadn't been able to find water, so he had continued on into the woods. He had traveled only about a hundred yards when the elf had leapt up from a bush and aimed an arrow at his heart.

The elf whistled like a goatsucker bird. Four other elves appeared, jumping up from behind bushes and trees. All had bows, all bows had arrows and all the arrows were aimed at Theros.

"Look, I'm not going anywhere, all right?" Theros said. He was wearing a battle-axe in a holster on his back, but he did not have it drawn. He would be dead five times over if he reached for the weapon.

The first elf lowered his bow and came forward. He circled around Theros slowly, examining him. Taking Theros's duffel bag, the elf opened the drawstring on top. He quickly rummaged through the contents. He did not, apparently, find anything of interest.

"Remove your axe and put it down," the elf commanded.

Theros reached back and flipped the axe forward in a well-practiced move. The elf backed up, thinking that Theros was about to attack. Instead, Theros tossed the weapon onto the ground in front of him. He looked up to see the other elves relax the tension in their bows. They did not remove the arrows, but they did bring their bows down.

"That proves I'm not an enemy. I'm just passing through," Theros said.

"It proves nothing, human, except that you fear for your life. And with good cause. You will come with us."

The elf slung his bow over his shoulder and picked up the large battle-axe. He staggered, nearly dropped it. After a brief struggle, he managed to heft the weapon and half-carry, half-drag it.

Theros shrugged and picked up his pack. He wasn't in any hurry to get to Solace. He had no appointment, no one to see, no one waiting for him. In fact, he knew very little about Solace. He knew only that most people referred to the town as a place where people went when they had nowhere else to go. Perhaps people like that could use a good blacksmith. It sounded like a business opportunity to Theros. He followed the elf.

The party of five elves and Theros wound through the now-darkening woods. The sun was setting in the west, the red ball of fire just barely visible through the trees of the great Qualinesti forest.

They walked for almost an hour. By the time they reached their destination, the forest was thick with night's shadows. They entered an ancient elven village built into the trees. The buildings were actually *part* of the trees, as if they had been woven into shapes the elves wanted. Theros had never seen anything like it.

The village was bathed in light coming from several firepits in the center of a circle. All of the buildings surrounded this circle, as far as Theros could see. The entire village probably held no more than a hundred people, or so he guessed.

They entered the largest building, which was made out of the largest tree. Inside, the tree had been hollowed into a room. A narrow spiral staircase, carved out of the tree, led upward.

"Leave your belongings here, and come with me."

The elf began to climb the spiral staircase. Theros followed. The other four elves came after him, all keeping wary eyes on him, their hands on their weapons. He considered trying to escape. He could take out the elf above him with a single blow of his fist, then kick the elves below him, send them tumbling down the stairs. He would be out into the night before the elves knew what hit them. He considered this, then let the plan drop. He was curious to see what the elves wanted with him.

Years ago, when he had been a slave of the minotaurs, he had fought elves in the Silvanesti forest. He had seen how the minotaurs had been beaten in battle and then humiliated in defeat. He had no love for Silvanesti elves. These were Qualinesti, their cousins. He assumed they would be the same, but these elves were different. They had the same delicate features, but their dress, their language, even their weapons were different from the Silvanesti.

The stairs led to a large circular room about fifteen yards in diameter. Two elves sat in chairs next to a stone fireplace that had been built into the wooden wall. A third sat behind a desk that appeared to have been crafted from the side of the tree.

Theros stopped in the center of the room. The elf who had captured him placed the battle-axe on the desk, then began to talk with the elf behind the desk in what Theros assumed was the Qualinesti tongue.

The elf behind the desk nodded, and the five elves who had been with Theros since his capture left the room, heading back down the spiral staircase.

"Sit down," the elf said, speaking Common.

Theros took the chair offered. There was no point in jumping around, demanding his release. He would learn more from just sitting and listening.

The elf continued. His voice was cool. It was obviously an effort for him to converse with a human. "I am called Gilthanas. I am a member of the royal family of Qualinesti. What is your name?"

Theros looked around the room. The two elves by the fire wore leather armor with metal cuirasses. Each had an ornately carved elven sword laid across his lap. They watched Theros intently. These must be the bodyguards.

He had done nothing wrong and had nothing to hide. "I am called Theros Ironfeld," he stated simply.

"What are you doing in Qualinesti territory, Master Ironfeld?" The elf spoke in clipped tones, but his grasp of the language was excellent.

"I'm traveling to Solace. I've heard that it is a good place to do business."

The elf raised an eyebrow. "What business would that be, Master Ironfeld?"

"I am a smith. I craft both weapons and armor. I've heard that there's a lot of demand for such items. I think I can make a reasonable living."

Theros's answer seemed to intrigue Gilthanas. He spoke with the other two elves by the fire. They each responded, but Theros could not make out any of what they said.

Finally, Gilthanas turned his attention back to Theros. "Tell me about your history. Where have you practiced your trade, and for whom?"

Theros thought for a moment, trying to decide what to say and what to keep quiet. Most of his story was, he realized, not suitable for elven pointed ears.

After he had left Moorgoth's army, he had returned to Sanction to try to find Marissa, only to discover that she had vanished. She had disappeared the very day Moorgoth's soldiers had marched out of town.

"We thought she had run off with the army," the innkeeper told Theros. "She got a message from one of Moorgoth's men that day. She left and never came back."

Theros was sick at heart and outraged. He remembered Moorgoth's look of displeasure when Marissa had publicly kissed Theros. Theros would never be able to prove it, but he had no doubt that Moorgoth was responsible for Marissa's disappearance. There was nothing now to keep Theros in Sanction. He made a brief stop at Yuri's family's home, to tell them that their son had found a girl, was going to be married. That was all he told them.

He was leaving the town, bitterly disappointed, when he ran headlong into one of the Sanction guardsmen, formerly a customer. Moorgoth had left troops behind to rule Sanction in his stead.

"Say, Ironfeld." The guardsman recognized him. "Didn't I hear you joined up with Moorgoth? What are you doing back in town? His army is way up north."

Theros mumbled something about Moorgoth having found another smithy, tried to get away.

The guardsman attached himself like a leech. "Now isn't this fortunate? You know Yagath? He's been looking for a good smith for his army. He told me he'd pay well to find one. Suppose I give him your name?"

"Suppose you don't," Theros said.

Yagath was a southern barbarian whose mounted horde descended on its enemies like a fiery wind, left nothing behind. Theros wanted no part of any more armies, especially not Yagath's. He started to walk away.

"Suppose I let Moorgoth know where he can find you." The guardsman sneered.

Theros turned, stared at the man.

"I heard you deserted," the guardsman said.

"Then why don't you turn me in?"

"Because Yagath'll give me more for you alive than Moorgoth would dead. Like I said, Yagath needs a smith."

Theros was given the choice of signing on with Yagath, or being turned over to Moorgoth's men. He had no money, no way to earn any money. The woman he loved had vanished. She'd either been sold into slavery or was, if she was lucky, dead. Theros figured he had nothing to lose.

* * * * *

Theros worked for Yagath for five years, setting up a base camp and running a smithy from a mountain valley near Neraka. Throughout that time, armies were massing in the Neraka and Sanction areas. Many secrets were boiling in Yagath's army, but Theros was blind, deaf and dumb. He made no enemies. He made no friends. He kept to himself, did his work, took his pay. He had learned what could go wrong when he stuck his nose into other men's affairs.

Theros concentrated on his craft. The armor and swords he produced were second to none.

Five years after he had started working for Yagath, the war, which would eventually be called the War of the Lance, started. Most of the fighting forces, under the leadership of a man known as Ariakan, moved north or east, to conquer the more populated areas. Yagath's army went with them, never to return.

Yagath was dead, shot by an elf sharpshooter. The rest of

the army had joined other forces. Theros packed up and went on his way. He felt much as he had when the minotaurs freed him. He was pleased to be his own man again, but what was he to do with himself now?

He was headed back to Sanction, when he stumbled across a force of hobgoblins marching north. He had drawn his axe, prepared to fight for dear life, only to find that the hobgoblins treated him as if he were some sort of god. They carried him, an honored guest, into their camp.

Clan Brekthrek was moving to a secure part of Nordmaar, and they needed a smith.

"We have heard much good of you," the clan leader said, poking Theros in the chest. "You come. Work for us."

Theros refused. He had little use for hobgoblins, considering them uncouth, crude and smelly.

The clan leader offered Theros the sum of one thousand steel pieces if he would join them.

"And," said the hobgoblin, with a leer, "I *won't* tell Baron Moorgoth where he can find you."

Theros rued the day he had ever become involved with Moorgoth. The man had cast an evil curse on Theros's life.

Theros became a member of Clan Brekthrek. The hobgoblins had never seen such finely crafted weapons and armor as Theros made. In fact, the armor and swords were too finely crafted for the clan leader to waste on his goblins. The rank and file of Clan Brekthrek needed no more than crude swords, spears and leather jerkins for armor. The hobgoblin sold or bartered most of the weapons to the humans in the armies of Ariakan.

The hobgoblin garrison in Nordmaar grew wealthy. Theros made certain that he was included in the cut. He converted all of his steel into gems, and kept them with him at all times. He hoped that someday he would find the chance to get away, to travel somewhere and start life over.

Theros left the clan two years later, when they moved to garrison duty inside Neraka. Theros was not allowed to remain with the army, though the hobgoblin had begged hard to keep his smith. Very few humans were allowed into Neraka. If Brekthrek knew why, which Theros doubted, the hobgoblin refused to tell. Theros heard hints of strange and terrible deeds performed in the temples of Neraka. He had no idea what they were, and didn't care. It was none of his business.

It wasn't a very good story to tell these elves. If they discovered he'd worked for hobgoblins, those ornate swords would be stuck in his heart.

"I'm from Nordmaar," Theros said. "My father was a fisherman. I was taken captive by minotaurs, worked as a slave to them on their ships for years."

Was he wrong, or did the elf appear suddenly extremely interested?

"I was with the minotaur Third Army that attacked Silvanesti. I was freed by a Silvanesti elf champion. I remain grateful to him."

It was the truth—the bare bones of the truth. The elves listened, made no comment. He couldn't tell if they believed him or not.

"I've knocked around a bit, here and there. I'm traveling south, looking for a good place to set up business. Bad things going on up in the north. Armies marching. Even rumors of dragons."

He smiled as he said that. The rumors always made people laugh.

The elves did not smile.

"What brought you here?" Gilthanas asked.

"Everywhere I went, I heard about Solace. Travelers I met on the roads all seemed to be going to Solace or coming from Solace. The name of the town drew me." Theros shrugged. "I've led a rough life. I could use some solace." Again, a small joke. Again, the elves didn't seem to think it was funny.

He continued. "I passed through Thorbardin, traveled through Pax Tharkas. Everywhere, I kept hearing talk of war. I don't like it." That was, indeed, the truth. He was sick to death of war, sick of the fighting and the killing.

Gilthanas looked over to the other two elves in the room. Both nodded. He turned his attention back to Theros.

"Master Ironfeld, to be honest, when we first brought you here, we thought you were an agent for Verminaard."

"Verminaard?" Theros repeated the name. "I heard of

him. Some sort of new cleric, isn't he?"

"He is a cleric of evil and the commander of the army in Pax Tharkas." Gilthanas was grim, stern. "This Verminaard has only one stated goal. He wants to eradicate all of the Qualinesti elves."

Gilthanas watched for Theros's reaction.

Theros grunted. "Not even the minotaurs wanted to do that. They wanted only to establish a colony."

This time, Gilthanas smiled. He gazed at Theros, somewhat perplexed. "I have a question. You might consider it strange."

Theros shrugged. "Go ahead."

"Why did the elf champion free you, Master Ironfeld? Ordinarily, our Silvanesti cousins would kill a human as swiftly as they would a minotaur. I find this very mysterious."

Theros thought for a moment. "It was a fair battle, an honorable defeat. I spared his life, when I could have killed him. He repaid me in kind."

"I see." Gilthanas regarded Theros thoughtfully. Theros had the idea that the elf did, indeed, see. Perhaps he saw more from that incident than Theros did.

Theros stifled a yawn. He wished they'd get on with this. He needed sleep in order to be back on the road to Solace in the morning.

Gilthanas stood and walked around to the other side of the desk. The other two elves stood also. "You will be our guest for this evening, Master Ironfeld. Hirinthas and Vermala will show you to your room for the night."

This was not an invitation to be declined. Theros was unarmed, alone, in an armed camp. He shrugged and accepted the offer. As long as the elves provided him with food and a warm place to sleep, he would go along with the plan—for the night, at least. He'd slept in much worse places.

Hirinthas and Vermala led Theros back down to the entry area. Theros glanced about for his belongings. They were gone.

"Do not worry, Master Ironfeld," said Vermala, "your possessions will be returned to you in the morning."

The elves led Theros across the center village circle to another building made of a hollowed-out tree. He was taken inside, led up another set of winding stairs that reached a trapdoor at the top. Vermala opened the door.

"Here is your room, Master Ironfeld. We will retrieve you in the morning."

Theros climbed inside. The elves closed the door behind him. Theros looked around. The room was clean, neat, with a straw-covered bed on one side and a small stand with a washbasin on the other. A low table beside the bed had a bowl of bread and fruit. He grimaced. He'd lived with the minotaurs long enough to have a taste for meat, but he was well aware that elves rarely ate animal flesh.

He ate, then washed. He had been traveling for the better part of a week, sleeping out in the open. A bed was a luxury.

He slept quite soundly through the night.

Chapter 27

Theros was dressed and ready when the knock at the door came. The trapdoor opened. An elf gestured.

"Please follow me, Master Ironfeld."

The elf walked swiftly down the narrow stairs. Theros, not used to living in tree houses, moved much more clumsily. He had a hard time keeping up.

They crossed back over to the first tree house. The elf once again led Theros up the stairs. The room had not changed in appearance. On the desk was his battle-axe, and beside it, his bag.

"Sit down. Can I offer you some food and drink?" Gilthanas asked. His voice was a shade warmer than it was yesterday, and yesterday, he had not offered Theros anything to eat.

Theros was hungry, though not particularly for more fruit and nuts. But he took care to eat the food and drink the water. He knew enough about elven customs to realize that this made him an official guest and that, as a guest, he was entitled to elven protection for as long as he remained in their company.

As it turned out, the food was surprisingly good. The water tasted as sweet as wine. The nuts and berries were as satisfying as any venison steak.

Gilthanas would not discuss business matters during a meal, when the body was supposed to concentrate on the important act of nourishing and replenishing itself. Instead, he spoke about his family.

"I am the youngest. I have an elder brother, Porthios, and a sister whose name in your language is Laurana."

"She must be very beautiful, your sister," said Theros, knowing what was expected of a guest. "She must have many suitors."

"One too many, if you ask me," said Gilthanas dryly.

He said nothing more about his sister, and Theros, seeing that the elf appeared displeased, did not ask.

When Theros declared himself finished eating, Gilthanas politely pressed him to eat more and was equally politely refused. Gilthanas then seated himself behind the desk. It was time to talk business.

"Master Ironfeld, I have a proposition for you. I have checked your story with the limited time and resources available to me, and so far, you appear to be telling the truth."

Theros shifted uncomfortably.

Gilthanas, seeing the man's uneasiness, gave a faint smile. "I am certain you have things to hide in your past. What man doesn't? But at least I have learned enough about you to know that you are a man who can be trusted. No, don't ask how. I have my sources.

"If we were in my homeland, in the old days, we would start the negotiations this morning and they would last for several days, maybe even weeks. But we do not have that luxury. Time is critical. I will be blunt and come straight to the point. My people need someone with your skills, Master Ironfeld. Would you be interested in working for us?"

Theros sat back, astounded. He certainly wasn't expecting this. He did not relish the idea of working for another army, especially an elven army. He could see Hran, cut down by elven blades. . . .

"Look, Gilthanas, thank you for the offer and all, but what I really want to do is set up a smithy in Solace and sell my services and wares to civilians. I've had my fill of fighting. I want to lead a peaceful life. I don't think I'm interested." Theros stood up, thinking all had been said and it was time to go.

Gilthanas did not agree. "Please, hear me out."

Reluctantly, Theros sat back down.

Gilthanas sighed. "I have not told you the entire story yet. I have told you of Verminaard's stated goal of exterminating the Qualinesti peoples. What I did not tell you is that he is coming very close to succeeding in that goal. Still, I do not need you to manufacture weapons. I doubt, in fact, if your limited human skills would suit us. I mean no offense, but human weapons are quite crude and clumsy, compared to those our people use." He glanced disdainfully at the axe as he spoke.

Theros sputtered at the insult, but the elf wasn't listening.

"You said you were from Nordmaar. You were taken aboard a minotaur ship, and you worked aboard it for some years."

Theros nodded. "Yes, I was a slave for the minotaurs from the age of eight until I was freed. Many of those years, I served aboard one ship. I told you all that."

"I wanted to confirm it. That is excellent. My people need your help to evacuate Qualinesti. You see"—Gilthanas spread his hands—"we know very little of ships and sailing."

Theros was astonished. The elves had been in Qualinesti as long as there had *been* a Qualinesti. Maybe longer. "What do you mean, evacuate? Where would you go?"

"Only a small handful of people know of the plan. We are going to remove most of the population to a region of

Southern Ergoth, a place we call Qualimori. We are not a seafaring people. We need your help."

Theros frowned. "I can't build ships, if that's what you're asking. I sailed on them. I didn't build them."

Gilthanas explained. "We have a shipwright from Northern Ergoth who has designed the ships. He already has a team of elves helping him assemble them. He has asked for a metalsmith who can manufacture the necessary metal parts. None of our people possess such skills. I know that you are a weapons-smith, but could you do the job? He would provide all of the specifications. You would be well paid."

Theros thought it over. "If this Verminaard is winning and I help out the losing side, my life wouldn't be worth much, now, would it? Not much good making money if I don't live to spend it."

"Very true," Gilthanas said, and he almost smiled. "I promise you that we will keep your work with us secret. We will take you to our camp on the western shores. We will pay you twenty steel pieces a day, plus five hundred to join. I would ask you to aid us for only a few months, after which, if you want to continue on to Solace, we would help you to reach it. Will you join our cause?"

Theros thought this over for a long moment. He didn't want to have anything to do with other people's causes. He wanted to start a business for himself. How was it that he kept tumbling into these predicaments? Would he ever in his life have a cause of his own? Still, the pay was good, and he would be away from any fighting. And it would be for only a few months.

"All right, I'll sign on with you," he said.

Gilthanas was pleased. "Thank you, Master Ironfeld. I remind you that it is important that you say nothing of this to anyone, even among my own people, until you reach the building site at Quivernost."

Theros picked up his axe, reseating it in the back holster he wore. He briefly opened his bag, noting that everything appeared to be in order. Downstairs, he met Hirinthas and Vermala, the two elves who had escorted Theros the night before.

"These two are warriors from the Royal Court of Qualinesti. They will ensure you safe passage to Quivernost. You will leave immediately."

To seal their deal, Gilthanas handed Theros a large felt bag. The bag was heavy. Theros opened it, saw the steel pieces. He did not bother to count them. He attached the bag to his pouch, hoisted his pack over his shoulder. Then the three of them headed off into the forest.

As he walked, his mind went to the making of pulleys and winches and nails. . . .

* * * * *

Theros and his companions traveled fast through the forest, heading west. Each night they stopped only after dark, and rose just before dawn to begin again. The two elf warriors carried all of the food, as well as their own bedrolls and weapons. Theros, who had thought them delicate, was impressed by their strength and stamina. He also had the feeling that the elves were forced to keep their pace slow because of him, and he was walking as rapidly as he could.

These elves were obviously not accustomed to being around humans, not like Gilthanas. They rarely spoke to Theros, and then only to give him some instructions or to ask if he would like more bread at dinner. They talked between themselves in their own language. Despite being part of a trio, Theros had never felt more alone.

"We will stop here for the night," Hirinthas announced on the third day.

Theros glanced around. The site was beautiful. A creek bubbled past a meadow surrounded by trees. Beside the creek was a small pit with ashes at the bottom. It had been used as a firepit many times before.

"Why are we stopping here?" Theros asked. It was early afternoon. "We could cover a lot more ground before dark."

Hirinthas began to unload his pack. "We are an easy day's walk from Quivernost. We should be safe this far west. This site has been used by travelers for centuries. We will camp here for the night."

Theros shrugged. He had no say in the matter. If it were up to him, he would have carried on. It was not up to him, however. Though the two elves treated him with respect, he was well aware that they did not trust him. He was never permitted to stand watch. Whenever his hand reached for his axe, an elven hand would always reach for a knife. They watched him constantly. Frankly, he was getting tired of it. Hobgoblins had treated him better than this!

"I'll go get some wood," Theros offered, dropping his bag. He headed into the forest, looking for fallen branches. Vermala had informed him earlier that he was not to cut any trees in the forest for firewood. The spirits of the trees would cry out, tortured, if their living limbs were savagely hacked off. Only those branches that had already fallen, dead branches that the tree had sloughed off, were acceptable for use.

Theros grinned to himself. He would have loved to have told that silly tale to old Hran. The minotaur would have laughed his horns off.

Naturally, because the campsite was so much in use, the area around the site was picked clean of any large firewood. Theros ventured farther into the forest. He wasn't worried about getting lost. The two elves would find him easily enough. He wouldn't be surprised if one of them was tracking him now.

A hundred feet farther, he came across the fallen trunk of an oak tree. The branches lay scattered around, most rotten beyond any use. The trunk was dried out and looked fine for burning. He removed his battle-axe from the holster.

A rustling of leaves in a bush caught his attention. He had just told himself it was nothing but his elf watchdogs, when he caught a flash of color—maroon.

Theros crouched down. There it was again—a patch of maroon behind a tree in the late afternoon sun. Elves wore greens and browns that blended into the forest. Theros kept completely still.

He waited for almost a minute before the maroon color moved again. A man—a human—emerged from behind the tree and cautiously walked forward ten paces, then crouched down. He wore black breeches with a maroon surcoat.

"Sargas take me!" Theros swore to himself. "I'd recognize that uniform anywhere! One of Moorgoth's men. What is he doing in these parts?"

He gripped the axe tighter. The soldier rose and cautiously padded forward again. This time Theros walked forward, too, keeping behind the soldier.

As he crept along, Theros looked around to see if he could spot any other soldiers about. He was certain that there must be more than one. This man wasn't a spy or a scout. By his uniform, he was part of a patrol. His comrades would be nearby.

There can be only one explanation, Theros thought. Moorgoth has hooked up with this Verminaard. And these elves and I have walked right into a trap!

Common sense urged him to run. Let the damned elves fend for themselves. He knew Moorgoth well enough to know that he would never forgive, never forget. A vivid picture of the tortured knights came to Theros's mind. Compared to what Moorgoth would do to him, those men had died easy.

All I ever wanted to do was become a civilian, set up an honest shop in an honest town. Where do I keep going wrong?

Slowly, he crept along behind the soldier. Theros did not recognize the man, but that wasn't surprising. It had been nearly ten years since he had served in Moorgoth's army. And he wasn't surprised at the direction the soldier was taking. He was heading straight for the elven campsite. Another ambush.

Theros stood up, keeping his axe concealed behind his back. "Looking for elves?" he said in a loud voice.

The startled soldier jumped and hit his head on a low tree branch. Wincing, he turned to face Theros.

The soldier stared, then he grinned. "Well, if it isn't the traitor Ironfeld. We've been dogging your steps for days. Moorgoth has offered a fat reward for your hide. I'll be the one to collect, it seems."

The soldier drew his sword and lunged straight at Theros.

"I wouldn't count your money yet!"

Theros brought his axe around and widened his stance. He sidestepped the soldier's attack and took a swing himself. The axe clanged off the soldier's sword blade.

The two faced each other, circling. The soldier had the advantage in that his sword could be used for thrusting as well as slashing. He tried to close with Theros.

Theros let him come. The soldier thrust at Theros, who narrowly avoided the blow. Unfortunately, he lost his footing, tripped over a branch, and fell heavily on his side. The soldier raised his sword for the kill. Theros tangled his legs with the soldier's legs, upended the man, and dumped him on the ground.

Leaving his axe where it lay in the grass, Theros jumped forward. The soldier saw him coming and tried to roll out of the way. Theros missed landing on him in a body blow, but he was able to knock the soldier's weapon out of his grasp. Now the combat was hand-to-hand.

The soldier went for the dirk at his side. Theros saw the move and smashed the man in the face with his fist. Blood spattered from his broken nose. Theros leapt on top of the man. They both crashed to the ground, Theros pinning the soldier with his weight. He wrapped his huge hands around the soldier's neck, started to slowly strangle him.

The man panicked. He thrashed for air. His hands tried to beat Theros off, but Theros was too big for him. The man twisted and tried to turn to free himself. His eyes were wild.

At last, Theros released the pressure, but he kept his hands around the man's neck.

The soldier breathed in a huge gulp of air.

"How many soldiers are with you?" Theros asked.

The soldier began to stutter. Theros squeezed his hands tight again, cutting off the man's air. His eyes bulged. At the last moment, Theros released the pressure again.

"There are four of us," the man gasped when he could talk. "Please don't tell them I told you so. They'd kill me! Please, let me go."

"And you'll run off and be a good little boy? Somehow I don't quite believe that. Are you here to ambush the elves?"

The soldier nodded. "General Moorgoth—"

"So he's a general now," Theros grunted.

"General Moorgoth heard that the elves were bringing people in to do some secret project on the western banks by the ocean. We're to kill or capture anyone going in that direction."

"You say Moorgoth has a reward out for me?" Theros asked. "How did he find me? And how do you know who I am? I've never seen you before in my life."

"Moorgoth's been getting reports on you for years. This was the first time he was ever able to act on them. He put out a description of you to all the soldiers. A big man with skin like the night and a voice like rumbling thunder. That's what he said."

Theros sighed. He removed the dagger from the man's belt and then let the man stand up.

"Right, take off your boots and remove the laces. Quickly!"

The man did as he was told.

Theros collected his axe and the soldier's sword. He tied the soldier to a tree with the bootlaces, both hands and feet. He didn't bother to gag the man. There was no point. If he cried out, he'd only attract the attention of the elves, and that was probably not the sort of attention he wanted.

The sound of clashing steel reminded Theros that he was not alone in the woods. He thrust his axe back in its holster and charged back to the campsite, sword in hand.

He arrived at the campsite and found Hirinthas and Vermala battling two soldiers. A third soldier lay dead on the ground. Vermala was covered with blood and was obviously faltering. Theros yelled a war cry and leapt into the fray.

The two soldiers were caught in a vice, elves in front, Theros behind. Startled by his yell, they looked back to see their new enemy. Hirinthas took advantage of their distraction to thrust his sword into the man's rib cage, bringing the first soldier down. The second soldier parried Vermala's blow and backed up against a tree.

"Surrender," Theros ordered. "You're outnumbered three to one."

The soldier lowered his sword. "All right. Take me prisoner. You won't get anything out of me."

Hirinthas removed the man's sword and forced him to sit down on the ground. Theros took the man's dagger. Vermala slumped to his knees. He had a wound in his side. Blood had soaked through his clothes.

Hirinthas took a surcoat from one of the dead soldiers and pressed it against Vermala's wound. Theros bound the soldier fast, then went to retrieve his own captive. He tied them up back-to-back. His prisoners safe, he built a fire.

The sun was starting to set. Vermala was pale and shivering. His wound was serious.

Theros stoked the fire, thought back to another time when he'd watched over another wounded soldier. The only difference was that one had been a minotaur. Remembering Huluk's orders that day, Theros looked over at Hirinthas. "You said you are within a day's march of your people. You've got to go and get help. Vermala needs medical attention. I've done all I can for him. I'll guard him and keep these two tied up until you get back."

Hirinthas was not pleased with this suggestion. "No, my job is to protect you through Silvanesti. I cannot leave my charge—"

"Damn you! You don't care one thing for me," Theros bellowed. "You don't trust me! That's it, isn't it?"

Hirinthas cast a scathing glance at the two soldiers. "Why should I trust you, human?"

"Because Vermala will die if you don't! Look, if I was going to kill you, I would have already done it. I could have joined up with these two and their buddies anytime. I swear to you by"—he almost said by Sargas, but thought better of it—"I swear to you on my mother's grave that I'll defend Vermala with my life!"

Hirinthas was smart enough to understand that what Theros had said was logical. If Theros was in league with these humans, Hirinthas would be dead by now. He could also see that his comrade was in very bad shape.

"Very well, Ironfeld, but if I return and find you have betrayed me, the world of Krynn itself will not be a large enough place for you to hide. I would follow you even into the Abyss."

Hirinthas stood and sprinted off into the night.

The four who remained sat by the fire and waited for morning.

No one talked much.

Chapter 28

The sun rose strong and warm the next day. Not a cloud was in the sky. Vermala lay huddled near the fire, shaking so much that his teeth rattled. Theros leaned over him, bathed his burning face in cold water, did what he could to make him more comfortable.

Fever was setting in. The elf had lost a lot of blood, and would not survive much longer.

The two prisoners were fast asleep, still tied together. At one point during the night, they had thought that Theros had fallen asleep. They had rolled to one side and began working on the knots that bound them together. A kick to the head informed the prisoners that they'd made a slight miscalculation.

"Wake up," Theros said to Vermala, afraid that perhaps the elf had fallen into the strange sleep trance from which one never awakens. "Keep awake, if you can."

Vermala opened his eyes. "I'm thirsty," he whispered.

He spoke the words in elven, his knowledge of the Common language lost in his pain. Theros didn't understand the words, but he guessed the intent.

The big man was relieved that Vermala was awake and worried at the same time. The waterskin was empty. He was wondering if he dared risk leaving and going to fill it, when the trees around him seemed to come alive. He sprang up, his axe in the ready position.

Elves burst out from the trees and ran into the glade. Hirinthas was in the lead. More elves were running out of the woods and joining them.

Hirinthas hurried forward and knelt beside Vermala, who was fluttering back and forth from consciousness to unconsciousness. A second elf sat down beside his injured comrade. He started to hum a strange tune. Removing a bag from his belt, he began laying out all manner of herbs, potions and concoctions.

"Will he live?" Theros asked in Common.

The healer elf ignored him for a moment, continuing to apply ointments to the wound. He then forced a potion down Vermala's throat that must have tasted terrible, judging by the expression on the elf's face. The healer spoke something in elven.

Hirinthas translated. "The next few minutes will tell all."

Hirinthas turned to the rest of the elves, now numbering around twenty, who had gathered in the glade. He issued instructions rapidly, in elven, then, glancing at Theros, translated. "I have told them to encircle the area. I want this area secure until we are ready to move out."

"Good idea," Theros said.

The elves disappeared into the woods, sliding among the trees more quietly than the wind. The wind rustled a leaf now and then. The elves never did. One elf was detailed to remain with the two prisoners, to ensure that they did not attempt escape. The prisoners were now wide awake and not looking terribly pleased at this turn of events.

Theros kept an anxious watch on the injured elf. The healer continued singing softly. Although Theros couldn't understand the words, he felt the music soothe him, ease away his troubles. He had not slept at all during the night and was starting to drift off when a voice spoke next to him, startling him to wakefulness.

Hirinthas was saying his name. "Master Ironfeld."

Theros blinked, turned. "Sorry, I must have dozed off."

Hirinthas looked ill at ease. The words were obviously not coming easily. "I want to . . . extend my thanks to you for remaining with my cousin. Not only that, but you saved our lives yesterday. I was . . . ungracious." The elf straightened. "I wish to apologize."

Theros smiled, shrugged. "Sure. I understand. I guess you haven't had much cause to trust humans lately."

Hirinthas gave a short nod and then went to sit beside his cousin.

Vermala suddenly gasped and lurched over sideways, the brown potion he'd drunk spewing from the side of his mouth. The wounded elf began to convulse. The healer elf inserted a stick in Vermala's mouth, so that he wouldn't bite his tongue, and tried to hold the elf down. The tremors were too violent. Theros knelt in front of Vermala. As gently as he could, he held the elf's shoulders pinned to the ground.

After half a minute, the elf lay still. At first, Theros thought he was dead, but then Vermala's eyes opened. He glanced around, looking first at Theros and then over to the healer.

"What happened? Is he going to be all right?" Theros asked, shaken.

"His fever is broken, the toxic spirits have been purged from his body. He will begin to heal." The healer started to pack up his herbs and potions.

"Looks to me like the cure's near as bad as the injury," Theros stated.

The healer was wrapping more bandages around the wound. "In the old days, our people had healers who could ease pain with a song, heal torn flesh by touching it, even restore life to the dead, if you believe the stories. And then came the Cataclysm and the gods left us. Now we must fall back on our wits. And even then, very often, my skill is not enough."

The healer looked over at Theros. "You did what was necessary for Vermala. You kept him warm, kept him awake."

"I've seen wounds like his before," said Theros gruffly. "Too many times. Too many." He shook his head.

The healer helped Vermala to drink some water. "He is out of danger. He can be moved. He should be carried back to Quivernost."

Vermala motioned for the healer to come closer, so that he could speak. In whispered tones, he conversed with the healer. Then the wounded elf reclined, closing his eyes. He sighed and fell asleep.

The healer sat back on his heels, gazing thoughtfully at Theros, who had the impression the conversation had been about him.

"If he was thanking me," said Theros, embarrassed and wishing these elves weren't so damned polite, "just tell him not to give it a second thought."

The healer tucked a blanket securely around Vermala's shoulders. "He asked me to thank you. He then thanked me for my services, and passed on to me the burden of your safe passage through the forest. I am now charged, along with Hirinthas, with your safekeeping."

Rising to his feet, the elf made a formal bow. "My name is Berenthinis. I am the healer for the village of Quivernost."

Theros bowed clumsily. Something the elf had said disturbed him. "I'm having a little trouble understanding. Did you say that you are *the* healer for the village? Do you mean that there's only one and you're it?"

The elf nodded. "That is true. The task of attending to the sick is considered an onerous one among my people. It reminds them constantly that the gods have left them. They know it must be done, but there are few willing to do it."

"And you'd abandon your people in order to escort me? What if someone needs you? What if a child falls ill? What if someone's injured?"

Berenthinis raised an eyebrow. "That is not your concern, Master Ironfeld. I have accepted the charge. I am honor bound."

Theros scratched his beard. Blasted elves! No common sense. Plus, Theros was getting tired of the fact that these elves apparently considered him a babe in the woods, likely to come to harm without their careful guidance.

"Look, healer." Theros had completely forgotten the elf's name. They all sounded alike to him anyway. "I'm responsible for my own well-being. I appreciate that you have given me safe passage, but you're needed back with your people. I'm here to help you, not be a burden to you. *I* am going to take Vermala's responsibility. You are released from your obligation."

The healer studied Theros a moment, then bowed again. "As you wish," was all he said.

Well, at least he hadn't argued. Theros guessed that it wasn't difficult for the elf to give up the responsibility. It was a rare elf indeed who would relish the job of keeping a human alive, no matter how grateful they were to him.

Theros and Hirinthas constructed a stretcher with two pine branches loosely held together with leather straps. They laid pine boughs over the straps, providing a bed for the wounded elf.

Hirinthas whistled like a bird. Within minutes, the elves guarding the perimeter had returned. They had been so silent, Theros had forgotten they were out there. Two were assigned to carry Vermala. Theros untied the prisoners and allowed them to put their boots back on. The elves bound the prisoners' hands behind their backs with strips of leather. They formed into a column, with Hirinthas at the head, and Theros taking up the position of rear guard.

They traveled slowly, moving carefully so as not to jar the injured elf. Theros carried his pack, his axe in its holster on his back. He kept a close eye on the prisoners, wondered what he was going to do about them, about Moorgoth. The prisoners' mouths were gagged, for which Theros was grateful. If the prisoners started talking about Theros having worked once for Moorgoth, they could make Theros's life very difficult. He'd have a tough time explaining that to the elves.

All these years, Theros had been living with a price on his head and he'd never known it. Ignorance is bliss—or so the kender say.

They reached Quivernost just after nightfall. The healer ordered Vermala to be taken to the healer's house. Berenthinis followed after the stretcher. Before he left, Theros stopped him, placing his hand on the elf's shoulder.

He felt the elf flinch beneath his touch, hastily removed his hand.

"Listen, I just want you to know that I appreciate you taking on my safety as your responsibility. It was an honorable thing to do. But you have a greater responsibility to these people. I don't have to tell you that. Still, you did me a great honor today." Theros bowed clumsily to the elf.

Berenthinis appeared taken aback. He studied Theros. "You are a strange man, Master Ironfeld. It is rare these days to hear anyone speak of honor, much less a human."

He returned the bow, then hurried to catch up with the stretcher-bearers.

Theros chuckled, but only to himself. "I've probably ruined that poor elf's whole philosophy concerning us savage humans."

Hirinthas was hovering at Theros's elbow. "Come with me, Master Ironfeld. I will introduce you to the other human who will be working with you."

Theros followed Hirinthas to a meeting hall built into a huge tree trunk. They entered a large room filled with elves, eating and drinking. It was mealtime, and the room was evidently used as the town tavern when not used for official business.

Hirinthas looked around the room. The only other human in the place sat at a table, eating bread and shrimp. Another elf sat with him, also eating. The two were not engaged in conversation and Theros had the feeling that the elf was some sort of guard. The human looked up as they approached, and his face brightened at the sight of Theros.

Rising to his feet, the man wiped bits of shrimp tails off his hands and extended his hand to Theros. "I'm Koromer

Vlusaj. They've brought me on here as the shipwright. Pleasure to see another human! No offense, there." He nodded to Hirinthas. "But it's good to see your own kind."

Theros sat down next to Koromer. The man was big, almost as big as Theros. Koromer's face was honest and open. His skin was bronzed from outdoor work and his hair bleached blond by the sun. He had a booming laugh that shook the tree in which they sat; it invariably startled the elves. Koromer's laugh went off like a crack of thunder.

They all sat down, Hirinthas taking his seat next to Theros and across from the elf sitting with Koromer. A serving maid brought both Hirinthas and Theros a bowl of shrimp and some bread. She returned with two glasses of a sweet elven wine and a jug of water. Theros thanked the woman, who stared at him blankly. Obviously she didn't understand a word. She was quick to leave.

"I hear you're an ironsmith." Koromer said.

Theros nodded. "I can do ironsmithing, but I was trained as a weapons-smith. Still, I'll be able to produce whatever you need, as long as I've got the forge, the tools, and the steel to do the job."

Koromer described what tools were available. Theros considered them, decided he could use a few more. He turned to Hirinthas. "Look, when you go back to Solace, please see if you can find a—"

Hirinthas said quietly, "I'm not going back to Solace, Master Ironfeld. However, I will be glad to find someone who is, and have him perform the task."

Koromer jerked a thumb toward the elf sitting with him. Theros understood.

He grunted. "So I'm to have my own personal watch-dog, is that it?"

"It is for your own safety," Hirinthas replied, a faint flush mantling his cheeks. Even he had the grace to feel somewhat ashamed. "My charge was to see you safely through the forests of Qualinesti. You are still here. Until you leave, I will be your guard. The same is true of Taranthas here. We will protect both you and Master Vlusaj until you leave our service."

Theros could guess what the elf's statement really

meant: *And we will protect our people from contact with you humans.*

Koromer and Theros exchanged glances. It wasn't worth arguing with the elf over the matter. He had his orders. And Theros had to admit that the thought of having a guard was somewhat comforting. The elves were at war, and there was no reason that he should become a casualty. He'd just have to view Hirinthas as a bodyguard, not a prison guard.

Theros turned back to Koromer, and together they began to map out a strategy to build the first elven fleet.

Chapter 29

"She's not pretty, but she'll do." Theros said.

"Aye, that she will," said Koromer, regarding their work with pride.

They looked out over the pier at the last of the evacuation ships. Her elven name was *Spiriniltan'thimis*. Koromer, who had difficulty with the language, did not even try to pronounce it. He just called it "Spirit."

Theros stood with the shipwright and their two ever-present elf bodyguards. They had spent the last eleven months producing the ships for the evacuation of Qualinesti. This one would join her sisters, now sailing the run between Quivernost, on the shores of the Qualinesti Nation, and Qualimori, on the southern end of Southern

Ergoth. A crew of elves were busy aloft, finishing the rigging of the ship.

"She'll make her first run in three days. She's a fine ship. But I've got to admit you're right, Theros. She sure isn't pretty." Koromer had designed the ship to be long and flat, with only two main sail masts, the same as the three previous ships. "But she'll do the job."

The run to Qualimori took only three days across open ocean. The ship was not designed to stay at sea for months or even weeks. This design permitted the maximum load capacity. She could carry eight hundred elves, with minimal provisions, or five hundred with a full cargo load.

Hirinthas could not share in the compliments. The squat, rolling vessel obviously offended his sensibilities. He said something to his fellow elf in their native tongue. Theros understood, although he pretended he didn't. He'd managed to pick up quite a bit of the elven language during his stay among them, but he was careful not to flaunt his knowledge. He couldn't ever learn to pronounce the words the way the elves did, and they always winced when they heard him butcher their beautiful language.

"Like the others, it is obviously a human-designed ship," Hirinthas said.

Had this been an elven ship, it would have been as sleek as a flying fish and just as useless. This was one of the reasons, Theros guessed, that Gilthanas had hired humans to build the ships. They did not have time to manufacture beautiful ships—just functional ships.

Theros had set up his forge in a building near the pier. He made all of the nails, pulleys, chains and metal braces. Koromer specified each piece with a diagram, and the two discussed the size and feel and weight of the piece. Theros then built one for testing. Once Koromer approved, Theros began to produce them in the quantities needed.

Eventually, they had built a fleet of four ships. Gilthanas calculated that it would take four of these ships, each running day and night, to evacuate the main population of the Qualinesti Nation in time. Already, fifteen thousand elves had made the crossing to Qualimori. They had started as soon as the first ship was operational and kept going. Now, with three ships in operation, they were ferrying over two thousand elves across every week. With this fourth ship, they could take nearly three thousand.

The first ship had been the hardest to build. They worked from a preliminary design that Koromer had developed. Changes were made daily to the working design as they found problems or ideas that just didn't work. Theros and Koromer almost came to blows over a rudder fitting that Koromer had Theros build, then rebuild, then build again, all because of changes in design. The final version worked, and they settled their differences. Now, after four successful launches, they counted on each other as friends.

And one morning, Theros woke up and realized that, for the first time in his life, he was happy. After years of living in a stinking, crowded city, he enjoyed being back near the sea again, hearing the endless song of the waves and the cries of the birds, breathing in the clean, fresh sea air. He worked hard during the day and spent his nights eating and drinking and talking with Koromer.

Now, seeing the final ship nearly launched, Theros went aboard to inspect her. He found her to be seaworthy and left the finishing of the work and the cleaning up to the elven crew. He turned his thoughts and steps toward a well-earned dinner. The sun had already started to set by the time he arrived at the meeting hall.

A cheer went up as Theros entered. Koromer was already seated at a table, holding a large mug. Theros smiled, bowed to the crowd of elves, and headed straight for Koromer.

"Hey! Where did you get that?" Theros demanded, staring into Koromer's mug. If his eyes didn't deceive him, Koromer was drinking ale! It had been many months since Theros had tasted ale.

Koromer pointed to a small keg sitting on the floor beside him. He took a spare mug from the table and filled it with dark, foaming ale. Theros's mouth began to water.

"Gilthanas brought us a present! He says it's from a place in Solace known as the Inn of the Last Home. Here, try it. It's beyond compare!"

Theros lifted the mug and drained it in a swallow. The ale was woodsy and bitter and cut through the salt tang that always seemed to be in his mouth. He had never in his life tasted anything so delicious. Putting down the mug, he wiped his eyes, unable to speak for a short time.

Koromer, laughing, filled the mug again.

"This is really good. Did you say Gilthanas is here?"

"Yes, he's over in the corner, talking to Hirinthas," Koromer said.

"I'm going to talk to him. Want to come?"

Koromer shook his head emphatically. "I'm not leaving this keg until it's empty!"

Theros laughed. Taking his foaming mug, he headed over to the corner Koromer had indicated.

Gilthanas actually did him the honor of rising to greet him. "Theros Ironfeld. It is good to see you. We owe you much, not only for your work, but for your loyalty and your patience. I know that living among our people cannot have been easy for you."

He spoke in Qualinesti elven, obviously expecting that Theros would understand him. Theros glanced at Hirinthas. The elf was more observant than Theros had realized.

Theros made a suitable reply, also in Qualinesti, doing his best to pronounce the slippery words. As he did, he studied Gilthanas. The elf looked much thinner than when Theros had seen him last. He was haggard, gaunt and seemed tired to the point of exhaustion. Still, he held himself straight, demonstrating his royal lineage.

"Thank you," said Theros. "It was good to work on a project that will truly benefit people. The *Spiriniltan'thimis*"—he stumbled over the name—"is the best of the four ships. We were able to trim the sails differently on this one so that it is more efficient in the water. She'll do several knots faster than the others. So, tell me about the war against this Verminaard."

Gilthanas was grim. "I cannot say it is going well. Still, we fight on. Verminaard has pushed into the southern portion of the forest, and we cannot rout him. It has been nearly a month since we were able to mount a raid on Pax Tharkas. I don't think we can afford the manpower to do that again. He is growing stronger and we are growing weaker. Still, the evacuation is ahead of schedule, thanks to you and Koromer. The Nation of Qualinesti and I owe you a great debt."

Theros smiled. "I did what needed doing. I'm just glad it's working out."

Gilthanas nodded. "Your work here is finished, Theros Ironfeld. Now that the fourth ship is ready for sailing, I am here to fulfill my promises to you. In the morning, I will give you your well-earned steel, plus a little extra—a gift from my father, the Speaker of the Suns, to show our thanks for staying until all four ships were completed. You did not have to do that. Hirinthas and Vermala will escort you to Solace, assuming that is where you still want to go."

Theros drank from his mug. "Truth be told, I haven't really thought about where I'll go next. I've been too busy getting these ships ready to sail. I don't have any plans."

It was on the tip of his tongue to offer to stay here, but he abandoned that. The elves were grateful for his services, they liked him well enough and probably trusted him by now. But they didn't want him living among them. They didn't want any humans living among them.

"Sure," he said offhandedly, "I think I would like to set up shop in Solace. I hear it's a good place to do business. People from all over go through there. I can make a fine business in weapons and armor. And if there's an inn there that sells ale like this—well, I think I might spend the rest of my life there!"

He returned to Koromer and they held their own private party, which lasted well into the evening. He went back to his quarters late, long after Solinari had set.

Two hours after sunrise, however, he was in his smithy. Hirinthas and Vermala came searching for him.

"We didn't expect to find you here," Vermala said. "You're all packed, I see. Are you ready to go?"

Theros nodded. It was hard leaving this place. He had truly enjoyed working here. "Is Koromer coming with us? Has he decided yet?"

"He has accepted our offer to stay on for a while, to conduct repairs, if any are necessary. And he has agreed to come with us to Qualimori when we go." Hirinthas paused, then said, "We would like to issue you an invitation to visit us in Qualimori, Theros Ironfeld. Or perhaps live with us, if you do not find Solace to your liking."

Theros stared in astonishment. He had never expected anything like this. He was pleased beyond his ability to express his feelings—in either Common or Qualinesti.

Hirinthas smiled. "Gilthanas wanted to meet with you before we left. He will be here shortly."

Theros didn't have to wait long, before Gilthanas entered the smithy. He carried a small velvet bag hand-embroidered in golden thread. Gilthanas handed the bag to Theros.

"Add this to the other treasures on your belt."

Theros took the bag, spent a moment admiring the delicate workmanship.

"My sister did the embroidery," Gilthanas said proudly.

"That makes it all the more valuable," Theros said. "I would like a chance to meet your sister someday."

Gilthanas said something meaningless and polite. Obviously, such a thing would never happen—a smith being introduced to an elf princess!

Theros looked inside the bag. Four diamonds caught the sunlight, sparkled with dazzling radiance. Each gem was the size of a walnut. Theros looked up in amazement. The gems were easily worth ten times what he was owed.

"I can't take this. You could give me just one and still overpay me." He started to return the gift.

Gilthanas stopped him. "You have ensured that the Qualinesti Nation will live. These four jewels are the least that we owe you. We can never repay our true debt."

Theros added the pouch to the other three pouches in which he kept all of his treasures. He carried nearly five thousand steel worth of gems and coins, not counting the diamonds.

Gilthanas then did something remarkable. Reaching out, he grasped Theros by the hand. Not only did he shake hands warmly, but he also retained Theros's large hand in his small one, pressed it tightly.

"Listen, my friend, you will be in great danger—even in

Solace—if anyone finds out that you were aiding us here in the Qualinesti Nation. Be careful. Speak no word to any man. Trust no one. Hirinthas and Vermala will guide you safely to the northern corner of the forest. From there, you will be on your own, just as any other traveler. I wish you the best of luck."

Gilthanas shook the big man's hand again.

For a moment, Theros couldn't speak. The elf had called him "friend."

"On to Solace, then," Theros said, when he found his voice.

Book Five

Chapter 30

Theros was taking a break from his labors, drinking a large mug of tepid water, when two men entered his shop. He paused in his swallowing to look at them, thinking he'd never seen a stranger pair in his life. One was a warrior, a mercenary by the looks of him, and he was one of the biggest men Theros—who was no small man himself—had ever seen. Big and jovial, he had a bluff, frank face on which every emotion registered like wind ruffling the surface of placid water.

Theros marked the big man as a customer and gave him a nod over the water mug. The smith's gaze turned to the person accompanying the big man and Theros frowned. The big man's comrade was a wizard, wearing red robes and carrying an odd-looking staff. Theros didn't normally pay much attention to staves, unless they needed a new iron shoe for the bottom, but the Seeker guards had been around asking questions about a staff, and so Theros took note of this one.

The staff itself was plain enough—ordinary wood—but the top was adorned with a crystal clutched in what appeared to be a dragon's claw. The staff was magic; of that, Theros had no doubt. He could have called the Seeker guards, earned himself a steel piece. But Theros's credo was "live and let live."

It wasn't unusual to see a mage in Solace, though it was unusual to see one in the company of a warrior. Solace had become a haven for wanderers. The elves had evacuated the lands to the south, and Verminaard, who was now calling himself a Dragon Highlord, was ravaging the area. Most of Theros's customers were either from Verminaard's army, or were heading over to join up. Business was booming in the arms trade.

Solace was a town built entirely in the vallenwood trees. All of the shops and homes were nestled in the limbs and trunks of the trees. Walkways connected the trees to each other, making it easy to get from place to place. Staircases were built from the ground up in various places near the main road through the town.

Theros's smithy was the only business located on the ground in Solace. There was no way to put a steel forge in a vallenwood tree without the wood igniting. Besides, the weight of the steel and finished products would be too much to move up and down the stairs. His shop looked out onto the main road that ran through the town, and onto the town square beyond.

The two customers stood in the doorway, blinking in the bright light of the forge fire. The big man began looking around. His gaze went immediately to the swords Theros had out on display.

The mage, standing somewhat behind the larger man, said, in an irritable voice, "Get on with it, Caramon. You know I cannot breathe this foul air."

Theros was about to tell the mage he could go wait at the

bottom of Crystalmir lake, if he preferred it, when the big man spoke up.

"You Theros Ironfeld?" he asked.

"That's my name," said Theros.

"I've heard you are the best weapons-smith in Solace."

"I am," Theros said coolly. "What can I do for *you*?" He laid emphasis on the word "you," pointedly excluding the mage.

"My name's Caramon. This is my brother Raistlin. Maybe you've heard of us? We used to live in Solace, but we left about five years ago to—"

"Caramon!"

The mage spoke his rebuke in a soft, whispering voice, but it had the effect of immediately silencing the warrior. Theros tried to get a look at the mage's face, but the man kept his red hood pulled low over his head. The hand that held the staff was thin and the skin, in the firelight, glistened a peculiar color, had a metallic cast to it.

"Uh, yeah, sure, Raist," the big man mumbled.

He held a long sword in his hands, still in the scabbard. The loop that attached the scabbard to his belt had worn off. When he drew out the blade, Theros saw that it had broken near the middle.

"It's served me well for years," the warrior said, "but an ogre proved too much for it. Creature had an iron ring around its neck."

Theros eyed the weapon. "You want a new blade, I take it. Do you want that scabbard repaired, as well?"

Caramon handed over the sword and scabbard to Theros. The leather had rotted and ripped. Theros examined the sword carefully.

"Very fine workmanship on the hilt," Theros said. "But it's already had one new blade and whoever made that wasn't the same person who made the original sword. Want to sell it? Or maybe trade it for one of these new ones over here?"

Theros was always looking for a bargain. He could easily repair and sell a weapon of this quality in Solace. The town was full of soldiers, mercenaries and hobgoblins.

"No, I wouldn't sell that sword if I was down to my last

steel coin," said Caramon, regarding it fondly. "This sword has kept me alive for five years. All I want is a scabbard and a new blade. What will it cost me?" The warrior sounded somewhat anxious.

Theros cast a glance at the man's well-worn clothing and the lean money pouch hanging from the belt. He was about to name his price, when suddenly the mage began to cough. It wasn't the cough of a winter chill. It was a hacking cough that nearly doubled the young man over.

"What's the matter with him?" Theros asked, nodding in the direction of the mage.

The big man looked worriedly at his brother. "You all right, Raist?"

"No, I am not all right, Caramon!" The mage spoke the words in gasps. "This air is poison! I'll . . . wait for you outside! Be as quick as you can."

Leaning heavily on his staff, the mage left the forge, went back out into the fresh air. He seemed to take a shadow with him. Theros wasn't sorry to see him go.

Theros studied the leatherwork. "I can make you a leather scabbard for two steel pieces, or a metal one for ten. The blade will cost you twenty-five."

Caramon was aghast. "Why so much for such simple work?"

"My scabbards don't fall apart, and my blades don't fall apart, like these." Theros held up the broken weapon and the torn scabbard.

Caramon frowned, then thrust his hand into his money pouch. He pulled out twenty steel. "Here, this is for the blade and the leather scabbard. The rest when you finish."

Outside, his brother could be heard having another coughing fit. Caramon, looking concerned, was about to hurry out.

Theros shouted after him, "Hey! What he's got—it's not catching, is it?"

"No, no, nothing like that," Caramon said hurriedly.

Theros nodded. "Come back this afternoon! Alone," he added.

Caramon nodded and dashed out the door.

After his customer left, Theros went back to his work. He

was forging a number of swords, twenty in all. They were huge blades, made according to a strange design insisted on by one of the Seekers—Hederick, the High Theocrat. He had wanted them finished in less than a week. Theros worked the steel quickly and efficiently, crafting the weapons according to the specifications. He would need more steel, though, to complete the job. In the meantime, he repaired the warrior's sword with a new blade and drew out a suitable leather scabbard from his back stock.

Later that afternoon, Theros climbed the stairs up the largest of the enormous vallenwood trees, heading for the Temple of the True Seeker. The temple was actually one of Solace's finer houses, donated to the cause by someone hoping for a blessing in the afterlife. Theros admired the house, which extended upward into the branches of the tree. It reminded him of the houses in which the elves had lived in Quivernost. Theirs weren't as fine as this, of course, but the architecture was the same delicate handiwork.

Theros knocked on the door. A servant popped his head out, took note of Theros—still dressed in his grimy leather apron—and told him to wait.

"Outside," added the servant, with a scathing glance at the smith's dirty boots.

Theros, grinning to himself, sat down on a bench built into the walkway between two vallenwood branches.

Before long, the door opened and the servant showed Theros into the antechamber, then into a room just off of it on the lower floor. There, a man sat at a desk. Theros recognized the man as Hederick, the High Theocrat. Obviously annoyed at being interrupted, he barely glanced up. He was flanked by two Seeker guards, who looked extremely bored.

"What do you want?" the High Theocrat snapped.

"Sir, my name is Theros Ironfeld. I'm the weaponssmith, come to report on the order that you gave me two days ago for swords."

Hederick was a gaunt, middle-aged man. The flush on his cheeks and his nose indicated that he enjoyed his ale, perhaps a bit too much. Theros was much more interested in the desk than the man. Although Theros didn't work with wood, he could recognize expert craftsmanship when he saw it, and this desk was one of the finest pieces he'd ever seen. It was a beautifully inlaid vallenwood desk that appeared to have been formed out of the living tree.

Hederick was responsible for the souls of the people of Solace, or so he said. In fact, through religious fervor and his troops of bullying guards, he had secured a near-dictatorship over the entire population.

The High Theocrat was a high-ranking member of the Seekers—the clerics who claimed that they were the only ones of their kind left on Krynn. The "new gods," as Hederick called them, had placed him in this position and he was to educate the populace of Solace in the true ways. As far as Theros could tell, the Seekers were more interested in money than souls and the only true way appeared to be through Hederick's purse.

"Yes, yes, I recall." Hederick looked up with more interest. "How are the swords coming? Are they ready yet?"

Theros hid a smile. Twenty swords in two days! It was obvious the High Theocrat had no idea of the difficulty of the work involved in making weapons.

"No, sir, they are not ready yet. Further, I need more steel. I have enough for only fifteen of the twenty blades. I will have to wait until my next shipment comes in from Thorbardin—"

"Nonsense!" the High Theocrat interrupted. "We shall get you what you need immediately. Guard, tell your commander to convey a shipment of steel to Mister Ironfeld's forgery—"

"Smithy, sir," Theros corrected. "I'm not in the business of making counterfeit money."

Hederick didn't get the joke. "Yes, yes," he snapped. "Steel to Mister Ironfeld's smithy by tomorrow."

The guard appeared baffled. "Where are we to obtain the steel, sir?"

Hederick glared at the man. "There is, as I recall, a shipment bound for Thorbardin. Confiscate it."

"The dwarves won't be happy about that, my lord," said the guard dubiously.

"It is not my life's work to make dwarves happy!" Hederick roared. "Tell them it is the will of the Seekers and the new gods!"

The guard left to carry out his orders. Another took his place in the office.

"Thank you, sir. If I get the required steel by tomorrow, I will have the weapons ready in time. A good day to you, sir." Theros bowed. Two more guards escorted him out.

According to Hederick, the High Theocrat was a position of spiritual leadership within the community. In fact, he was a bureaucrat with power, and the will to use it for his own personal gain. He ruled Solace with a mailed fist, his hobgoblins keeping the townsfolk in line, and the mercenaries under his command keeping the peace according to Hederick's rules.

The weapons that Theros was making weren't going to be used to protect the people of Solace. They weren't meant for the Seeker guard. No humans and few hobgoblins could effectively wield a weapon of the size called for by the specifications. The only soldiers whose strength and sheer size allowed them to wield such weapons were those in the armies of the Supreme Circle of the Minotaurs. However, minotaur warriors usually preferred axes. So who could be needing such weapons, and why this far south?

Ogres, maybe, but Theros doubted the swords were meant for ogres. The hilts of the weapons were specifically designed to be used by someone—or some *thing*—with a clawed hand. Claws, not fingers.

Hederick was selling these weapons for a profit, a personal profit. The temple would see little of the money. No one would question the matter. No one dared. Several people who had been foolish enough to defy Hederick were either languishing in prison or had simply disappeared.

Bad times were coming for Solace. Theros could feel the tension mount in the town from day to day. It was the same sort of atmosphere that he remembered from living in Sanction and near Neraka. There was a taint of evil in the air, like smoke drifting in from a nearby fire.

War was coming, though the people of Solace were

doing their best to try to deny it. Theros was engaged in his own personal, internal struggle. War would catch up with him again; there was no place he could go to avoid it. Already, he'd been discreetly approached by the emissaries of the Dragon Highlord Verminaard. Theros's reputation as a fine weapons-smith had spread far. Theros had turned them down flat.

He wondered at himself, wondered at his reasons.

Theros was familiar with evil. He had served in armies led by evil commanders, and lived in places that were sink-holes of evil. Still, he could not reconcile evil with honor, the guiding principle of his life.

And what was the nature of evil? Theros had often asked himself that question. He had finally decided that, for himself, evil was denying the rights of other people. It was the determination that what you believed was right and that everyone else was wrong. And because they were wrong, they no longer mattered.

The minotaurs had raised Theros to believe that because he was human, he was inferior. He had even come to think that himself. Now that he was older, he realized that he had truly admired minotaurs like Hran and Huluk because they made him feel that he had worth. They made him feel almost equal.

Almost. And then only because Theros had gone out of his way to prove himself to them.

Now the minotaur army was on the march again, delighting in conquering, enslaving, subjugating. Sargas wanted Theros to be a part of this evil army. But Sargas also demanded that Theros be honorable. How could one maintain honor by denying another the right to live in freedom? The minotaurs did not seem to have any problem with this dichotomy, but Theros did.

Theros wished he could find someone to advise him on this. Someone to share his doubts and feelings with. But no one in Solace knew of Sargas, the minotaur god, or of any other of the "old" gods, for that matter. According to the High Theocrat, the old gods had abandoned the people at the time of the Cataclysm, some three hundred or more years ago. Now new gods ruled Krynn, gods who didn't appear to have much interest in good, evil or honor. All these new gods seemed to care about was money.

Theros couldn't see how a money-grubbing bureaucrat would know anything about gods. Then again, how would a weapons-smith know anything more? Sargas had come to Theros twice. The second time—when Theros had just left the army of Baron Dargon Moorgoth—was when Theros first began to have doubts. Sargas may have been a god of honor, but he was also a god of vengeance, retribution, and cruelty.

Since seeing Sargas last, Theros had decided to go his own way. He did not abandon his faith. He did not believe in these "new" gods. He still believed in Sargas, but he no longer prayed to Sargas for assistance. And Theros dreaded the day he had to face Sargas again.

He walked back to his shop, taking the overhead walkways. When he could look down upon the smithy, he climbed down the spiraling staircase to the ground. He was headed over to his smithy, when, out of the corner of his eye, he caught movement in the underbrush near several outlying trees. Odd. People in Solace didn't usually spend time on the ground if they could help it. He stopped and looked, thinking perhaps it was children, who sometimes liked to hang about the forge. Theros didn't like having children around. The forge was a dangerous place and he was always afraid one of them would get burned.

He peered intently into the trees, saw nothing.

He entered the forge to find that he had customers. A hobgoblin was stomping about impatiently, waiting for Theros to return. It was truly a bother not having an assistant to deal with such matters. Theros had come to know himself, however. He knew that he didn't have the patience needed to train an apprentice. He would always feel guilty for the way he had abused Yuri first in Sanction and then in the army of Dargon Moorgoth. Theros's temper ran away with him when he tried to work with someone else in his smithy. He could not give up the control that he needed to trust and work with an assistant. The bother of not having an assistant was the price he had to pay for remaining in control. It was a compromise that he could live with.

"Ironfeld!" The hobgoblin snarled. "I wait an hour. Where the devil—"

"Just a minute, please," Theros said curtly.

Pushing past the outraged hobgoblin, Theros went through the forge and back into the storage room. There he had a window that looked out over the forest—right where he had seen movement. Theros carefully cracked the shutter and stared out. He waited. Nothing.

The hobgoblin shouted for Theros to hurry. "I want my dagger sharpened. This blade is dull! Hurry up!"

"You'll wait as long as I want you to wait, or you can come and wrestle me if you like," Theros shouted back.

The hobgoblin fell into a seething silence. Theros, with his massive chest and muscles well toned from use, could easily best a flabby hobgoblin.

Theros kept watching out the window. Suddenly, he spied the movement again. An elf stood up from a crouching position and glided silently back into the woods. The elf appeared to have been keeping a watch on the forge.

"Elves? In Solace?" Theros muttered to himself.

He thought they had all evacuated to Qualimori on Southern Ergoth.

Very curious. Very curious, indeed.

He went back to his customer. "Now, about that dagger . . ."

Chapter 31

Curious doings were the theme of the week, it seemed. First, there was the order for the odd weapons that Theros had accepted from the High Theocrat. Second was the sighting of an elf near Solace, an elf keeping watch on Theros's forge. And the third curious event was yet to come.

For the time being, Theros had his hands full of hobgoblins. Not for the first time, he wondered who had let these creatures into Solace.

First had been the hobgoblin with the dagger. A few swipes on the sharpening stone had honed the weapon. Theros had been about to tell the creature it could sharpen the weapon itself, when he realized that it probably had been the hobgoblin's attempt at sharpening that had dulled the blade.

Next came five hobgoblins hauling with them two large blocks of steel. Theros pointed to the corner of the shop. The hobgoblins shuffled under the strain, then dumped the steel in the area indicated. They just missed dropping the steel on their feet, but only because their commander, a hobgoblin named Glor, reminded them to watch their toes.

"So where did you get this from?" Theros asked.

"Bunch of dwarves. They not like it when we take, but High Theocrat order us to bring it to you. He say that you need it. Now you can finish job. Hey, you make me new sword now?"

The hobgoblin held up a sword. It looked like a dagger in the hobgoblin's huge hand. Theros took the weapon, a finely crafted piece, and studied it. It was of dwarven make. He carried it with him into the storeroom in the back. He pulled out a long sword that had been made to order, but never claimed. The sword was a good one, but the dwarven-made weapon was a masterpiece. It was easily worth double the long sword.

Theros returned, carrying the long sword.

"Here, Glor, take this one in trade for the other."

Glor looked at the blade with awe. He had never owned anything like this in his whole life. He had stolen most of what he possessed, but Theros guessed that the hobgoblin wasn't the most successful of thieves. Glor nodded and babbled his thanks. Then he shooed out his four helpers, following them into the sunshine.

Theros turned back to his work. He felt guilty using the steel, but if he refused, Hederick would send his henchmen over to "convince" Theros that this was the wish of the new gods. Theros didn't want trouble. He determined that, as soon as he was finished, he'd track the dwarves down and at least pay them for their loss.

He placed a large melting pot on the forge, placed one of the new steel blocks inside it. He began melting the steel, and poured it into prepared molds for the swords.

Hours later, the blades were cool enough and solid enough to be knocked from their molds. Wearing thick leather gloves, wielding a mallet, he broke the steel from the wood. He plunged the steel into the water barrel that stood near the forge. Steam rose from the water as the liquid absorbed the heat. As it turned out, he wouldn't need that other block of steel.

"Maybe I can return that to the dwarves," he said to himself. He went over to the corner, bent down to retrieve the excess block of steel. Happening to glance out the window, he stood up straight at the sight of something curious.

Two barbarians, a man and a woman—humans known as Plainspeople—were walking along the ground beneath the vallenwood trees. Accompanying them was a knight in full armor. Theros stared. He'd heard of the Plainspeople, but he'd never in his life seen them. They kept to themselves, distrusting strangers, and he had never heard of them leaving their own lands. The male barbarian was exceedingly tall; he could have looked eye to eye with a minotaur. The woman was difficult to make out, for she was heavily bundled in a fur cape.

Theros's gaze passed over the barbarians. After his initial astonishment, he was far more interested—from a professional viewpoint—in the knight.

The armor he wore was extremely well made, but very old-fashioned in design and workmanship. Theros almost wept with pleasure at seeing such fine work, and his hands itched to hold the marvelous sword the knight wore proudly at his side. The armor marked the man as a Solamnic Knight, but he wore no surcoat denoting his order.

Theros was suddenly taken back through the years to the night he had met Sir Richard Strongmail, the same night that honorable man had died from torture at the hands of Dargon Moorgoth's soldiers. It was the last time that Theros had encountered a Knight of Solamnia. The knights were not welcome in Solace. According to the High Theocrat, the knights were a contributing cause to the Cataclysm and had personally destroyed the ancient holy empire of Istar.

And so this young man was a mystery. He wore armor nearly as old as the Cataclysm, or older, as far as Theros could tell. The sword handle was indicative of an ancient blade, too. Yet the man wore no badge of a liege lord. He was definitely a Solamnic, though. Theros could tell by the long mustache.

The Knights of Solamnia prided themselves on their mustaches, much as a minotaur prided himself on his horns. This young man's long mustache flowed over a stern and serious mouth, the sort that seemed to have smiled rarely in its entire existence.

What was a knight doing in Solace? And why was he in the company of two barbarians? And was there a possibility that he would be interested in selling his sword and armor? Theros decided that he would buy those pieces if it took every last steel coin in his possession.

He considered calling out to the knight through the window, but was afraid that the noise might draw unwanted attention, both to himself and to the knight. Better to have their conversation in some private place.

He decided to follow them. He shut up his shop, walked out into the roadway and followed the three up the steps leading to the walkways on the upper level. It seemed as if the knight knew the town of Solace well. He did not hesitate or pause to ask directions, but knew exactly where he was going.

The three moved north, then east, along the walkways, finally turning off on one which Theros knew well. It led to the Inn of the Last Home. Theros ate and drank there often. The innkeeper, Otik, made the best spiced potatoes Theros had ever eaten, and the ale—which he had first tasted in Quivernost—was the best in Ansalon. Besides, there was a red-headed girl there named Tika, who was every bit as pretty as Marissa.

The knight and two barbarians entered the inn. Theros hesitated. This wasn't exactly the place he'd had in mind for a private talk, but perhaps this was better. Theros entered the common room. He was walking toward the back, when a yell and a screech stopped him in his tracks.

"My hat! You've stepped on my hat!"

Theros turned. An old man dressed in shabby, mouse-colored robes was quivering all over with rage, pointing a trembling finger at Theros's feet.

Theros looked down to find that he was standing on a

gray hat, which, by the looks of it, had been stood on, stomped on, trampled and generally mistreated many times before.

Bending down, Theros picked up the hat and made an attempt to return it to a semblance of its original shape. As this appeared impossible, he set the hat on the table.

"Excuse me, sir. I didn't see your hat."

"My hat!" The old man clutched it to his chest. Then, looking up at Theros, the old man winked. "You'll be seeing a lot more interesting things tonight. Much more interesting than my hat!"

A loony, thought Theros, then headed for his usual table. He wasn't surprised. The day had been filled with such fools.

He sat down at his usual table, but shook his head when Tika looked his way. He couldn't stay long. He would have to get back to those swords for the Theocrat. He watched, hoping to have a chance to catch the knight alone. The knight and the barbarians had parted company. The barbarians sat alone, apart from the others. The knight was receiving a warm welcome from several other new faces in the tavern, one of which was a kender. Alarmed, Theros checked his purse.

"Good, still there," he said to himself.

Theros was interested to see that the big warrior who had ordered the new blade put on his sword was one of this group, as was the red-robed mage. A dwarf quaffed ale and argued with the kender. Near the dwarf sat a half-elf, who was obviously trying to hide his elven heritage by wearing a beard. Theros had lived among the elves long enough to recognize the traits.

They were laughing and talking together warmly, with the exception of the red-robed mage, whom everyone else in the group seemed to avoid. Still, even he was part of the circle of friendship that seemed to surround these men like the bright glow of the fire.

Theros, watching them, felt suddenly very much alone. He had never, in his life, had friends like that. Friends who, he felt, would be willing to lay down their lives for each other. He wanted very much to meet these men, to get to know them better, but he felt that his presence would be an intrusion.

It was time to get back to work. He'd be working late tonight getting those weapons finished.

Theros stood and made his way to the door. As he walked past the group, he tried to listen in on what they were saying. He wasn't the only person eavesdropping. The old man in the mouse-colored robes seemed to have a similar interest in the group, judging by the fact that he was leaning so far out of his chair to hear that it was a wonder he didn't tumble out of it. His hat was, once again, on the floor.

The half-elf was speaking.

". . . good to see you again, old friend. Any word of your father's inheritance?"

Theros didn't hear the knight's answer, although he had some idea now as to the nature of the sword and armor. He doubted now if the knight would want to sell. Theros paused on his way out and retrieved the old man's hat.

"Here, Father. Someone's liable to step on it again."

"Eh? Oh, thank you, my boy. Say, could you do me one small favor?"

"What is it, Father?" Theros asked, thinking that he was going to be conned into buying the old man a mug of ale.

"Just pop down to Hederick's office, will you? Tell him that he should come see who's at the inn tonight." The old man nodded toward the group of friends.

"Why should I do that?" Theros asked, astonished and displeased. "I'm no tell-tale."

"Why in Sargas's name should you?" asked the old man jovially, and he prodded Theros with a long, pointed finger. "Because if you do, you may get your wish. Just see to it, will you? There's a good boy."

Theros, grunting, pushed open the door and left.

He headed down the walkway, intending to go back to his forge. But then he heard the old man's voice.

Why in Sargas's name should you? Sargas! Was this a messenger from Sargas? Impossible! The minotaur god was not likely to use decrepit old humans in his service. But then, why had the old man mentioned Sargas? How could he know of a minotaur god? And what wish was he talking about?

It was all very confusing. Theros found himself stepping onto a crossing walkway that led to the High Theocrat's office. He knocked on the door. This time, the servant immediately let him in.

The guard jumped to attention, but the High Theocrat waved him to sit down. "Relax, Sergeant. This is Theros Ironfeld, our smith and a well-known weapons-maker in Solace. To what do I owe this second visit today? Have you finished the swords?"

"They will be ready by tomorrow night." Theros tried to focus his thoughts, which seemed as shapeless as the old man's hat. He opened his mouth, but at the last moment, he couldn't bring himself to say anything about the knight or his friends. To do so would be to perhaps get them into trouble and that would be most dishonorable. "That's . . . all I wanted."

Theros mumbled and was on his way out when a guard burst in, nearly knocked the smith to the ground.

"Theocrat, there is a strange group of travelers in the Inn of the Last Home! One of them is a Solamnic Knight!"

Theros paused to hear the response. The bureaucrat nearly toppled over backward in his chair. "What did you say? A Solamnic Knight, here, in Solace? It is they that caused the anger of the gods, and now they suffer the wrath of civilized peoples throughout Ansalon. I cannot abide this! Not only that, but Lord Verminaard has also offered a reward for knowledge of the whereabouts of any Solamnic Knight."

The High Theocrat started for the door. The guard started to go with him.

"No," Hederick said. "We can't go charging in there. They may be armed. I don't want any trouble. I'll observe them and listen to their talk. When they're good and drunk, you come in and arrest them."

The High Theocrat hastened down the walkway toward the Inn of the Last Home. Theros, pondering all the strange things that had happened to him on this day, took his time walking back to his smithy.

He went to work on his mysterious blades. The raw steel

was now crudely shaped, but the process of heating and hammering to put a fine edge on the blades was a slow one.

He lifted the first blade, and to hold it still, he thrust it into the grillwork that covered half the forge. Next, he began to pump the leather bellows at the end of the forge, heating up the coals. Soon, the blade was hot enough to work. Theros took the blade out of the fire and began hammering it on the anvil.

He closed the forge so that he could work undisturbed. The town was quiet after sundown. Most of the townsfolk had gone home or over to Otik's inn for ale and food. Even at some distance from the inn, Theros could hear the sounds of merriment whenever he paused in his hammering.

He continued for another hour, finishing the shaping and hardening of the blade's metal. He let the fire die down and decided to call it a night. Closing up the shop's shutters, he locked the front door on the way out.

Suddenly, a dreadful scream came from the direction of the Inn of the Last Home. Theros's heart lurched. He'd heard that kind of scream before. It had been wrenched from the knights tortured by Uwel Lors. Theros ran to see what was going on.

He was on the ground level, and it took him several minutes to reach the base of the stairs at the inn. Above him, a commotion was in progress. People were yelling and shouting. A screeching voice—it sounded like the old man in the mouse-colored robes—shouted for the town guard.

Theros looked around to see a startled hobgoblin turn and run back in that direction, fumbling for his sword. Patrons started streaming out of the inn, running across the walkways.

Theros moved aside as several people tumbled down the stairs, trying to get away. They wanted no part of the town guard.

"What happened?" Theros asked.

"The High Theocrat!" a woman answered, gasping. "They're attacking the High Theocrat!"

Theros looked up to see Hederick come stumbling out of the door. He was clutching a wounded hand and babbling about blasphemers and witches. The High Theocrat stumbled down the walkway toward his office and home.

Twenty or so hobgoblins poured out of the guardsmen's hut, all running toward the inn. They were joined by the Seeker guards. All had their weapons drawn.

Theros circled around the base of the huge vallenwood tree to give the soldiers enough room to maneuver. The last thing he wanted was to be accidentally skewered by a battle-lusting hobgoblin. He made his way around to the back, below the kitchen.

It was then that he saw the strangers. The town guard was coming in the front of the inn. The same group of friends he had seen earlier in the day were making their escape out through the kitchen. Theros, standing in the shadows, watched them.

The barmaid, Tika, was showing them how to lower themselves down by a rope normally used to haul up huge casks of ale. The friends were all together, and accompanying them were the two barbarians. They took the same route, with the exception of the mage, who floated down as light as a feather.

Theros shivered and shook his head. "Mages," he muttered with distaste.

The knight and the half-elf were the last to descend. The knight seemed displeased by the idea of running from trouble instead of confronting it. The half-elf was endeavoring to explain that they were outnumbered and that there was a lady to protect.

Curious indeed, Theros thought as he watched from below. They must be the ones who attacked Hederick.

Theros considered shouting out, alerting the guards to their presence, turning them in. The guards were nearby. One shout and they could be here within moments.

Theros kept silent. He watched the friends disappear into the night, and in his heart, he wished them well. After all, he had run away from trouble in his own time, and no one had turned him in.

He remained in the shadows, pondering. It had indeed been a curious day.

Chapter 32

Theros waited a long time in the shadows beneath the kitchen, long after the strangers had fled, thinking about them and wondering why he felt as if they had brushed their fingers across his soul. He came up with no good answer, and, at length, he shook off his preoccupation, told himself it was all nonsense, and marched back to his smithy. He could tell, by the way the hobgoblins and human guards were running about in every direction—jumping into bushes and sprinting up and down staircases—that the group had made good its escape.

Theros returned to his smithy and was making certain that all was well for the night, when the hobgoblin Glor came dashing up and poked his ugly head in the window.

"Master Ironfeld. You see strange people? They hide in your shop?"

Theros suppressed his smile. "No, Glor, there's no one hiding in my shop. Come in and look around if you like."

"Oh, thank you, Master Ironfeld. I have to. Boss says so."

The hobgoblin looked around the forge, pointedly avoiding dark corners, trapdoors and large barrels—any place where someone might actually hide. The hobgoblin wasn't looking for a fight, especially with a Solamnic Knight, who—so Glor maintained—was as tall as a minotaur, with a sword the size of a vallenwood.

Theros didn't want a fight, either, with the knight or anyone else. His fighting days were over. He had become older and wiser, or so he told himself. No need to go looking for glory when there was plenty of money to be made in the honest trade of weapons and armor.

It was known far and wide that if a person wanted a special piece, be it weapon or armor, said person went to Theros Ironfeld. He kept requests confidential, and produced on time and according to specification. With the presence of strange armies up north and rumors—or facts—of war, the demand for weapons was the highest it had been in years. Unfortunately for the citizenry, but fortunately for Theros, it was clear he would have plenty of work for a long time.

He covered the firepit, letting the coals slowly cool and the smoke curl up the chimney, then walked back behind the shop to the large trunk of the vallenwood tree that served as his home. He lived in the lower trunk, completely carved out to provide a living area and small kitchen. He couldn't explain it, but unlike everyone else in Solace, he never felt secure sleeping in the tops of trees.

Theros lived alone. Some nights he thought of Marissa, the woman he had met in Sanction those many years ago. He had never found another woman that was her equal, though it was not as if he had tried very hard. It seemed that he was not destined to find a perfect mate.

"Once I am wealthy," he told himself, "I will have my pick of women, to be sure. They will fall all over themselves to have me court them.

"Oh, who am I kidding? Women would just get in the way of my work. It is a patient woman, indeed, who could put up with the dirt and smell and soot and rough, calloused hands of a weapons-smith."

He entered his home. It was dark inside. Leaving the door open to let in the lambent light, he groped about, looking for a candle. A noise behind him caught his attention.

He turned to see a group of people glide past him in the darkness. The people did not see him. He moved silently to the door to watch their passage. They were heading out of town, traveling north.

He recognized them easily. The half-elf and the knight led the way. None of them made a sound except for an occasional smothered giggle that could have come only from the kender; he was immediately shushed by the gruff scoldings of the dwarf. All in all, they were the most peculiar band of fugitives from justice Theros had ever seen.

And once again, as they passed, unaware of his existence, they touched him.

* * * * *

Early the next day, after a night of fitful and not particularly restful sleep, Theros paid a visit to the High Theocrat's office. He banged on the door, but there was no reply. He put his ear to the door and listened. Sure enough, he heard voices inside. He banged again.

The door opened. The captain of the guard, a warrior in black leather armor, glared at him. "What do you want?"

"I will have the swords ready soon," Theros said in a tone that indicated he was angry at being kept waiting. "Where do I have them delivered?"

That was just an excuse. In reality, Theros was consumed with curiosity to know what had happened at the inn last night. Peering over the guard's head, which was easy for a man of Theros's height, he could see the High Theocrat sitting in a chair, propped up by pillows and cushions. He looked as pale as a ghoul and he was nursing an arm swathed in bandages.

"I'm sorry, Captain. I didn't realize. Is the High Theocrat all right?" Theros asked. "Is he injured?"

The captain nodded. "He was assaulted by a band of criminals last night in the Inn of the Last Home. Do you know anything about—"

"Is that Ironfeld?" yelled the High Theocrat from inside. "Bring him in, Captain."

Theros entered and couldn't help but stare at the bandaged hand of the High Theocrat. The bandage didn't quite cover the fingertips; they were blackish and swollen. "What happened, Your Holiness?" Theros asked.

"It was that damned barbarian woman and that blue cryshtal shtaff." Hederick was obviously using dwarven spirits as a painkiller, for his voice was slurred and his gaze unfocused. "Captain, you know that I have ishued ordersh to confishcate anyone with a blue cryshtal shtaff. With a shtaff of any short. Snort. Sort. How did thish woman shneak into town with it, Captain?" Hederick banged his good hand on the table. "Ansher me that!"

The captain looked long-suffering, as if he already had explained it fifty times and probably would be called upon to explain it fifty more. "When she and her companion and the Solamnic Knight were stopped on the road outside of Solace, the staff appeared to be nothing more than a plain wooden walking stick, High Theocrat. We still have a warrant for the arrest of any of the party you described. If they show themselves, they will answer to me, and then to you, High Theocrat."

Hederick grunted with displeasure. The soldier bowed his head in apologetic submission, all the while rolling his eyes when he thought the High Theocrat wasn't looking.

"What do you know of thish, Ironfeld?" Hederick demanded.

"I'm sorry, Your Holiness," Theros said, apologizing in his turn. "I know nothing at all. Did . . . did the staff cause that injury to your hand?"

"No!" Hederick drew himself up with pride. "I did that myshelf."

Theros stared. He knew a severe burn when he saw one—even the tips of one. It looked as if Hederick had stuck his hand into the white-hot coals of the forge.

"You . . . did that yourself, Your Holiness?"

"Yesh, but she made me!" Hederick was frothing at the mouth. "That witch!"

"I see," Theros said, though he didn't.

"All right, then, off you go!" Hederick scowled. "If you shee any of them, report to me. And don't dawdle over those shwords." Hederick reached out his good hand for the dwarven spirits.

The captain opened the door and ushered Theros out.

* * * * *

It was a week before the High Theocrat returned instructions to Theros on what to do with the swords.

Upon completion, Theros returned, once again, to the High Theocrat's office.

Hederick appeared to be feeling better, though his hand was still bandaged and would, Theros knew from experience, bear the scars of that encounter for life.

Theros said that the swords were ready for delivery, mentioned the agreed-upon price, and then couldn't help trying to satisfy his curiosity.

"Your Holiness, who are these weapons intended for? They are too unwieldy for your guards."

"These are official secrets," said Hederick, looking about to make certain that they weren't overheard. "I shouldn't be telling you, but . . ."

He was too self-important to keep anything to himself. He motioned Theros closer.

"You've heard of Lord Verminaard and his campaign against the god-cursed elves?"

"Yes," Theros said in a calm, even tone. "I heard that when he was finished with the elves he would move on to Solace."

"I am a personal friend of Lord Verminaard," Hederick claimed. "And he has told me several times that he will most certainly leave Solace in peace, under my expert care and guidance."

Theros certainly hoped this was true. "Are the swords

for the forces in the north or for Verminaard's troops? I ask because the weapons are so—"

The High Theocrat hushed him. "Quiet there, Master Ironfeld. As I said, these are official secrets. These weapons are going to the war effort. You need not worry about who they are for. That's a secret! All you need to know is that you have been paid and paid well for your time and effort."

To emphasize his words, the High Theocrat handed Theros a bulging felt bag.

"The little extra is for your fine work, Master Ironfeld."

Theros took the money, resisted the temptation to look in the bag. He trusted it contained good steel, not worthless copper or what was more commonly known as kender-coin. "Thank you, High Theocrat. I am most grateful for your patronage. And now, if you could tell me where you want these weapons delivered?"

Theros hoped to get a glimpse of the buyer.

The High Theocrat smiled sourly. "Glor will pick them up. Have them ready by noon sun, Master Ironfeld." He made a gesture. Theros was dismissed.

Returning to his shop, Theros began to crate up the weapons for transport. So these weapons were meant for Verminaard. Theros thought back to Gilthanas and Vermala and the other elves. Perhaps one of these very swords would be used to slay his friends. In effect, Theros might prove to be the death of those he had worked so hard to save.

Bah! That was ludicrous. Theros had done a job, nothing more. He had to earn a living. Gilthanas himself could not fault Theros for that.

But it would be easy to follow that imbecile Glor when he left town, Theros thought.

Realizing what he was plotting, Theros snorted. He was trying to recapture the excitement of youth! He had no real need to know anything about the new owners of the weapons he had just made, other than that they had paid the High Theocrat a large sum, and he himself had made a good salary.

"Silly, damned silly," he thought. "You'll get yourself

whacked over the head with a club if you're not careful, Theros Ironfeld." He firmly intended to remain in the forge.

* * * * *

Right on time, Glor came with the wagon. He and Theros loaded the three cases of swords onto the back of the flat wagon. Glor tied the crates down with ropes so that they would remain stable during the ride across the ruts and bumps of the road.

Glor mounted the wagon. The hobgoblin was in a good mood, happy that the troublemakers had vanished without a trace.

Theros waited until Glor had driven the horse and wagon a good hundred yards down the road, then started off on foot, following behind, keeping to the shadows of the trees on the side of the road.

As it was, Theros needn't have bothered to hide. Glor never once looked back. Theros followed the slow-moving wagon up the road and out of town, to where farmers' fields stretched out far into the distance.

Theros lost track of the wagon twice, as gentle, rolling hills obscured his line of sight. When he crested the second hill, he saw the wagon stopped at the bottom, off to the side of the road. He was so close that even a numbskull like Glor couldn't miss seeing him.

Theros ducked hastily into the brush. He flattened down on his belly and crawled forward to get a better look at Glor's customers. By the time he was near enough to see, the wagon was empty and Glor was starting to turn the empty horse and wagon around.

"Damn!" Theros muttered.

He had missed the transaction. Whoever had picked up those weapons must have disappeared into the woods. Once the wagon was turned, Glor stopped again, gathered up the three crates, now empty, and carried them back.

Still, Theros knew his suspicions had been correct. The crated weapons weren't going to be used for the war in the north. If they were, they would have been kept in their packing cases and shipped on ahead. No, the weapons had just been delivered for more urgent needs closer to home.

Theros remained hiding in the brush as Glor and the wagon passed by. Again Theros followed the hobgoblin, this time back into Solace. When Theros entered town, he climbed the stairs of the nearest tree and ran across the catwalks, heading for his smithy.

Glor had already pulled the wagon up in front of the shop. He went inside. A minute later, the hobgoblin came out, looking around and shouting for the smith. Theros descended the nearest tree.

"Over here, Glor! Are you looking for me?" Theros asked casually.

"Oh, yes, Master Ironfeld. I have wood boxes that swords come in. Where you want them?"

"Put them behind the shop, will you, Glor?" He tossed Glor a silver piece.

The hobgoblin caught it, grinned from hairy ear to hairy ear.

"Were your customers pleased with the swords?" Theros asked, fishing for information.

"Me don't know. They don't tell Glor. They think me slave. They say 'do this' and 'do that' and me supposed to hop. I go now. Drink and eat."

The hobgoblin left and Theros went back into his shop, not much wiser than when he'd started out. He was breathing heavily and sweating. Glor hadn't seemed to suspect anything, however.

"I'm out of shape," Theros muttered to himself. "Haven't been in the field toughening up like in the old days! And I made the mistake of letting that damned hobgoblin get too far ahead of me."

He caught himself smiling, though, and was forced to admit that he'd actually enjoyed his clandestine excursion. It took willpower to go back to his mundane business.

* * * * *

At sundown, Theros headed over to the Inn of the Last Home and ordered his usual—spiced potatoes and salt pork. The meal was a good one, and the ale up to its usual fine standards. The talk at the inn was the same as ever—rumors of war to the north. Some told tales of evil creatures, the likes of which had never been seen before on Krynn, swarming down on unsuspecting villagers. Others claimed their friends had family who knew others who had heard that dragons were attacking the North Keep.

Theros chuckled to himself. He had been up in that area with the armies of Dargon Moorgoth and with Clan Brekthrek. He had never seen a dragon, nor any other creature. He ate and drank in silence, listening to the talk that customers with common sense termed "kender tales."

Later in the evening, Theros paid his tab and went back to his forge to take a last look around before retiring for the night. Unlocking the door, he went inside, not bothering to light any of the lamps. He could see well enough by the glow of the coals in the firepit, the lights in the town square and the reflected light of the moons.

All seemed fine. He turned to leave and noticed that he had not locked the back shutters. He pulled in the shutters, and as he did so, he thought he heard a rustling sound back in the bushes where he had seen—or thought he had seen—an elf the week before.

Elf or hooligan, kender or hobgoblin, Theros didn't like the idea of anyone snooping around his forge and his stock of swords, daggers and finely tooled scabbards. He bolted the shutters and went back into the main room in the smithy. Finding his old leather webbing, he strapped it on. Theros went back to the display board, unclipped the massive battle-axe from the center of the wall, and slid it into the back holster.

By Sargas, he was going to find out what was going on!

Chapter 33

Theros moved silently out into the night. He skirted around the now-dark smithy and headed past his home built into the vallenwood tree. Crouching, he slid into the bushes, paused to listen.

Nothing. Theros moved deeper into the woods. He walked very slowly, placing the toe of his foot first, rolling gently onto the heel, making very little noise. He made his destination the trunk of an enormous vallenwood, black against the night.

He crept to the tree and halted. Putting his back to the trunk, he listened. He didn't hear anything at first, then slowly, over a period of minutes, he became aware that he could hear very faint high-pitched voices.

Elves. It had to be.

He endeavored to locate the direction of the voices. Once he did so, he moved on, as quietly as before.

Ahead, several bushes clumped together to form a large mass of shadows in the darkness. Theros went down on his hands and knees and began to crawl slowly forward through the intertwined branches and twigs. Every few feet, he stopped to listen, fearful that even the small amount of noise he was making would scare off the object of his attention.

Apparently, they hadn't heard. The talking continued. Theros spoke Qualinesti from his time with the elves, but through lack of use, he had forgotten much of it. He tried to make out the words.

It was definitely Qualinesti. Theros recognized specific words here and there. His time spent with the elves had taught him to listen for inflection more than word use.

He was slipping forward again, trying to get close enough to hear more, when a twig caught Theros full in the face, nearly poking out his eye. He caught his breath, bit his tongue to keep from cursing with the pain. Rubbing his watering eye, he kept silent and moved forward again.

He found himself in a small clearing, nestled in the foliage. The bushes had receded from around a once-proud vallenwood tree that had toppled many years earlier. The branches had been removed, used for everything from furniture to walking staves. Only the rotten trunk remained on the forest floor.

Theros stared ahead. The moons cast enough light through the high leaf cover to swathe the area with great shadows. He couldn't quite make out any distinct shapes, and the sounds had ceased. He grabbed his axe, placed it across his lap, and kept still.

At length, Theros found them. First he saw one elf, sitting cross-legged, with a bow across his thighs. He was looking around, as if searching for something. Then three more elves came into view, seeming to materialize out of the darkness.

The elves resumed talking. He thought he recognized the voice of one of them. He was straining to hear, straining to understand what they were saying, when something moved right behind him.

Someone else was watching the elves, it seemed.

Theros slid from behind one small tree to the next, and waited. He was as curious about another watcher as he was about the elves themselves.

Out of the bushes crawled a large humanoid form. The light of Lunitari shone on it clearly. Theros recoiled from the ghastly sight. He'd never seen anything so hideous. It was the size of a minotaur, but it had the head of a lizard. It wore leather armor and carried a large sword in its hand.

Not just any sword. It carried one of the swords that Theros had delivered that very day. Theros shuddered with the shock. He had been making weapons for monsters! The beast reeked of the Abyss.

The elves did not hear or see the lizard man crawling through the underbrush. Theros rose quietly to his knees, then carefully and slowly moved to a standing position. He took two steps forward, raising his battle-axe over his head. He no longer worried about keeping silent. The monster heard him and turned. Theros brought the axe down hard into the lizard man's back. The monster screeched in pain and fury.

The elves jumped to their feet, dropping their bows and drawing swords and daggers.

"Who goes there?" one elf shouted in Common.

Theros's axe killed the monster with one swing. The axe head remained embedded in the lizard man's back. Theros straightened and pulled on the axe to free it. To his surprise, his axe blade was stuck fast.

Alarmed, fearing more of the creatures might be around, he tugged and yanked on his axe. It wouldn't budge. Frustrated, he kicked at the monster's body lying on the forest floor. His foot hit solid rock.

The corpse had turned to stone!

"Damn!" he muttered. He looked up to find an elven blade pointed at his throat. For the moment, Theros didn't care about that. Impatiently, he shoved the sword blade to one side. He wasn't about to lose his battle-axe.

"I'm not your enemy," he said in Qualinesti, the words

coming back to him in a flood.

"Theros?" said the elf, staring at him in the moonlight. "Theros Ironfeld?"

"Gilthanas!" Theros was pleased to see his friend, but this wasn't exactly the time for a reunion. "What the devil is going on here? What is this thing?"

Lowering his sword, the elf looked down at the immobile form. "It is called a draconian. Its appearance here augurs impending doom. Careful!" Gilthanas was on guard, glancing around warily. "Where there is one, there are probably more."

"Great! Just great!" Theros grunted, frantically trying to pry his weapon free from the stone corpse. "Draconian? I've never heard of such a beast and I've done a fair share of traveling. And what are Qualinesti doing in Solace?"

"Look out!" one of elves yelled.

Another huge draconian leapt out of the shadows, cutting down the elf with a huge, jagged sword that was also of Theros's making. Two more loomed out of the night, and Theros could hear another crashing through the bushes.

He gave up trying to free his axe. Reaching down, he grabbed the large sword that lay next to the dead draconian. Another one of the elves was dead. Theros prepared to defend himself. Gilthanas stood at his back, slender elven sword raised to attack.

The other remaining elf spirited away into the bushes, sidestepping a draconian's savage blow. The draconian, having lost its prey, stood and gazed about. Reptile eyes glistened red in the moonlight. The lizard man was not more than ten feet to Theros's right. The other three were circling around him, trying to surround him and Gilthanas.

Theros lunged for the draconian on his right. The beast easily parried the blow, but that had just been a feint. Theros's arm muscles bulged with the effort of turning the draconian's enormous blade—a good blade, as Theros had cause to know.

As Theros struggled with the draconian, he saw, out of the corner of his eye, another leap out of the bushes. Theros shouted a warning, but it was too late. The draconian struck Gilthanas over the head with the flat of his sword. The elf crumpled like a sack of coal. Helpless to assist his friend, Theros watched in frustration as the draconian slung the elf's comatose body over its shoulder and made off.

Theros's sword slid up from the draconian's lower right side, catching the monster in the right hip. The wound bit deep into the scaled hide, but it didn't kill. Theros tried to see what was happening behind him, even as he kept close watch on his opponent, who was shouting at its comrades in a strange, guttural language.

Two of the draconians to Theros's rear dashed off, probably pursuing the elf who had managed to escape. That left the wounded draconian to his front and one more behind him. Theros skirted around the large beast in front of him, trying to position himself before both of the draconians. They saw what was happening, and the wounded draconian backed up to try to keep Theros between them.

To Theros's astonishment, the draconian spoke to him, in decent-sounding Common. "Surrender now, human, and you will be treated well as a prisoner of the Dark Queen."

"To the Abyss with you and your Queen," Theros said. He lunged at the wounded draconian, and at the same time, ducked his head low.

Sure enough, the draconian behind him had swung. The blade whistled past inches away from Theros's ears.

Theros's attack missed, but the draconian, in trying to avoid it, stumbled backward and fell. Theros spun around to face his other opponent. The draconian sidestepped Theros's attack. It swung its sword ineffectively.

Theros could sympathize. They were both using new swords, and neither was accustomed to the feel of them yet. But Theros was at the disadvantage. He was not used to fighting with a sword, had not fought anyone in a long time. The huge blade was not suited to his style, nor fit to his size.

The draconian kept pressing its advantage and pushed Theros back into the underbrush. Theros heard movement, remembered the other draconian, and turned too late. The swing came from his left. Theros ducked, diving into the bushes. The blade scraped his left arm, not a serious injury. He rolled to his side, then got up and ran.

He had never run from a fight before. He could almost

see Hran and Huluk—not to mention Sargas—glaring at him in disapproval. Theros didn't care. This was a time for human common sense, not minotaur notions of honor. Theros was outnumbered by foes twice his size. He had no decent weapon and was wounded. He had to escape, or he would die.

He sprinted through the trees, tripping several times, but clamoring to his feet in a hurry. He had the feeling that the draconians would not want to show themselves in Solace. Otherwise, they would have been in the town, not skulking about in the woods outside it.

Theros was right. As soon as the lights of Solace came into view, he heard the draconians that pursued him halt. Theros made it back into town and immediately climbed the first stairs he came to, and groped his way down the walkway to the center of town. Turning toward home, he descended the staircase to the ground level.

He kept looking behind him, but the draconians had not followed. Unlocking the door, he hurried inside. His hands shaking, he managed to light a candle and examine his wound. The blood flow had stopped, but it hurt like hell. Clumsily, he washed the wound out and bound it.

"Draconians!" he muttered to himself. "Where did such monsters spring from? And the elves—Gilthanas. What was Gilthanas doing in Solace?"

Questions flooded Theros's mind. He had no answers. He wondered if he shouldn't warn someone about the monsters lurking in the forest, and then he realized that there was no one to warn. The High Theocrat had sold Theros's swords to these monsters. He was in league with them, as were his Seeker guards and the hobgoblins.

Suddenly, a gust of wind blew in from the window, dousing Theros's candle. The wind was hot and unnatural and it raised the hair on his neck and arms. With the wind came darkness, such darkness as Theros had never before known. It was as if the moons and the stars had all been swept from the sky. A terrible rumbling began outside, to the north of the town. The rumbling shook the ground. If it was thunder, then this was going to be a storm like none Theros had ever witnessed.

He went to the window. An enormous fireball exploded, right before his eyes. A huge vallenwood tree in front of him burst into flame. He could hear the people in the houses in the tree's branches begin to scream in terror. What in the name of Sargas was going on?

He heard another explosion, and another.

Theros ran outside. In the north section of town, many buildings were on fire. People, panic-stricken, were leaping from the burning walkways. He could see them silhouetted against the flames, falling—sometimes to their deaths—below.

It was then that he first felt the fear. Terror like none he had known before washed over him, filling his veins with ice water. He began to shake. A roaring sound came from overhead. Barely able to move from fright, he lifted his head and looked up. Monstrous beasts flew through the night sky, belching fire and smoke from their gaping maws.

Dragons! He had heard the tales, even as far back as his childhood in the fishing village in Nordmaar. But these were not creatures of imagination. The dragons were here, and they were real.

Fires now burned everywhere. Through the flames, Theros saw an army entering the town, marching on the ground, moving in column formation. He stared in horror, recognizing the soldiers. The attacking forces were draconians. Hundreds of them were swarming into town, accompanied by humans dressed in maroon uniforms.

Draconians marched with the troops of Baron Dargon Moorgoth. It seemed that fate had caught up with Theros at last.

The fear known as dragon awe nearly drove Theros mad. With no clear idea of what he was doing or where he was going, he ran through the smoke and flames. Instinct, apparently, led him back to his forge. He was relieved to find that it was still standing. And then he saw the reason why. A squad of draconians and hobgoblins stood around it, guarding it. Of course! To the armies, the forge was the most valuable building in Solace.

Theros turned to escape, but it was too late. They'd seen him.

"That's him!" Glor screeched. "That's the smith!"

The draconians dashed out to capture him. Exhausted, his lungs burning from the smoke that clouded the air, he was an easy capture.

The attack on Solace ended as quickly as it had started. Most of the town was ablaze. Theros's smithy was left unscathed, but his home, not twenty yards away, burned like a torch in the night. Squads of draconians began going door to door, rounding up survivors and herding people off the streets and into the town square.

Theros remained inside his forge, a prisoner of the draconians, a blade of his own making held at his throat. A human officer marched in. He was wearing black leather armor adorned by a black helm and a black metal cuirass with a dragon insignia. Theros was thankful to see the uniform wasn't maroon.

"Put that dagger down," the officer ordered the draconian. He faced Theros. "You are the smith, Ironfeld?"

Theros nodded. "I am."

The officer appeared pleased. "Good! I am glad you survived the fire. You have been supplying quality blades to my soldiers. Fewmaster Toede, the new commander of the Solace Military District, wants you to continue. In return, your smithy has been spared destruction. Cooperate with us and you will be handsomely rewarded. Resist and you will be killed. Any questions?"

Theros couldn't think of any questions after that. Not with five draconians standing in his forge.

"I'll make weapons for you, but on one condition. Forget your money. People are wounded out there. I've some skill at healing from my days in the army. Let me aid those in need, and then I'll serve you."

The human officer grunted. "A foolish bargain, human. You could have made your fortune, grown wealthy enough to own this miserable town. Still, we're getting the best of it. Lord Toede is always pleased to save money. Go along with him," the officer ordered the draconians. "See to it that he doesn't try to escape."

Theros went out into the night to do what he could to aid the victims of the attack.

Chapter 34

Theros went out into a night he would never forget, a night of horror and terror, a night of pain and suffering. There were so many homeless, so many injured, so many dying, that he felt helpless to know where to begin. He stood in the bright light of the burning fires and stared, anger flaring in his heart hotter than the fiercest forge fire.

A soldier knows his duty before going into battle. A soldier knows the risks and makes his peace with them. Here were defenseless children, burned and bleeding. Here were new mothers, clutching dead babies to their breasts. Here were old men, driven from their dwellings. Here were shopkeepers, with lifetimes invested in their small holdings, whose fortunes had vanished in a whoosh of flame.

These people had done nothing and they were the victims. What kind of monster made war upon the innocent?

A Seeker guard—looking dazed and bewildered—told Theros that a command center, of sorts, had been established at the Inn of the Last Home. The inn had been lifted from its perch in the tree by the claws of a dragon and deposited on the ground. Men were busy shoring up sagging timbers, doing what they could to make the building stable, for it was the only place large enough to shelter the wounded. Theros went to find out who was in charge, to offer his help. The first person he saw was Hederick, the High Theocrat.

"Your Holiness!" Theros shouted. "We need guidance! Tell us what to do."

But Hederick, shocked at the treachery of those he had considered allies, sat mumbling to himself, tears streaming down his soot-stained face. Theros shook his head and was on his way to assist with the carpentry work, when the barmaid, Tika, grabbed hold of him.

She was frightened, but managing to remain calm in the midst of the turmoil around her. She was carrying a basin of bloodstained water, in which floated used bandages.

"They need men to fight the fires," she told Theros.

He wasted no words, but left immediately.

Many of the single dwellings in the mighty vallenwoods were burning. The people feared that the fires, unless contained, would consume the entire forest, and with it, all of Solace. Men and women formed bucket brigades, drawing water from the well near the Inn of the Last Home. Under Theros's direction, teams were formed to drive wagons to Crystalmir lake and bring water back in large barrels. Working through the long, exhausting, dreadful night, they at last brought the blazes under control.

The draconian soldiers, along with those wearing maroon coats and those in black armor, stood around and watched and laughed. It was all Theros could do to keep from wringing their necks.

A cry drew Theros's attention. A woman, standing in front of a burning dwelling perched high among the branches, was holding a baby in her arms. Citizens below had spread out a blanket like a safety net and were urging her to drop the baby and then to jump to escape the fire.

At that moment, a soldier in a maroon coat walked up, and with his sword, slit the blanket up the middle.

"Now jump, lady!" he called, laughing. He held his sword like a spit. "Or, better yet, throw me the baby!"

The soldier was Uwel, Moorgoth's whipcracker.

Theros experienced then what the minotaurs call battle-rage, the madness that overtakes warriors and leads them to fling themselves into danger without a thought for their own safety. Theros saw Uwel torturing the knights; he saw him now tormenting this poor mother. The other citizens were fearful, holding back, muttering to themselves. Unarmed, they could do nothing. The woman was weeping and pleading.

Theros stalked over. Grabbing Uwel by the shoulder, Theros doubled up his fist and slammed it into the man's head. In that blow, Theros expended all his pent-up fury and frustration, his anger like a mailed glove over his hand.

If Uwel Lors had a chance to think anything at all, in those last few moments of his life, it must have been that he was struck by a thunderbolt from the heavens. Theros felled the man in a single blow. His only regret was that Uwel didn't suffer as he had made others suffer. Theros hoped that some god saw to that matter in what the smith devoutly wished was a long and tormented afterlife.

Uwel was dead before he hit the ground. Theros stood, breathing heavily, looking down at the body.

"Quick!" someone said. "Before anyone finds him."

With great presence of mind, they flung the torn blanket over the body, and two men dragged it off into the woods. Others climbed the tree, rescued the mother and her child. Theros shook the pain from his hand and went back to work, a little glow of satisfaction replacing the searing anger.

No one ever found Uwel's body. The maroon-coated troops searched and searched, and at last concluded that he must have deserted. Baron Moorgoth, who was running his army from the safety of Pax Tharkas, was said to have publicly cursed Uwel's name and was offering a large reward for the man, either dead or alive.

As the sun came up, the last few fires were allowed to burn out. Everyone was weary almost past endurance. People slumped down on the ground, slept where they fell. After a few hours of sleep, they'd be awakened to form burial parties.

Only the inn, Theros's smithy, and a few other sites—those the attacking army thought might be useful—were spared from destruction.

His work finished, Theros returned to his smithy and collapsed upon a cot in the back room. His wound pained him, but it was nothing compared to the pain in his soul. He lay on the cot, too tired for sleep to come readily to his aching body, and tried to make sense of what had transpired.

Why had the dragons attacked the town? An army that large could have simply marched in and taken over. Why the need to commit such terrible slaughter? To wreak such havoc? Where was the honor in murdering children?

There was none. There could be no excuse. This was done for the delight of evil, nothing else.

That settled, he wondered what had happened to Gilthanas. Why were the elves in Solace? Was he being held prisoner or was he dead?

Still seeing the light of flames against his closed eyelids, Theros drifted off into a fitful sleep.

* * * * *

Three days later, most of the army had moved on, leaving behind those who would exert Verminaard's authority. Solace was starting, painfully, to rebuild. The wondrous trees were useless now, mostly burned-out husks. The walkways had all been destroyed, which didn't matter—there were few homes or businesses left. Soot and ash lay thick in the streets. The stench was terrible—it seemed to permeate everyone's clothes—and the food and drinking water tasted of smoke.

Using his last block of steel, Theros forged hundreds and hundreds of nails, hinges and tools. He gave these away, receiving some satisfaction from the fact that Hederick's stolen steel was now going to a good use. He kept a few swords lying about, which he grabbed whenever any of Verminaard's troops were near so he could pretend to be working on weapons. He guessed this wouldn't fool anyone for long. He was right.

The new "ruler" of Solace, a fat hobgoblin who was known by the grandiose title of Fewmaster Toede, came storming into Theros's smithy late one afternoon. Theros had been expecting this visit. He gazed with no friendly aspect on the hobgoblin, who was nowhere near as tall as Glor, but twice as wide. His self-importance was about three times wider than he was.

"Smith," said Toede, glancing balefully about the shop with little red, piggy eyes. "What are you doing, wasting your time on worthless stuff like this?" He held up a handful of half-made nails. "You were ordered to make and mend weapons for my troops. I realize that you're making a fine profit—"

"I am," Theros said coolly, with barely a glance at the little beast. "But not in money. I am sorry to disappoint you, Fewmaster, but the needs of the people in this town you just destroyed come first. Give me a week, then I'll get back to the business of making weapons and armor."

Armor that would mysteriously fall apart, swords that would shatter at the first blow. A smith knows how to do these things.

Toede snorted. "A week! You will start work now, this minute. You see"—he interrupted Theros's protest—"I know a little secret about you, Master Theros Ironfeld. I am told that you are an elf-lover. That you helped build the ships that took those slimy, pointy-eared demons out of the reach of our justice."

Toede puffed up, tapped himself on the chest. "I am, so far, the only person who knows about this crime. Make my weapons and I'll see to it that Lord Verminaard doesn't hear about it. If he does, you see, I'm afraid that not even the fact that you're a skilled weapons-maker would be enough to induce him to spare your miserable, elf-loving life."

Theros didn't have to take any time to think over Toede's proposition.

"You can tell your Lord Verminaard from me that he can go roast his feet in the Abyss for all I care."

"Come, you don't mean that, Master Ironfeld," the hobgoblin said. Toede became confidential. "Look, Ironfeld, your weapons would fetch me a great price on the open market. What is it you want? A cut of the take? Very well. I can be reasonable. Begin making my weapons by tomorrow, or your secret will no longer be a secret. I'll have you hauled to Pax Tharkas for what you've done. I'm sure Lord Verminaard would love to meet someone who aided the evacuation of the elves to Southern Ergoth."

Theros didn't bother to respond. He picked up a hammer, a large hammer, and began twirling it around and around.

Toede, glancing at the hammer, gulped and started to sidle out of the smithy.

"You just remember what I said, Theros Ironfeld!" the hobgoblin yelled, from a safe distance.

Theros went back to the work of making a large saw.

* * * * *

The next day dawned gray and gloomy. A chill, dank fog hung over the town. The day before, a caravan of cages on wagons had arrived in the town. Fewmaster Toede's soldiers herded men and women deemed to be a "threat" into the cages, to be taken to Pax Tharkas. More cages were waiting to be loaded today.

Theros rose from his temporary quarters in the back of the smithy, and dressed. He drew some water from his rain bucket and shaved, then went out to stoke up the forge.

An hour later, he had the steel hot enough to pour into the molds he used to make nails. He was just about to lift the cauldron when the door to the smithy swung open, and three draconians entered.

Theros had no fear of the slimy hobgoblins, but he couldn't help feeling a shiver in the presence of the lizard men.

The first draconian picked up one of the molds for making nails and threw it out the window. The second draconian picked up a hammer and knocked a hole in the wall. The third lifted a heap of nails and tossed them back into the melting pot.

So this was it. The day had come at last. The draconians continued wrecking his shop. Theros watched, seemingly too frightened to intervene or protest. His hand closed over the hilt of a sword he had concealed beneath his leather apron.

When the shop was in ruins, the draconians turned to Theros.

"You will come with us. You are under arrest for crimes against the Dragon Highlord Verminaard. You have been ordered to stand trial in Pax Tharkas by decree of Fewmaster Toede, commander of the Solace Military District."

Theros drew his sword with one hand, his throwing knife with the other. The draconians stared in amazement. Few in the town had dared resist them. They fumbled for their own swords.

Theros loosed his knife. It flipped end over end, and the blade bit deep into the first draconian's skull. The other two ducked out the open door. Theros, figuring that now he had nothing to lose, pursued them into the street. The fog swirled around them. Citizens scattered in alarm. Other draconians came running. All had their weapons drawn.

Four combatants circled Theros. One draconian suddenly vanished in the fog. Theros assumed that the monster was going to try to get behind him. Theros couldn't worry about that now. He concentrated his attention on the draconian nearest him.

Leaping to the attack, Theros swung his sword in a furious blow that would have swept the weapon from the hand of a human opponent. The draconian parried the blow easily. Theros advanced, swinging again, then feinted. He had managed to fool the draconian, who had left himself unguarded.

Before Theros could strike, the draconian he'd lost in the fog materialized behind him. The draconian swung his blade in an arc. The blade hacked into Theros's right arm, just below the shoulder. Theros's hand went numb and useless. Astonishingly, at first, he felt no pain. He looked over to see what was wrong with his arm and saw that it was hanging from the shoulder, connected only by several tendons.

The draconian swung again. Theros's arm fell off.

Theros stood and stared at his severed limb lying on the ground. And then blackness rolled in like the ocean waves and swallowed him. He felt no pain, but he could hear himself shouting, then screaming.

Then there was only silence.

* * * * *

Theros woke up to find himself lying on the ground beneath a dome of luminous, pale pearl gray. The ground was soft and perfectly smooth. He looked over and saw that his arm was missing, but he did not feel any pain, nor was he afraid.

He stood up and looked around. He could see nothing—nothing to define distance in any direction. The ground was gray. The dome above the ground was gray. The light came from the sky and the ground.

Theros looked over to where his right arm had been. The first thought that came to his mind was that he would never be a smith again.

I will be a cripple for the rest of my life, he thought.

It was only then that it occurred to him that there was no rest of his life. He was dead.

"Welcome to the Hall of the Gods, Theros Ironfeld."

Theros looked up to see Sargas, the minotaur god, materializing from the gray, looming up in front of him. He was surprised to hear Sargas speak aloud—previous words from the god had resounded only in his head.

Sargas was more magnificent, more enormous, than Theros remembered. In one hand, the minotaur god held the handle of a giant battle-axe; in the other, he cradled the axe head. The god appeared displeased.

"You have not fulfilled the promise I saw in you as a

child, Theros Ironfeld. You have, I must admit, lived by my code of honor. This does you honor, and it does me honor as your god.

"However, I am also the god of vengeance and retribution! You have not served me well. You are merciful, forgiving. You tend to run from a fight, rather than seek glory in battle. You show compassion instead of evincing the wrath of a true warrior of Sargas!"

Anger was building in Theros, anger similar to that which he had felt in striking down Uwel Lors.

"I never asked to be a follower of Sargas!" Theros shouted up into the gray dome. "You want me to be something I am not. It is not honorable to punish without cause. It is not honorable to show wrath where kindness is warranted. A Solamnic Knight called Sir Richard Strongmail showed me true honor, he showed me courage and compassion, and he showed me that true strength lies in decency. He is what I want to be like, not you!"

Sargas glared down at Theros, who could not help but tremble at the baleful stare.

"I should punish you for your disloyalty. However, I am a god of honor and I told you early in your life that you were a man of destiny.

"It is clear that I am no longer your god. You do not worship me. But you have kept faith in me all these years. You have, by your courage and honor, earned your place at the table of my warriors, Theros Ironfeld. I give you one more chance to pledge your allegiance to me."

Theros bowed his head. "I cannot, great Sargas. Forgive me."

The giant minotaur glowered. Then he said something astonishing. "I reward your faith, when other men might have abandoned it. I grant you the freedom to choose to follow a different god."

"Sargas, you confuse me. I thought that you were the one and only god," Theros said humbly.

Sargas smiled. "No, man of destiny. As I told you before, there are many gods. Just as I am the god of honor, there is a god of guile. Just as I am the god of evil, there is a god of good. And there are more. There are gods of creation, of destruction, of life and death. I will introduce them to you."

A circle of beings appeared, forming a ring around Theros. They all shone with an inner radiance, though sometimes that brilliance was cloaked with darkness. Each god seemed to take on different forms, even as Theros stared at them. One was a dwarf in fancy clothing, another a horrible skeleton, hideous to look upon. One was a fat merchant, another a gentle creature with eyes like a doe.

"We are the gods of Krynn. We control all aspects of life. Two of the gods are not present. Paladine seeks to defeat the Queen of Darkness in her attempt to return to the world from which she and her dragons were long ago banished. They have taken physical form and are manipulating events in the great conflict to come."

Sargas laughed. "As you may suspect, I am the Dark Queen's champion and ally."

Theros looked around at the circle of beings. Their power and majesty made it difficult for him to think. He wanted to do what was right, but he had no idea what that was.

"I will introduce to you the gods. I start with Gilean, God of Neutrality," Sargas said.

A man stepped forward. He carried a large book in which he constantly wrote. He lifted his eyes, gazed at Theros briefly, and returned to his work.

"This mortal knows his true nature," Gilean said. "You are right, Sargas. He must be free to choose."

Sargas introduced the rest of the pantheon of neutral gods: Sirrion, the god of flame; Chislev, the goddess of nature; Zivilyn, the god of wisdom; Shinare, the goddess of wealth and money; and Lunitari, the god of neutral magic. Every one of them had something to offer Theros, if he would choose to serve him.

But none of them felt right to Theros. He respected them and understood that each was important, but none embodied what was in his heart. They did not represent what he knew himself to be. These were not the gods he could follow.

Sargas did not appear surprised. The last of the neutral

gods he introduced was Reorx, the Forge.

"Reorx is the forger of creation and tools. I think you would be well suited to Reorx, Theros Ironfeld. You will become his follower."

Reorx, a powerful dwarf in shining gold armor, rubbed his beard and thoughtfully regarded the big man. The dwarf shook his head.

"No, this man is not for me. I appreciate a master of steel and a forger of weapons, but he will not be a worshiper of mine."

Sargas looked angry.

"He is my disciple, and until I release him, he goes where I send him."

Reorx shook his head. "No, Sargas, this human is not your disciple. Mark my words, Sargas. Do not attempt to interfere."

"He owes me his very life!" Sargas snarled. "He will obey me."

Reorx stood his ground.

"You must let him choose, and choose freely. He will anyway, regardless of what you try to do."

Sargas marched Theros around the circle, took him past the gods of evil. They offered Theros power, immortality, fabulous riches, dark magic. But they did not want mere worshipers. They wanted slaves.

Theros shook his head. One by one, the gods of neutrality and evil drifted into the gray, disappearing from sight.

Sargas introduced the remaining gods.

"This is Majere, the god of monks. Next to him is Kiri-Jolith, the god of warfare. He favors knights. Next, Habbakuk, the god of animals and the sea. Branchala is the god of music, and Solinari is the god of good magic."

Theros's gaze continued down the line. His heart felt rested, but still something about each was not quite right. Theros wanted nothing to do with magic, and he had little care or knowledge of animals. He continued looking until his eyes came to a woman who stood at the end of the line.

She was, at the same time, all women in his life, all women who had ever meant something to him. She was his loving mother. She was the charming Marissa. She was the courageous Telera. She was, strangely, the woman in the burning tree, clutching the baby. She was Tika, cool and calm in the midst of chaos. Theros felt drawn to this woman.

Sargas noticed his interest.

"This is Paladine's companion and adviser, Mishakal. She is the goddess of healing and light."

Theros began to cry. His lower lip quivered, his eyes filled with tears. He sank to his knees. He tried to cover his face with his hands, in spite of the fact that he had only one arm.

Mishakal stepped forward.

"He has made his choice now, Sargas. You have done well to teach him honor. Let him now rekindle that part of his soul he knew he had but could not develop."

Sargas bowed and disappeared into the gray.

Mishakal knelt down in front of Theros and took him into her arms. She let him cry, cradling him, letting his anger and sorrow and fear and pain flow into her. She absorbed them all, and washed them away with Theros's tears.

"Yes, Theros, your mother is a follower of mine. She rests in a very special place in my hall. She is to be honored for the work she did on the face of Krynn in her time, and for giving you the inner strength to pursue your own destiny."

Theros looked up through tear-flooded eyes at the radiant woman.

"Theros," she said softly, "do you have the will to live?"

His heart fluttered. Mishakal saw the spark of life within him, growing stronger by the moment.

"You must make the choice this day, Theros Ironfeld. You must choose what you will do. You may remain with me in my great hall and be with your mother. She sends her love and wants you to know that you have always been loved. She is proud of you.

"Or you can return to the world of the living. It will be difficult. You will go back to terrible pain, to the bitter knowledge that you are a cripple. You go back to a world torn apart by war. But you are a man of destiny, Theros, and you can make a difference there."

Theros felt Mishakal's peace soothe his heart and his soul. He made his choice.

* * * * *

Theros woke up to unbelievable pain and agony. The gray dome was gone. He was lying inside a cart drawn by two elk. The cart had metal bars, forming a cage. He groaned and tried to sit up, but firm hands pushed him back down.

The pain of his terrible wound was almost unbearable. He coughed, hacking up phlegm. He lifted his eyes and looked up to see a person bending over him.

It was a barbarian woman, the one he'd seen walking into Solace that night.

"Who are you?" Theros asked, dazed.

"I am called Goldmoon. I am a follower of the goddess Mishakal. She has restored you to life."

Theros smiled and let himself drift into a healing sleep. Before he slept, he murmured something.

"What did he say?" asked a man known as Tanis Half-elven.

"You won't believe this," said a warrior known as Caramon. "I could swear he said, 'Thank you, Sargas!' "

If you enjoyed reading *Theros Ironfeld*, be sure to read these other books in the DRAGONLANCE® Warriors Series.

In *Knights of the Crown* a spell thief named Sir Pirvan the Wayward begins an unlikely quest to become one of the Knights of Solamnia. His training starts as a squire of the Knights of the Crown, who have much to teach him about the virtue of loyalty. (ISBN 0-7869-0108-X)

Sir Pirvan's attempt to join the greatest order of chivalry in the history of Krynn continues in *Knights of the Sword.* To achieve the Order of the Sword, Pirvan must begin his training in the virtues of courage and heroism. He also finds himself serving as a mentor for another whose prospects for knighthood seem dubious. (ISBN 0-7869-0202-7)

Maquesta Kar-Thon details the exploits of a young woman who must capture a deadly sea monster for a minotaur lord in order to save her father's life. At eighteeen, Maq is forced to become the captain of a ship and to battle pirates, Blood Sea imps and other evil creatures of the deep. Her quest must be successful. Her father's life depends on it. (ISBN 0-7869-0134-9)